ACPL Laramie, WY 09/2015
39092055255691
Somoza, Jos*e Carlos,
The Athenian murders /
Pieces: 1
WITHDRAWN

1%

This item was purchased with monies provided from the optional 1% sales tax.

THE ATHENIAN MURDERS

THE ATHENIAN MURDERS

TRANSLATED BY SONIA SOTO

José Carlos Somoza

FARRAR STRAUS GIROUX
NEW YORK

ALBANY COUNTY
PUBLIC LIBRARY
LARAMIE, WYOMING

Farrar, Straus and Giroux
19 Union Square West, New York 10003

Copyright © 2000 by José Carlos Somoza
Translation copyright © 2001 by Sonia Soto
All rights reserved
Originally published in 2000 by Alfaguara, Spain, as La caverna de las ideas
English translation originally published in 2002 by Abacus, Great Britain, as
The Athenian Murders
Published in the United States by Farrar, Straus and Giroux
First American edition, 2002

Library of Congress Cataloging-in-Publication Data
Somoza, José Carlos, 1959–
[Caverna de las ideas. English]
The Athenian murders / José Carlos Somoza ; translated by Sonia Soto.— 1st American ed.
p. cm.
ISBN 0-374-10677-0 (hc : alk. paper)
I. Soto, Sonia. II. Title.

PQ6669.O56 C3813 2002
863'.64—dc21

2001054480

Designed by Abby Kagan

www.fsgbooks.com

1 3 5 7 9 10 8 6 4 2

There is an argument which holds good against the man who ventures to put anything whatever into writing on questions of this nature; it has often before been stated by me, and it seems suitable for the present occasion.

For everything that exists there are three instruments by which the knowledge of it is necessarily imparted; fourth, there is the knowledge itself, and, as fifth, we must count the thing itself which is known and truly exists. The first is the name, the second the definition, the third the image. . . .

—PLATO, EPISTLE VII

THE ATHENIAN MURDERS

THE CORPSE lay on a fragile birch-wood litter.[1] The torso and belly were a confusion of splits and tears crusted with congealed blood and dried mud, but the head and arms appeared unblemished. A soldier pulled aside the corpse's robes for Aschilos to examine it. Onlookers gathered, slowly at first, then in great numbers, forming a circle around the macabre remains. A cold shiver ran over Night's blue skin, and the golden manes of the torches, the dark edges of the chlamyses, and the thick horsehair crests on the soldiers' helmets waved in the Boreas. Silence had open eyes: All gazes followed Aschilos's movements as he performed the terrible examination. As gently as a midwife, he parted the lips of the wounds, then probed the horrific cavities with meticulous attention, like a reader sliding his finger over inscriptions on papyrus. His slave held a lamp over him, shielding it from the buffeting wind with his hand. All were silent save old Candaulus. When the soldiers had appeared with the corpse, he had started shouting in the middle of the street, waking the neighborhood, and there now remained a

1. The first five lines are missing. In his edition of the original text, Montalo noted that the papyrus was torn here. I'm beginning my translation of *The Athenian Murders* with the first sentence of Montalo's text, which is the only version we have. —TRANS.

faint echo of his earlier raving. He limped around the circle of onlookers, apparently unaffected by the cold, though nearly naked, dragging his withered left foot—a blackened satyr's hoof. He held out reedy, emaciated arms, leaning on the others' shoulders, crying, "Look at him! He must be a god! This is how the gods descend from Olympus! Don't touch him! Didn't you hear me? He's a god. . . . Swear your allegiance, Callimachus! You, too, Euphorbus!"

A great mane of white hair grew untidily on his angular head like an expression of his madness. It waved in the wind, half-covering his face. But the crowd paid him little attention—people preferring to look upon the corpse rather than at the madman.

The captain of the border guard emerged with two of his men from the nearest house, replacing his long-maned helmet: He believed it appropriate that he should display his military insignia in public. He peered through his dark visor at the gathered crowd. Noticing Candaulus, he gestured dismissively, as if brushing away a bothersome fly.

"Silence him, by Zeus," he said, not addressing any of the soldiers in particular.

One of them approached the old man and, raising his lance, with a single horizontal blow, struck the wrinkled papyrus of his abdomen. Candaulus gasped midsentence and doubled up soundlessly, like hair flattened in the wind. He lay writhing and whimpering on the ground. The crowd was grateful for the sudden quiet.

"Your report, Physician?"

The doctor, Aschilos, took his time to answer, not even looking up at the captain. He disliked being addressed as "Physician," even more when the speaker seemed contemptuous of every man save himself. Aschilos might not be a soldier, but he came from an old aristocratic family and had had a most refined education: He was conversant with *The Aphorisms,* observed the Hippocratic oath, and had spent long periods on the island of Cos, studying the sacred art of the Asclepiads, disciples and heirs of Asclepius. He was not, therefore, someone a captain of the border guard could easily humiliate. And he already felt insulted: He had been awakened by soldiers in the dark hours of the early morning and called to examine, in the middle of the street, the corpse of the young man brought down on a litter from Mount Lycabettus. And he was no doubt expected to draw up some kind of report. But as everyone well knew, he, Aschilos, was a doctor of the living, not the dead, and he believed that this shameful task discredited his profession. He lifted his hands from the mangled body, trailing a mane of bloody humors. His slave hurriedly cleansed them with a cloth moistened with lustral water. He cleared his throat twice and said, "I believe he was attacked by a hungry pack of wolves. He's been bitten and mauled. . . . The heart is missing. Torn out. The cavity of the hot fluids is partially empty."

The murmur, with its long mane, ran through the crowd.

"You heard him, Hemodorus," one man whispered to another. "Wolves."

"Something must be done," his companion replied. "We will discuss the matter at the Assembly."

"His mother has been informed," the captain announced, the firmness of his voice extinguishing all comments. "I spared her the details; she knows only that her son is dead. And she is not to see the body until Daminus of Clazobion arrives. He is the only man left in the family, and he will determine what is to be done." Legs apart, fists resting on the skirt of his uniform, he had a powerful voice, accustomed to imposing obedience. He appeared to address his men, but also evidently enjoyed having the attention of the common people. "As for us, our work here is done!"

He turned to the crowd of civilians and added, "Citizens, return to your homes! There is nothing more to see! Sleep if you can. . . . Part of the night remains!"

Like a thick mane of hair ruffled by a capricious wind, each strand waving independently, the humble crowd gradually dispersed, some leaving separately, others in groups, some in silence, others commenting on the horrifying event.

"It's true, Hemodorus, wolves abound on Lycabettus. I've heard that several peasants, too, have been attacked."

"And now this poor ephebe! We must discuss the matter at the Assembly."

A short, very fat man remained behind, standing by the corpse's feet, peering at it placidly, his stout, though neat, face impassive. He appeared to have fallen asleep. The departing crowd avoided him, passing without looking at him, as if he were a column or a rock. One of the soldiers went to him and tugged at his cloak.

"Return home, citizen. You heard our captain."

The man took little notice, and continued to stare at the corpse, stroking his neatly trimmed gray beard with thick fingers. The soldier, thinking he must be deaf, gave him a slight push and raised his voice. "Hey, I'm talking to you! Didn't you hear the captain? Go home!"

"I'm sorry," said the man, though actually appearing quite unconcerned by the soldier's command. "I'll be on my way."

"What are you looking at?"

The man blinked twice and raised his eyes from the corpse, which another soldier was now covering with a cloak. He said, "Nothing. I was thinking."

"Well, think in your bed."

"You're right," said the man, as if he had woken from a catnap. He glanced around and walked slowly away.

All the onlookers had gone by now, and Aschilos, in conversation with the captain, swiftly disappeared as soon as the opportunity arose. Even old Candaulus was crawling away, still racked with pain and whimpering, helped on his way by the soldiers' kicks, in search of a dark corner to spend the night in demented dreams. His long white mane seemed to come alive, flowing down his back, then rising in an untidy snowy cloud, a white plume in the wind. In the sky, above the precise outline of the Parthenon, Night lazily loosened her mane, cloud-decked and edged with silver, like a maiden slowly combing her hair.[2]

But the fat man whom the soldier seemed to have woken from a dream did not follow the others into the mane of streets that made up

2. I'm struck by the excessive use of metaphors relating to "manes" and "hair" throughout the text, from the beginning. They may point to the presence of eidesis, but I can't be sure at this stage. Montalo didn't seem to have noticed anything, as he didn't mention it in his notes.—TRANS.

the tangled central district. Instead, he appeared to hesitate, to think twice about his course of action, before setting off unhurriedly around the small square. He headed toward the house that the captain of the guard had left moments earlier and from which there now emerged—he could hear it clearly—a terrible wailing. The house, even in the dim light of dawn, revealed the presence of a family of considerable wealth—it was large, on two floors, and had a vast low-walled garden spread out before it. At the entrance, a short flight of steps led up to a double door flanked by Doric columns. The door was open. A torch hung on the wall, and a little boy was sitting on the steps beneath it.

As the man approached, an old man appeared, staggering, at the door. He wore the gray tunic of a slave. At first, because of his unsteady gait, the fat man thought he must be either drunk or crippled, but then he realized that the slave was weeping bitterly. The old man barely glanced at him as he passed; clasping his face in his filthy hands, he stumbled up the garden path to a small statue of the guardian Hermes, mumbling disjointedly. The man could occasionally make out "My mistress!" and "Oh, woe!" The man turned his attention back to the boy, who was still sitting on the steps, his small arms crossed over his legs, watching without a trace of shyness.

"Are you a servant in this house?" he asked, showing him a rusty obol.

"Yes, but I could just as well be a servant in yours."

The man was taken aback by the swift answer and clear, defiant voice. The child couldn't be more than ten years old. A strip of cloth was tied around his head, only just controlling unruly blond hair the color of honey, although it was difficult to tell the exact shade in the torchlight. His small pale face bore no signs of Lydian or Phoenician origins, indicating instead that he was of northern, possibly Thracian, descent. With his small furrowed brow and lopsided smile, his expression was full of intelligence. He wore only a gray slave tunic, but seemed not to feel the cold, despite having bare arms and legs. He caught the obol skillfully and tucked it in the folds of his tunic. He remained sitting, swinging his bare feet.

"For the moment, all I need is for you to announce me to your mistress," said the man.

"My mistress is not receiving anyone. A big soldier, the captain of the guard, came and told her that her son is dead. Now she is screaming and tearing out her hair, and cursing the gods."

And, as if his words required proof, a prolonged chorus of shrieks was suddenly heard, coming from deep inside the house.

"Those are her slave women," said the boy calmly.

The man said, "Listen. I was a friend of your mistress's husband, and—"

"He was a traitor," said the boy, interrupting him. "He died a long time ago. He was condemned to death."

"Yes, that's how he died: He was executed. But your mistress knows me well, and, since I'm here, I'd like to offer her my condolences." He took another obol from under his tunic, and it changed hands as swiftly as the first. "Tell her that Heracles Pontor is here to see her. If she doesn't wish to see me, I'll leave. But you must go and tell her."

"I will. If she doesn't receive you, do I have to return the obols?"

"No. Keep them. But I'll give you another if she sees me."

The boy jumped to his feet.

"You know how to do business, by Apollo!" And he disappeared through the dark doorway.

The untidy mane of clouds in the night sky hardly changed shape while Heracles awaited his answer. Soon, the boy's honey-colored head appeared in the darkness.

"Give me that third obol." He smiled.

Inside, the house was a dark labyrinth of corridors framed by stone arches like great open maws. The boy stopped in one of the gloomy passages to place his torch in the mouth of a hook, but he couldn't quite reach it. Although the young slave didn't ask him for help—he stood on tiptoes, straining to reach it—Heracles took the torch from him and slid it smoothly into the iron ring.

"Thank you," said the boy. "I am not yet fully grown."

"You will be soon."

Issuing from unseen mouths, the clamor, roar, echo of grief seeped through the walls, as if all the occupants of the house were lamenting as one. The boy—Heracles couldn't see his face as he walked in front, diminutive, vulnerable, like a lamb heading into the open jaws of some enormous black beast—suddenly sounded as deeply affected as the rest.

"We were all fond of the young master," he said, without looking around. "He was very kind." And he gave a little gasp—or it could have been a sigh, or a sniff—and Heracles wondered if he was crying. "He only ever had us beaten when we did something really bad, and he never punished me or old Iphimachus. . . . Did you see the slave who came out of the house as you arrived?"

"I didn't pay him much heed."

"Well, that was Iphimachus. He was the young master's pedagogue. He's very upset by the news." And he added, more quietly, "Iphimachus is a good man, if a little stupid. I get on well with him, but then, I get on with almost everyone."

"That doesn't surprise me."

They came to a chamber.

"You must wait here. The mistress will be with you presently."

Wide-necked amphorae were set about the room, a windowless cenacle, modest in size, lighted unevenly by small lamps on stone brackets. It also contained two old couches that did not exactly invite one to comfortable repose. Once Heracles was alone, he began to feel oppressed by the dark, cavelike room, the ceaseless weeping, the stale air like a sick man's breath. The entire house seemed attuned to death, as if lengthy daily funerals had always been held there. What is that smell? he wondered. A woman's weeping. The room was filled with the damp odor of mourning women.

"Is that you, Heracles Pontor?"

A shadow stood in the doorway to the inner chambers. The dim lamplight revealed nothing of her face save, by some strange chance, the area of her mouth. So the first part of Itys that Heracles saw was her lips. They opened for her words to issue, forming a black spindle-shaped hole, like an empty socket watching him from a distance, or the eye of a painted figure.

"It is a long time since you have crossed the threshold of my modest home," said the mouth without waiting for a reply. "Welcome."

"Thank you."

"Your voice . . . I remember it well. And your face. Yet it is so easy to forget, even seeing each other often."

"But we don't meet often," said Heracles.

"That's true. Though your house is nearby, you are a man and I am a woman. I have my position as a *despoina,* a husbandless mistress of a house, and you yours as a man who discusses matters in the Agora and speaks at the Assembly. I am a mere widow. You are a widower. We both do our duty as Athenians."

The mouth closed, and the pale lips formed into a curve so fine, it was almost invisible. A smile perhaps? Heracles found it impossible to tell. Two slave women appeared behind Itys's shadow; both wept, or sobbed, or intoned a single choking note, like the wail of an oboe. I must endure her cruelty, he thought, for she has just lost her only son.

"Please accept my condolences," he said.

"Thank you."

"And my help. In anything you might need."

He knew immediately that he shouldn't have added it. He had gone beyond the limits of his visit, attempted to bridge the infinite distance, to sum up in a few words all their years of silence. The mouth opened—a small but dangerous animal suddenly sensing prey.

"You are thus repaid for your friendship with Meragrus," she said dryly. "You need not say anything more."

"This has nothing to do with my friendship with Meragrus. . . . I consider it my duty."

"Oh, a duty." This time, the mouth formed into a faint smile. "A sacred duty, of course. You talk as you always have, Heracles Pontor!"

She stepped forward, and the light revealed the pyramid of her nose, her cheeks—marked with recent scratches—and the black embers of her eyes. She hadn't aged as much as Heracles had expected.

The hand of the artist who made her is still apparent, he thought. The *colpos* of her dark peplos spilled in slow waves over her breast. One hand was hidden beneath her shawl; she clutched both edges of the garment with the other, and it was in the hand that Heracles saw signs of age, as if the years had flowed down her arms, blackening the ends. There, and only there, in the enlarged knuckles and crooked fingers, Itys was old.

"I am grateful for your sense of duty," she murmured. There was deep sincerity in her voice for the first time, and it shook him. "How did you find out so soon?"

"There was a great commotion in the street when they brought the body. It woke the neighborhood."

There was a scream. Then another. For a moment, absurdly, Heracles thought they came from Itys's mouth, which was shut; as if she had roared internally, and her thin body were shuddering and resonating with this sound produced in her throat.

But then the scream, deafening, entered the room; clad in black, it pushed the slaves away, crawled from one side of the room to the other, then collapsed in a corner, writhing, as if seized by a holy madness. At last, it dissolved into an endless lamentation.

"It's much worse for Elea," said Itys apologetically, as if to excuse her daughter's conduct. "Tramachus was more than a brother; he was her *kyrios,* her legal guardian, the only man Elea has ever known and loved."

Itys turned toward the girl, who was crouching in a dark corner, her legs gathered tightly to her, as if she wanted to take up as little space as possible, or to disappear into the shadows like a black cobweb, her hands raised in front of her face, her eyes and mouth wide open (her features were three black circles filling her entire countenance) as she shook with violent sobs. Itys said, "That's enough, Elea. You are not to leave the gynaeceum—you know that—particularly in such a state. Displaying your grief before a guest . . . Such behavior does not befit an honorable woman! Return to your chamber!" But the girl's weeping grew louder. Raising her hand, Itys exclaimed, "I will not repeat my order!"

"Allow me, mistress," said one of the slaves. She knelt hurriedly beside Elea and murmured something to her that Heracles could not make out. Soon, the girl's sobs became incomprehensible mumbling.

When Heracles looked at Itys again, he saw that she was watching him.

"What happened?" asked Itys. "The captain of the guard told me only that a goatherd found him dead a little way from Lycabettus."

"Aschilos, the doctor, claims it was a wolf attack."

"It would take many wolves to kill my son!"

And not a few to overcome you, oh noble woman, he thought.

"Doubtless there were many," he said.

Itys began speaking in a strangely gentle voice, not addressing Heracles, as if she were alone, intoning a prayer. The mouths of the cuts on her pale, angular face were bleeding again.

"He left two days ago. I bade him farewell, as I had many times before, unconcerned—he was a grown man, well able to take care of himself. . . . 'I'm going to spend the day hunting, Mother,' he told me. 'I'll fill a knapsack with quails and thrushes for you. I'll set traps with my nets for hares.' He said he would return that night, but he did not. I was going to chide him, but—"

Her mouth opened suddenly, as if about to pronounce an enormous word. She remained thus a moment, jaw tensed, the dark ellipse of her maw[3] motionless in the silence, before closing it gently and murmuring, "But now I cannot face and rebuke Death . . . because it will not return with my son's countenance to ask my forgiveness. My beloved son!"

Slight tenderness in her is more terrible than Stentor's roar, Heracles thought admiringly.

"The gods can be unjust at times," he said, because he felt he had to say something, but also because, deep down, he believed it.

"Don't speak of them, Heracles. . . . Do not speak of the gods!"

3. As the attentive reader may already have noticed, all the metaphors and images in the second half of this chapter relate to "mouths" and "maws," as well as to "screams" and "roars." What we have here, obviously, is an eidetic text.—TRANS.

Itys's mouth trembled with rage. "It was the *gods* who sank their teeth into my son's body, and smiled as they tore out and devoured his heart, breathing in the warm scent of his blood with relish! Oh, do not speak of gods in my presence!"

It was as though Itys was trying, vainly, to subdue her own voice, issuing as a powerful roar from her maw, imposing silence all around her. The slaves had turned to look at her; even Elea was silent, listening to her mother with mortal reverence.

"Cronius Zeus has brought down the last great oak of this house while it was yet in leaf! *I curse the gods and their immortal caste!*"

She raised her arms, hands open, in a fearsome, precise gesture. Then, slowly lowering them and her voice, she added with sudden contempt, "The highest praise the gods may expect from us is our silence!"

The word *silence* was torn by a triple clamor, which penetrated deep into Heracles' ears and remained with him as he left the terrible house—a ritual, threefold scream, from the slaves and from Elea, their mouths open, jaws almost unhinged, forming a single throat rent by three distinct, high-pitched, deafening notes—the funereal roar of the maw.[4]

4. I find it surprising that, in his scholarly edition of the original, Montalo should have made no mention of the powerful eidesis present in the text, at least throughout the first chapter. But maybe he didn't know about this strange literary device. It's not unusual to find translators, even among the most erudite, who are not familiar with a literary technique that may, in any case, have been used by only a handful of Greek writers—in some ways the most celebrated ones—and whose main feature is precisely that it is only noticed by those who know about it. By way of example for the curious reader, and also to be honest about how I came to discover the image hidden in this chapter (for the translator must be honest in his notes; lying is the author's prerogative), I will recount the brief conversation I had yesterday with my friend Helena, whom I respect as a learned and highly experienced colleague. The subject of work came up, and I told her enthusiastically that *The Athenian Murders,* the novel I had just begun translating, was an eidetic text. She stared at me for a moment, holding one of the cherries on the nearby plate by its stalk.

"A what?" she asked.

"Eidesis," I explained, "is a literary technique invented by the ancient Greeks to transmit *secret* messages or keys in their works. It consists in repeating, in any text,

---

metaphors or words that, when identified by a perceptive reader, make up an idea or image that's independent of the original text. Arginusus of Corinth, for example, used eidesis to hide a detailed description of a young woman he loved in a long poem apparently about wildflowers. And Epaphus of Macedonia inserted his will by means of eidesis in an epic tale describing the death of the hero Patroclus. And Euphronius of—"

"How interesting." Helena smiled, bored. "And would you care to tell me what's hidden in your anonymous *Athenian Murders*?"

"I won't know until I've translated the whole thing. In chapter one, the eidesis mainly involves 'hair' or 'manes,' 'mouths' and 'maws' that 'scream' and 'roar,' but—"

" 'Manes' and 'maws that roar'?" she asked simply, interrupting me. "It could be referring to a lion, couldn't it?"

And she ate the cherry.

I hate the way women always arrive at the truth effortlessly, by the shortest route. It was my turn to go very still and stare.

"A lion, of course," I muttered.

"What I don't understand," Helena went on casually, "is why the author thought the idea of a lion so secret that he had to hide it through eidesis."

"We'll find out once I've translated it. An eidetic text can only be fully understood once you've read all the way through." As I spoke, I was thinking, A *lion,* of course. Why didn't I think of that?

"Right." Helena considered the conversation at an end. She bent her long legs, which had been stretched out on a chair, put the plate of cherries on the table, and stood up. "Get on with the translation and let me know how it goes."

"What's surprising is that Montalo didn't notice anything in the original manuscript," I said.

"Why don't you write to him?" she suggested. "It'll make you look good and bring you some kudos."

And, although at the time I pretended not to agree (I didn't want her to know she'd solved all my problems at a stroke), this is exactly what I have done.—TRANS.

2[1]

SLAVES PREPARED THE BODY of Tramachus, son of the widow Itys, according to custom: The horrific lacerations were glossed with ointments from a *lekythos;* agile-fingered hands slid over the ravaged flesh, anointing it with essences and perfumes; it was wrapped in a delicate shroud and arrayed in clean clothes; the face was left uncovered, the jaw firmly bandaged to prevent the horrifying rictus of death; an obol to pay for Charon's services was placed beneath the slimy tongue. The corpse was then laid out on a bed of myrtle and jasmine, feet toward the door, watched over by the gray presence of a guardian Hermes; the wake would last all day. At the garden gate, the *ardanion,* the amphora of lustral water, served to make public the tragedy and to cleanse the guests of contact with the beyond. From midday on, the hired mourners intoned their sinuous canticles, and tokens of condolence rained down. By afternoon, a line of men snaked the length of the garden path. All stood in silence beneath the cold damp of the trees, awaiting their turn to enter the house, file past

1. "The surface is sticky; one's fingers slide over it as if smeared with oil; the central area is fragile, like scales," stated Montalo regarding the pieces of papyrus that make up the manuscript at the opening of the second chapter. Could it have been made from leaves from different plants?—TRANS.

the body, and offer their condolences to the family. Tramachus's uncle, Daminus, of the deme of Clazobion, acted as host; he possessed a considerable fortune in boats and in silver mines in Ergasteria, and his presence drew many. Few, however, attended in memory of Meragrus, Tramachus's father, condemned and executed as a traitor to democracy many years earlier, or out of respect for the widow Itys, who had inherited her husband's dishonor.

Heracles Pontor arrived at sunset, for he had decided that he, too, would take part in the *ecphora,* the funeral procession, always held at night. Slowly, ceremonially, he entered the dark vestibule—damp and cold, the air oily with the scent of unguents—and circled the corpse once, following the winding line of guests. He embraced Daminus and Itys; she was wrapped in a black peplos and large-hooded shawl. They did not speak. His embrace was one among many. As he processed, he recognized some of the guests but not others. There was Praxinoe and his son, the beautiful Antisus, said to have been one of Tramachus's closest friends; also Isiphenes and Ephialtes, well-known merchants, there, no doubt, because of Daminus; and—a presence he found most surprising—Menaechmus, the sculptor-poet, dressed as carelessly as usual, who broke with protocol by stopping to whisper a few words to Itys. And lastly, as he emerged into the cold damp garden, he thought he saw the sturdy figure of the philosopher Plato waiting to enter with the others. Heracles assumed he had come in memory of his old friendship with Meragrus.

The procession that set off for the cemetery along the Panathenaic Way looked like a giant sinuous creature; the head consisted of, first, the corpse, on a swaying bier carried by four slaves; behind it, the immediate family—Daminus, Itys, and Elea—deep in silent grief; then the oboe players, young men in black tunics, awaiting the start of the ceremony to begin playing; and lastly, the white peploses of the four weepers. Friends and acquaintances of the family, advancing two by two, made up the body.

In the cold damp evening mist, the cortege headed out of the city through the Dipylon Gate and set off along the Sacred Way, leaving the lights of the houses far behind. The tombstones of the Ceramicus rippled in the torchlight; all around, there rose statues of gods and heroes delicately oiled with the night dew, tall steles inscribed and embellished with undulating figures, and urns of solemn outline with ivy snaking over them. The slaves carefully placed the corpse on the funeral pyre. The sinuous notes of the oboes slid through the air; the hired mourners, in formation, tore at their garments while intoning their cold, oscillating chant. Libations were made in honor of the gods of the dead. The guests dispersed to observe the ceremony. Heracles chose to stand beside a huge statue of Perseus; Medusa's decapitated head, which the hero clutched by her mane of vipers, was level with Heracles' face and appeared to be watching him through empty eyes. The chanting concluded, the final words were uttered, and the golden heads of four torches were lowered at the edge of the pyre: The many-headed fire rose up, writhing, its numerous tongues waving in the cold damp air of the night.[2]

The man knocked on the door several times. No one answered, so he tried again. Clouds with many heads began to twist in the dark Athenian sky.

The door was opened at last; a figure appeared, swathed in a long black shroud, with a featureless white face. Confused and intimidated, the man stammered, "I wish to see Heracles Pontor, known as the Decipherer of Enigmas."

The figure slipped back into the shadows; still hesitant, the man entered the house. Outside, now and then, thunder boomed.

Heracles Pontor sat at the table in his small room. He had stopped reading and was absorbed in tracing the sinuous path of a large crack that ran from the ceiling halfway down the opposite wall. The door opened gently and Ponsica appeared.

2. "Cold" and "damp," together with "undulating" and "sinuous" movement, in all its variants, appear to dominate the eidesis in this chapter. This could easily be a sea image (which would be very characteristic of the Greeks). But what about the recurring "stickiness"? Let's move on and see.—TRANS.

"A guest," said Heracles, deciphering the graceful undulating movements of his masked slave's slender, agile-fingered hands. "A man. Wishes to see me." Both hands fluttered at once, the ten heads of her fingers conversing in the air. "Yes, show him in."

The man was tall and thin. He wore a humble woolen cloak, upon which the cold damp night had deposited a layer of its slimy scales. His well-formed head was bald and shiny, and his chin sported a neatly trimmed beard. His eyes were bright, but the weariness of age was apparent in the lines around them. Once Ponsica had left, still silent, the man, who had been watching her in amazement, turned to Heracles.

"Is what they say of you true?"

"And what do they say?"

"That the Decipherer of Enigmas can read the faces of men and the look of things as if they were papyri. That he knows the language of appearances and can translate it. Is that why your slave hides her face behind a blank mask?"

Heracles got up to get a bowl of fruit and a krater of wine. He smiled slightly and said, "By Zeus, I would not want to deny such a reputation, but my slave covers her face more for my own tranquillity than for hers. She was kidnapped by Lydian bandits when she was no more than a baby, and during a night of drunkenness, they amused themselves by burning her face and tearing out her small tongue. . . . Please, help yourself to fruit. . . . It seems one of the bandits took pity on her, or discerned there might be profit to be made, and adopted her. Later, he sold her as a slave for domestic work. I bought her in the market two years ago. I like her because she's as silent as a cat and as obedient as a dog, but her ruined features displease me."

"I understand," said the man. "You feel sorry for her."

"Oh no, it's not that," said Heracles. "They distract me. My eyes are too often tempted by the complexity of all that they see. For example, just before you arrived, I was engrossed in following the path of that interesting crack on the wall—its course and tributaries, its origin. . . . Well, my slave's face is an endless, twisted confusion of cracks, a constant enigma for my tireless gaze, so I decided to have her hide it by making her wear a mask. I like to be surrounded by simple things: the rectangle of a table, the circles of goblets . . . simple geometric shapes. My work consists in exactly the opposite—deciphering the complicated. Please, make yourself comfortable on the couch. Do try some of this fresh fruit, especially the sweet figs. I adore figs, don't you? I can also offer you a goblet of undiluted wine."

The man had listened to Heracles' calm words with growing surprise. He now reclined slowly on the couch. In the light from a small oil lamp on the table, his bald head cast a perfectly round shadow on the wall. The shadow of Heracles' head—a thick cone with a short tuft of hair on top—stretched to the ceiling.

"Thank you. I'll take the couch for now," said the man.

Heracles shrugged. He pushed aside some scrolls and drew the bowl of fruit toward him. He sat down and took a fig.

"Now, how can I help you?" he asked pleasantly.

Thunder clamored harshly in the distance. After a pause, the man said, "I'm not sure, in truth. I've heard that you solve mysteries. I've come to present you with one."

"Show it to me," said Heracles.

"What?"

"Show me the mystery. I solve only enigmas that I can see. Is it a text? An object?"

Again, the man looked astonished, frowning, mouth open, as before. Meanwhile, Heracles neatly bit off the head of the fig.[3]

"No, nothing like that," he said slowly. "The mystery I've brought you is something that was but is no longer. A memory. Or the *idea* of a memory."

"How can you expect me to solve such a thing?" Heracles smiled. "I only translate what my eyes can see. I don't go beyond words."

The man stared at him hard, as if challenging him.

3. I have translated "the head of the fig" literally, although I'm not quite sure what our anonymous author was referring to. He might have meant the round fleshy part, or, just as easily, the end with the stalk. Or it might simply be a writer's trick to draw attention to the word *head,* which, it seems increasingly likely, is the next eidetic word.—TRANS.

"There are always *ideas* beyond words, even if they're invisible," he said. "And they are all that matters."[4] The man bowed his head and the round shadow moved down the wall. "We, at least, believe in the independent existence of ideas. But let me introduce myself. My name is Diagoras, from the deme of Mardontes. I teach philosophy and geometry at the school in the gardens of Academe run by Plato. You may have heard of it—it's known as the 'Academy.' "

Heracles nodded.

"I have heard of the Academy and I am acquainted with Plato," he said. "Although I have to admit that, lately, I haven't seen him often."

"I'm not surprised," replied Diagoras. "He's very busy with the next book in his dialogue on the ideal government. It's not him I've come about, however, but . . . one of my students, Tramachus, son of the widow Itys. The young man killed by wolves a few days ago. Do you know whom I mean?"

In the dim lamplight, Heracles' fleshy face remained expressionless. Ah, so Tramachus attended the Academy, he thought. That's why Plato went to offer Itys his condolences. He nodded, then said, "I know his family, but I wasn't aware that he was a student at the Academy."

"He was," said Diagoras. "And a good one."

Intertwining the heads of his thick fingers, Heracles said, "And the mystery you've brought me has to do with Tramachus."

"Directly," replied the philosopher.

Heracles thought a moment, then waved his hand vaguely. "Now, tell me about it as best you can, and we'll see."

Diagoras of Mardontes gazed at the pointed head of the flame—a cone rising from the wick—as he reeled off the words: "I was Tramachus's principal tutor, and I was very proud of him. He possessed all the noble qualities that Plato requires of those who aspire to be wise

4. It occurs to me that, quite apart from their purpose within the fiction of the dialogue, these last sentences—"There are always *ideas* beyond words . . ." and ". . . they are all that matters"—could also be a message from the author to emphasize the presence of eidesis. Montalo, as usual, doesn't seem to have noticed anything. —TRANS.

guardians of the city: He was beautiful, as only one who has been blessed by the gods can be; he debated intelligently; his questions were always pertinent, his conduct exemplary; his spirit vibrated in harmony with music and his slender body was shaped by exercise in the gymnasium. He was about to come of age and burned with impatience to serve Athens as a soldier. Although it saddened me to think he would soon be leaving the Academy—I held him in great esteem—my heart rejoiced in the knowledge that his soul had learned all that I had to teach and was well prepared for life."

Diagoras stopped. His gaze remained fixed on the gently undulating flame. Then he went on wearily. "But about a month ago, I began to notice something strange happening to him. He seemed preoccupied. He wasn't concentrating during classes. In fact, he would stand well away from his classmates, leaning against the wall farthest from the front of the room, ignoring the forest of arms that rose, like heads on long necks, when I asked a question, as if he were no longer interested in knowledge. At first, I didn't attach too much importance to his behavior. As you know, at that age, problems are numerous, but they bubble up and then subside smoothly and swiftly. But his lack of interest continued, and even worsened. He often missed classes; he didn't go to the gymnasium. Some of his classmates, too, noticed he had changed, but they didn't know why. Could he be sick? I decided to speak to him, although I still believed that his problem was trivial . . . possibly amorous in nature—you know what I mean—it's common at that age." To Heracles' surprise, Diagoras blushed like a young man. He swallowed before continuing. "One afternoon, in the interval between classes, I found him alone in the gardens, beside the statue of the Sphinx."

In among the trees, the young man was oddly still. He appeared to be staring at the head of the stone figure, the woman with a lion's body and eagle's wings, but his prolonged immobility, so like the statue's, showed that his mind must be far away. The man found him standing with heels together, arms by his sides, head slightly tilted. It was cold in the twilight, but the young man wore only a short, light tunic—similar to the Spartan chiton—which flapped in the wind, leaving his arms and pale thighs uncovered. His chestnut curls were tied with a ribbon. He wore beautiful leather sandals. Intrigued, the man came closer. As he did so, the younger man became aware of his presence and looked around.

"Ah, Master Diagoras, it's you."

He made as if to leave, but the man said, "Wait, Tramachus. I wanted to speak to you alone."

The young man stopped, his back to Diagoras, white shoulders uncovered, and turned slowly. The man, eager to appear affectionate, noticed that the boy's smooth limbs were tense, so he smiled reassuringly. He said, "Are you not rather lightly dressed? It is a little cold."

"I'm not cold, Master Diagoras."

The man fondly stroked the undulating muscles of his pupil's left arm.

"Are you sure? Your skin is icy, my poor child . . . and you seem to be trembling."

Emboldened by affection for the boy, he moved a little closer and, with a gentle, almost motherly, movement of the fingers, brushed aside the chestnut curls flopping over his forehead. Once again, he marveled at the flawless beauty of his face, the loveliness of the honey-colored eyes staring at him, blinking. He said, "Listen, my child. Your classmates and I have noticed that something is the matter. You haven't been yourself lately."

"No, Master, I—"

"Listen," insisted the man softly. He stroked the youth's smooth oval face, taking his chin in his hand as carefully as he would a goblet of pure gold. "You are my best student, and a teacher knows his best student well. For a month now, nothing seems to have interested you; you haven't taken part in dialogues. . . . Wait, don't interrupt. You've grown distant with your classmates, Tramachus. Of course something is the matter, my child. But tell me what it is, and I swear before the gods that I will help you, for my energies are considerable. I won't tell anyone if you don't wish me to. You have my word. Do confide in me."

The boy's brown eyes, open very wide (perhaps too wide), were fixed on the man's. For a moment, all was stillness and silence. Then the boy moved his lips—pink, moist, and cold—as if about to speak. But he said nothing. He continued to stare, eyes bulging like small ivory heads with huge black pupils. The man saw something strange there and was so absorbed that he hardly noticed the young man step back, still holding his gaze, his white body still rigid, lips tense.

The man stood motionless for a long time after the young man had fled.

"He was terrified," said Diagoras after a deep silence.

Heracles took another fig from the bowl. Thunder shook in the distance like the sinuous vibration of a rattlesnake.

"How do you know? Did he tell you?"

"No. I told you, such was my confusion that he ran away before I could say another word. But, though I lack your ability to read men's faces, I have seen fear too many times not to recognize it. Tramachus's fear was more terrible than any I have ever seen. His eyes contained nothing else. When it was revealed to me, I didn't know what to do. It was as if . . . as if the terror in his eyes turned me to stone. When I looked around, he'd disappeared. I never saw him again. The following day, one of his friends told me he had gone hunting. I was a little surprised, since his state of mind the evening before did not seem conducive to the enjoyment of such a pastime, but—"

"Who told you he had gone hunting?" Heracles asked, interrupting Diagoras. He seized the head of another fig from among the many poking over the edge of the bowl.

"Euneos, one of his closest friends. And Antisus, son of Praxinoe."

"Both students at the Academy?"

"Yes."

"Fine. Please go on."

Diagoras ran his hand over his head (on the shadow on the wall, a creature slithered over the slimy surface of a sphere) and said, "I wanted to talk to Antisus and Euneos that day. I found them at the gymnasium."

Hands rising, writhing, playing in a shower of tiny scales; wet, slender arms; multiple laughter, banter interspersed with the sound of water, eyelids tightly closed, heads raised; a shove, and, again, laughter spilling forth. From above, the image brings to mind a flower formed of adolescent bodies, or a single body with several heads; arms like undulating petals; multiple slimy nakedness caressed by steam; a tongue of water sliding slickly from the mouth of a gargoyle; the flower of flesh moves, gestures sinuously. A thick breath of steam suddenly clouds our view.[5]

The vapor clears. We see a small room—a changing room, judging by the collection of tunics and robes hanging on the whitewashed walls—and several young male bodies in varying degrees of undress; one of them lies facedown on a couch, quite naked, and avid dark-skinned hands slide over it, slowly massaging the muscles. There is laughter: The young men jest after their shower. The hiss of steam from the cauldrons of boiling water diminishes until it ceases. The curtain at the door is drawn back, and the multiple laughter stops. A tall, thin man, with a shiny bald head and neatly trimmed beard, greets the young men, who hasten to answer. The man speaks. They listen, continuing their various activities: dressing, undressing, rubbing their well-formed bodies with cloths, oiling their undulating muscles.

The man addresses two of the young men in particular—one, pink-cheeked, with thick black hair, is bending down, tying his san-

5. This strange paragraph, which would seem to be a poetic description of the young men having a shower at the gymnasium, contains, in concise summary and strongly emphasized, almost all the eidetic elements of chapter 2: "damp," "head," and "undulation," among others. Also noteworthy is the repetition of "multiple" and "scales," which appeared earlier on. The "flower of flesh" image is, I believe, simply a metaphor and has nothing to do with the eidesis.—TRANS.

dals, while the other is the naked ephebe who is being massaged. His face (we can see it now) is extremely beautiful.

The room, like the bodies, exudes heat. Then a snake of mist swirls before our eyes, and the vision disappears.

"I asked about Tramachus," explained Diagoras. "At first, they didn't quite understand what I wanted, though they both admitted that their friend had changed, but they didn't know why. Then Lisilus, another Academy student who happened to be there, made an incredible revelation: For some months, in secret, Tramachus had been seeing a hetaera from Piraeus called Yasintra. 'Perhaps it is she who has changed him, Master,' he added spitefully. Antisus and Euneos reluctantly confirmed the existence of the relationship. I was astounded and, in some ways, hurt. But I was also relieved; that my pupil should keep from me his shameful visits to a prostitute in the port was indeed worrying, considering his distinguished education, but I reflected that if the problem amounted to nothing more, there was no need to worry. I decided to speak to him again, at a more propitious moment, and to discuss reasonably how his spirit had erred. . . ."

Diagoras paused. Heracles Pontor lighted a wall lamp, and the shadows of their heads multiplied: Heracles' truncated triangles moving, together, on the adobe wall, and Diagoras's circles, thoughtful, still, their perfect outline marred by the hair spilling over his head, and by the neatly trimmed beard. When Diagoras resumed his story, his voice was barely audible.

"But that night, almost at dawn, the border guards knocked at my door. A goatherd had found his body in the forest, near Lycabettus, and notified the guard. Once they'd identified him, they called me, as there was no man at his house to receive the news, and his uncle, Daminus, was out of the city. . . . "

He paused again. The distant storm and the sound of another fig being smoothly beheaded could be heard. His face was contorted, each word now a great effort. He said, "Strange as you may find it, I felt guilty. If I'd gained his trust that afternoon, and persuaded him to tell me what was the matter, maybe he wouldn't have gone hunting . . . and he would still be alive." He looked up at his obese interlocutor, who sat listening, leaning back in his chair, looking so tranquil, he might have been about to fall asleep. "I confess I have spent the past two days tortured by the thought that Tramachus may have decided upon his fateful hunting trip to escape from me and my tactless questions. So, this afternoon, I made a decision: I have to find out why he was so terrified, and how I could have helped. That's why I've come to you. In Athens, the saying goes that to know the future, you need the oracle of Delphi, but to know the past, you simply need the Decipherer of Enigmas."

"That's ridiculous!" exclaimed Heracles.

His unexpected reaction startled Diagoras. Heracles stood up quickly, dragging all the shadows of his head after him, and paced briskly about the cold damp room, thick fingers stroking the sticky fig he'd just taken from the bowl. He went on irritably: "I only decipher the past if it's something I can see—a text, an object, a face. But you talk of memories, impressions, and . . . opinions! What kind of guidance can they provide? You say that for a month your disciple had seemed 'preoccupied,' but what does that mean?" He raised an arm abruptly. "Just before you entered the room, I was staring at that crack, and it might have seemed that I, too, was 'preoccupied.' You claim you saw terror in his eyes. . . . Terror! I ask you this: Was terror written out in Ionic characters in his pupils? Is the word *fear* engraved in the lines on our foreheads? Is it a line like that crack on the wall? A thousand different emotions might have produced the expression that you attribute to fear alone!"

Diagoras replied, a little uneasily, "I know what I saw. Tramachus was terrified."

"You know what you *thought* you saw," pointed out Heracles. "Knowing the truth is knowing how much of the truth we can know."

"Socrates, Plato's teacher, believed something similar," admitted Diagoras. "He said that all he knew was that he knew nothing. In fact, we all agree. But the mind, too, has eyes, and with it we can see things that our physical eyes cannot."

"Is that so?" Heracles stopped abruptly. "Very well then, tell me what you see here."

He quickly held something up to Diagoras's face: A sticky dark green head protruded from between his thick fingers.

"A fig," said Diagoras after a moment of surprise.

"A fig like any other?"

"Yes. It looks intact. It has a good color. An ordinary fig."

"Ah! That's the difference between you and me!" cried Heracles triumphantly. "I look at this fig and am of the opinion that it *seems* like an ordinary fig. I may even believe that it is *very likely* an ordinary fig, but I stop there. If I want to know more, I have to open it up . . . as I did with this one while you were speaking."

He gently parted the two halves of the fig that he'd been holding together: In a single sinuous movement, multiple tiny heads rose up angrily from its dark interior, emitting a very faint hiss. Diagoras's face contorted in disgust. Heracles said, "And when I do so . . . I'm not as surprised as you when the truth turns out to be different from what I expected!"

He put the fig back together and placed it on the table. Suddenly calm again, as at the beginning of the conversation, the Decipherer went on: "I pick them out myself at a metic's stall in the Agora. He's a good man and almost never cheats me, I assure you; he knows very well that I'm an expert when it comes to figs. But nature sometimes plays tricks."

Diagoras was flushed again. He cried, "Are you going to accept the job, or would you rather go on about that fig?"

"Please understand. I can't take on something like this." The Decipherer picked up the krater and poured a cup of thick, undiluted wine. "I'd be betraying myself. What have I to go on? Mere suppositions . . . and not even my own, but yours." He shook his head. "Impossible. Would you care for some wine?"

But Diagoras was already standing, straight as a reed. His cheeks were flushed a deep red.

"No, I wouldn't. Nor do I want to take any more of your time. I realize now that I was wrong to ask you. I'm sorry. We have both done our duty—I in setting out my offer, and you in rejecting it. I bid you a good evening."

"Wait," said Heracles casually, as if Diagoras had left something behind. "I said I couldn't take on *your* job, but if you'd like to pay me for a job of *my own,* I'd be happy to accept your money."

"Is this some kind of joke?"

The heads of Heracles' eyes emitted multiple glints of mockery, as if all he had said up till then had, indeed, been nothing but an immense joke. He explained: "The night the soldiers brought Tramachus's body, an old madman named Candaulus roused the whole neighborhood. Like everyone else, I went outside to find out what was going on, and I saw the corpse. A doctor, Aschilos, was examining it, but the incompetent fool couldn't see beyond his own beard. I, however, did see *something* that I thought strange. I'd forgotten all about it, until now." He stroked his beard thoughtfully. Then, as if he'd suddenly come to a decision, he cried, "Yes, I accept! I will solve the mystery of your disciple, Diagoras, but not because of what you *thought* you saw when you spoke to him, but because of what I *saw* when I looked at his corpse!"

The Decipherer would answer none of the multiple questions that had formed in Diagoras's head, saying only, "Let's not discuss the fig until we've opened it up. I may be mistaken, so I'd rather say nothing more for now. But trust me, Diagoras: If I solve *my* enigma, it's likely that yours, too, will be solved. If you like, I'll visit you to discuss my fee."

They confronted the multiple heads of the financial side of the matter and reached an agreement. Then Heracles said he would begin his investigation the following day—he'd go to Piraeus and try to find the hetaera Tramachus frequented.

"May I go with you?" Diagoras asked eagerly. And, as the Decipherer stared at him in amazement, Diagoras added, "I know it's not necessary, but *I would like to.* I want to work with you. It would make me feel I was helping Tramachus. I promise to do exactly as you say."

Heracles Pontor shrugged and smiled. "Very well. It's your money, Diagoras, so I suppose you have every right to take part in the investigation."

And at that moment, the multiple snakes coiled at his feet raised their scaly heads and flicked out their slimy tongues in fury.[6]

6. I'm sure readers were as surprised as I was by these last lines! We should definitely not see them as a complicated metaphor, but neither should we take them too literally—it really would be going too far to believe that "multiple snakes" were "coiled" on the floor of Heracles' room and that the entire conversation between Diagoras and the Decipherer of Enigmas therefore took place in "a place full of snakes slithering, cold and slowly, up the arms and legs of the protagonists while they talk on, oblivious," as Montalo put it. (This distinguished expert in Greek literature offered an absurd justification: "Why shouldn't there be snakes in the room if the author *so wishes*? It is the author who has the last word over what takes place in the world of his novel, not us.") But the reader shouldn't worry: The sentence about the snakes is pure fantasy. As are all the previous ones, of course, this being a work of fiction, but let us be clear: This sentence is a fantasy in which the reader *is not to believe,* while the others, equally fictitious, are to be *believed,* at least during reading, in order for the story to make sense. In fact, the only purpose of this ridiculous last sentence is, in my view, to emphasize the eidesis. The author wanted us to see the image hidden in this chapter. Even so, it's a deceptive device, and the reader should not jump to the *obvious conclusion*! This morning, before I had reached this stage of the translation, Helena and I unexpectedly discovered not only the correct eidetic image but also—or so I believe—the key to the whole book. We immediately told Elio, our boss.

" 'Damp cold,' 'sliminess' or 'stickiness,' 'sinuous' and 'slithering' movements—it could be a snake, couldn't it?" suggested Elio. "Chapter one: a lion. Chapter two: a snake."

"But what about 'head'?" I objected. "Why all the 'multiple heads'?" Elio shrugged. So I showed him the little statue I'd brought from home. "Helena and I think we know. This is a statue of the Hydra, the mythical monster with many snake heads that multiplied when they were cut off. Hence the emphasis on the 'beheading' of the figs."

"But there's more," said Helena. "Defeating the Lernaean Hydra was the second labor performed by Hercules, the hero of many Greek legends."

"So what?" said Elio.

I went on excitedly: "*The Athenian Murders* has twelve chapters, and, according to legend, Hercules performed twelve labors in all. His Greek name was Heracles. The name of the novel's central character is Heracles, too. And the first labor of Hercules, or Heracles, consisted in slaying the Nemean lion . . . and the hidden image in chapter one is a lion."

"And in chapter two, it's the Hydra," said Elio quickly. "It does all seem to fit—for now, that is."

"What do you mean 'for now'?" I was slightly annoyed by this qualification.

Elio smiled calmly.

"I agree with your conclusions," he said, "but eidetic works can be treacherous. You have to remember that you're dealing here with things that are entirely imaginary, not even words, but ideas. Distilled images. How can we be sure what final key the author had in mind?"

"Simple," I replied. "We just have to prove our theory. In most versions, the third labor is the capture of the Erymanthian boar. If the image hidden in chapter three turns out to be a boar, that's one more item of proof."

"And so on until the end," said Helena confidently.

"I have one objection." Elio scratched his bald head. "The labors of Hercules weren't a secret when this work was written. Why use eidesis to hide them in the text?"

There was silence.

"A valid point," admitted Helena. "But let's suppose that the author created an eidesis of the eidesis, and that the labors of Hercules are, in turn, hiding another image."

"And so on ad infinitum?" asked Elio. "If that's so, we'll never find the original idea. You have to stop somewhere. According to that view, Helena, any written thing can refer the reader to an image, which, in turn, can refer him to another, and another. It would make reading impossible!"

They both looked at me expectantly. I admitted I didn't understand, either.

"Montalo edited the original text," I said, "but, unbelievably, it doesn't seem that he noticed anything. I've written to him. His thoughts may prove useful."

"Did you say Montalo?" Elio raised his eyebrows. "I'm afraid you've wasted your time. Montalo died last year. Didn't you know? It was big news. . . . You didn't know, either, Helena?"

"No," admitted Helena. She glanced at me sympathetically. "That's bad luck."

"Isn't it?" agreed Elio. He turned to me. "And since his was the only edition of the original and so far yours is the only translation, it seems that finding the final key to *The Athenian Murders* is entirely up to you."

"What a responsibility," joked Helena.

I didn't know what to say. And I'm still going over it in my mind.—TRANS.

3[1]

IT SEEMS APPROPRIATE to interrupt the swift progress of the story for a moment and say a few quick words about the central characters, Heracles, son of Phrynichus, from the deme of Pontor, and Diagoras, son of Iampsachus, from the deme of Mardontes. Who were they? Who did they think they were? Who did others think they were?

With regard to Heracles, let us say that[2]

As for Diagoras[3]

1. "Haste, carelessness. The handwriting here is uneven and, at times, illegible, as if the scribe had been in a hurry to get to the end of the chapter," Montalo said of the original text. I, for my part, am looking out to see if I can "capture" my wild boar in these sentences. I'm now beginning to translate chapter 3.—TRANS.

2. "There follow five indecipherable lines," stated Montalo. Apparently, the handwriting in this section was dreadful. Montalo could only make out five words in the entire paragraph: *enigmas, reason, wife,* and *fat man.* The editor of the original text added, not without irony: "The reader must try to reconstruct Heracles' biography from these five words, a task that seems both very easy and enormously difficult." —TRANS.

3. The three lines the anonymous author devoted to the character of Diagoras were also illegible. Montalo could make out only the following: *Did he live?* (including the question mark), *spirit,* and *passion.*—TRANS.

Now that the reader is fully acquainted with the details of the lives of our protagonists, let us swiftly resume our story with an account of what occurred in the port of Piraeus, where Heracles and Diagoras went in search of the hetaera named Yasintra.

They sought her down narrow streets, along which the smell of the sea traveled swiftly; in dark spaces left by open doors; here and there, among small clusters of silent women who smiled as the two men approached but grew abruptly serious on being questioned; up and down rises and hillsides that sank to the sea's edge; on corners where a shadow—man or woman—waited silently. They asked old women with painted faces, whose hard, blank countenances, daubed with white lead, seemed as ancient as the houses; they placed obols in trembling palms as cracked as papyrus; they heard the jangle of golden bracelets as arms were waved in the direction of a place or person: "Ask Kopsias." "Melitta knows." "Maybe at Thalia's." "Amphitrite is looking for her, too." "Eos has lived longer in this neighborhood." "Clito knows her better." "I'm not Thalia; I'm Merope." And all the while, their eyes, beneath lids thick with pigments, always half-closed, swiftly moving, surrounded by black lashes and patterns of saffron or ivory or red-gold, as if the women were free only in their gazes, as if they reigned only behind the black of their pupils. The still features and brief answers concealed their thoughts; only the eyes were sincere and fleeting, quick, eager.

The afternoon steadily drained away. Rubbing his arms beneath his cloak with swift movements, Diagoras said, "The day has passed quickly and soon it will be night."

Heracles said nothing.

They walked up a narrow, sloping street. Beyond the rooftops, the sea's end was revealed by a purple sunset. The crowds and frenetic rhythms of the port, and the places frequented by those seeking pleasure and amusement, were all left behind. They were now in the neighborhood where *they* lived, a forest with stone paths and adobe trees, through which darkness ran swiftly and night rose up prematurely; a place of peopled desolation, hidden, full of quick glances.

"Your conversation is entertaining at least," said Diagoras, not even attempting to hide his irritation—he felt as if he'd been talking to himself for hours. His companion simply walked along, grunting from time to time and working through the figs in his knapsack. "You have a gift for dialogue, by Zeus." He stopped and looked around, but only the echo of their footsteps followed them. He exclaimed in disgust, "These revolting, foul-smelling alleys, piled with rubbish! Where is the 'well-constructed' city, as Piraeus is always described? Is this the famous 'gridiron' layout of streets designed, it is claimed, by Hippodamus of Miletus? By Hera, I haven't even seen any district inspectors, *astynomi,* or slaves or soldiers, not like in Athens! I feel I am not among Greeks, but in a world of barbarians. And this is more than my impression; this really is a dangerous place. I can smell danger as distinctly as the sea." He glanced at Heracles again and added dryly, "Of course, I'm reassured by your animated chatter. Your conversation is so comforting, it makes me quite forget where I am."

"You're not paying me to chat, Diagoras," said Heracles with absolute indifference.

"Thanks be to Apollo. I hear your voice!" said the philosopher sarcastically. "Pygmalion could not have been as astonished when Galatea spoke! I will sacrifice a goat tomorrow in honor of—"

"Be quiet," ordered the Decipherer abruptly. "That's the house."

A cracked gray wall stood precariously on one side of the street, with a conclave of shadows gathered by the door.

"The seventh house, you mean," grumbled Diagoras. "I've asked after her in six previous houses, to no avail."

"Well, with your great experience, you should have no difficulty questioning these women."

The dark shawls concealing their features swiftly revealed gazes and smiles when Diagoras approached. A blush colored the philosopher's cheeks. He began clumsily, "Excuse me. My friend and I seek the dancer Yasintra. We were told—"

Just as the careless foot of a hunter crunching on a branch causes his prey to disappear in a flash into the undergrowth, Diagoras's words had an unexpected effect on the women: One of them ran off down the street at great speed, while the rest hurried into the house.

"Wait!" Diagoras shouted after the fleeing shadow. "Is that Yasintra?" he asked the other women. "Wait, by Zeus! We just want to—"

The door slammed shut. The street was now deserted. Heracles walked away slowly, and Diagoras followed him reluctantly. A moment later, he said, "Now what are we to do? Why are we still walking? She's gone. Run away! Do you imagine you can catch her at this pace?" Heracles grunted and calmly took another fig from his knapsack. Utterly exasperated, the philosopher stopped and shouted angrily, "Listen to me! We've spent all day searching for the hetaera, in the streets on the seafront and inland, in houses of ill repute, in the upper district and in the lower. We've rushed here, there, and everywhere, trusting the false word of mediocre souls, uncultured spirits, coarse procuresses, and wicked women! And now that Zeus seems to have allowed us to find her, we've lost her again! Yet you plod on, like a contented dog, while—"

Heracles interrupted placidly: "Calm down, Diagoras. Have a fig. It'll give you the strength to—"

"I've had enough of your figs! I want to know why we're still walking! I think we should try to talk to the women who went into the house and—"

"No. The woman who ran away is the one we want," said the Decipherer calmly.

"So why aren't we chasing her?"

"Because we're very tired. At least I am. Aren't you?"

"If we're so tired," said Diagoras, growing yet more irritable, "why don't we stop?"

Heracles trudged on, eating his fig in silence.

"You're so Socratic, Diagoras," he said at last.

They walked on awhile in the smoothly approaching night. The street rolled on uninterrupted between two rows of dilapidated houses. Very soon, they would be in absolute darkness, unable even to make out the surrounding buildings.

"Athena knows where that woman has got to!" muttered Diagoras, rubbing his hands briskly to warm them. "She was young and agile. I believe she could have run without stopping until she was out of Attica."

He imagined her running for the nearby forest, leaving prints of her bare feet behind her, by the light of a moon as white as a lily in the hands of a young girl. She would be unconcerned by the dark (she must know the way), her breath leaping in her chest, the sound of her steps muffled by the distance, her fawnlike eyes wide. Unafraid, she would shed her clothes so as to run more swiftly, her lily white body a delicate flash of lightning shooting through the undergrowth, dodging the trees, her loose hair barely catching on their antlers (slender as stems or a girl's fingers), quite naked and resplendent, like an ivory flower held by a young girl as she runs.[4]

They soon reached a crossroads. Beyond it, the street narrowed to a passage strewn with stones. An alley started to the left. To the right, a small bridge between two tall houses created a tunnel, its end lost in shadow.

"What now?" inquired Diagoras irritably. "Do we draw lots to decide on the way forward?"

He felt a pressure on his arm and, in compliant silence, allowed himself to be led quickly to the street corner nearest the tunnel.

4. The original text is missing several words (written so "hastily" they prove "illegible," according to Montalo), making this mysterious paragraph difficult to interpret. The implicit eidesis seems to relate to "speed," which has featured since the beginning of the chapter, but there are also images of deer (though not wild boar): "fawnlike eyes," the "antlers" of the trees, suggesting not the third labor of Hercules, but the *fourth,* the capture of the Arcadian stag. I don't find it too surprising that the order of the labors should have been altered, as this was often the practice of writers in antiquity. But a new metaphor stands out: a young girl holding a lily. Is this an eidetic image? And if so, what does it have to do with the hunting of the stag? Did the author intend it to represent the purity of the goddess Artemis, to whom the stag was sacred? In any case, I don't think one can dismiss it, as Montalo did, "as an instance of poetic license of no real significance."—TRANS.

"Let's wait here," whispered Heracles.

"But what about the woman?"

"Waiting can be a means of pursuit."

"Surely you don't believe she's going to retrace her steps?"

"Of course she is." Heracles captured another fig. "Everyone always returns. And speak a little lower—we don't want to frighten off our quarry."

They waited. The moon's white horns appeared. A brief gust of wind disturbed the stillness of the night. The two men wrapped their cloaks tightly around them. Diagoras suppressed a shiver, even though the moderating presence of the sea made it milder here than in the city.

"Someone's coming," whispered Heracles.

It sounded like the supple rhythm of a girl dancing in bare feet, tiptoeing over the stones. But it was a flower, not a person, that emerged from the streets beyond the crossroads, a lily damaged by the rough hands of the wind. It fell apart as it brushed the wall near their hiding place, and, scattering petals, it went quickly on its way through air that smelled of foam and salt. It disappeared, carried by the Zephyr as if by a beautiful young girl—eyes of sea, hair of moonlight—wearing it in her hair.

"It was nothing. Just the wind," said Heracles.[5]

For a brief moment, time stopped, spent. Diagoras, now chilled to the bone by the damp cold, gave himself away by whispering to the Decipherer's stout shadow: "I never would have believed that Tramachus . . . I mean, you understand. Purity was one of his greatest virtues, or so it seemed. This is the last thing I would have expected.

5. Of course it's something! Our protagonists can't see her, of course (she's a purely fictional figure), but here, once again, we have the girl with the lily. There can no longer be any doubt that this is another eidetic image, and a very powerful one at that, since it crosses over into the reality of the story, like a ghost. What can it mean? I have to admit that this sudden apparition makes me a little uneasy; I even struck the text, just as Pericles is said to have done to Phidias's chryselephantine statue of Athena to get her to speak: "What does it mean? What do you mean?" The paper, of course, yields no answers. I've calmed down now.—TRANS.

To associate with a vulgar . . . He was still a boy! It hadn't occurred to me that he might be experiencing the normal desires of an ephebe. When Lisilus told me—"

"Quiet," Heracles' shadow said suddenly.

Quick scraping sounds came from the tunnel, as if someone were walking over rubble. Diagoras felt the Decipherer's warm breath in his ear just before he heard his voice.

"Jump on her quickly. Protect your crotch with your hand and watch her knees. Try to calm her."

"But—"

"Do as I say, or she'll get away again. I'll back you."

What does he mean? wondered Diagoras, undecided. But there was no more time for questions.

Agile, quick, silent, a shadow, thrown by the trace of moonlight, spread like a carpet over the ground at the crossroads. Diagoras flung himself upon it, and, without warning, it turned into a body. A mass of perfumed hair swung in his face, like a slap, and a muscular form struggled in his arms. Gripping tightly, Diagoras pushed her against the opposite wall.

"That's enough, by Apollo!" he cried. "We're not going to hurt you! We just want to talk to you. Calm yourself." The figure became still, and Diagoras backed away slightly. He could not see her face, as it was masked by her hands, but her eyes peered through fingers as slender as the antlers of a young stag. "We want to ask you a few questions. About an ephebe named Tramachus . . . You knew him, didn't you?"

Calmer now, Diagoras thought she would eventually open the delicate doors formed by her hands and show her face.

Then came a flash of lightning in his lower abdomen. The pain, at first, was a perfect, blinding light that flooded his eyes like liquid spilling, relentless, over the edge of a krater. The sensation took a little longer, crouching between his legs before stretching furiously and exploding into his consciousness as if spewing shards of glass. He fell, coughing, to the ground, and didn't even feel his head strike the paving stones.

There was a scuffle. Heracles Pontor threw himself upon the figure. He was far less gentle than Diagoras, grabbing her slim arms and pushing her roughly against the wall. She moaned—a manly gasp. Again he slammed her against the wall. The figure tried to strike back, but Heracles leaned his fat body against her so that she couldn't use her knees. He saw Diagoras struggle to his feet. He spoke quickly to his prey: "I'll only hurt you if you give me no choice. And if you strike my companion again, I'll have no choice." He turned to Diagoras and said, "Keep a tight hold of her this time. I told you to watch out for her knees."

Diagoras muttered to the shadow, gasping painfully with each word: "My friend . . . speaks the truth. . . . We don't wish to hurt you. . . . Do you understand?"

The shadow nodded, but the philosopher kept a firm grip on her arms.

At last, the struggle subsided, just as cold relinquishes the muscles in a rapid race. Panting, Diagoras felt the flat, anonymous, blurred figure that he held firmly against the wall turn quickly into a woman. He sensed the volume of her breasts, the narrowness of her waist, the different smell, the smooth firmness. He observed curly hair, slender limbs, curves. Lastly, he made out her face.

His first thought was that her face was strange. He realized that, for some reason, he had imagined she would be very beautiful. But she wasn't: Her curly hair was an untidy mat of fur; her eyes were too large and pale, like those of a swift, timid animal, although in the darkness he could not tell their color; her thin cheeks hinted at the skull beneath the taut skin. He drew back, confused, the pain still throbbing dully in his abdomen, and asked, "Are you Yasintra?"

The cold clothed his words in steam.

She didn't answer.

"You knew Tramachus," insisted Diagoras. "He came to see you."

"Watch her knees," Heracles' voice warned from a great distance.

The girl stared in silence.

"Did he pay for his visits?"

Diagoras wasn't sure why he asked that, but it was the first question to receive an answer:

"Of course he did," she said. Both men reflected that many ephebes had a less masculine voice than she; it was the echo of an oboe in a cavern. "The rites of Bromios are paid for in paeans; the rites of Cypris in obols."

Diagoras didn't know why, but he felt offended. Perhaps it was because the girl seemed unafraid. And were the full lips mocking him in the darkness, or was he imagining it?

"When did you meet him?"

"At the last Lenaea. He saw me dancing in the procession to the god and sought me out afterward."

"He sought you?" asked Diagoras in disbelief. "But he was not yet a man!"

"Many youths seek me."

"Perhaps you refer to someone else."

"Tramachus, who was killed by wolves," said Yasintra. "I speak of him."

Heracles said impatiently, "Who did you think we were?"

"I don't understand." Yasintra turned her liquid gaze upon him.

"Why did you run away when we asked for you? You don't look like one who flees from men. Whom were you expecting?"

"Nobody. I run away if I want to."

"Yasintra," pleaded Diagoras, "we need your help. We know that Tramachus was in some kind of trouble. A very grave matter was tormenting him. I— We were his friends and we want to find out what it was. Your relationship with him no longer matters. We simply want to know if Tramachus spoke of his worries."

He wanted to add, Oh please, help me. I care about this more than you can imagine.

As vulnerable and fragile as a lily in the hands of a maiden, he felt he could have pleaded for help a hundred times. His spirit, stripped of all pride, was like a young girl with blue eyes and shining hair, imploring on her knees: "Help me, please, help me." But, gentle as the brush of a girl's white tunic against a flower, and yet, as ardent as the girl's delectable nubile body, his wish was not translated into words.[6]

"Tramachus never spoke much," she said. "But he didn't seem anxious."

"Did he ever ask for your help?" inquired Heracles.

"No. Why would he?"

"When did you see him last?"

"One moon ago."

"He never talked about his life?"

"Who ever talks to women like me?"

"Did his family approve of your relationship?"

"There was no relationship. He came to see me, paid, and left."

"But perhaps his family disliked the idea that its noble son was coming to you for solace, even if only once in a while."

"I don't know. It wasn't his family I had to please."

"Maybe his father knew about you," suggested Heracles calmly.

"He had no father."

"You're right," said Heracles. "I meant his mother."

"I don't know her."

There was a short silence. Diagoras looked at the Decipherer for help. Heracles shrugged.

"Can I go now?" asked the girl. "I'm tired."

Although they said nothing, she moved away from the wall and hurried away. Swathed in a long dark shawl and tunic, she had the loose stride of a wild animal in the forest. Her bangles and bracelets

6. The powerful eidetic image of the girl with the lily persists! And now the idea of "help"—repeated three times in this paragraph—seems to have joined it. The author described the young girl according to the rules of eidesis—in other words, scattering adjectives throughout the text for the reader to collect at the end and create the complete image. The image here, I believe, is that of a "young girl," with eyes as "blue" as the sea, "shining" hair or hair of "moonlight," and a "delectable" and "smooth" body, wearing a "white tunic" and holding a "lily." Obviously a very beautiful young girl . . . But why is she running away? And who or what is threatening her?—TRANS.

jangled with every step. Just as she was about to be swallowed by the darkness, she turned and said to Diagoras, "I didn't want to strike you."

It was late at night by the time they returned to the city, following the Long Walls.

"I'm sorry you got hurt," said Heracles a little guiltily. The philosopher had been silent since their conversation with Yasintra. "Are you still in pain? I did warn you. . . . I've come across that type of hetaera before. They're very agile and quite capable of defending themselves. When she ran away, I knew she'd attack if we got near her."

He paused, expecting Diagoras to say something, but his companion walked in silence, head bowed, chin resting on his chest. They had left the lights of Piraeus behind some time ago. The great paved road (which, according to Heracles, though empty, was safer and quicker than the more commonly used route), lined by walls built by Themistocles, destroyed by Lysander, only to be rebuilt again, rolled on smoothly in the dark winter's night. In the distance, to the north, the walls of Athens stood out like a dream, gleaming faintly.

Heracles went on quickly: "Now it's you, Diagoras, who has said nothing in a long while. Have you lost heart? Didn't you say you wanted to help with the investigation? My investigations always begin like this: We seem to have nothing, but then . . . Maybe you thought it a waste of time questioning the hetaera? Pah! I can tell you from experience that following up a lead is never a waste of time, quite the opposite. Hunting is knowing how to follow a trail, even though it seems to lead nowhere. Then, contrary to what most people believe, shooting the deer with the arrow turns out to be the easiest—"

He was interrupted by Diagoras's muttering: "He was a boy," he said, as if answering some question from Heracles. "Still too young to be an ephebe. His gaze was pure. His soul seemed as if burnished by Athena herself."

"Don't blame yourself. Even at that age, we seek outlets."

The philosopher raised his eyes from the dark road for the first time and glanced disdainfully at Heracles.

"You don't understand. We teach the boys at the Academy to love wisdom above all else and to reject dangerous pleasures and their fleeting rewards. Tramachus knew virtue; he was aware that it is infinitely more useful and profitable than vice. How could he ignore this?"

"And how did you teach virtue at the Academy?" asked the Decipherer.

"Through music and the enjoyment of physical exercise."

After another silence, Heracles scratched his head and remarked, "Well, let's just say that Tramachus thought the enjoyment of physical exercise more important than music."

Diagoras ignored him and began to speak quickly and pedantically, as if reciting a tedious lesson to a group of dull students. "Ignorance is the root of all evil. Who would choose the worst while fully aware that it was the worst? If reason, through learning, made you see that vice was worse than virtue, falsehood worse than truth, immediate pleasure worse than the lasting kind, why would you consciously choose the former? You know, for instance, that fire burns. Would you, of your own free will, hold your hand over flames? It's absurd. An entire year visiting that . . . woman! Paying for his pleasure! I don't believe it. The hetaera lied to us. I assure you of that. . . . What are you laughing at?"

"Forgive me," said Heracles. "I was remembering someone I once watched hold his hand over flames by choice. An old friend from my deme, Crantor of Pontor. He believed quite the opposite: He claimed that reason is not enough to make a man choose the best, since he lets himself be guided by desires, not ideas. One day, he felt like burning his right hand, so he held it over the fire and burned it."

There was a long silence. Then Diagoras said, "And you . . . do you agree with him?"

"Not at all. I always believed my friend was mad."

"And what became of him?"

"I don't know. He suddenly had an impulse to leave Athens, so he left. And he hasn't returned."

After another silence and several hurried steps along the paved road, Heracles asked, "What do you think of the hetaera?"

"She's a strange, dangerous woman." Diagoras shuddered. "Her face . . . Her gaze . . . I looked into her eyes and saw horrible things."

In his vision, she was dancing on the snowy peaks of Parnassus, to a rapid beating of drums, her only clothing a thin deerskin. Her body moved without thought, without will almost, a flower in the fingers of a young girl, spinning dangerously close to the slippery edge of the abyss.

In his vision, she could ignite her hair and dangerously lash her own back with it; she could throw back her head so that the bone in her neck protruded from between the muscles like a lily stem; she could shout as if asking for help, calling Bromios, with his deer hooves; she could intone the quick paean from the evening *oreibasia,* the ritual dance tirelessly performed by maenads on mountaintops in winter, handling dangerous, swiftly poisonous snakes and knotting their tails beautifully, just as a young girl, without help, weaves a crown of white lilies.

In his vision, she was a naked form, bloodied by flames from the fires and juice from the grapes. As she moved, she traced hasty, bold words in the snow with her bare feet, ignoring the urgent cries of Prudence, who appeared before her like a slender young girl clad in white, to warn her, vainly, of the danger of the dances. "Help me!" called the little voice, to no avail, for to the eyes of a maenad, danger is as a gleaming lily placed on the opposite bank of an impetuous river. She would not resist the temptation to swim across swiftly, without even seeking help, and claim the flower. "Take care. There is danger here!" calls the voice of reason. But the young girl pays no heed, for the lily is too beautiful.

This was all part of his vision, and he took it to be true.[7]

7. Diagoras's latest vision brings together all the eidetic images that have appeared so far: speed, the stag, the young girl with the lily, and the plea for help. Now we have the word *danger,* as well! What can it all mean?—TRANS.

• • •

"What strange things you see in the gazes of others, Diagoras!" mocked Heracles good-humoredly. "Our hetaera may dance in the Lenaean processions from time to time, but believing that she frolics with the maenads in dangerous ecstasies in honor of Dionysus is going too far. I fear your imagination has keener sight than Lynceus."

"I told you what I saw with my mind's eye," retorted Diagoras. "It can discern the idea itself, and you shouldn't be so quick to despise it, Heracles. The idea itself is superior to reason. It is the light before which all beings and things are no more than vague shadows. And sometimes that idea may only become known to us through myth, fable, poetry, or dreams."

"Perhaps, but your 'idea itself' is of no use to me, Diagoras. I'm concerned only with what I can see with my own eyes and reason with my own logic."

"So what did you see in the girl?"

"Very little," said Heracles modestly. "Only that she was lying."

Diagoras halted his rapid march and turned to look at the Decipherer. Smiling a little guiltily, like a child caught playing a dangerous prank, Heracles explained.

"I set her a trap by mentioning Tramachus's father. As you know, Meragrus was condemned to death years ago, accused of dangerous collaboration with the Thirty."[8]

"I know. It was a harsh trial, like that of the admirals from Arginusae, because Meragrus paid for the crimes of many others." Diagoras sighed. "Tramachus was always reluctant to talk about his father. It was a dangerous subject for him."

"That's what I mean," said Heracles. "Yasintra claimed Tramachus hardly spoke to her, but she knew very well that his father died in disgrace."

8. Dictatorship established in Athens, under Spartan supervision, after the Peloponnesian War, made up of thirty citizens. The reader should note that the word *danger* seems to have left a sort of eidetic "echo" since its first appearance (the same happened with the word *help*), indicating that its presence is important.—TRANS.

"No. She knew only that he was dead."

"Not at all! As I've explained, Diagoras, I decipher only what I can see. But I see what someone says as clearly as I'm now seeing the torches at the city gate. Everything that we do or say is a text that can be read and interpreted. Do you recall her exact words? She didn't say, 'His father is dead,' but 'He had no father'—wording we would usually use to deny the existence of someone we didn't wish to recall. The kind of expression Tramachus would have used himself. Now, if Tramachus mentioned his father to a hetaera from Piraeus—a matter so intimate that he didn't even wish to share it with you—why did she tell us he hardly spoke to her?"

While Diagoras was pondering the question, Heracles added, "And there's something else: Why did she run away when we asked for her?"

"I'm sure she had plenty of reasons," answered Diagoras. "What I still don't understand is how you knew she was hiding in the tunnel."

"Where else? I knew we'd never catch her. She's young and agile, whereas we're old and clumsy. I refer mainly to myself, of course." He quickly raised a fat hand, forestalling Diagoras's objection. "So I deduced that she wouldn't need to run far. She simply had to hide somewhere until the danger was past. And what better place than a dark tunnel close to her house? But why did she flee? Now, that's what I don't understand. She earns her living precisely by not fleeing from any man."

"More than one dangerous crime must weigh on her conscience," said Diagoras gravely. "You may laugh, Decipherer, but I have never seen such a strange woman. The memory of her gaze still makes me shudder. . . . What's that?"

A procession of torches was running through the streets near the city gate. The participants wore masks and carried tabors.

"The start of the Lenaea," said Heracles. "The time is upon us."

Diagoras shook his head disapprovingly.

"Always in such a hurry to amuse themselves."

Having identified themselves to the soldiers, they went through the gate and headed toward the center of the city. Diagoras asked, "What do we do now?"

"We rest, by Zeus. My feet ache. My body was made for rolling from place to place, not walking. Tomorrow, we'll talk to Antisus and Euneos. I mean, you'll talk and I'll listen."

"What am I to ask?"

"Not so fast. Let me think about it. I'll see you tomorrow, good Diagoras. Relax; rest your body and your mind. And may anxiety not rob you of sweet sleep. Remember that you have engaged the best Decipherer of Enigmas in all Hellas."[9]

9. I managed to speak to Helena during one of her breaks this afternoon (she teaches Greek to a class of thirty). I was so agitated that I told her immediately what I'd found out.

"There's a new image in chapter three, in addition to the stag: a young girl holding a lily."

Her blue eyes widened.

"What?"

I showed her the translation.

"She appears mainly in the visions of one of the central characters, a Platonist philosopher called Diagoras. But she manages to enter reality in one scene. It's a very powerful eidetic image, Helena. A girl holding a lily, calling for help and warning of danger. According to Montalo it's a poetic metaphor, but it's obviously eidetic. The author provided a description—golden hair and eyes as blue as the sea, a slender body, dressed in white—dispersed throughout the chapter. See? Here he mentioned her hair. Here 'a slender young girl clad in white'— "

"Wait a minute," said Helena, interrupting. "The 'slender young girl clad in white' in this paragraph represents Prudence. It's a poetic metaphor in the style of—"

"No!" I confess I raised my voice a little more than I would have liked. Helena stared at me in amazement (I hate to think of it now). "It's not a metaphor; it's an eidetic image!"

"How can you be so sure?"

I thought for a moment. My theory seemed so obvious that I'd forgotten to gather any proof to back it up!

"The word *lily* is repeated ad nauseam," I said. "And the girl's face—"

"What face? You just said the author mentioned only her eyes and hair. Did you dream up the rest?" I opened my mouth to answer, but suddenly didn't know what to say. Helena went on: "Don't you think you're taking this eidesis business a bit too far? Elio warned us, remember? He said eidetic novels can be treacherous, and he's right. You start thinking that all the images are significant simply because they're repeated.

But that's ridiculous. In the *Iliad,* Homer described the form of dress of many of his heroes in minute detail, but that doesn't mean it's an eidetic treatise on clothing."

"Helena, look." I pointed at my translation. "Here we have the image of a young girl asking for help and warning of danger. . . . Read the whole chapter. Please."

So she did. I waited, biting my nails. When she'd finished, she again turned her painfully sympathetic gaze upon me.

"Look, you know I'm not as well versed as you in eidetic literature, but as far as I can see, the idea of 'speed' is the main hidden image here. This alludes to the fourth labor of Hercules, the capture of the Arcadian stag, which ran extremely fast. I also find hunting images, referring to the same thing: 'trail,' 'prey,' 'hunter.' And the stag itself is mentioned a few times: 'antlers,' 'white horns,' 'mat of fur.' . . . But the 'young girl' and the 'lily' are clearly poetic metaphors used—"

"Helena—"

"Let me finish. They're poetic metaphors used by the author to represent the rather artless nature of the philosopher Diagoras."

I wasn't convinced.

"But why specifically a 'lily'?" I objected, annoyed. "Why is it repeated so often if it's not an eidetic word? And why the repetition of 'help' and 'danger'?"

"I think you're confusing eidesis with repetition." Helena smiled. "Writers sometimes repeat words in a paragraph out of carelessness, or because they've run out of imagery."

She stopped when she saw the look on my face.

"Helena, I can't prove it, but I'm *sure* the girl with the lily is an eidetic image. . . . It's awful."

"What is?"

"That you hold a completely different view after having read the *same* text. It's awful that the images, the ideas formed by the words in books, should be so fragile! I *saw* a deer as I read, and I *also* saw a girl holding a lily and crying for help. You see the

---

stag, but not the girl. If Elio read this, perhaps only the lily would catch his attention. What might another reader see? And Montalo . . . what did Montalo see? Only that the chapter was copied out carelessly! But"—I thumped the papers in an unforgiveable moment of anger—"there *has* to be a *final* idea that doesn't depend on our opinions, surely? In the end, the words *must* make up a precise idea!"

"You sound like a man in love."

"What?"

"You've fallen in love with the girl with the lily, haven't you?" Helena's eyes sparked with derision. "Remember, she's not even a character in the novel. She's an idea that you've pieced *together* as you translate, an image woven from separate words." And, pleased to have shut me up, she went back to her classes, just turning to add, "Some advice: Don't get obsessed with it."

Now, in the evening, in the peace and comfort of my study, I believe Helena's right: I'm just the *translator.* Someone else would, with utter confidence, produce a different version, with different words, evoking different images. And why not? Perhaps, in my eagerness to follow the trail of the girl with the lily, I've created her with my own words. Because, in a way, a translator is also a writer . . . or rather (and it amuses me to think so), the *eidesis* of a writer—always present, yet always invisible.

Maybe. But why am I so *sure* that the girl is the *true* hidden message in this chapter, and that her cry for *help* and her warning of *danger* are so important? I'll find out only if I carry on.

For now, I'll follow the advice of Heracles Pontor, Decipherer of Enigmas: "Relax. . . . And may anxiety not rob you of sweet sleep."—TRANS.

THE CITY was preparing for the Lenaea, the winter festival in honor of Dionysus.

The servants of the *astynomi* decorated the streets, scattering hundreds of flowers over the Panathenaic Way, but the violent to-ing and fro-ing of men and beasts turned the iridescent mosaic to a pulp of crushed petals. Singing and dancing contests, announced on marble tablets on the monument to the Eponymous Heroes, were held in the open air, although the singers' voices were generally displeasing to the ear, and most of the dancers executed their leaps clumsily and furiously, disobeying the oboes. As the archons did not wish to vex the people, street entertainment, though frowned upon, was permitted. Young men from different demes staged rather poor theatrical acts in competition with one another, and people gathered in the squares to watch amateurs per-

1. A good night's sleep does wonders. I woke up thinking I could see Helena's point. Now that I've reread chapter 3, it doesn't seem so obvious that the girl with the lily is an eidetic image. Perhaps my imagination was playing tricks on me. I'm now starting chapter 4. Montalo said about this particular papyrus: "Battered, creased in places—could it have been trampled by a beast? It is a miracle that the text has come down to us in its entirety." As the usual order of the labors has been altered, I don't yet know which one I'm dealing with here. I'll have to go very carefully.—TRANS.

forming violent pantomimes based on ancient myths. The Theater of Dionysus Eleuthereus opened its doors to both new and established authors, mainly of comedies (the great tragedies being reserved for the Festival of Dionysus) so full of brutal obscenities that, usually, only men attended. And everywhere, though particularly in the Agora and Inner Ceramicus, from morning till night, there was a mingling of noise, shouting, laughter, wine, and people.

The city prided itself on its liberality, which set it apart from the barbarians and even from other Greek cities, so slaves were permitted their own, much more modest, festivals. They ate and drank better than during the rest of the year, held dances, and, in the noblest houses, were sometimes allowed to go to the theater, where they could watch themselves, as masked actors playing the parts of slaves clumsily derided the populace.

But the activity of choice during the festival was religion. The processions in honor of Dionysus Bacchus combined mysticism and savagery: Priestesses carried brutal wooden phalluses through the streets, dancing girls performed frenzied dances simulating the religious ecstasy of the maenads or bacchae—crazed women, in which all Athenians believed but none had ever seen—and men in masks mimed the god's threefold transfiguration (into serpent, lion, and bull), sometimes using the most obscene gestures. Rising above all the strident violence, the Acropolis remained silent and virgin.[2]

It was a cold, sunny day. That morning, a troupe of coarse Theban performers was granted permission to entertain people outside the Poikile Stoa. One, a rather old man, juggled with daggers, but his grip often failed and the knives fell to the ground, clashing violently; another man, huge and almost naked, despite the cold, swallowed the flames from two torches and expelled them violently through his nose;

2. The Acropolis (where the great temples to Athena, patroness of the city, stood) was mostly reserved for the Feast of the Panathenaea, although I suspect the patient reader already knows this. The words *violence* and *clumsiness* feature prominently. They must be the first eidetic images of this chapter.—TRANS.

the others played tunes on battered Boeotian instruments. After the opening act, they donned masks and performed a poetic farce about Theseus and the Minotaur. The gigantic fire-eater played the Minotaur, lowering his head and charging, playfully threatening to gore the spectators gathered around the columns of the stoa. Suddenly, the mythical monster drew a broken helmet from a sack and made a great show of placing it on his head. Everyone recognized it—a Spartan hoplite's helmet. Just then, the old man with the daggers, playing Theseus, flung himself at the beast, and struck it until he brought it to the ground. It was a simple parody, its meaning perfectly clear to the audience. Someone shouted, "Freedom for Thebes!" The actors chorused the cry wildly while the old man stood triumphantly over the masked beast. Confusion broke out among the increasingly restless crowd, and the actors, fearing the arrival of soldiers, stopped the pantomime. But spirits were running high: Slogans against Sparta were chanted, someone forecast the imminent liberation of the city of Thebes (which had suffered under the Spartan yoke for years), and others invoked the name of General Pelopidas—rumored to be in exile in Athens since the fall of Thebes—calling him "Liberator." There was a violent commotion, in which reigned equally the old bitterness toward Sparta and the jolly confusion caused by the wine and the feast. Some soldiers intervened, but when they heard that the cries were not against Athens but against Sparta, they restored order only reluctantly.

During all the violent tumult, one man had remained motionless and indifferent, oblivious to the clamor of the crowd. He was tall and thin, and wore a humble gray cloak over his tunic. With his pallor and shiny bald head, he resembled one of the polychrome statues adorning the vestibule of the stoa. A second man—short and fat (the exact opposite, in fact, of the first man), with a thick neck and a head that was slightly pointed at the crown—strolled up to him. They greeted each other briefly, as if expecting to meet, and, as the crowd dispersed and the shouting—now crude insults—subsided, they headed down the street and out through one of the narrow gates of the Agora.

"The furious plebeians insult the Spartans in Dionysus's honor," remarked Diagoras contemptuously, clumsily attempting to slow his impetuous steps to Heracles' plodding pace. "They mistake drunkenness for freedom, revelry for politics. What do we care about the fate of Thebes, or any other city, when we have shown that Athens herself matters not to us?"

Heracles Pontor, who had some interest in politics and, as a good Athenian, took part in the violent debates at the Assembly, said, "We're bleeding from the wound, Diagoras. In fact, our desire for Thebes to throw off the Spartan yoke shows that Athens matters very much to us. We may have been defeated, but we will not forgive open insults."

"And why were we defeated? Because of our absurd system of democracy! If we had allowed the best among us to govern, instead of the people, we would still have an empire."

"I prefer a small assembly where I can cry out to a vast empire in which I must keep silent," Heracles said, then suddenly regretted not having a scribe on hand, because he felt rather pleased with this sentence.

"Why should you have to keep silent? If you were one of the best, you would be able to speak out, and if you were not, why not strive to be so?"

"Because I don't want to be one of the best, but I want to speak out."

"It's not a question of what you want, Heracles, but of the well-being of the city. For instance, who would you have decide a ship's course? The majority of sailors, or the man with the greatest knowledge of seamanship?"

"The latter, of course," Heracles replied, adding after a pause, "as long as I was allowed to speak up during the journey."

"But what good is the right to speak when you hardly ever exercise it?" cried Diagoras, exasperated.

"You forget that the right to speak consists, among other things, of the right to keep silent when one wishes. Let me now exercise that right, Diagoras, by cutting short this conversation. What I most hate in this world is wasting time, and though I don't really know what that is, discussing politics with a philosopher is, I imagine, what comes closest. Did you receive my message?"

"Yes. And I have to tell you that Antisus and Euneos haven't got lessons at the Academy this morning, so they'll be at the Colonos Gymnasium. Though, by Zeus, I thought you'd get here earlier. I've been waiting for you at the stoa since the shops opened, and now it's almost midday."

"Actually, I rose at dawn, but I've been busy making inquiries."

"Relating to my job?" Diagoras brightened.

"No, mine." Heracles stopped at a stall that sold figs. "Remember, Diagoras, that it's *my* job, even though the money is yours. I'm not investigating the causes of your student's supposed fear, but the enigma I thought I saw when I looked at his corpse. How much are the figs?"

The philosopher snorted impatiently while the Decipherer filled the small knapsack hanging at his shoulder, over his linen cloak. They set off once more down the sloping street.

"What have you found out? Can you tell me?"

"In truth, very little," confessed Heracles. "There is a tablet on the monument to the Eponymous Heroes announcing that it was decided at the Assembly yesterday to organize a battue to exterminate the wolves on Lycabettus. Did you know?"

"No, but it seems just. It's sad that Tramachus had to die for it to happen."

Heracles nodded.

"I've also seen the list of new recruits. It would seem Antisus is joining up immediately."

"That is so," said Diagoras. "He is now old enough to be an ephebe. By the way, if we don't go any faster, they'll have left the gymnasium by the time we arrive."

Heracles nodded again, but he continued at the same plodding pace.

"Nobody saw Tramachus set off hunting that morning," he said.

"How do you know?"

"They let me consult the registers at the Acharnian and Phile gates, which lead to Lycabettus. Let us pay a small homage to democracy, Diagoras! Such is our zeal for collecting information to discuss at the Assembly that we record the name and class of everyone carrying things in and out of the city every day. This creates long lists that include entries such as: 'Menacles, metic merchant, and four slaves. Wineskins.' We believe we can thus better monitor trade. Nets and other hunting equipment are scrupulously entered. But Tramachus's name isn't there. And nobody else left the city that morning carrying nets."

"Perhaps he didn't take any," suggested Diagoras. "Maybe he was only going to hunt birds."

"But he told his mother that he was going to set traps for hares. At least, that's what she told me. But I wonder: If he was hunting hares, wouldn't it have been sensible to take a slave with him to watch over the traps and drive out prey? Why did he go alone?"

"So what do you suppose? That he didn't go hunting? That somebody was with him?"

"At this hour in the morning, I'm not in the habit of supposing anything."

The Colonos Gymnasium was a large-porticoed building to the south of the Agora. The doors were engraved with the names of famous Olympic athletes and flanked by small statues of Hermes. Inside, the sun was beating down with violent ardor on the palaestra, a rectangular area of raked earth, open to the elements, where the pancratia were held. The dense smell of crowded bodies and massage oils filled the air. The place, though vast, was packed: older youths, some dressed, others naked; boys in full training; *paedotribes* in purple cloaks, carrying staffs, instructing their pupils. The ferocious din precluded conversation. At the far end, through a stone arcade, were the roofed inner chambers—changing rooms, showers, and massage and unguent rooms.

Two men were engaged in combat on the palaestra. Quite naked and glistening with sweat, they leaned against each other, as if trying to butt each other, the arms of each forming muscular knots around his opponent's neck; despite the clamor of the crowd, they could be heard roaring and bellowing with the prolonged effort; white threads of saliva hung from their mouths like strange barbarian adornments. The fight was savage, brutal, irrevocable.

No sooner had they entered than Diagoras tugged at Heracles Pontor's cloak.

"There he is!" he cried, pointing to a place in the crowd.

"Oh, by Apollo," murmured Heracles.

Diagoras saw his amazement.

"Did I exaggerate Antisus's beauty?" he asked.

"It wasn't your disciple's beauty that surprised me, but the old man talking to him. I know him."

They decided to question Antisus in the changing rooms. Heracles stopped Diagoras rushing over to him, and handed him a piece of papyrus.

"Here are the questions you are to ask. It's better if you do the talking; that way, I can study his answers."

Diagoras was reading the papyrus when a violent clamor in the crowd made them look toward the palaestra. One of the pancratiasts had savagely struck his opponent's face with his head. The sound was heard throughout the gymnasium, like a bundle of reeds cracking beneath the impetuous hoof of a huge animal. The fighter staggered and was about to fall, although he seemed surprised, rather than hurt, by the blow. He didn't even raise his hands to his crushed face, which looked first exhausted, then devastated, by the impact, like a wall smashed by the horns of an enraged beast. Instead, he stepped back, eyes open wide and fixed on his opponent, as if someone had played a joke on him, while, from his eyes down, the solid framework of features collapsed noiselessly and thick lines of blood ran from his lips and large nostrils. But still he didn't fall. The crowd shouted insults, urging him to fight back.

Diagoras greeted his disciple and said a few words in his ear. As they headed toward the changing room, the old man who had been conversing with Antisus, his body blackened and shriveled like one huge burn, widened his onyx black eyes in surprise on seeing the Decipherer.

"By Zeus and Apollo of Delphi, you here, Heracles Pontor!" he cried in a voice that sounded as if it had been dragged over rubble. "Let us make libations to Dionysus Bromios, for Heracles Pontor, the Decipherer of Enigmas, has deigned to visit a gymnasium!"

"Occasional exercise can be beneficial." Heracles bore the man's violent embrace with good grace. He had known the old Thracian slave for many years—he had served in Heracles' family home—and treated him like a freeman. "Greetings, O Eumarchus. I'm happy to see that you are as youthful in old age as ever."

"That is well worth repeating!" The old man had no trouble making himself heard above the violent clamor. "Zeus increases my age but reduces my body. In you, I see, the two go hand in hand."

"My head remains the same size, for now." They both laughed. Heracles looked around. "Where is the man who was here with me?"

"Over there, with my pupil." With a finger that had a nail as long and twisted as a horn, Eumarchus pointed to a place in the crowd.

"Your pupil? You're Antisus's pedagogue?"

"I was! And may the Benefactresses take me in should I be so again!" Eumarchus made a sign to drive away the bad luck brought by mentioning the Erinyes.

"You seem angry with him."

"And why shouldn't I be? He has only just enlisted, and the stubborn boy has decided suddenly that he wants to guard the temples of Attica, far from Athens! His father, the noble Praxinoe, has asked me to try to convince him otherwise."

"Well, Eumarchus, an ephebe must serve the city wherever he is most needed."

"By the aegis of blue-eyed Athena, Heracles, don't tease me at my great age!" yelled Eumarchus. "I can still butt your barrel of a belly with my calloused old head! Wherever he is most needed? By Cronius Zeus, his father is one of the *prytaneis* at the Assembly this year! Antisus could choose the most comfortable post of all!"

"When did your pupil make his decision?"

"A few days ago! I'm here to try to make him change his mind."

"Times and tastes have changed, Eumarchus. Who would want to serve Athens in the city itself? The young seek new experiences."

"If I didn't know you as I do," said the old man, shaking his head, "I'd think you meant it."

They made their way through the crowd to the entrance of the changing rooms. Heracles said, laughing, "You've quite restored my good humor, Eumarchus!" He placed a handful of obols in the slave's cracked palm. "Wait for me here. I won't be long. I'd like to engage you for a small task."

"I'll stand here as patiently as the boatman of the Styx awaiting the arrival of another soul," said Eumarchus, delighted at the unexpected gift.

Inside the small changing room, Diagoras and Heracles stood, while Antisus sat on a low table, legs crossed.

Diagoras said nothing for a moment, silently delighting in the breathtaking beauty of the perfect face, drawn with economy of lines and framed by blond curls arranged in the latest fashion. Antisus was clad in nothing but a black chlamys—the sign that he had recently become an ephebe—but he wore it carelessly, awkwardly, as if still unused to it. With smooth violence, the pristine whiteness of his skin showed through the irregular openings of the garment. He swung his bare feet furiously, the childish action belying his newly acquired adult status.

"We can talk while we wait for Euneos," said Diagoras. He pointed to Heracles. "He's a friend. You may speak before him in all confidence." Heracles and Antisus nodded at each other briefly. "Antisus, do you remember the questions I asked you about Tramachus, and how Lisilus told me he had been visiting a hetaera? I knew nothing of the woman. I wondered if perhaps there were other things I didn't know."

"What sort of things, Master?"

"Anything. Anything you know about Tramachus—what he was interested in, what he liked to do when he wasn't at the Academy. The anxiety I saw in his face during those last days disturbs me somewhat. I want to do everything I can to find the cause and make sure it doesn't happen to other students."

"He didn't spend much time with us, Master," replied Antisus sweetly. "As for his habits, I assure you they were honorable."

"Who could doubt it?" Diagoras put in quickly. "My boy, I know well the beauty and nobility of my students. Hence my surprise at Lisilus's words. But you all confirmed their truth. And as you and Euneos were his closest friends, I feel you must know other things that, either out of propriety or goodness of heart, you haven't dared reveal."

A wild crash, as of objects shattering, filled the silence: The pancratiasts' fight had evidently intensified. The walls seem to shake at the footsteps of some enormous beast. Just as calm returned, Euneos entered the room.

Diagoras immediately compared them, as he had many times before, for he enjoyed studying his students' very different beauties in detail. With curly coal black hair, Euneos looked younger yet more masculine than Antisus. His face resembled a healthy red fruit; his strong milky white body had matured into that of a man. The older of the two, Antisus had a more graceful and ambiguous figure, smooth and pink-skinned, with not a trace of hair. But Diagoras thought Ganymede himself, cupbearer of the gods, could not rival Antisus's beauty. The boy's face could appear a little mischievous, especially when he smiled, but when he became suddenly serious, as he did when listening attentively, its beauty sent a shiver down the spine. Their physical differences were reflected in their temperaments, although in a manner contrary to expectation: Euneos was shy and childlike, while Antisus, with the aura of a pretty young girl, possessed the forceful personality of the true leader.

"You called, Master?" said Euneos softly as he opened the door.

"Come in. I wish to speak to you, too."

Blushing furiously, Euneos said the *paedotribe* had summoned him, so he would have to change and leave shortly.

"This won't take long, my child, I assure you," said Diagoras.

He quickly explained what he wanted to know. There was a silence. Antisus swung his rosy feet faster.

"We know little else about Tramachus's life, Master," he said as sweetly as ever, though the contrast between his youthful firmness of character and Euneos's blushing timidity was obvious. "We heard rumors of Tramachus's relationship with the hetaera, but we didn't believe them. Tramachus was noble and virtuous."

"I know," said Diagoras.

Antisus continued: "He almost never met us after class at the Academy, as he had religious duties. His family worships the Sacred Mysteries."

"I understand." Diagoras attached little importance to this last piece of information. Many noble Athenian families worshiped the Mysteries of Eleusis. "But I was wondering about the company he kept. I don't know. . . . Other friends, maybe."

Antisus and Euneos glanced at each other. Euneos began removing his tunic.

"We don't know, Master."

"We don't know."

Suddenly, the entire gymnasium seemed to shake. There was a rumbling, as if the walls were about to collapse. Outside, the crowd was howling frenetically, urging on the fighters, whose frenzied roars were now clearly audible.

"One last thing: I'm surprised that Tramachus, in such a preoccupied state, should have gone hunting alone. Was he in the habit of doing so?"

"I don't know, Master," said Antisus.

"What about you, Euneos?"

As the trembling grew stronger, objects around the room fell to the floor: clothes, a small oil lamp, registration tokens for the contest draws.[3]

"I think he was," murmured Euneos, a blush spreading over his cheeks. The loud quadrupedal footsteps were getting closer. A little

3. What is going on? The author certainly took eidesis to the limit! The pancratiasts' fight has turned into an absurd thundering, suggesting the furious attack of a huge animal (which tallies with all the images of "violent" and "impetuous" charges that have appeared throughout the chapter, as well as those referring to "horns"). I think these are references to the seventh labor of Hercules, the capture of the wild, raging Cretan bull.—TRANS.

statue of Poseidon toppled off a shelf and shattered on the floor. The changing room door shook deafeningly.[4]

"Good Euneos, do you recall other similar occasions?" inquired Diagoras gently.

"Yes, Master. At least two."

"So Tramachus often went hunting alone? What I mean to say, my child, is that this was normal, even if something was worrying him?"

"Yes, Master."

The door bulged as something charged at it. There was a scraping of hooves, snorting, the powerful echo of an enormous presence outside.

Quite naked save for the perfect ribbon encircling his black hair, Euneos calmly spread a brick red unguent over his thighs.

After a pause, Diagoras remembered his final question: "Euneos, it was you who told me that Tramachus wouldn't be attending classes that day because he'd gone hunting, wasn't it, my child?"

"I believe so, Master."

The door endured another battering. Heracles Pontor's cloak was showered with splinters. There was a roar of rage outside.

"How did you know? Did he tell you himself?" Euneos nodded. "When? I mean, I understand he left at daybreak, but I talked to him the evening before and he said nothing about going hunting. When did he tell you?"

Euneos didn't answer immediately. His small Adam's apple charged at his shapely neck.

"That . . . same . . . evening, I think, Master."

4. I'll quickly explain to the reader what's happening. The eidetic image—here, an enraged bull—has taken on a life of its own and is charging at the door to the changing room where the conversation is taking place. I hasten to add that the "beast's" actions are purely eidetic and the characters cannot, therefore, perceive them, just as they are unaware, for instance, of the adjectives the author uses to describe the gymnasium. This is not a supernatural event, but simply a literary device, whose only purpose is to draw attention to the image hidden in this chapter (think of the "snakes" at the end of chapter 2). The reader should not, therefore, be too surprised if Diagoras and his students seem oblivious to the powerful attacks on the room, continuing their conversation as if nothing were happening.—TRANS.

"You saw him that evening?" Diagoras raised his eyebrows. "Did you often meet in the evenings?"

"No. It must have been . . . earlier."

"I understand."

There was a brief silence. Barefoot and naked, the glistening unguent like a second skin over his thighs and shoulders, Euneos carefully hung his tunic on a hook bearing his name. On the shelf above, there were a few personal belongings: a pair of sandals, alabaster jars of unguents, a bronze strigil for scraping oneself clean after exercising, and a little wooden cage containing a tiny bird. The bird was flapping its wings violently.

"The *paedotribe* is expecting me, Master," he said.

"Of course, my child." Diagoras smiled. "We, too, must leave."

Obviously uneasy, the naked youth glanced at Heracles out of the corner of his eye and apologized once again. Passing between the two men, he headed for the door—it was so damaged, it fell off its hinges as he opened it—and left the room.[5]

Diagoras turned toward Heracles, looking for a signal that they might leave, but the Decipherer was staring, smiling, at Antisus.

"Tell me, Antisus, what are you so afraid of?"

"Afraid, sir?"

Apparently highly amused, Heracles took a fig from his knapsack.

"Why, if not, would you have chosen an army post so far away from Athens? I, too, would try to leave were I as frightened as you. And I would choose a similarly plausible excuse, so that I should be considered not a coward, but quite the opposite."

"Are you calling me a coward, sir?"

"Not at all. I will call you neither cowardly nor brave until I know

5. As I've already said, the eidetic events—the savage charges, the battering of the door—are purely literary and, therefore, only perceived by the reader. Montalo, however, like the characters, noticed nothing. "The surprising metaphor of the *roaring beast*," he stated, "which seems literally to destroy the realism of the scene and interrupts the measured conversation between Diagoras and his students [. . .] on several occasions, seems to have no purpose other than satire—a scathing criticism, no doubt, of the savage pancratium matches held in those days." Need I say more!—TRANS.

exactly why you are afraid. The only difference between the brave man and the coward is the source of his alarm. The cause of your fear may be so horrifying that anyone in their right mind would choose to flee the city as soon as possible."

"I'm not running away from anything," said Antisus, stressing every word, although his tone remained gentle, respectful. "I've wanted to guard the temples of Attica for a long time, sir."

"My dear Antisus," said Heracles placidly, "I may accept your fear but not your lies. Don't for a moment think of insulting my intelligence. You made your decision only a few days ago, and your father has asked your former pedagogue to make you change your mind, when he might have tried to do so himself. Does that not imply that your decision took him completely by surprise, that he is overwhelmed by what he sees as a sudden and inexplicable change of opinion, and that, not knowing what to attribute it to, he has called upon the only person outside your family who knows you best? I ask myself, by Zeus, what could be the cause of such a brutal change? Could the death of your friend Tramachus have played a part?" And, quite unconcerned, he added, almost without pausing, as he wiped the fingers in which he had held the fig, "Excuse me, where might I clean my hands?"

Heracles selected a cloth from near Euneos's shelf, utterly oblivious to the silence around him.

"Did my father get you, too, to try to make me reconsider?" In the young man's gentle words, Diagoras noted that respect (like a frightened, cornered animal abandoning its usual obedience and charging violently at its owners) was turning to annoyance.

"Good Antisus, don't . . . be . . . angry," he stammered, casting a withering glance at Heracles. "My friend sometimes goes too far. You mustn't worry, my boy. You've come of age, so your decisions, even if misguided, always deserve the greatest consideration." He then whispered to Heracles: "Would you come with me, please?"

They hastily bade Antisus farewell. The argument began even before they were out of the building.

"It's *my* money!" said Diagoras irritably. "Or have you forgotten?"

"But it's *my* job, Diagoras. Don't forget that, either."

"I don't care! Can you explain your highly inappropriate remarks?" Diagoras was growing more and more angry. His bald head had turned quite red. He lowered his forehead, as if about to charge at Heracles. "You offended Antisus!"

"I fired an arrow in the dark and hit the bull's eye," said the Decipherer calmly.

Diagoras stopped him, pulling violently at his cloak.

"Let me tell you something. I don't care if you think people are merely papyri that you can read and solve like riddles. I'm not paying you to offend—and in my name!—one of my best students, an ephebe whose every lovely feature bears the word *virtue*. I disapprove of your methods, Heracles Pontor!"

"I fear I disapprove of yours, too, Diagoras of Mardontes. Instead of questioning those two boys, you seemed to be composing a dithyramb in their honor. And all because you find them so beautiful. I think you confuse beauty with truth."

"Beauty is part of truth!"

"Oh," said Heracles, waving a hand dismissively, indicating that he didn't want to start a philosophical discussion. But again, Diagoras tugged at his cloak.

"Listen to me! You're nothing but a miserable Decipherer of Enigmas. You simply observe material things, judge them, and conclude that something happened this way or that, for this or that reason. But you don't arrive at the truth itself, and you never will. You've never beheld it, nor had your fill of its vision of the absolute. Your skill consists merely in discovering shadows of the truth. Antisus and Euneos are not perfect creatures, and neither was Tramachus, but I have seen into their souls, and I can assure you that a great deal of the idea of virtue shines within them . . . and it shines in their eyes, their beautiful faces, their harmonious bodies. Nothing on earth, Heracles, could be as resplendent as they are without possessing at least a little of the golden riches that come only from virtue itself." He stopped, as if ashamed at his impassioned speech. He blinked several times, his face quite red, adding more calmly, "Don't insult the truth with your intelligence, Heracles Pontor."

Somewhere in the emptiness of the devastated, rubble-strewn palaestra,[6] someone cleared his throat. It was Eumarchus. Diagoras turned and headed impetuously toward the door.

"I'll wait outside," he said.

"By thundering Zeus, I've only ever heard two people argue like that when they were man and wife," said Eumarchus once the philosopher had gone. Inside his black sickle of a smile, a single obstinate tooth, curved like a small horn, persisted.

"Don't be surprised, Eumarchus, if my friend and I end up getting married," said Heracles, amused. "We're so different that I think the only thing that binds us is love." They laughed good-humoredly. "Now, Eumarchus, if you don't mind, let's take a little walk and I'll tell you why I asked you to wait."

They strolled around the gymnasium, which was strewn with rubble after the recent onslaught. Violent charges had cracked the walls in places; javelins and discuses lay among shattered furniture; colossal footprints were visible in the sand; the floor tiles were covered with the skin that had fallen away from the walls—huge limestone flowers the color of lilies. The fragments of a vessel lay buried beneath the wreckage. On one of them, the hands of a young girl, her arms raised, palms facing upward, appeared to be signaling for help or warning of imminent danger. A dust cloud swirled in the air.[7]

6. The eidesis in this chapter is so powerful that it has a devastating effect on the location of the scene: The palaestra is "rubble-strewn," destroyed by the passing of the literary "beast." The huge crowd seems to have disappeared. In all my years as a translator, I've never seen an eidetic catastrophe of this kind. The anonymous author obviously intended the hidden images to be uppermost in his readers' minds and wasn't remotely worried about the realism of the plot being jeopardized.—TRANS.

7. The author certainly enjoyed playing with his readers. Here we have proof that I'm right, disguised yet perfectly identifiable: the girl with the lily, another extremely important eidetic image in this novel! I don't know what it means, but here she is (her presence is unmistakable—note the proximity of the word *lilies* to the detailed description of the hands of the "girl" painted on a buried pot fragment). The discovery

"Ah, Eumarchus," said Heracles as they finished their conversation, "how can I pay you for this favor?"

"By paying me," answered the old man. They laughed again.

"One thing more, good Eumarchus. I noticed that there was a small caged bird on the shelf of your pupil's friend Euneos. A sparrow, a gift typically sent by a lover to his beloved. Do you know who Euneos's lover is?"

"By Phoebus Apollo, I don't know about Euneos, Heracles, but Antisus has received an identical gift, and I can tell you it was from Menaechmus, the sculptor-poet. He's besotted!" Eumarchus tugged at Heracles' cloak and lowered his voice. "Antisus told me about it some time ago, but he made me swear by all the gods that I would tell no one."

Heracles thought a moment.

"Menaechmus . . . Yes, the last time I saw that eccentric artist was at Tramachus's funeral, and I remember being surprised that he was there. So Menaechmus gave Antisus a little sparrow."

"Are you surprised?" shouted the old man in his rough voice. "By Athena's azure eyes, I'd give that beautiful Alcibiades with the golden hair an entire nest! Though being a slave and at my age, I doubt the gift would get me anywhere!"

"Right, Eumarchus," said Heracles, looking suddenly cheerful. "I have to leave. But do as I told you."

"Continue paying me as you have, Heracles Pontor, and your order is as good as saying to the sun, 'Rise every day.' "

Heracles and Diagoras made a detour to avoid the Agora, which would be packed because of the Lenaea at that time of the evening. Even so, their progress was hindered by an accumulation of public

---

moved me to tears, I have to admit. I stopped work and went over to Elio's house. I asked whether it would be possible to see the original manuscript of *The Athenian Murders.* He said I should talk to Hector, our publisher. He must have seen something in my eyes, because he asked me what was the matter.

"There's a girl in the text calling for help," I told him.

"And you're going to save her?" came the mocking rejoinder.—TRANS.

games, obstacles caused by improvised farces, a labyrinth of entertainments, and the slow, violent crowd charging at them. They walked in silence, both deep in thought. At last, as they came to the district of Scambonidai, where Heracles lived, he said, "Please accept my hospitality for the night, Diagoras. My slave Ponsica is not too bad a cook, and a leisurely meal at the end of the day is the best way of gathering strength for the next."

The philosopher accepted his invitation. As they entered Heracles' dark garden, Diagoras said, "I would like to apologize. I should have expressed my disagreement more discreetly at the gymnasium. I apologize for wounding you with unnecessary insults."

"You're my client and you're paying me, Diagoras," said Heracles as calmly as always. "Any problems I have with you, I consider part of the job. As for your apology, I accept it as a gesture of friendship. But it, too, is unnecessary."

As they crossed the garden, Diagoras thought, What a cold man. Nothing seems to touch his soul. How can someone who cares nothing for beauty and who is never, not even occasionally, carried away by passion arrive at the truth?

As they crossed the garden, Heracles thought, I have yet to determine whether this man is simply an idealist, or an idiot, as well. In any case, how can he boast of having discovered the truth, if he sees nothing of what goes on around him?[8]

Suddenly, the front door of the house opened violently and Ponsica's dark form appeared. Her featureless mask was as blank as ever, but she began gesticulating to her master with unusual energy.

"What's the matter? A visitor . . ." deciphered Heracles. "Calm yourself. You know I can't read you when you're agitated. Start again." An unpleasant snort came from inside the dark house, followed immediately by extremely high-pitched barking. "What's that?" Ponsica

8. I've really enjoyed translating this passage, as I think I have something of both protagonists in me. I wonder, can someone like me, to whom beauty *matters,* who is *carried away* from time to time by passion, and yet makes sure that nothing of what goes on around him goes *unnoticed,* discover the truth?—TRANS.

gestured frantically. "The visitor? My visitor is a dog? Oh, a man with a dog . . . But why did you let him in while I was out?"

"Don't blame your slave woman," bellowed a powerful voice with a strange accent from inside the house. "But if you think she should be punished, tell me and I'll leave."

"That voice . . ." muttered Heracles. "By Zeus and aegis-bearing Athena!"

The man, who was huge, emerged energetically from the doorway. His beard was so thick, it was impossible to tell if he was smiling. A small but frightening dog with a deformed head appeared, barking, at his feet.

"You may not recognize my face, Heracles," said the man, "but I'm sure you remember my right hand."

He held out his hand, palm upward: The skin at the wrist was violently twisted into a knot of scars, like the flank of an old animal.

"Oh, by the gods," whispered Heracles.

The two men greeted each other warmly. Afterward, the Decipherer turned to an open-mouthed Diagoras and said, "This is my friend Crantor, of the deme of Pontor," he said. "I told you about him. It was he who placed his right hand in the fire."

The dog was called Cerberus. At least that's what the man called it. It had a huge forehead, creased into folds, like an old bull, and it bared an unpleasant set of teeth inside a pink mouth that contrasted with the sickly whiteness of its face. It had the cunning, bestial little eyes of a Persian viceroy. Its body was a small slave dragging itself after its cephalic master.

The man's head, too, was very large, but his tall, sturdy body was a column worthy of such a capital. Everything about him was exaggerated, from his manner to his size. He had a high forehead and large nostrils, and his big face was almost entirely covered by a beard; thick veins ran over his immense tanned hands; torso and belly were similarly huge; his feet were solid, almost square, and his toes all appeared to be exactly the same length. He wore an enormous patched gray cloak, evidently a faithful companion during his travels, as it molded itself stiffly to his body.

In a way, man and dog resembled each other. There was, in both, a gleam of violence in their eyes; when they moved, it took one by surprise and it was difficult to predict where their movements would take them, for it seemed that they were unaware of it themselves. And both had a voracious, and complementary, appetite, as anything that one rejected was furiously devoured by the other, or sometimes the man picked up a bone from the floor that the dog hadn't finished gnawing and completed the task in a few quick bites.

And both man and dog smelled the same.

Reclining on one of the couches in the cenacle and holding a bunch of black grapes captive in his huge hands, the man was talking. His voice was thick, deep, with a strong foreign accent.

"What can I tell you, Heracles? What can I recount of the wonders that I've seen, the marvels that my Athenian eyes have witnessed and that my Athenian reasoning would never have accepted? You ask many questions, but I have no answers. I'm not a book, though I'm full of strange tales. I've traveled across India and Persia, Egypt and the kingdoms of the south, beyond the Nile. I've been to caves where lion-men dwell, and I've learned the violent language of serpents that think. I've walked barefoot over the sands of oceans that opened before me and closed behind me, like doors. I've watched black scorpions scratch their secret symbols in the dust. And I've seen magic bring death, and the many forms daemons take to manifest themselves to sorcerers, and I've heard the spirits of the dead speak through their loved ones. I swear, Heracles, there is a world outside Athens. And it is infinite."

The man seemed to create silence with his words, like a spider weaves a web with thread from its belly. When he stopped talking, nobody spoke immediately. A moment later, the spell broke and the lips and eyelids of his listeners sprang to life.

"I'm delighted to see, Crantor," said Heracles, "that you have managed to fulfill your original aim. When I embraced you in Piraeus all those years ago, not knowing when I would see you again, I asked for the umpteenth time why you were choosing to go into exile. And I remember that you answered, also for the umpteenth time, 'I want to be surprised every day.' It would seem that you have succeeded." Crantor grunted, no doubt signifying agreement. Heracles turned to Diagoras, who had remained silent and obedient on his couch, finishing his wine. "Crantor and I are from the same deme and have known each other since childhood. We were educated together, and although I became an ephebe before he did, we took part in identical missions during the war. Later, when I married, Crantor, who was extremely jealous, decided to travel the world. We bade each other farewell and so . . . until today. In those days, we were separated only by our desires." He paused and his eyes glinted with happiness. "Do you know, Diagoras? In my youth, I wanted to be a philosopher, like you."

Diagoras expressed sincere surprise.

"And I, a poet," said Crantor in his powerful voice, also addressing Diagoras.

"But he ended up becoming a philosopher."

"And he a Decipherer of Enigmas!"

They laughed. Crantor's was a dirty, awkward laugh. Diagoras thought it sounded like a collection of other people's laughs, acquired on his travels. He himself simply smiled politely, while Ponsica, shrouded in silence, removed the empty platters from the table and poured more wine. It was now dark inside the cenacle, save for the light of the oil lamps picking out the faces of the three men, creating the illusion that they were floating in the darkness of a cave. Cerberus crunched ceaselessly, and, occasionally, the violent cries of the crowds running through the streets shot like lightning through the windows.

Crantor refused Heracles' offer of a bed for the night. He explained that he was only passing through the city on his life of constant travel; he was heading north, beyond Thrace, to the barbarian kingdoms, in search of the Hyperboreans, and didn't intend to remain in Athens more than a few days. He wished to amuse himself at the Lenaea and go to the theater—"To the only good theater in Athens—

the comedies." He said he had found a lodging that would tolerate Cerberus. The dog barked hideously upon hearing its name. Heracles, who had no doubt drunk too much, pointed to the dog and said, "You've ended up married, Crantor. You, who always criticized me for taking a wife. Where did you meet your lovely partner?"

Diagoras almost choked on his wine. But Crantor's amiable reaction confirmed his suspicion that the impetuous current of a close childhood friendship, mysterious to the eyes of others, flowed between Crantor and the Decipherer, and that their years of distance and the strange experiences that separated them had not quite succeeded in stemming it. Not *quite,* because Diagoras also sensed—he couldn't have said how, but he often had such impressions—that neither was entirely at ease with the other; they had to return to the children they once were in order to understand, and even bear, the adults they now were.

"Cerberus has lived with me longer than you can imagine," said Crantor. His voice was different, lacking its usual violence, as if he were lulling a newborn baby to sleep. "I found him on a quay. He was alone like me, so we decided to join destinies." He glanced over at the dark corner where the dog was chewing violently, adding, to Heracles' amusement, "He's been a good wife, I assure you. He shouts a lot, but only at strangers." And he stretched out an arm and patted the small white patch affectionately. The animal barked shrilly in protest.

After a pause, Crantor went on, "About Hagesikora, your wife . . ."

"She died. The Moirai decreed that she should have a long illness."

There was silence. At last, Diagoras said he must leave.

"Don't do so on my account." Crantor raised his huge burned hand. "Cerberus and I will soon be off." And almost without transition, he asked, "Are you a friend of Heracles?"

"I am really a client."

"Ah, some mysterious problem to solve! You're in good hands, Diagoras. I know for a fact that Heracles is a wonderful decipherer. He's grown a little stouter since I last saw him, but I assure you he has the same piercing gaze and quick intelligence. He'll solve your enigma, whatever it may be, in a few days."

"By the gods of friendship," grumbled Heracles, "let's not speak of work tonight."

"So you are a philosopher?" Diagoras asked Crantor.

"What Athenian isn't?" rejoined Crantor, raising his eyebrows.

"Let us be clear, good Diagoras," Heracles said. "Crantor is a philosopher in deed, not in thought. He takes his convictions to their utmost limit, for he doesn't like to believe in anything that he can't put into practice." Heracles seemed to enjoy his speech, as if he had been talking of the trait he most admired in his old friend. "I remember . . . I remember one of your sayings, Crantor: 'I think with my hands.' "

"You remember it wrongly, Heracles. The sentence was, 'Hands think as well.' But it applies to the whole body."

"Do you think with your intestines, too?" Diagoras smiled. Wine had made him skeptical, as it often does to those who rarely drink it.

"And with my bladder, and my penis, and my lungs, and my toenails," said Crantor. And after a pause, he added, "I believe you, too, are a philosopher, Diagoras."

"I am a tutor at the Academy. Do you know of the Academy?"

"Of course. Our good friend Aristocles!"

"We've long known him by his nickname, Plato." Diagoras was pleasantly surprised to find that Crantor knew Plato's real name.

"I know. Tell him from me that he is fondly remembered in Sicily."

"Have you been to Sicily?"

"I've more or less come straight from there. It is rumored that the tyrant Dionysius has fallen out with his brother-in-law Dion because of your colleague's teachings."

Diagoras was delighted to hear it.

"Plato would be happy to know that his sojourn in Sicily is beginning to bear fruit. But I invite you to tell him so in person at the Academy, Crantor. Please pay us a visit whenever you wish. Come and dine with us. Then you can take part in our philosophical dialogues."

Crantor stared in amusement at his cup of wine, as if it contained something extremely funny or ridiculous.

"I thank you, Diagoras," he replied, "but I'll have to think about it. The truth is, your theories don't appeal to me." And he laughed quietly, as if he'd just made a hilarious joke.

Slightly confused, Diagoras asked pleasantly, "What theories *do* appeal to you?"

"Living."

"Living?"

Still staring at his cup, Crantor nodded. Diagoras said, "Living isn't a theory. To live, all one needs is to be alive."

"No. One has to learn how to live."

Having wanted to leave a moment earlier, Diagoras now felt a professional interest in the conversation. He leaned his head forward and stroked his neatly trimmed Athenian beard with the tips of his slender fingers.

"What you've just said is very curious, Crantor. Please explain, for I fear I don't understand. In your opinion, how does one learn to live?"

"I can't explain."

"But it would seem that you have learned how to do so."

Crantor nodded. Diagoras said, "How can one learn something which is then impossible to explain?"

Crantor suddenly revealed huge white teeth lurking in the center of his labyrinth of a beard.

"Athenians . . ." he grumbled, so low that Diagoras couldn't make out the rest of the sentence. But as Crantor spoke, his voice grew louder, as if he had been far away and was now charging violently toward them. "They never change, however long one stays away. . . . Athenians. Oh, your passion for word games, sophisms, texts, dialogues! Your way of learning, with your asses on a bench, listening, reading, deciphering, inventing arguments and counterarguments in one endless dialogue! Athenians . . . one people made up of men who think and listen to music, and another people, more numerous but governed by the first, who know pleasure and suffering but not how to read or write." He jumped up and went over to the window. The confused clamor of Lenaean reveling filtered through it. "Listen to it,

Diagoras. The true Athenian people—their history will never be recorded on funeral steles or preserved on the papyri that your philosophers use to compose their wonderful works. These people don't even speak; they bellow, roar like an enraged bull." He moved away from the window. Diagoras noted a savage, almost fierce, quality in his movements. "A people made up of men who eat, drink, fornicate, and enjoy themselves, believing they're possessed by the ecstasy of the gods. Listen to them! They're out there."

"There are different classes of men, just as there are different types of wine, Crantor," said Diagoras. "These people of whom you speak are incapable of reasoning. Men who can reason belong to a higher class, so they have no choice but to lead the—"

The cry was savage, unexpected. Cerberus barked loudly, echoing his master's stentorian outburst.

"Reasoning! What good is reasoning? Did you use reason in your war against Sparta? Were your imperial ambitions based on reason? Pericles, Alcibiades, Cleon—these men led you to the slaughter! Were they reasonable? And now, in defeat, what's left? Reasoning past glories!"

"You talk as if you weren't Athenian!" protested Diagoras.

"Leave, and you, too, will cease to be Athenian! One can only be Athenian within the walls of this absurd city! The first thing you find when you leave is that there is no single truth—every man has his own. And out there, you open your eyes, and all you see is the blackness of chaos."

There was a pause. Even Cerberus's furious barking ceased. Diagoras turned toward Heracles, as if about to say something, but the Decipherer appeared to be deep in his own thoughts. Diagoras assumed Heracles considered the conversation too "philosophical" and was therefore letting him do all the answering. He cleared his throat and said, "I understand what you're saying, Crantor, but you're wrong. The blackness you mention, in which you see only chaos, is simply your ignorance. You believe that absolute, immutable truths do not exist, but I can assure you they do, even though they may be difficult to perceive. You say every man has his own truth. I would counter that every man has his own *opinion.* You have come across a great many very different men who expressed themselves in different languages and had their own opinions about things, and you've come to the erroneous conclusion that nothing has the same value for all. The fact is, Crantor, you don't go beyond words, definitions, images of objects and beings. But there are ideas beyond words—"

"The Translator," declared Crantor, interrupting him.

"What?"

Illuminated from below by the lamps, Crantor's huge face looked like a mysterious mask.

"There's a widely held belief in many places far from Athens," he said, "that everything we do and say is words written in another language on a huge papyrus scroll. And Someone is reading the scroll right now, deciphering our thoughts and actions, and finding hidden keys to the text of our lives. That Someone is known as the Interpreter, or Translator. Those who believe in Him think that our lives have an ultimate meaning, of which we ourselves are unaware, but which the Translator discovers as He *reads* us. Eventually, the text comes to an end and we die, knowing no more than before. But the Translator, who has read us, discovers at last the ultimate meaning of our existence."[9]

Heracles broke his silence and said, "What good does believing in that stupid Translator do them if they die in the end?"

"Well, there are those who believe it's possible to *talk* to the Translator." Crantor smiled mischievously. "They say we can address Him in the knowledge that He is listening, since He reads and translates all our words."

"And those who believe it, what do they say to this . . . Translator?" asked Diagoras, who found the belief no less ridiculous than Heracles.

"It depends," said Crantor. "Some praise Him, or request things—that He should tell them what's going to happen to them in future

9. Though I've searched through all my books, I can't find a single reference to this supposed religion. The author must have invented it.—TRANS.

chapters, for instance. Others challenge Him, as they know, or think they know, that He doesn't really exist."

"And how do they challenge Him?" asked Diagoras.

"They shout out to Him," said Crantor. And suddenly, he raised his eyes to the dark ceiling. He seemed to be looking for something.

He was looking for you.[10]

"Listen, Translator!" he shouted in his powerful voice. "You, who are so sure you exist! Tell me who I am! Interpret my language and define me! I challenge you to understand me! You, who think we are merely words written long ago! You, who think that our story has a final, hidden key! Apply your reason to me, Translator! Tell me who I am—if, when you read me, that is, you can also *decipher* me!" Recovering his composure, he looked at Diagoras and smiled. "That's what they shout at this supposed Translator. But the Translator never answers, of course, because He doesn't exist. And if He does exist, He knows as little as we do."[11]

Ponsica brought in another krater and poured more wine. Making the most of the pause, Crantor said, "I'm going for a walk. The night air will do me good."

The deformed white dog followed him out. A moment later, Heracles said, "Don't pay him too much heed, good Diagoras. He was always very strange, very impulsive, and time and experience have accentuated his oddity. He never had the patience to sit down and discuss things at length; complex reasoning confused him. He wasn't like an Athenian, or even a Spartan, for he loathed war and armies. Have I

10. I have translated this literally, but I can't understand to whom the author was referring in this unexpected grammatical shift to the second person.—TRANS.

11. I really don't know why I'm suddenly feeling so uneasy. In Homer, for instance, there are numerous examples of unexpected shifts into the second person. This must be something similar. But the fact is, I felt rather tense as I translated Crantor's invective. I've come to the conclusion that *Translator* may be another eidetic word. If this is the case, the image that emerges from this chapter is more complex than I thought: the violent "charges" of an "invisible beast" (representing the Cretan bull), the girl with the lily, and now the "Translator." Helena's right: I've become obsessed with this book. I'm going to speak to Hector tomorrow.—TRANS.

told you how he went to live alone in a hut he built himself on the island of Euboea? It was around the time he burned his hand. But he wasn't happy as a misanthrope, either. I don't know what pleases or displeases him. I never have. I suspect he isn't happy with the part Zeus has allocated him in the great Play of life. I apologize for his behavior, Diagoras."

The philosopher made light of it and stood up to leave.

"What are we doing tomorrow?" he asked.

"You're not doing anything. You're my client and you've already done quite enough work."

"But I'd still like to help."

"That won't be necessary. I'm going to carry out a little investigation on my own tomorrow. I'll let you know if anything new turns up."

Diagoras stopped at the door:

"Have you found out anything you can tell me?"

The Decipherer scratched his head. "It's all going well," he said. "I have a few theories that will keep me awake tonight, but . . ."

"I know," said Diagoras. "Let us not speak of the fig before we open it up."

They bade each other good night like good friends.[12]

12. I'm becoming more and more anxious. I don't know why, I've never felt like this about a piece of work. But it might all be my imagination. I'll reproduce the brief conversation I had with Hector this morning, and leave it to the reader to decide.

"*The Athenian Murders.*" He nodded when I mentioned the work. "Yes, a classical Greek text by an anonymous author dating back to Athens just after the Peloponnesian War. I was the one who mentioned to Elio that it should be on our list."

"I know. I'm doing the translation," I said.

"How can I help you?"

I told him. He frowned and, like Elio, asked me why I wanted to check the original manuscript. I explained that I thought the novel was eidetic but that Montalo didn't seem to have noticed. He frowned again.

"If Montalo didn't notice, then it *can't be* eidetic," he said. "I'm sorry, I don't want to be rude, but Montalo was an expert on the subject."

I summoned all my patience to say, "The eidesis is very powerful, Hector. In some scenes, it affects reality and even the characters' conversations and opinions. It must mean something, surely? I want to find the key the author hid in the text, and I need the original to make sure that my translation is accurate. Elio agrees—he told me to talk to you."

Hector is very stubborn, but he gave in eventually, though he didn't give me much hope—the text had been in Montalo's possession, and after his death, all his manuscripts went to other libraries. He didn't have any close friends or family and lived like a hermit in an isolated house in the country.

"And it was precisely his desire to get away from civilization," he added, "that led to his death. Don't you agree?"

"What?"

"Oh, I thought you knew. Didn't Elio tell you?"

"All he said was that he was dead." Then I remembered Elio's words. "And that 'it was big news.' But I didn't understand why."

"Because he had a horrific death," said Hector.

I swallowed. Hector went on.

"His body was found in the forest near his home. He'd been torn to pieces. The police said he must have been attacked by a pack of wolves."—TRANS.

HERACLES PONTOR, the Decipherer of Enigmas, could fly.

He soared as light as air, high in the pitch-dark of a cave, in absolute silence, as if his body were a sheet of parchment. At last, he found what he was looking for. First, he heard the beats, as thick as the sound of oars cutting through muddy waters; then he saw it, floating in the dark, like him—a human heart, just ripped out and still beating. A hand held it as if it were a wineskin; thick trails of blood oozed through the fingers. But it was the identity of the man grasping it so tightly, rather than the naked organ itself, that concerned him. The arm to which the hand belonged, however, appeared to have been neatly cut off at the shoulder, and beyond, everything was in shadow. Curious, Heracles came closer: How could an unattached arm float in the air? Then he discovered something even stranger: He could hear only a single set of heartbeats. He looked down in horror and raised his hands to his chest. He found a huge empty hole.

He realized that it was his own heart that had been torn out.

He woke up screaming.

By the time a worried Ponsica entered the room, he was feeling better, and was able to reassure her.[1]

The young slave stopped to hang the torch in the metal hook. He jumped, reaching it this time before Heracles had a chance to help.

"You've taken a long time to return," the boy said, brushing dust from his hands. "But while you still pay me, I don't mind waiting for you until I am old enough to be an ephebe."

"You'll be one sooner than Nature intends, if you carry on being so shrewd," said Heracles. "How is your mistress?"

"A little better than when you last saw her, though not fully recovered." Along one of the dark corridors, the boy stopped and drew closer to the Decipherer with a mysterious air. "My friend Iphimachus, the old slave of the house, says she screams in her dreams," he whispered.

"I had a dream last night that made me scream," confessed Heracles. "It's odd, because it doesn't happen very often."

"It's a sign of age."

"Do you know the meaning of dreams, too?"

"No. It's what Iphimachus thinks."

They reached the cenacle where Heracles had been received before. Today it was cleaner and brighter. Lamps burned in alcoves and behind the couches and amphorae, as well as along the corridors that led to it, so that the room was bathed in golden light. The boy asked, "Aren't you taking part in the Lenaea?"

1. I had a dream last night, before I started on this section. I didn't see a heart, though. In the dream, I was watching the central character, Heracles Pontor, as he lay in bed dreaming. Suddenly, he woke up screaming, as if he'd just had a nightmare. Then I, too, woke up and screamed. Now, having read the opening of chapter 5, I find the similarity chilling. With regard to this scroll, Montalo noted: "The papyrus is smooth and very thin, as if fewer layers of the plant were used to produce it, or as if, with the passing of time, it has become fragile, porous, delicate, like the wing of a butterfly or small bird."—TRANS.

"Me? I'm not a poet."

"I thought you were. What are you, then?"

"The Decipherer of Enigmas," replied Heracles.

"What's that?"

Heracles thought a moment.

"On reflection, it's not unlike what Iphimachus does," he said. "Giving an opinion on mysterious things."

The boy's eyes sparkled, but then, as if suddenly remembering his duties, he lowered his voice and announced, "My mistress will see you presently."

"Thank you."

The boy left the room, and Heracles, still smiling, realized he didn't know his name. He occupied himself by observing the tiny weightless particles floating around the lamps—suffused with their light, they looked like gold filings. He tried to find some order or pattern to the motion of the specks, but soon he had to look away; he knew that his curiosity, hungry to decipher ever more complex images, risked losing itself in the infinite intimacy of things.

As Itys entered, her cloak flapped like wings in the draft. Though still pale and with shadow-ringed eyes, her face appeared less ravaged. Her gaze had lost some of its darkness and seemed clear and light. Her slave women bowed before Heracles.

"We honor you, Heracles Pontor. I apologize for my poor hospitality—good cheer sits ill with grief."

"I am grateful for your hospitality, Itys, and would not wish for any other."

She motioned toward one of the couches.

"At least let me offer you some undiluted wine."

"Not this early in the day, thank you."

She waved her hand and the slave women left in silence; then she and Heracles reclined on couches facing each other. As Itys arranged the folds of her peplos over her legs, she said, "You haven't changed, Heracles Pontor. You wouldn't risk a single drop of wine at an unaccustomed hour, even to offer a libation to the gods, in case it ruined even the most insignificant of your thoughts."

"You haven't changed, either, Itys: You still tempt me with the juice of the vine so that my soul should lose touch with my body and float free in the sky. But my body has grown heavy."

"Your mind, however, grows ever lighter, doesn't it? I confess, mine does, too. All my mind wishes to do is flee from within these walls. Do you allow yours to fly, Heracles? I can't keep mine locked up; it stretches its wings, and I tell it, "Take me wherever you like." But it always takes me to the same place: the past. You can't understand such things, of course, because you're a man. But we women live in the past."

"All of Athens lives in the past," rejoined Heracles.

"Meragrus would have said something similar." She smiled faintly. Heracles smiled, too, but then noticed her strange look. "What happened to us, Heracles?" There was a pause. He lowered his gaze. "Meragrus, you, your wife, Hagesikora, and I—what happened to us? We followed rules, laws laid down by men who didn't know us and to whom we didn't matter. Laws our fathers obeyed, and our fathers' fathers. Laws with which men must comply but may discuss at the Assembly. We women may not speak of them, even at the Festival of the Thesmophoria, when we leave our houses and gather in the Agora. We must remain silent and even abide by your mistakes. As you know, I am no better than any other woman. I cannot read or write; I have not seen other skies, other lands. But I like thinking. And do you know what I think? That Athens is made of laws that are as antiquated as the stones of ancient temples. The Acropolis is as cold as a cemetery. The columns of the Parthenon are the bars of a cage and birds cannot fly within it. Peace . . . yes, we have peace. But at what price? What have we done with our lives, Heracles? Things were better in the past. At least we all thought so. And so did our fathers."

"They were wrong," said Heracles. "Things were no better. Nor were they much worse. There was simply a war."

Motionless, Itys said quickly, as if answering a question, "You loved me then."

Heracles felt as if he were outside his body, watching himself as he reclined on a couch, very still, breathing calmly, a neutral look on his face. But he could feel how his body was reacting: His hands, for instance, suddenly felt cold and sweaty.

"And I loved you," she added.

Why had she changed the subject? he wondered. Was she incapable of having a reasonable, balanced conversation, like a man? Why now, suddenly, such personal questions? He shifted uneasily on his couch.

"Please forgive me, Heracles. Dismiss my words as the delusions of a lonely woman. But I wonder, have you never thought that things might have been different? No, that's not what I mean. I know that you've never thought about it. But have you never *felt* it?"

And now this absurd question! He decided he must have lost the habit of talking to women. He could hold a fairly reasonable conversation even with his latest client, Diagoras, despite the obvious incompatibility of their temperaments. But with women? What did she mean by such a question? Surely women couldn't remember each and every emotion they'd ever felt? And even if they could, what did it matter? Feelings, emotions, were like brightly colored birds: They came and went, as fleeting as dreams. He knew this, but she evidently did not. How was he to explain it to her?

"Itys," he said, clearing his throat, "when we were young, we had certain feelings, but now we have other, very different ones. Who can say for sure what would have happened in this case or that? Hagesikora was the woman my parents had me marry and, although she bore me no children, I was happy with her and mourned her when she died. As for Meragrus, he chose you."

"I chose him when you chose Hagesikora, for he was the man my parents imposed upon me," replied Itys. "And I was happy with him and mourned him when he died. And now . . . here we are, both moderately happy, not daring to speak of what we have lost, of every wasted opportunity, every slight to our instincts, every affront to our hopes . . . reasoning . . . inventing reasons." She paused and blinked, as if only just waking up. "But I ask you again to forgive my rambling. The last man of the house is gone and . . . what are we women without men? You are the first to visit since the funeral banquet."

So grief has made her talk of these things, thought Heracles with sympathy. He tried to sound kind: "How is Elea?"

"She can just about endure herself. But she is in torment when she thinks of her terrible solitude."

"And Daminus of Clazobion?"

"He is a man of commerce. He will marry Elea only when I am dead. The law would allow it. Since her brother's death, my daughter has legally become an *epiclera,* and she must marry to prevent our fortune passing to the state. As her uncle through the paternal line, Daminus has the right to take her as his wife. But he has never held me in great esteem, and it has been even worse since Meragrus's death. So he is waiting for me to die, circling like a vulture. I don't care." She rubbed her arms. "At least I'll have the certainty of knowing that this house will be part of Elea's inheritance. Anyway, I have no choice: As you may imagine, my daughter has few suitors, since the family has fallen into dishonor."

After a brief pause, Heracles said, "Itys, I have agreed to carry out a small investigation." She looked at him. He spoke quickly, sounding formal. "I can't tell you my client's name, but I assure you he is an honest man. And the investigation has to do with Tramachus. I thought I ought to take it on . . . and to tell you that I had."

Itys pressed her lips together.

"So you came to see me as the Decipherer of Enigmas?"

"No. I came to tell you. I will not trouble you further if you wish me to leave."

"What kind of mystery could there be surrounding my son? His life held no secrets for me."

Heracles breathed deeply.

"You mustn't worry—my investigation isn't centered on Tramachus, though it does hover around him. It would be a great help to me if you could answer some questions."

"Very well," said Itys reluctantly.

"Had your son seemed preoccupied over the last few months?"

She frowned, thoughtful. "No. He was the same as always. He didn't appear especially anxious."

"Did you spend much time with him?"

"No, although I'd wished to. I didn't want to stifle him. He had become very sensitive about such things—they say it happens to sons in households run by women. He wouldn't tolerate us interfering in his life. He wanted to fly far away." She paused. "He longed for the day when he would become an ephebe and leave. And, Hera knows, I never censured him."

Heracles nodded, briefly closing his eyes, as if to show that he understood how she felt without her having to put it into words. Then he said, "I know he attended the Academy."

"Yes. I wished him to study there, for his own sake, but also in memory of his father. As you know, Plato and Meragrus were fairly close friends. According to his tutors, Tramachus was a good student."

"What did he do in his spare time?"

After a brief pause, Itys said, "I would answer that I don't know, but, as a mother, I think I do, and whatever it was, Heracles, it can't have been very different from what any other boy his age did. Though he hadn't legally come of age, he had grown into a man. He ran his own life, just like any other man. He wouldn't let us women poke our noses into his affairs. 'Be satisfied with being the best mother in Athens,' he would say." Her pale lips showed the beginnings of a smile. "But, I repeat, he had no secrets. I was confident that he was being well educated at the Academy, so it didn't trouble me that he seemed distant. I let him fly free."

"Was he very devout?"

Itys smiled and shifted.

"Oh, yes, the Sacred Mysteries. Going to Eleusis is all I have left. You can't imagine what strength it gives me, poor widow that I am, having something to believe in, Heracles." His face remained blank. "But I haven't answered your question. Yes, he was devout, in his own way. He came to Eleusis with us, if that's what it is to be devout. But he trusted more in his own strengths than in his beliefs."

"Do you know Antisus and Euneos?"

"Of course. His best friends, fellow students at the Academy and scions of noble families. They sometimes came to Eleusis. I have the highest opinion of them: They are worthy."

"Itys . . . was Tramachus in the habit of going hunting alone?"

"Sometimes. He liked to prove that he was ready for life." She smiled. "And so he was."

"Please excuse the lack of order to my questions, but, as I said, my investigation isn't focused on Tramachus. Do you know Menaechmus, the sculptor-poet?"

Itys narrowed her eyes. She tensed, like a bird about to fly away.

"Menaechmus?" she said, and gently bit her lip. After a brief pause, she added, "I think . . . Yes, I remember now. He used to come to the house when Meragrus was alive. A strange man, but then, my husband had very strange friends. I don't include you, of course."

Heracles returned her thin smile before asking, "You haven't seen him since then?" Itys said no. "Do you know if he had any kind of relationship with Tramachus?"

"No, I don't think so. I'm certain Tramachus never mentioned him." Itys frowned anxiously. "Heracles, what is this? Your questions are so . . . Even if you can't tell me what you're investigating, at least tell me whether my son's death . . . I mean, Tramachus was attacked by a pack of wolves, wasn't he? That's what we were told. That was what happened, wasn't it?"

Still expressionless, Heracles said, "It was. His death has nothing to do with all this. But I won't trouble you further. Thank you for your help. May the gods be propitious."

He left hurriedly. He had a guilty conscience, for he had had to lie to a good woman.[2]

2. My conscience isn't troubling me in the slightest. Yesterday, I told Helena about the disturbing parallel between events in real life and those in the book. "You're such a fantasist," she complained. "How on earth could Montalo's death have anything to do with the death of a character in a two-thousand-year-old book? You're quite mad! Montalo's death was *real,* an accident. Whatever happens to the character in the book you're translating is pure fiction. Maybe it's another eidetic device, a secret symbol, or something." Helena's right, as usual. Her devastating common sense would demolish even Heracles Pontor's most intelligent arguments. And, by the way, fictional as he may be, he is rapidly becoming my favorite character, the only voice

• • •

They say something unprecedented happened that day: An oversight on the part of the temple priests caused hundreds of white butterflies to be released from the great urn of offerings to Athena Nike. That morning, beneath the cool, bright sun of an Athenian winter, their quivering wings, fragile and luminous, invaded the city. Some people saw them enter the unsullied sanctuary of Artemis Brauronia and seek the camouflage of the goddess's snow white marble; others caught sight of little white flowers flitting around the statue of Athena Promachos, waving their petals, yet not falling to the ground. The butterflies quickly multiplied, beleaguering, without risk of danger, the stone maidens who, needing no help, supported the roof of the Erechtheum. They nested in the sacred olive tree, a gift from aegis-bearing Athena; gleaming, they flew down the hillsides of the Acropolis. An army by now, they erupted, a gentle, feather-light nuisance, into everyday life. Nobody would do anything about them, because they were hardly anything: no more than flickering light, as if Morning had fluttered her delicate eyelashes, sprinkling the fine dust of her gleaming makeup over the city. Watched by the astounded inhabitants, they made their way unhindered through the impalpable ether, to the Temple of Ares and the Stoa of Zeus, the Tholus and the Heliaea, the Theseum, and the monument to the heroes, ever dazzling, flighty, reveling in their translucent freedom. After kissing the friezes of public buildings like capricious little girls, they occupied the trees and snowed, zigzagging, over the grass and the rocks in the springs. Dogs barked at them inoffensively, as they sometimes do at ghosts or whirling dust; cats leapt onto rocks out of their wavering path; mules and oxen raised their heavy heads to stare, but, without the capacity for dreams, they weren't saddened.

---

that makes sense of all this chaos. What can I say, astonished reader? It suddenly seemed terribly important to find out more about Montalo and his solitary life, so I wrote to Aristides, an academic who was a close friend of his. He replied promptly, saying he'd be happy to see me. I wonder sometimes if I'm trying to imitate Heracles Pontor by carrying out *my own* investigation?—TRANS.

At last, the butterflies alighted on men and began to die.[3]

When Heracles Pontor returned home at midday, he found his garden covered with a smooth shroud of butterfly corpses. The birds nesting in the cornices or high up in the pines had, in fact, already begun to devour them—hoopoes, cuckoos, goldcrests, rooks, wood pigeons, crows, nightingales, goldfinches—heads bent over the delicacy, busying themselves like artists at their pigments, turning the fine grass green again. It was a strange sight, but Heracles thought it neither a good nor a bad omen, for, among other things, he didn't believe in omens.

As he walked up the garden path, a flapping of wings to his right caught his attention. A hunched black shadow emerged from behind the trees, frightening the birds.

"So you like to jump out and startle people now, do you?" Heracles smiled.

"By Zeus's pointed lightning bolts, I swear I don't, Heracles Pontor." Eumarchus's old voice crackled. "You hired me to be discreet, to spy on others without being seen, didn't you? Well, I've learned my trade."

Startled by the noise, the birds took wing, abandoning their feast. As they rose, their tiny agile bodies alighted up in the air, then beat down vertically toward the earth, and the two men blinked, dazzled by the glare of the midday sun at its zenith.[4]

3. This invasion of white butterflies (which is quite absurd—there is no historical evidence to suggest that butterflies were ever used as an offering to Athena Nike) must be eidetic: The ideas of "flight" and "wings"—present from the beginning of the chapter—invade the reality of the story. The final image, in my view, is that of the labor of the Stymphalian birds, in which Hercules has to chase away the myriad birds plaguing the lake of Stymphalus, which he does by clashing bronze cymbals. And has the reader noticed the cleverly disguised presence of the girl with the lily? Please tell me if you do, reader, or am I imagining it? The "little white flowers" and the "maidens" (the caryatids of the Erechtheum) are there, as well as those essential words, *help* ("needing no help") and *danger* ("beleaguering, without risk of danger"), always closely linked with this image!—TRANS.

4. The birds, like the butterflies, are eidetic, so they have now turned into rays of sunlight. The reader should note that there is nothing miraculous or magical about it; it's as much of a literary device as the change of meter in a poem.—TRANS.

"That horrible mask you have for a slave gesticulated that you were out," said Eumarchus, "so I patiently awaited your return. I came to tell you that my work has borne fruit."

"Did you do as I ordered?"

"As your hands obey your thoughts. Last night, I became my pupil's shadow. I followed him, tirelessly, at a prudent distance, like a female falcon accompanying her young on their first flight. I was a pair of eyes tied to his back as he threaded his way through the crowded streets. He met his friend Euneos at nightfall by the Stoa of Zeus and they set off across the city. They were not walking for pleasure, if you understand me; their volatile steps had a clear destination. But Father Cronius could inflict on me Prometheus's fate, tying me to a rock for a bird to peck out my liver daily with its black beak, and still I could not have imagined a stranger destination, Heracles! I can tell by the faces you're making that you're growing impatient with my tale. Don't worry, I'll get to the point. I found out, at last, where they were going! I'll tell you and you'll be as amazed as I."

The light of the sun pecked lazily at the grass before landing on a branch and trilling a few notes. A second nightingale alighted beside it.[5]

At last, Eumarchus finished his story.

"Explain to me, O great Decipherer, what it all means," he said.

Heracles pondered a moment before saying, "Now, I still require your help, good Eumarchus. Follow Antisus's footsteps at night and report to me every two or three days. But first, fly hurriedly to my friend's house with this message."

"I am grateful to you, Heracles, for agreeing to have our meal outside," said Crantor. "Do you know, I can no longer endure the gloomy interiors of Athenian houses? The inhabitants of villages south

5. The metamorphosis of bird into light here takes place the other way around. Readers encountering an eidetic text for the first time may find these sentences confusing, but, I repeat, this isn't a miracle, but simply a question of language.—TRANS.

of the Nile cannot believe that in our civilized Athens we live cloistered within adobe walls. They believe that only the dead need walls." He took another piece of fruit from the bowl and drove the sharp beak of his dagger into the table. After a moment, he said, "You're not in a talkative mood."

The Decipherer seemed to awaken from a dream. In the intact peace of the garden, a small bird warbled a tune. Sharp clattering gave away Cerberus's presence in a corner, as he licked the remains from his dish.

They were dining on the porch. Obeying Crantor's wishes, and aided by the guest himself, Ponsica had brought out the table and two couches from the cenacle. The air was growing cold, for the sun's chariot of fire was completing its journey, its curved trail of gold stretching, unbroken, across the band of sky above the pines, but it was still possible to sit outside and enjoy the sunset. Though his friend had certainly been loquacious, entertaining even, recounting numerous Odyssean anecdotes and allowing him to listen in silence without having to contribute, Heracles had ended up regretting his invitation: The details of the enigma he was on the verge of solving were tormenting him. And he had to keep a constant watch over the sun's curved trajectory, as he was concerned not to be late for his appointment later that evening. But his Athenian sense of hospitality prompted him to say, "Crantor, my friend, I apologize for being such a poor host. I have let my thoughts fly elsewhere."

"Oh, I don't want to disturb you, Heracles. I assume you've been pondering a matter relating to your work."

"I have. But I am ashamed of my inhospitable behavior. So let me now perch my thoughts on a branch and partake in conversation."

Crantor wiped his nose with the back of his hand and finished his piece of fruit.

"Are things going well? In your work, I mean."

"I can't complain. I'm treated better than my colleagues in Corinth and Argos. They do nothing but decipher the enigmas of the Delphic oracle for a few rich clients. Here, I'm much in demand: to solve a mystery in an Egyptian text, establish the whereabouts of a lost object, identify a thief. There was a time, just after you left, at the end of the war, when I had barely enough to eat. . . . Don't laugh; it's true. . . . So I, too, turned to solving the riddles of Delphi. But now, in peacetime, we Athenians have nothing better to do than decipher enigmas, even when there are none. We gather in the Agora, or the gardens of the Lyceum, or at the Theater of Dionysus Eleuthereus, or simply in the streets, and question one another incessantly. And when no one has an answer, they engage a decipherer."

Crantor laughed again. "You, too, have chosen the life you wanted, Heracles."

"I don't know, Crantor, I don't know." He rubbed his bare arms beneath his cloak. "I think this way of life has chosen me."

Ponsica brought another jug of undiluted wine. Her silence seemed to infect them. Heracles noticed that his friend (Was Crantor still his friend? Were they not now strangers reminiscing about mutual friends?) was watching the slave. The last pure rays of sun alighted on the gentle curves of the featureless mask; slender but in constant movement, her snow white arms emerged from the symmetrical openings of the black floor-length cloak with pointed edges. Ponsica placed the jug gently on the table, bowed, and left. From his corner, Cerberus barked furiously.

"I can't . . . I couldn't . . ." muttered Crantor suddenly.

"Couldn't what?"

"Wear a mask to hide my ugliness. I assume your slave wouldn't either if you didn't force her to."

"The complex pattern of her scars distracts me," said Heracles. He shrugged, adding, "She is my slave, after all. Others make them do their work naked. I've covered her up completely."

"Does her body distract you, too?" Crantor smiled, tugging at his beard with his burned hand.

"No, but all I want from her is efficiency and silence. I need both so that I can think in peace."

The invisible bird whistled three sharply distinct notes. Crantor turned his head toward the house.

"Have you ever seen her naked?" he asked.

Heracles nodded.

"When I inquired about her at the Phaleron market, the trader stripped her. He thought her body more than made up for her ruined face and that I would therefore pay more. But I said to him, 'Have her dress. I simply need to know if she can cook and run a modest-sized house without help.' The merchant assured me that she was very efficient, but I wanted her to tell me so herself. When I saw that she didn't answer, I realized that the man had been trying to hide the fact that she couldn't speak. Embarrassed, he quickly explained that she was a mute and told me the story of the Lydian bandits. He added, 'But she expresses herself with a simple alphabet of signs.' So I bought her." Heracles paused and sipped his wine, adding, "It's the best purchase I've ever made, I assure you. But she's gained, too: I have arranged that she should be set free upon my death and have, in fact, already allowed her considerable freedom. Occasionally, she even asks for permission to go to Eleusis, as she worships the Sacred Mysteries, and I happily grant it." He concluded with a smile: "We're both happy."

"How do you know?" said Crantor. "Have you ever asked her?"

Heracles looked at him over the curved edge of his cup.

"I don't need to," he said. "I deduce that she is."

Sharp musical notes filled the air. Crantor narrowed his eyes and said after a pause, "Always deducing, Heracles." He tugged at his mustache and beard with his burned hand. "That's all you ever do. Things appear before you masked and mute, and you insist on deducing from them." He shook his head and looked oddly at his friend, as if he admired him for it. "You're so incredibly Athenian, Heracles. At least the Platonists, like that client of yours the other day, believe in absolute, immutable truths that they cannot see. But you? What do you believe in? In what you deduce?"

"I only believe in what I can see," said Heracles simply. "Deduction is another way of seeing things."

"Imagine a world full of people like you." Crantor smiled and paused, as if really imagining such. "How sad it would be."

"It would be quiet and efficient," retorted Heracles. "Now, a world of Platonists would be sad: They'd walk through the streets as if they were flying, eyes closed and minds set on the invisible."

They laughed. Crantor was the first to stop, saying in a strange tone, "So the best solution is a world full of people like me."

Heracles raised his eyebrows, amused. "Like you? They might suddenly feel the urge to burn their hands, or their feet, or to bang their heads against a wall. Everyone would be wandering around maimed. And who knows, some might start maiming others."

"No doubt they would," said Crantor. "It is, in fact, what happens everywhere every day. For instance, we maimed the fish you served for dinner this evening with our sharp teeth. The Platonists believe in what they cannot see; you believe in what you can see. But when you eat, you all mutilate meat and fish. And figs."

Ignoring the gibe, Heracles ate the fig he'd raised to his mouth. Crantor went on: "You think, and reason, and believe, and have faith. But the truth . . . where is the truth?" He laughed loudly, his chest shaking. A few birds detached themselves, like pointed leaves, from high branches.

After a pause, Crantor turned his black eyes to Heracles. "I've noticed you staring at the scars on my hand," he said. "Do you find them distracting, too? Oh, Heracles, how glad I am that I did what I did that afternoon in Euboea, as we discussed similar matters! Do you remember? We sat, just you and I, beside the small fire inside my cabin. I said, 'If I had an urge to burn my right hand and *did so,* I would prove to you that some things can't be reasoned.' You replied, 'No, Crantor, because it would be easy to *reason* that you were doing so in order to prove that there are things that can't be reasoned.' So I stretched out my arm and placed my hand in the flames." He did likewise, holding his right arm over the table, and went on: "Astounded, you leapt up and cried, 'Crantor, by Zeus, what are you doing!' And I, my hand still in the flames, replied, 'Why are you so surprised, Heracles? Is it because, against all reason, I am *burning my hand*? Or that, despite all the logical explanations that your mind may devise as to my motive, the fact is, the *reality* is, Heracles Pontor, that I am *burning my hand*?' " He burst out laughing again. "What good is reasoning when you see Reality burn its hand?"

Heracles looked down at his cup. "Actually, Crantor, there is an enigma that defies my powers of reasoning," he said. "How is it possible that we're *friends*?"

They laughed again, with restraint this time. Just then, a small bird alighted on the end of the table, flapping its delicate dun-colored wings. Crantor gazed at it in silence.[6]

"Observe this bird, for example," he said. "Why has it landed on the table? Why is it here, with us?"

"It must have a reason. Maybe we should ask it."

"I'm being serious. From your point of view, you might see this little bird as more important in our lives than it seems."

"What do you mean?"

"Perhaps . . ." Crantor said enigmatically, "perhaps it's part of the key that explains our presence in the great Work that is the world."

Heracles smiled, though he felt in poor humor. "Is this what you believe in now?" he asked.

"No. I'm looking at things from your point of view. But you know, he who always seeks explanations runs the risk of inventing them."

"No one would invent something quite so ridiculous, Crantor. How could anyone believe that the presence of this bird is part of—how did you put it?—the key that explains everything?"[7]

Crantor didn't answer. Slowly, hypnotically, he stretched out his hand, opening it as it neared the bird. In a single lightning move, he caught the little animal in fingers with sharp, curved nails.

6. As the reader must already realize, there is nothing fortuitous about the bird's presence. On the contrary, together with the butterflies and the eidetic birds in the garden, it is there to draw attention to the hidden image of the Stymphalian birds. The obvious repetition of the words *pointed, curved,* and *sharp,* evoking their beaks, contributes to this.—TRANS.

7. The cunning author was playing with his readers again! Unaware of the truth—that is, that they are merely characters in a book with a hidden key—the characters make fun of the eidetic presence of the bird.—TRANS.

"Some *do* believe it," he said. "Let me tell you a story." He held the little head up to his face and peered at it strangely (it was impossible to tell whether with tenderness or curiosity). "Some time ago, I met a mediocre man, the son of a writer no less mediocre than he. This man aspired to be a writer like his father, but the Muses didn't bless him with talent. So he learned languages and turned his hand to translating—the profession that most resembled his father's. One day, the man was given an ancient papyrus and told to translate it. He set to eagerly, working day and night. It was a work in prose, quite an ordinary story, but the man, perhaps because he could not create anything of his own, *wanted* to believe that it contained a hidden key. And thus began his agony. Where was the secret hidden? In the characters' speech? In the descriptions? Deep within the words? Or in the images? At last, he thought he'd found it: I've got it! he said to himself. But then he thought, Might this key not lead to another, and another, and another? Like myriad birds that are impossible to catch." Crantor's eyes, suddenly dull, were staring at a point somewhere beyond Heracles.

They were staring at you.[8]

"What happened to him?"

"He went mad." Beneath the bristly chaos of his beard, Crantor's lips formed into a sharp-curved smile. "It was terrible. No sooner did he think he'd found the final key, than another very different one landed in his hands, and another, and another. In the end, completely insane, he stopped translating the text and fled from his home. He roamed the forest for several days like a blinded bird. In the end, he was devoured by wild beasts."[9] Crantor looked down at the tiny fren-

8. I suddenly felt a little dizzy and had to stop work. It's nothing, just a stupid coincidence—it so happens that my late father was a writer. I can't describe my feelings as I translated Crantor's words, written thousands of years ago on an old papyrus by an unknown author. *He's talking about me!* I thought for one crazy moment. When I got to the sentence "They were staring at you"—another jump into the second person, as in the previous chapter—I leapt away from the paper as if it might burn me and had to stop translating for a while. Then I reread the words, several times, until, at last, my absurd terror abated. I can go on now.—TRANS.

9. Like Montalo?—TRANS.

zied creature in his hand and smiled again. "This is the warning I give to all those who so eagerly seek hidden keys: Take care, or you might not notice that you're flying blind, so confident are you of your wings." Slowly, almost tenderly, he moved his pointed thumbnail toward the little head poking from between his fingers.

The bird's agony was tiny and horrific, like the screams of a child tortured underground.

Heracles sipped his wine placidly.

Afterward, Crantor tossed the bird onto the table, like a *petteia* player flinging down a counter.

"That is my warning," he said.

The bird was still alive, but it was shivering and chirping frenziedly. It made two clumsy little leaps and shook its head, scattering bright red clots.

Heracles greedily seized another fig.

Eyes half-closed, Crantor might have been thinking of quite trivial things as he watched the bird shake its bloody head.

"Beautiful sunset," said Heracles, somewhat bored, scanning the horizon. Crantor agreed.

The bird suddenly flew off, but then it crashed, as if flung, brutally, into the trunk of a nearby tree. It left a crimson mark and let out a cry. It took off again, colliding with the lower branches. It fell to the ground, then rose once more, only to fall again, trailing garlands of blood from its empty eye sockets. After several futile leaps, it rolled on the grass and lay still, waiting, hoping for death.

With a yawn, Heracles remarked, "It really isn't too chilly."[10]

Suddenly, Crantor got up from the couch, as if the conversation

10. It seems Heracles hasn't noticed that Crantor has gouged out the bird's eyes. One must therefore deduce that this brutal act of torture has taken place at an eidetic level, like the attacks of the "beast" in the previous chapter and the coiled snakes at the end of chapter 2. This is the first time, however, that a *character* in the novel has done something like this. I find this intriguing. As a rule, literary acts are carried out by the author, as the characters' behavior must at all times remain as close to real life as possible. But it seems that Crantor's anonymous creator couldn't have cared less whether his character was realistic or not.—TRANS.

were at an end. But he added, "The Sphinx devoured anyone who gave the wrong answers to her questions. But do you know the worst thing, Heracles? The Sphinx had wings, and one day she flew away. Since then, we men have experienced something *much worse* than being devoured: not knowing whether our answers are right." He stroked his beard with one of his enormous hands and smiled. "Thank you for the meal and for your hospitality, Heracles Pontor. We will have occasion to see each other again before I leave Athens."

"I trust we will," said Heracles.

And man and dog headed out through the garden.[11]

Diagoras was at the agreed-upon place by nightfall, but, as he expected, he had to wait. He was thankful, however, that the Decipherer had not chosen as crowded a spot as the last. This time, it was a deserted corner beyond the metic traders' quarter, facing alleys leading into the districts of Kolytos and Melitta. And it was well away from the stares of the crowds, whose noisy reveling could be heard—far more loudly than Diagoras would have wished—coming mainly from the Agora. The night was cold and capriciously, impenetrably misty. The dark peace of the streets was occasionally disturbed by the unsteady footsteps of a drunk. And there were also the comings and goings of the *astynomi's* servants, always in pairs or groups and carrying torches and sticks, and of small detachments of soldiers returning from guarding some religious service. Diagoras looked at no one and no one looked at him. One man, however, approached him. He was

11. Why this eidetic cruelty to the bird, whose presence—let us not forget—is also eidetic? What was the author trying to convey? Crantor says it's a "warning," but from whom to whom? Fine, if Crantor is part of the plot, but if he's simply the author's mouthpiece, the warning begins, terrifyingly, to sound like a curse: "Translator or reader beware: Don't reveal the *secret* contained in these pages . . . or something unpleasant may befall you." Maybe Montalo found out what it was and . . . That's ridiculous! The book was written thousands of years ago. How could a curse have power after all this time? My head's full of (eidetic) birds. There must be a simpler answer: Crantor is one more character; he's just *badly drawn*. Crantor is a mistake. He may not even have anything to do with the main theme.—TRANS.

short and wore a threadbare cloak that also served as a hood. From its folds, he cautiously slid a long, bony arm, his hand outstretched, like a crane's leg.

"By the warrior Ares," he croaked, "I served in the Athenian army for twenty years, survived Sicily and lost my left arm. But what has my Athenian homeland done for me? Thrown me out on the streets to scavenge for bones like a dog. Have more mercy than our rulers, good citizen!"

With dignity, Diagoras reached under his cloak for some coins.

"May you live as long as the sons of the gods!" the beggar said gratefully, and walked away.

Just then, Diagoras heard his name. The obese figure of the Decipherer of Enigmas stood, edged with moonlight, at the end of an alley.

"Come on," said Heracles.

They walked in silence toward the district of Melitta.

"Where are we going?" asked Diagoras.

"I want you to see something."

"Have you learned more?"

"I think I know everything."

Though Heracles was as laconic as ever, Diagoras thought he heard tension in his voice and wondered at the cause. Perhaps he has bad news, he thought.

"Just tell me whether Antisus and Euneos are implicated."

"Wait. Soon you will be able to tell me yourself."

They walked down a dark street lined with smithies that were shut for the night. They left behind the Pidea bathhouse and the small shrine to Hephaestus. They turned into an alley so narrow that a slave carrying two amphorae on a pole across his shoulders had to wait for them to pass before he could enter. They crossed the little square dedicated to the hero Melampus. The moon guided them down a sloping street lined with stables and through the dense darkness of a street of tanneries. Always uncomfortable on these silent walks, Diagoras said, "By Zeus, I hope we're not going to have to chase another hetaera."

"No. We're almost there."

They stopped in a street of ruined houses, their walls staring empty-eyed into the night. Heracles pointed to one of them.

"Do you see those men with torches at the door?" he asked. "That's where we're going. Now, do as I tell you. When they ask what you want, say, 'I've come to see the performance,' and give them a few obols. They'll let you in. I'll be doing likewise."

"What does this all mean?"

"As I said, you can tell me yourself afterward. Come on."

Heracles was first to reach the door. Diagoras repeated his words and gestures. Inside the gloomy hallway of the dilapidated house, they could see a narrow flight of stone steps leading below. Several men disappeared down them. Unsteadily, Diagoras followed the Decipherer and descended into darkness. For a moment, he was aware of nothing but his companion's stout back, as the steep steps required all his attention. Then he heard chanting, reciting. Down below, the darkness was different, as if created by a different artist, and it called for different eyes. Unaccustomed to it, Diagoras's eyes could make out only confused shapes. A strong smell of wine combined with the odor of bodies. There were tiers of wooden benches, and they took seats in one of the rows.

"Look," said Heracles.

At the back of the room, on a small stage, a masked chorus was reciting verses around an altar. The members of the chorus had their hands raised, palms upward. Through the slits in the masks, their eyes, though dark, appeared watchful. The rest of the scene was lost in the glare of torches in the corners, but, squinting, Diagoras could make out another masked figure at a table covered in scrolls.

"What is this?" he asked.

"A theatrical performance," replied Heracles.

"I can see that. I mean what—"

The Decipherer gestured to him to be silent. The chorus concluded the antistrophe and stood in a line, facing the audience. Diagoras began to feel as if he were stifling; but he was disturbed by more than the unbreathable air: There was, too, the tangible *zeal* of the spectators. They were few in number—there were many empty seats—but they acted in unison: craning their necks, swaying in time to the chanting, drinking wine from small wineskins. One of them, beside Diagoras, sat there panting, eyes bulging. This was *zeal*.

Diagoras remembered having witnessed it for the first time at performances by the poets Aeschylus and Sophocles: an almost religious sense of participation, a tacit, unspoken intelligence, as resides in the written word, and a certain—what exactly? Pleasure? Fear? Elation? He couldn't understand it. He felt, at times, that the immense ritual was more ancient even than man's understanding. It wasn't exactly theater, but something preexistent, chaotic. There were no fine verses for a cultured audience to translate into beautiful images. The plot was almost always irrational: Mothers fornicated with their sons, sons murdered their fathers, and wives entangled their spouses in bloody nets; one crime repaid another; vengeance was eternal; the Furies hounded the guilty and the innocent; corpses remained unburied. Howls of pain everywhere from a merciless chorus, and terror as huge and oppressive as that of a man lost at sea. Theater like a Cyclops's eye, watching the audience from its cave. Diagoras had always felt uneasy before these tortured works. No wonder Plato disliked them so much! Where, in such performances, were the moral teachings, the rules of conduct, the duty of the poet to educate the people, the—

"Diagoras," whispered Heracles. "Look at the two chorus members on the right, in the second row."

One of the actors approached the figure at the table. His high cothurni and complicated mask indicated that he was the Coryphaeus. He began a stichomythia with the seated actor.

CORYPHAEUS: *Come, Translator, search for the keys, if there are any.*
TRANSLATOR: *Long have I sought them. But the words confound me.*
CORYPHAEUS: *So you think it useless to persist?*
TRANSLATOR: *No, for I believe that all that is written may be deciphered.*
CORYPHAEUS: *Are you not afraid of reaching the end?*
TRANSLATOR: *Why should I be afraid?*
CORYPHAEUS: *Because there may be no answers.*
TRANSLATOR: *While I have strength, I will continue.*

CORYPHAEUS: *Oh, Translator, you drag a rock that will only roll back down the mountain!*

TRANSLATOR: *It is my Destiny. In vain would I try to rebel!*

CORYPHAEUS: *It would seem you are driven by blind faith.*

TRANSLATOR: *There must be something behind the words! There is always a meaning!*

"Do you recognize them?" asked Heracles.

"Oh gods," murmured Diagoras.

CORYPHAEUS: *I see it is futile to try to make you change your mind.*

TRANSLATOR: *You are not mistaken. I am bound to this chair and to these scrolls.*

There was a clashing of cymbals. The chorus began a rhythmic stasimon.

CHORUS: *I weep for you, Translator. Your fate ties your eyes to the words, making you believe that you will find a key to the text you translate! Why did owl-eyed Athena bestow luminous knowledge upon us? There you are, unfortunate, reaching fruitlessly for your reward, but the meanings elude both your outstretched hands and your skilled gaze! Oh, torture!*[12]

Diagoras had seen enough. He stood up and went to the door. There was a clash of cymbals so loud that the sound turned to light, and everybody blinked. The members of the chorus raised their arms.

CHORUS: *Beware, Translator, beware! You are being watched! You are being watched!*

"Diagoras, wait!" cried Heracles Pontor.

12. Torture indeed. Is this a message from the author to his possible translators? Could the secret of *The Athenian Murders* be such that its anonymous creator wanted to play it safe by trying to discourage anyone who might attempt to decipher it? —TRANS.

CHORUS: *Danger awaits you! You have been warned, Translator!*[13]

Out in the cold, dark street, under the watchful eye of the moon, Diagoras took several deep breaths. Coming up behind him, the Decipherer was also gasping for air, but in his case, it was due to the effort of climbing the stairs.

"Did you recognize them?" he asked.

Diagoras nodded.

"They were wearing masks, but it was them."

They walked back through the deserted streets. Heracles said, "So what does it all mean? Why do Antisus and Euneos come here at night, wrapped in long dark tunics? I expect you can explain it to me."

"At the Academy, we believe that theater is an imitative and vulgar art," said Diagoras slowly. "Our students are expressly forbidden to attend, let alone participate in, theatrical performances. Plato believes—we all believe—that most poets are rather careless and spend their time setting the young a bad example by depicting characters who are noble yet full of despicable vices. To us, true theater is not coarse entertainment intended to make the populace laugh and shout. In Plato's ideal government, the—"

"Apparently not all your students agree," said Heracles.

Diagoras looked pained and closed his eyes.

"I never would have believed it," he murmured. "Antisus and Euneos . . ."

"And probably Tramachus, too. I'm sorry."

"But what kind of grotesque . . . play were they rehearsing? And what place was that? The only indoor theater in the city I know of is the Odeon."

13. This might sound—and probably actually is—amusing, but alone in my house at night as I was, bent over my papers, I stopped translating when I came to these words, and glanced around nervously. Nothing but darkness, of course (when I'm working, I have a single light on at my desk and nothing else). I can only attribute my behavior to the powerful spell cast by literature, which at such time of night, can confuse one's mind, as Homer might have said.—TRANS.

"Ah, Diagoras, Athens breathes while we think!" exclaimed Heracles with a sigh. "There is much that our eyes do not see, but that also belongs to the people: ridiculous entertainment, improbable professions, irrational activities. You never leave your Academy, and I never leave the confines of my brain, which comes to the same. But Athens, my dear Diagoras, is not our *idea* of Athens."

"So now you agree with Crantor?"

Heracles shrugged. "What I'm trying to say, Diagoras, is that there are strange places where you and I have never been. The slave who found out about all this assured me that there are several illegal theaters like this one in the city. Most are old houses bought cheaply by metic merchants, who then rent them out to poets, paying their high taxes with the proceeds. The archons forbid these activities, of course, but, as you've just seen, there is an audience for such things. The theater is a fairly lucrative business in Athens."

"As for the play itself . . ."

"I don't know the title or the subject, but I do know the author: It's a tragedy by Menaechmus, the sculptor-poet. Did you spot him?"

"Menaechmus?"

"Yes. He was the man sitting at the table, playing the Translator. His mask was small, so I could see who it was. A strange man. He has a workshop in the Ceramicus and earns his living making friezes for the houses of noble Athenians. And he writes tragedies that can never be performed officially, but only for a 'select' few, mediocre poets like himself, in these underground theaters. I've made some inquiries in his neighborhood. It seems his workshop is used for more than work—he holds Syracusan-style gatherings there in the evenings, orgies that would make the most debauched blush. The main guests are the youths who serve as models for his sculptures and as the chorus in his plays."

Diagoras turned toward Heracles. "You wouldn't dare to imply that—"

Heracles shrugged and sighed, as if reluctantly about to impart bad news.

"Come," he said. "Let us stop here and talk."

They were in a wide-open area, beside a stoa with walls decorated with forms suggesting human faces. The only features the artist had retained were the eyes, open and watchful. The moon looked down, and, in the distance, a dog barked.

"Diagoras," said Heracles slowly, "though we have been acquainted only a short time, I believe I know you slightly, and I suspect you could say the same about me. What I'm about to say will displease you, but it's the truth, or part of it. And it's what you paid me to find out."

"Speak," said Diagoras. "I will listen."

His voice as gentle as the wings of a small bird, Heracles began: "Tramachus, Antisus, and Euneos led—still lead—a somewhat dissolute life. Don't ask me why. I don't think you, as their tutor, should feel responsible. But the fact is, the Academy advises them to reject the vulgar emotions aroused by physical pleasure, and not to take part in plays, and yet they associate with hetaeras and act as chorus members." He raised a hand quickly, anticipating an interruption. "In theory, there's nothing wrong with that, Diagoras. Some of your colleagues may even know about it and allow it. After all, the young will do that sort of thing. But in Antisus's and Euneos's case—and no doubt Tramachus's, too—let's just say they've taken it too far. They met Menaechmus—I still don't know how—and became fervent . . . disciples at his . . . unusual evening 'classes.' The slave I engaged to follow Antisus last night told me that, after leaving the theater, Euneos and Antisus accompanied Menaechmus to his workshop, where they held a little party."

"A party . . ." Watchfully, Diagoras's eyes moved, as if wanting to take in the whole of the Decipherer at a glance. "What kind of party?"

The old man's eyes watched, bulging. . . . the sculptor's workshop . . . a man of mature years . . . several youths . . . laughing . . . the glare of lamps . . . the youths waited . . . a hand . . . waist . . . The old man licked his lips. . . . a caress . . . a boy, much more beautiful . . . quite naked . . . spilled wine . . . "Like that," he said. . . . Surprised, the old man . . . meanwhile, the sculptor . . . moving closer . . . slowly, gently . . . gentler still . . . "Ah," he moaned. . . . at the same time, the other boys . . . roundness. Then, on their backs . . . strange position . . . legs . . . exasperating . . . in the half-light . . . with sweat . . . "Wait," he heard him whisper. . . . Incredible, thought the old man.[14]

"That's ridiculous," said Diagoras hoarsely. "In that case, why don't they leave the Academy?"

"I don't know." Heracles shrugged. "Perhaps they want to think like men in the morning and to enjoy themselves like animals at night. I really don't know. But that's not the main problem. The fact is, their families have no idea that they're leading double lives. The widow Itys, for instance, is happy with the education Tramachus received at the Academy. As are Antisus's father, the noble Praxinoe, who is one of the *prytaneis* at the Assembly, and Euneos's father, Trisipus, the venerated old general. What would happen, I wonder, if your students' nighttime escapades became public?"

"It would be terrible for the Academy," muttered Diagoras.

"Yes, but what about for them? It would be even worse now that they're old enough to become ephebes, when they acquire legal rights. How do you think their noble fathers would react, when they so wished for them to be educated according to Master Plato's ideals? Those most concerned that none of this should become known are your students . . . not to mention Menaechmus himself."

And, as if he had nothing more to say, Heracles set off down the deserted street. Diagoras did likewise, watching the Decipherer's face

14. "Most of this passage—undoubtedly describing Menaechmus's party with the youths, as watched by Eumarchus—has been lost. A more soluble kind of ink was used and many of the words have simply evaporated over time. The blanks are like bare branches where before words perched like little birds," stated Montalo about this corrupt passage. He went on: "How will the reader reconstruct his own orgy with the remaining words?"—TRANS.

closely. Heracles added, "What I have just told you comes very close to the truth. I will now explain the hypothesis I consider most likely. In my opinion, all was going well until Tramachus decided to give them away."

"What?"

"He may have had a guilty conscience about betraying the principles of the Academy. Who knows? Whatever it was, my theory is this: Tramachus decided to talk. To tell everything."

"That wouldn't have been so terrible," said Diagoras quickly. "I would have understood—"

Heracles interrupted: "Remember, we don't know what *everything* is. We don't know the exact nature of the relationship they had—still have—with Menaechmus. . . ." Heracles paused significantly.

Diagoras murmured, "Do you mean to tell me that . . . his terror in the garden . . ."

Heracles' expression showed that this wasn't what he considered most important. "Yes, perhaps," he said. "Remember, though, it was never my intention to investigate the terror you claim to have seen in Tramachus's eyes, but—"

"What you saw when you looked at his corpse and which you've never seen fit to tell me," Diagoras said impatiently.

"Exactly. But now everything has fallen into place. I didn't tell you about it because its implications were so unpleasant that I wished to devise a theory to explain it first. I think the time has come to reveal it to you."

Heracles suddenly raised his hand. Diagoras thought the Decipherer was about to cover his mouth so as not to say any more. But Heracles stroked his small silver beard and went on: "At first sight, it seems very straightforward. Tramachus's body, as you know, was covered in bite marks, but . . . *not all over.* What I mean is, his arms were almost *untouched.* That was what surprised me. The first thing we do when attacked is raise our arms, so that's the first place we're injured. How do you explain that an entire pack of wolves *attacked* poor Tramachus but barely touched his arms? There's only one possible answer: Tramachus was unconscious *at the very least* when the wolves found him, so he didn't put up a struggle. The beasts went straight for his heart, ripping it out."

"Please, spare me the details," said Diagoras. "But I don't understand what this has to do with—" He stopped. The Decipherer was watching him closely, as if he could read his thoughts. "Wait. You said that when the wolves found him, Tramachus must have been 'unconscious *at the very least.*' "

Heracles went on impassively. "Tramachus didn't go hunting. My theory is that he was going to tell everything. Menaechmus—and I'd like to think that *it was Menaechmus*—probably arranged to meet him on the outskirts of the city in order to come to some arrangement with him. There was an argument, maybe even a fight. Or perhaps Menaechmus had already decided to silence Tramachus in the worst possible way. Then, by chance, wolves destroyed the evidence. Now this is just a theory."

"True. Tramachus may simply have been asleep when wolves chanced upon him," said Diagoras.

Heracles shook his head.

"A man asleep can always wake up and defend himself. No, I don't think so. Tramachus's wounds show that *he didn't defend himself.* The wolves came across an inert body."

"But it could be that—"

"That he was unconscious for some other reason? That's what I thought at first, so I didn't want to tell you what I suspected. But if that is so, why have Antisus and Euneos become so afraid since their friend's death? Antisus has even decided to leave Athens."

"Perhaps they fear we'll find out about their double life."

Heracles replied quickly, as if Diagoras's suggestions were entirely predictable: "You're forgetting one last thing: If they're so afraid of being found out, why are they continuing with their activities? I don't deny that they might be scared of being discovered, but I think they're *much more* scared of Menaechmus. As I said, I've made some inquiries about him. He's violent and irascible, and unusually strong, despite his slight build. It may be that Antisus and Euneos now know what he's capable of, and they're frightened."

The philosopher shut his eyes and pressed his lips together. He was boiling with rage. "That . . . wretch," he muttered. "What do you suggest we do? Accuse him publicly?"

"Not so fast. First we have to establish the degree of guilt of each of them. Then we have to find out exactly what happened to Tramachus. And lastly . . ." Heracles had a strange look. "The most important thing: I have to hope that the feeling lurking uncomfortably inside me since I began this investigation—as if a huge eye were watching my every thought—is unjustified."

"What kind of feeling?"

Heracles' gaze, lost in the night air, was inscrutable. After a pause, he answered slowly, "The feeling that I may, for the first time in my life, be *completely wrong.*"[15]

There it was: His eyes could see it in the darkness. He'd searched for it watchfully, tirelessly, among the opaque stone spirals of the cave. It was the same one, there was absolutely no doubt. As before, he recognized it by the sound: a muffled beating, like the leather-covered fist of a boxer rhythmically pounding the inside of his head. But this wasn't what mattered: What was absurd, illogical, and what his rational eye refused to accept, was the floating arm whose hand was gripping the organ. There, beyond the shoulder, that was where he should be looking. But why was that exactly where the shadows thickened? Darkness be gone! He had to find out what was hiding in that clot of blackness, what body, what image. He moved closer and put out his hand. The heartbeats grew louder. Deafened, he awoke abruptly . . . and found, to his disbelief, that he could still hear them.

15. The words *eyes* and *watchful* have both been repeated frequently in this last section, and they echo the verses that the author has the Chorus speak: "You are being watched." So there is a double layer of eidesis in this chapter. On one hand, the theme of the labors of Hercules continues with the image of the Stymphalian birds. On the other, there is mention of a "Translator" and of watchful eyes. What can it mean? Does the "Translator" have to "watch" out for something? Is somebody watching him? Montalo's learned friend Aristides has agreed to see me tomorrow.—TRANS.

Someone was pounding on his front door.

"What . . ."

He wasn't dreaming; someone was knocking insistently at the door. He felt for his cloak, which was neatly folded on a chair by the bed. Dawn's watchful gaze slipped through the crack of window. As he came out into the corridor, he saw an oval face, its only features black slits for eyes, floating toward him.

"Ponsica, open the door!" he said.

At first, stupidly, he wondered why she didn't answer. By Zeus, I'm still asleep: Ponsica can't speak. The slave gestured nervously with her right hand; she held an oil lamp in her left.

"What? Fear . . . You're afraid? Don't be stupid! We must open the door!" Grumbling, he pushed past the woman and went into the hallway. The knocking began again. There was no light—Ponsica had the lamp—so when he opened the door, his terrifying dream of only a few moments before (so similar to the one the previous night) brushed his memory, like a cobweb caressing the unwary eyes of someone moving through a dark old house. But at the door, he found not a hand gripping a beating heart, but the figure of a man. Ponsica came up behind him with the lamp and the man's face was revealed: middle-aged, with watchful, sleep-filled eyes. He wore the gray cloak of a slave.

"I have a message for Heracles of Pontor from my master, Diagoras," he said with a strong Boeotian accent.

"I am Heracles Pontor. Speak."

Intimidated by Ponsica's appearance, the slave replied hesitantly, "The message is, 'Come immediately. There's been another death.' "[16]

16. This is the end of chapter 5. I finished translating it after my conversation with Professor Aristides, an amiable man with wide gestures but brief smiles. Like Ponsica in the novel, his hands are expressive, while his face remains blank. Perhaps his—I was going to say "watchful"—eyes (the eidetic words have slipped into my thoughts now) . . . as I said, his eyes may be the only mobile, human feature of his plump face with its small pointy black beard. He received me in his large living room. "Welcome," he said, smiling briefly and indicating one of the chairs by the desk. I told him about *The Athenian Murders,* written by an anonymous author after the Peloponnesian War. No,

---

he hadn't heard of it, but the subject sounded unusual. He settled the matter with a vague shrug, saying that if Montalo spent time on the text, it must have "some merit."

When I mentioned that it was eidetic, he looked more interested.

"Strangely, Montalo spent the last years of his life studying eidetic texts. He translated a good many and established the definitive version of several original texts. I would even go so far as to say that he became quite obsessed with the subject. I'm not surprised—some of my colleagues have spent their whole lives trying to find the final key to an eidetic work. I assure you, these texts can become the worst poison literature has to offer." He scratched his ear. "I'm not exaggerating. I've translated some of them myself and have ended up dreaming about the images I've found. They can play tricks on you. I remember a treatise on astronomy by Alceus of Quiridon in which the word *red,* and all shades of the color, recurred throughout, nearly always teamed with another two words: *head* and *woman.* Sure enough, I started dreaming about a beautiful red-haired woman. I could see her face quite clearly—it tormented me." He frowned. "In the end, I discovered through another text, which came my way by chance, that a former mistress of the author had been wrongly sentenced to death. Using eidesis, the poor man had hidden the image of her beheading in the text. You can imagine what a shock it was. Instead of a beautiful ghost with red hair, I now saw a decapitated head pouring blood." He arched his eyebrows and looked at me, as if inviting me to share his disappointment. "Writing is a strange business, my friend. In my opinion, it's one of the strangest, most terrible things a man can do." And he added, again giving me his economical smile, "Reading is another."

"But getting back to Montalo—"

"Yes, yes. He took his obsession with eidesis much further. He believed that eidetic texts constituted irrefutable proof of Plato's Theory of Ideas. I expect you know it."

"Of course," I replied. "Everyone does. Plato claimed that ideas exist independently of our thoughts. He said they were real entities, more real than human beings and objects."

He didn't look too pleased with my summary of Plato's philosophy, nodding his small chubby head.

"Yes . . ." he said hesitantly. "Montalo believed that if an eidetic text evokes the *same* hidden idea in *all* readers—that is, if we all find the *same* final key—that *proves* that ideas have their own independent existence. Childish as his reasoning may seem, he was on the right track: If everyone finds a desk in this room—the *same* desk—that means that the desk exists. In addition—and this is what most interested Montalo—should there be such a consensus among all readers, it would prove, too, that the world is rational and therefore good, beautiful, and just."

"I don't get that last point," I said.

"It's a consequence of my previous point. If we all find the same idea in an eidetic text, then ideas exist, and if ideas exist, then the world is rational, as Plato and most ancient Greeks believed. And what is a rational world, made according to our thoughts and ideals, if not good, beautiful, and just?"

"So for Montalo," I murmured, amazed, "an eidetic text was nothing less than . . . the key to our existence."

"Something like that." Aristides gave a short sigh and gazed at his neat little nails. "I hardly need tell you that he never found the proof he was looking for. Perhaps it was frustration that caused his illness."

"What illness?"

He raised one eyebrow expertly.

"Montalo went insane. He spent the last years of his life shut up in his house. We all knew that he was ill and never saw anyone, so we left him alone. One day, his body was found in the forest near his house—he'd been attacked by wild animals. He must have been wandering aimlessly, during one of his attacks, and fainted and . . ." His voice trailed off as if to emphasize (eidetically?) his friend's sad end. He finished, almost inaudibly: "What a horrible way to die."

"Were his arms untouched?" I asked, stupidly.—TRANS.

[1]

IT WAS THE CORPSE OF A YOUNG GIRL. She wore a veil, a peplos that covered her head, and a cloak around her shoulders. She lay on her side, on top of an endless, erratic outline of rubble and, from the position of her legs—they were uncovered to the thigh and, in a way, it still seemed improper to look at them, even in these circumstances—one might almost believe that death had surprised her as she ran or leapt, her peplos hitched up. Her left hand was clenched, as in a children's game where something is hidden in the fist, but her right gripped a dagger with a blade, of a hand span in length, that seemed wrought entirely from blood. She was barefoot. As to the rest, there seemed to be no part of the slender body, from her neck to her calves, that wounds had not marked—short, long, straight, curved, triangular, square, deep, superficial, light, grave. The entire peplos had been ravaged; the edges of the torn cloth were bloodstained. The sight, while sad, was merely a preamble; naked, the body would no doubt display the horrific mutilations suggested by the gruesome bulges in the clothing where humors had congealed—dirty excrescences that

1. "The papyrus is dirty, riddled with corrections, stains, and illegible or corrupt sentences," noted Montalo about chapter 6.—TRANS.

looked like aquatic plants seen from the surface of crystal-clear water. Surely the death could yield no more surprises.

But there *was* a surprise: When Heracles parted the veil, he found a man's face.

"You are astonished, Decipherer!" cried the *astynomos,* effeminately pleased. "By Zeus, I do not criticize you for it! I did not want to believe it myself when my servants told me! But may I ask you why you are here? This kind gentleman," he said, indicating a bald man, "assured me that you would want to see the body. But I don't understand why. There is nothing to decipher here save the obscure motive that prompted this ephebe—" he turned toward the bald man— "What did you say his name was?"

"Euneos," said Diagoras as if in a dream.

"Nothing to decipher save the obscure motive that prompted Euneos to dress as a courtesan, get drunk, and inflict these dreadful wounds upon himself. . . . What are you looking for?"

Heracles was gently lifting the edges of the peplos.

"Ta, ta, ta, ba, ba, ba," he hummed softly to himself.

The corpse appeared taken aback by the humiliating exploration: It gazed up at the dawn sky with its remaining eye, while the other, torn out and hanging by a viscous string, stared at the inside of an ear. Split in two, the muscle of the tongue protruded, mocking, from the open mouth.

"What are you looking at?" cried the *astynomos* impatiently, for he wished to complete his task. He was charged with cleansing the city of excrement and litter, and with supervising the final destination of any bodies that sprouted among them. The early-morning appearance of a corpse on a piece of land strewn with rubble and waste in the district of the Inner Ceramicus was, therefore, his responsibility.

"How can you be so sure, *astynomos,* that all this was self-inflicted?" asked Heracles, now busy opening the corpse's left hand.

The *astynomos* savored the moment, a grotesque smile smeared over his smooth small face.

"I don't need a decipherer to tell me what happened!" he shouted. "Can't you smell his filthy clothes? They stink of wine! And there are *witnesses* who saw him slashing himself with the dagger."

"Witnesses?" Heracles didn't seem impressed. He'd found a small object in the corpse's left hand and had put it away under his cloak.

"Highly respectable witnesses. I have one of them right here."

Heracles looked up.

The *astynomos* was pointing at Diagoras.[2]

They offered their condolences to Trisipus, Euneos's father. The news had spread quickly, so there were a lot of people there when they arrived, mostly family and friends, for Trisipus was highly respected. He was remembered for his exploits as a general in Sicily and, more importantly, he was one of the few who returned to tell of them. Should anyone have doubted him, his history was engraved in dirty scars on the tombstone of his face, which, as he would say, was "blackened at the siege of Syracuse." One scar in particular was the source of more pride than all the honors received in his lifetime—a deep, oblique fissure running from the left side of his forehead to his right cheek and distorting the moist eye in its path, the result of a blow from a Syracusan sword. While unpleasant to behold, his weathered face, with its pale cleft and eyeball resembling a raw egg, was a badge of honor, and many a handsome youth envied it.

There was a great stir at Trisipus's house, but one got the impression that it was always thus, that it mattered not that this was an exceptional day. As Diagoras and the *astynomos* arrived (with the Decipherer lagging behind—for some reason, he had been reluctant to accompany them), two slaves emerged carrying bulging baskets of rubbish, the result, perhaps, of one of the many large banquets held by

2. "The sentences appear deliberately vulgar. The lyricism of the previous chapters has been lost, and instead we have satire, vacuous mockery, causticity, foulness. The style is no more than a residue of the original, a scrap tossed into this chapter," stated Montalo, and I couldn't agree more. I would add that the images of "dirt" and "rubble" seem to suggest the labor of the stables of Augeas, in which the hero must clean out the filthy stables of the king of Elis. Montalo had to do much the same here: "I've removed all the corrupt sentences and polished certain expressions; the text is, if not exactly gleaming, a little cleaner as a result."—TRANS.

the military hero for the great men of the city. It was almost impossible to enter, due to the piles of people deposited at the door—they asked questions; they were baffled; they expressed opinions but knew nothing; they watched; they complained when the ritual wailing of the women interrupted their conversations. There was another subject, apart from death, at the animated gathering: There was, above all, the *stench*. Euneos's death *reeked*. Dressed as a courtesan? But . . . Drunk? Insane? Trisipus's eldest son? Euneos, the general's son? The ephebe from the Academy? A knife? But . . . It was still too early for theories, explanations, enigmas. For now, general interest was focused on the facts of the case. And those facts were like rubbish piled under the bed. No one knew exactly what they were, but everyone was aware of the bad smell.

In the cenacle, Trisipus sat like a patriarch, surrounded by family and friends, receiving tokens of condolence, paying little heed to the givers. He held out one hand or both, kept his head high, expressed thanks. He looked confused—not sad or angry, but confused (and this made him worthy of compassion), as if he were disconcerted by the presence of so many people, and preparing to make the funeral speech. Grief had turned the bronze face, with its disheveled gray beard, darker still, highlighting the dirty white scar, and making him appear poorly constructed, as if disparate pieces had been stuck together. He weakly requested silence and, seeming to have found the appropriate words at last, said, "My thanks to you all. Had I as many arms as Briareus, I would use them—heed me well—to clasp you all tightly to me. To my joy, I see that my son was well loved. . . . And now allow me to honor you with a few brief words of praise."[3]

3. There is a gap in the text at this point. According to Montalo, "There is a large dark brown stain, elliptical in shape and quite unexpected, covering thirty whole lines. What a shame! Trisipus's speech has been lost to posterity!"

I'm now back at my desk after an odd incident: I was writing this note, when I noticed something move in the garden. The weather is fine, so the window was open—I like, even at night, to see the row of little apple trees that marks the boundary of my modest plot. Although my nearest neighbor is only a stone's throw away from the trees, I'm not used to seeing anyone, particularly in the early hours. Anyway, I was immersed in Montalo's words, when I glimpsed a shadow out of the corner of

• • •

"I thought I knew my son," said Trisipus, nearing the end of his speech. "He worshiped the Sacred Mysteries, though he was the only devout member of our family. And he was considered a good student at Plato's school. His tutor, here with us, can testify to it."

All faces turned toward Diagoras, who reddened.

"Indeed he was," he said.

Trisipus paused, sniffing and summoning a little more dirty saliva. When he spoke, he expelled some, with calculated precision, from a corner of his mouth—the least firm of the sides, although he may have alternated corners at each pause in his lengthy speech. Since he always spoke as a military man, he never expected anyone to talk back. He therefore went on too long, when the subject was more than exhausted. Just then, however, even the greatest advocate of concision would have hoped for more. Indeed, everyone was listening with an almost unhealthy interest.

"I am told that he was inebriated . . . that he was wearing women's clothing and slashed himself with a dagger." Spitting out tiny drops of saliva, he continued: "My son? My Euneos? No, he would never do something so . . . *foul-smelling.* You must mean another, not my Euneos! I am told that he lost his mind! That he lost his mind in a single night and desecrated the temple of his virtuous body. By Zeus and aegis-bearing Athena, it is a lie! If not, am I to believe that my son was a stranger to his own father? And, further, that you are all as mysterious to me as the designs of the gods? If such rubbish is true, I will, from now on, take it that your faces, your expressions of grief and sympathy, are as foul as carrion!"

---

my eye, an indistinct figure moving among the apple trees, as if searching for the best spot from which to spy on me. Needless to say, I got up and went to the window; just then, I saw someone emerge from the trees to the right and run away. I shouted, futilely, at him to stop. I've no idea who he was—I saw little more than an outline. I'm starting work again, feeling distinctly nervous—I live alone, so I'm an easy target for burglars. I've closed the window now. Oh well, it was probably nothing. I'm continuing the translation, starting with the next legible line: "I thought I knew my son."—TRANS.

There were murmurs. Judging by their looks of indifference, it seemed as if almost everyone was happy to be considered "carrion," and that no one was prepared to alter their opinion of events even slightly. There were reliable witnesses, such as Diagoras, who claimed, though reluctantly, that they had seen Euneos drunk and crazed, wearing a peplos and linen cloak, slashing himself with a dagger. Diagoras added that it had been a chance meeting: "I was returning home last night when I saw him. At first, I thought he was a hetaera; then he greeted me, and I recognized him. But I realized he was drunk, or insane. He was cutting himself with a dagger, but he was laughing, so I didn't appreciate the gravity of the situation immediately. By the time I thought of stopping him, he had fled. He was heading toward the Inner Ceramicus. I hurried to get help and found Ipsilus, Deolpos, and Archelaus, former students. They, too, had seen Euneos. We called the soldiers, but it was too late."

Once Diagoras was no longer the center of attention, he looked around for the Decipherer. He was making his way through the crowd, heading toward the door. Diagoras rushed after him and managed to catch up with him outside, but Heracles wouldn't stop. Diagoras tugged at his cloak.

"Wait! Where are you going?"

The look on Heracles' face made him step back.

"Engage another decipherer to listen to your lies, Diagoras of Mardontes," he said with icy fury. "I will take half of the money you have paid me so far as my fee and will have my slave return the rest to you at your convenience. Good day."

"Please!" begged Diagoras. "Wait! I—"

The cold, severe gaze intimidated him once more. Diagoras had never seen the Decipherer so angry.

"I'm offended not by the deceit itself, but by your foolish belief that you could *deceive me.* That, Diagoras, is unforgivable!"

"I haven't tried to deceive you!"

"In that case, my congratulations to Master Plato, for he has taught you the difficult art of lying unintentionally."

"You are still working for *me*!" said Diagoras irritably.

"Again, you've forgotten that it's *my* investigation."

"Heracles—" Diagoras spoke more quietly, realizing that a crowd of onlookers had piled up around them like litter. "Heracles, don't abandon me now. After all that's happened, you're the only person I can trust!"

"Tell me again that you saw that ephebe in women's clothing, slicing himself up before your eyes, and I swear by the peplos of Athena Polias that you will never hear from me again!"

"Come, I beg you. Let us find a quiet place to talk."

But Heracles continued: "A strange way to assist your students, O tutor! Do you think that smearing the truth with dung will help to uncover it?"

"My concern is the *Academy,* not the students!" Diagoras's round head had turned quite red; he was panting, and tears had risen to his eyes. And he had accomplished a strange feat: He had shouted noiselessly, smudging his voice until he achieved an internal howl, letting Heracles (but only him) know that he had shouted. Repeating his vocal trick, he added, "You must swear that the *Academy* will be kept out of this!"

"I'm not in the habit of pledging my word to those who lie so freely!"

"I'd kill," cried Diagoras at the peak of his inverse scream, his stentorian whisper. "Hear me well, Heracles. I'd kill for the *Academy*!"

Heracles would have laughed had he not felt so indignant. He thought Diagoras must have discovered the "ultramurmur"—a means of deafening one's interlocutor with spasmodic whispers. The stifled screams reminded Heracles of a child who is terrified of having a precious toy snatched away by a schoolmate and does everything he can to prevent it, but without the teacher noticing. But in this case, the "toy" was the Academy (and it was at the word *Academy* that Diagoras's voice became almost completely inaudible, so that Heracles knew what he was saying only from the movement of his lips).

"I'd kill!" repeated Diagoras. "What is a lie, compared with harming the *Academy*? The worst must give way to the best! That which is worth less must be sacrificed to that which is worth more!"

"Then sacrifice yourself, Diagoras, and tell me the truth," said Heracles calmly, sarcastically. "Because I assure you that you have never seemed to be worth less than you do now."

They walked through the Poikile Stoa. At that hour, it was being swept, with slaves moving their brooms rhythmically, clearing the day's litter. Heracles wasn't sure exactly how, but the repetitive commonplace sound, so like the chattering of old women, seemed to mock Diagoras in his impassioned state. Incapable as ever of taking anything lightly, the philosopher was now comporting himself with the solemnity he felt was appropriate to the situation—head hung low, using language befitting a speaker at the Assembly and sighing deeply.

"I . . . In truth, I last saw Euneos at the play last night. This morning, just before dawn, one of my slaves woke me to tell me that the *astynomos's* servants had found his body among the rubble on land in the Inner Ceramicus. When I heard the details, I was horrified. My first thought was for the honor of the Academy."

"So it is preferable for a family to suffer dishonor, rather than an institution?" asked Heracles.

"Do you not believe it is? If, as in this case, the institution is so much more qualified than the family to govern and educate men nobly, should not the institution have priority over the family?"

"But how would the Academy be harmed if it became public that Euneos was murdered?"

"If you found that one of those figs was filthy"—Diagoras pointed at the one Heracles was about to eat—"but you didn't know how it became so, would you have confidence in the other figs from the same tree?"

"Maybe not." Heracles reflected that if you asked a Platonist a question, you ended up answering his questions.

"But if you found a dirty fig on the ground," Diagoras continued, "would you blame the fig tree for its filthy state?"

"Of course not."

"Well, that's what I thought. I reasoned as follows: If Euneos alone was responsible for his own death, the Academy will not be harmed; people will even be relieved that the bad fig has been removed. But if someone was behind Euneos's death, how can we avoid chaos, panic, suspicion? And what if one of our critics—of whom we have many—started making dangerous comparisons with Tramachus's death? Can you imagine what would happen if word spread that someone was murdering our students?"

"You're forgetting one small thing." Heracles smiled. "With your actions, you're contributing to Euneos's murder going unpunished."

"No!" cried Diagoras, triumphant for the first time. "That's where you're wrong. I intended to tell *you* the truth. You would continue the investigation in secret, with no risk to the Academy, and you would catch the culprit."

"A masterly plan," said the Decipherer sarcastically. "Tell me, Diagoras, how did you do it? I mean, did you place the dagger in his hand?"

Reddening, the philosopher looked gloomy once more.

"No, by Zeus, I would never have touched the corpse! When the slave led me to the place, the *astynomos* and his servants were there. I told them the version of events I had devised on the way, and named several former students, who I was sure would confirm everything I said, if the need arose. When I saw the knife in his hand and smelled the strong odor of wine, I thought my explanation was plausible. Could that not, in fact, be what happened, Heracles? The *astynomos* who examined the body said that all the wounds were within reach of his right hand. There were no cuts on his back, for instance. In truth, it would seem that he himself—"

Diagoras fell silent on seeing that the Decipherer again looked angry.

"Please don't insult my intelligence, Diagoras, by quoting the view of a miserable rubbish collector like the *astynomos*. I am the Decipherer of Enigmas."

"What makes you think Euneos was murdered? He smelled of wine; he was wearing women's clothes; he held a dagger in his right hand and could have caused all those wounds himself. I know of several horrible cases of the effects of wine on the young. This very morning, I remembered an ephebe from my deme who became inebriated for the first time during the Lenaea one year and killed himself by dashing his head against a wall. So I thought—"

"You started thinking, as always," stated Heracles placidly. "While I simply examined the body. There you have the difference between a philosopher and a decipherer."

"So what did you find?"

"His clothing. The slashed peplos . . ."

"Yes?"

"The slashes bore no relation to the wounds *beneath*. Even a child would have noticed. Well, maybe not, but I did. A simple examination was all it took for me to see that beneath a straight cut in the cloth lay a round wound, and that a large puncture mark concealed a light, straight cut on the skin. Somebody obviously *dressed him* as a woman *after* he was stabbed, first slashing the clothes and covering them in blood, of course."

"Incredible," said Diagoras, truly impressed.

"It's merely a question of knowing how to look at things," replied the Decipherer, indifferent. "As if that were not enough, our murderer made another mistake: There was no blood around the corpse. If Euneos had stabbed himself so savagely, there would have been a trail of blood over the rubble and rubbish, at least close to him. But there was no blood on the ground. It was clean, if you like. Which means that Euneos was stabbed *somewhere else* and then moved to that derelict part of the Inner Ceramicus."

"Oh, by Zeus . . ."

"But perhaps this last mistake was *crucial*." Narrowing his eyes and stroking his neat silver beard thoughtfully, Heracles added, "Though I still don't understand why they dressed him in women's clothing and placed *this* in his hand."

He took an object from under his cloak. They both stared at it in silence.

"Why do you think someone else put it there?" asked Diagoras. "Euneos could have picked it up before."

Heracles shook his head impatiently.

"Blood was no longer dripping from Euneos's body. Rigor mortis had set in," he explained. "If Euneos had been holding *this* when he died, the fingers would have been too stiff for me to remove it as easily as I did. No. *Someone* dressed him in women's clothing and slipped this into his hand."

"But, by the sacred gods, why?"

"I don't know. And I find that disconcerting. I haven't translated that part of the text yet, Diagoras. Although I assure you, in all modesty, I'm not a bad translator." Suddenly, Heracles turned and set off down the steps of the Stoa. "Now everything has been said, so let us waste no more time! We've got another labor of Hercules to perform!"

Diagoras hurried after him.

"Where are we going?"

Heracles replied, "To meet a very dangerous man who may help us! We're off to Menaechmus's workshop!"

As he walked away, he put the withered white lily back under his cloak.[4]

In the darkness, a voice asked, "Is anybody there?"[5]

4. I could help you, Heracles, but how to tell you all that I know? How are you to know, clever as you are, that it isn't a clue *for you,* but *for me,* for *the reader* of an eidetic novel in which *you yourself,* as a character, *are just one more clue*? Your presence, I now realize, is also *eidetic*! You're there because the author decided to put you there, like the lily that the mysterious murderer placed in his victim's hand, to convey more clearly to the reader the idea of the labors of Hercules, which is one of the central themes of the novel. So, the labors of Hercules, the girl with the lily (with her cry for "help" and warning of "danger"), and the Translator—all three mentioned in the last few paragraphs—are, so far, the main eidetic images. What can they mean? —TRANS.

5. I've stopped translating, but *I'm still writing,* so that, whatever happens, I'll leave a record of my plight. Briefly, *someone has gotten into the house.* I'll recount the events leading up to this (I'm writing in a hurry, so it may be a bit of a mess). It's evening, and I was just about to start the final part of this chapter, when I heard a slight, but unfamiliar, noise somewhere in my empty house. I ignored it, and set to work. I had only written two sentences when I started hearing regular rhythmic sounds, like *footsteps.* My first instinct was to check the hall and the kitchen, since the sounds seemed to come from there, but then I thought I ought to write down what was happening, because—

• • •

In the darkness, a voice asked, "Is anybody there?"

It was dark and dusty. The floor was strewn with rubble and possibly rubbish—things that sounded and felt like stones when trodden on, and things that sounded and felt soft, crumbly. The darkness was total, and it was impossible to see where they were going. The place might have been huge, or very small. There might have been an exit other than the portico through which they had entered, or there might not.

Another sound!

I'm back now after looking around. There was no one there, and nothing appeared to have been moved. I don't think I've been burgled. The lock on the front door hasn't been forced. True, the kitchen door, which leads to a little yard, was open, but I may have left it open myself, I don't remember. I had a good look around. I could make out the familiar shapes of my furniture in the dark (I didn't want my visitor to know where I was, so I didn't turn on any lights). I checked the hall and the kitchen, the library and the bedroom, calling out, "Is anybody there?" several times.

Reassured, I switched on a few lights. It seems to have been a false alarm. Now, back at my desk, my heart is gradually settling down. I must have imagined it. But then I think back to last night: *Someone* was spying on me from behind the trees in the garden, and now . . . I don't think it was a burglar, though anything's possible. Surely a burglar would concentrate on *burgling,* not watching his victims. Maybe he's preparing his masterstroke. He's in for a shock (I laugh at the thought): Apart from a few ancient manuscripts, there's nothing of any value in my house. I'm rather like Montalo in that respect. Well, actually, in lots of other respects, too.

I've found out a little more about him in the last few days. There are many similarities between us: both choosing to live alone in the country, in a large house with an internal and external courtyard, like the mansions of rich ancient Greeks in Olynthus or Troezen. And both of us passionate about translating ancient Greek texts. Neither of us has enjoyed (or suffered) the love of a woman, or had children, and our friends (Aristides, for instance, in his case; Helena—with a few *obvious* differences—in mine) are, above all, colleagues. A few queries spring to mind: What *happened* to Montalo during the last years of his life? Aristides said he was obsessed with using an eidetic text to prove Plato's Theory of Ideas. Perhaps he found the proof he was looking for in *The Athenian Murders,* and it made him lose his mind. But why, if he was an expert on eidetic texts, did he not seem to have noticed that *The Athenian Murders* was one?

I'm not sure why, but I'm more and more convinced that the answer to these questions is *hidden* in *the text.* I must carry on translating.

I apologize to the reader for the lengthy interruption. I'll start again from the sentence "In the darkness, a voice asked."—TRANS.

"Heracles, wait," whispered another voice. "I can't see you."

In the darkness, the slightest sound made them jump uncontrollably.

"Heracles?"

"I'm over here."

"Where?"

"Here."

In the darkness, finding that *there really was somebody there* almost made them scream.

"What's the matter, Diagoras?"

"Oh gods. For a moment, I thought—it's just a statue."

Heracles groped his way closer, stretched out a hand, and touched something. Had it been a real face, his fingers would have gone straight into the eyes. He felt the sockets, recognized the geometric slope of a nose, the undulating outline of lips, the cleft promontory of a chin. He smiled and said, "You're right, it *is* a statue. There must be quite a few around. We're in his workshop."

"Indeed," said Diagoras. "I can almost see them now. My eyes are growing used to the dark."

And so they were: Sight, like a paintbrush, had begun to render white figures in the blackness, sketches, rough drafts. Choked by dust, Heracles coughed and poked the dirt at his feet with the tip of his sandal—a sound like a box of beads being shaken.

"Where can he be?" Heracles asked.

"Why don't we wait for him in the hallway?" suggested Diagoras, made uneasy by the inexhaustible darkness and the slowly looming statues. "I'm sure he won't be long."

"He's *here,*" said Heracles. "If not, why was the door open?"

"This is a very strange place!"

"It's simply an artist's workshop. But it's odd that the shutters are closed. Come on."

They moved forward. It was easier now. Gradually, they discerned islands of marble, busts on high wooden shelves, bodies that had yet to emerge from the stone, slabs to be carved for friezes. The space that contained them was becoming visible, too. The room was large, with a door at one end opening onto a hallway, and what appeared to be heavy hangings or curtains at the other. One wall was scarred by gold filaments, faintly gleaming marks spreading over huge closed wooden shutters. Sculptures, or the blocks of stone in which they gestated, stood everywhere, rising out of the remains of artistic endeavor—fragments, splinters, pebbles, sand, tools, rubble, rags. A large wooden podium, with a couple of shallow steps on either side, stood in front of the curtains. On it, a row of white sheets was being besieged by a large container of rubble. The air in the workshop was cold and actually *smelled* of stone—a strangely dense, dirty smell, as if one had sniffed the ground and inhaled the light, prickly specks of dust.

"Menaechmus?" Heracles Pontor called out.

A sound shattered the silence—immense, jarring with the mineral gloom. Someone had removed the plank barring one of the vast windows—the one nearest the podium—and let it fall to the floor. As fierce as a god's curse, the resplendent midday sun cut across the room unhindered, clouds of chalky dust swirling around it.

"My workshop is closed in the afternoons," said the man.

There must have been a door hidden behind the hangings, for neither Heracles nor Diagoras had seen him enter.

He was thin, with an unhealthy, slovenly appearance. Dirty tufts of gray sprouted unevenly in his untidy hair. His pale face was stained with dark circles under the eyes. There was not one detail of his appearance that an artist would not have been tempted to alter: the sparse, uneven beard, the irregular cuts in the cloak, the worn-out sandals. His sinewy brown hands displayed a motley collection of stains, as did his feet. In fact, his entire body was a worn tool. He coughed, and tried to smooth down his hair; he blinked, his eyes bloodshot. He turned his back on his visitors, ignoring them, and went to a tool-strewn table by the podium, where he began, it seemed—though there was no way of knowing for sure—selecting the ones he needed. They made a variety of ringing sounds, like out-of-tune cymbals.

"We are aware of it, good Menaechmus," said Heracles with studied gentleness. "We haven't come to purchase a statue."

Menaechmus turned, directing the remnants of his gaze at Heracles.

"What are you doing here, Decipherer of Enigmas?"

"Simply conversing with a colleague," answered Heracles. "We are both artists—your skill lies in carving the truth, mine in discovering it."

The sculptor turned back to the table and rummaged clumsily among the tools.

"Whom have you brought with you?" he asked.

Diagoras began with dignity: "My name—"

"He's a friend," said Heracles, interrupting the philosopher. "You can believe me when I say that I am here, in great part, due to him. But let us waste no more time."

"Good," said Menaechmus, "for I must work. I have a commission from a noble family from the Scambonidai, which must be completed within a month. And many other things." He coughed again. The cough, like his words, was dusty, damaged.

He suddenly stopped what he was doing—his movements always abrupt, ungainly—and climbed the stairs to the podium. Heracles said in an friendly tone, "I simply wish to ask you a few questions, my dear Menaechmus, and if you help me, we'll finish more quickly. Does the name Tramachus, son of Meragrus, mean anything to you? Or Antisus, son of Praxinoe, or Euneos, son of Trisipus?"

Up on the podium, Menaechmus stopped removing sheets from the statue.

"Why do you wish to know?"

"Oh, Menaechmus, if you answer my questions with questions, how will we ever finish? Let us proceed in an orderly fashion: You answer my questions; then I will answer yours."

"I know them."

"Through your work?"

"I know many ephebes in the city." He broke off to tug at a sheet that was caught. He was impatient. His movements had an agonistic quality. Objects seemed to defy him. He granted the cloth the opportunity of two more brief attempts, almost warnings. Then he clenched his teeth, braced himself, and, with a dirty grunt, pulled with both hands. The sheet came away from the statue, making a sound that was like a pile of rubbish being knocked over, disturbing ephemeral deposits of dust.

The sculpture, uncovered at last, was elaborate: a man sitting at a table covered with papyrus scrolls. The unfinished base writhed formlessly, the pure marble undefiled by the chisel. Apparently intent on some task, the figure had its back to Heracles and Diagoras, and of the head, only the crown was visible.

"Did any of them pose for you?" asked Heracles.

"Occasionally," came the terse reply.

"But not all your models perform in your plays."

Menaechmus was back at the tool table, setting out a row of chisels of different sizes.

"They are free to choose," he said, not looking at Heracles. "Sometimes they do both."

"Like Euneos?"

The sculptor turned his head abruptly. Diagoras reflected that Menaechmus seemed to ill-treat his own muscles, like a drunken father battering his children.

"I have just heard about Euneos, if that's what you mean," said Menaechmus. His eyes were two shadows fixed on Heracles. "I had nothing to do with his fit of madness."

"Nobody is claiming you did." Heracles raised his hands, palms outward, as if Menaechmus were threatening him.

The sculptor returned to his tools, and Heracles said, "Incidentally, did you know that Tramachus, Antisus, and Euneos had to perform in your plays in secret? Their tutors at the Academy forbade it."

Menaechmus shrugged his bony shoulders. "I've heard something to that effect. It's nonsense!" And with that, he bounded up the steps to the podium. "Nobody has the right to prohibit art!" he cried, striking a corner of the marble table impulsively, dangerously, with his chisel. It left the vestige of a musical note in the air.

Diagoras was about to retort, then seemed to think better of it. Heracles said, "Were they afraid of being discovered?"

Menaechmus circled the statue eagerly, as if seeking another disobedient corner to punish. He said, "I suppose so. But I took no interest in their lives. I simply gave them the opportunity to be in the chorus. They accepted without hesitation, and the gods know I was grateful: My tragedies, unlike my statues, bring me neither fame nor fortune, only pleasure, and it's difficult finding actors to play in them."

"When did you meet them?"

After a pause, Menaechmus replied, "During visits to Eleusis. I worship the Mysteries."

"But your relationship with them went beyond the sharing of religious beliefs, didn't it?" Heracles was strolling around the workshop, pausing to examine several sculptures with the casual interest of a Maecenas.

"What do you mean?"

"I mean, O Menaechmus, that you loved them."

The Decipherer stood before an unfinished statue of Hermes complete with caduceus, petasus, and winged sandals. He said, "Particularly Antisus, from what I see."

He pointed to the god's face, with its beautiful, slightly malevolent smile.

"And that head of Bacchus, crowned with grapes?" continued Heracles. "And this bust of Athena?" He went from figure to figure, gesticulating like a trader trying to raise his price. "A great many of the gods and goddesses of sacred Olympus seem to bear Antisus's beautiful countenance!"

"Antisus is loved by many." Menaechmus resumed his work furiously.

"And praised by you. I wonder, how did you deal with Tramachus's and Euneos's jealousy? I should imagine they weren't too happy about your obvious preference for their friend."

For a moment, in the midst of the clinking of chisels, it seemed as if Menaechmus was panting vigorously, but when he turned, Heracles and Diagoras saw that he was smiling.

"By Zeus, do you think I mattered to them that much?"

"Yes, since they agreed to model for you and perform in your plays, thus disobeying the sacred precepts laid down by the Academy. I believe they admired you, Menaechmus. They posed for you naked or dressed in women's clothing, and once the work was finished, they displayed their naked bodies or their androgynous attire for your pleasure. And in so doing, they risked being discovered and dishonoring their families."

Still smiling, Menaechmus cried, "By Athena! Do you really believe I'm worth that much, either as an artist or a man, Heracles Pontor?"

Heracles replied, "Young spirits, unfinished, like your sculptures, can take root in any soil, Menaechmus of Carisio. And best of all is well-manured soil."

Menaechmus appeared not to listen. He was concentrating intensely on sculpting some of the folds in the statue's garments. *Ching! Ching!* Suddenly, he began talking, but as if addressing the marble. His rough, uneven voice daubed the workshop walls with echoes.

"Yes, I am a mentor to many ephebes. Do you think our young men don't need mentors, Heracles? Is the world"—his growing anger seemed to make him strike the stone ever harder: *Ching!*—"they're going to inherit a pleasant place? Look around you! Our art here in Athens . . . What art? Our statues used to be charged with power. We imitated the Egyptians, always so much wiser than we!" *Ching!* "But now, what do we do? We draw geometrical forms, figures that comply strictly with the canon! We've lost spontaneity, strength, beauty!" *Ching! Ching!* "You say my works are unfinished, and you're right. Do you know why? Because I can't create anything in accordance with the canon!"

Heracles tried to interrupt, but the clean opening of his speech was lost in a quagmire of blows and exclamations from Menaechmus.

"And the theater! It used to be an orgy in which even the gods took part! But with Euripides, what did it become? Cheap dialectics to suit the noble minds of Athens!" *Ching!* "Theater that is a thoughtful meditation rather than a sacred celebration! As an old man, at the end of his life, Euripides himself conceded that it was so!" He stopped chiseling and turned to Heracles with a smile. "He changed his views completely. . . ."

And, as if this last sentence alone had required a pause, he resumed striking the marble even harder than before, and went on: "In old age, Euripides gave up philosophy and turned to making real *theater*!" *Ching!* "Do you remember his last play?" And, brandishing the word as if it were a precious stone that he had found in the rubble, he cried, "*Bacchae*!"

"Yes!" a voice rang out. "*Bacchae*! The work of a madman!" Menaechmus looked at Diagoras, who seemed to be scattering his shouts in great agitation, as if his silence until then had cost him a great effort. "Euripides lost his faculties in old age, as happens to many, and his work deteriorated to an inconceivable degree! In his middle years, his pure, reasoning spirit was devoted to the search for philosophical truth, but over time, its noble foundations collapsed . . . and his last play was, like those of Aeschylus and Sophocles, a reeking heap of rubbish teeming with all the sicknesses of the soul and flowing with innocent blood!" Red in the face after his impassioned speech, he glared at Menaechmus.

After a short silence, the sculptor asked quietly, "Would you mind telling me who this idiot is?"

Heracles raised his hand to forestall his companion's angry reply: "Forgive us, good Menaechmus, we didn't come to discuss the plays of Euripides. . . . No, let me finish, Diagoras!" The philosopher could barely contain himself. "We wanted to ask you—"

He was interrupted by thunderous echoes. Menaechmus was shouting, pacing up and down the podium, occasionally pointing at one of the two men with his small hammer, as if he might throw it. "What of philosophy? Think of Heraclitus! 'Without strife, there can be no existence'! That was the view of the philosopher Heraclitus! Philosophy, too, has changed! It was once a driving force! But what is it now? Pure intellect! What fascinated us in the past? Matter itself: Thales, Anaximander, Empedocles! We used to ponder matter itself! But now what do we think about?" His voice was horribly distorted as he said, "The world of ideas! Ideas exist, of course, but they're somewhere else, far away! They're perfect, pure, good, and useful!"

"They are!" screamed Diagoras. "They are, whereas you are imperfect, vulgar, contemptible, and—"

"Please, Diagoras, let me speak!" cried Heracles.

"We mustn't love ephebes, oh no!" mocked Menaechmus. "We must love the *idea* of ephebes! We must kiss the thought of lips, caress the definition of a thigh! And let us not create statues, by Zeus! That's nothing but vulgar imitative art! Let us create *ideas* of statues! This is the philosophy that the young will inherit! Aristophanes was right to place it in the *clouds*!"

Diagoras spluttered with indignation.

"How can you express an opinion with such confidence about something of which you know nothing?"

"Diagoras!" Heracles' firmness caused a sudden silence. "Can't you see that Menaechmus is trying to keep us off the subject? You must let me speak!" And, surprisingly calm, he went on: "Menaechmus, we came to question you about Tramachus's and Euneos's deaths." He sounded almost apologetic, as if he regretted having to mention such a trivial matter to someone so important.

After a brief silence, Menaechmus spat, wiped his nose, and said, "Tramachus was killed by wolves while out hunting. As for Euneos, I'm told he got drunk and the fingers of Dionysus gripped his brain, forcing him to stab himself repeatedly. What have I to do with any of that?"

Heracles replied quickly, "Together with Antisus, they came to your workshop in the evenings and took part in your strange amusements. All three admired you and responded to your amorous demands, but you favored one of them. They probably argued; perhaps threats were even made. The entertainments you organize with your ephebes don't exactly have a good reputation, so they wouldn't have wanted any of it to become public. Tramachus didn't go hunting, but the day he left Athens, your workshop was closed and you were nowhere to be seen."

Diagoras raised his eyebrows and turned to Heracles. He had been unaware of this last fact. But Heracles went on, as if intoning: "Tramachus was in fact murdered, or beaten into unconsciousness and left to the mercy of wolves. Last night, Euneos and Antisus came here after your play. Your workshop is the building nearest to where Euneos was found this morning. I know for certain that Euneos, too, was murdered, and that his murderer committed the crime elsewhere and then moved the body. And one can assume that the two locations were not far apart, for who would think of crossing Athens with a corpse slung over his shoulder?" He paused and opened his arms wide, in an almost friendly gesture. "So you see, good Menaechmus, you have rather a lot to do with it."

Menaechmus's face was impossible to read. He might almost have been smiling, but his gaze was somber. Without a word, he slowly turned away from Heracles and resumed striking the marble with deliberate blows of his chisel. When he spoke, there was amusement in his voice: "Oh, what a wonderful, exquisite piece of reasoning!" He stifled a laugh. "I'm guilty by syllogism! Better still, I'm guilty because my house is close to the potters' plot of land." Still chiseling, he shook his head slowly and laughed again, as if the sculpture or his work on it were cause for amusement. "This is how we Athenians construct truths nowadays: We talk of distances; we make calculations based on emotions; we apply reason to the facts!"

"Menaechmus—" said Heracles gently.

But the sculptor continued: "It will be said, in years to come, that Menaechmus was found guilty because of a matter of length! Nowadays, everything obeys a canon. Haven't I said so many times? Justice is now simply a question of distance."

"Menaechmus," insisted Heracles, still gently. "How did you know that Euneos's body was found on the potters' plot of land? I didn't say so."

Diagoras was surprised by the sculptor's violent reaction: He turned toward Heracles, eyes wide, as if the Decipherer were a stout Galatea suddenly come to life. For a moment, he said not a word. Then he cried, with the remnants of his voice: "Are you insane? The whole neighborhood is talking about it! What are you implying?"

Heracles again sounded meek, apologetic: "Nothing, don't worry. It was part of my reasoning regarding the distance." And then, as if he'd remembered something, he scratched his conical head and added, "What I don't quite understand, good Menaechmus, is why you focused on what I said about the distance but not on my statement regarding the *possibility* that *someone murdered* Euneos—a far stranger idea, by Zeus, and one that is not being talked about in the neighborhood, but which you seem to have readily accepted. You began by criticizing my argument regarding distance, but you didn't ask: 'Heracles, how can you be so sure that Euneos was murdered?' I really don't understand, Menaechmus."

Diagoras felt no compassion for Menaechmus as he watched the Decipherer, with his merciless deductive powers, miring the sculptor in his own frenzied words, gradually sinking him into total confusion, as if into one of the putrid pools where, according to travelers' tales, those who try to free themselves by frantic contortions are swallowed all the faster. In the dense silence that followed, he felt the urge to make a mocking, trivial remark to underline their victory over the wretch. Smiling scornfully, he said, "What a beautiful sculpture you're working on, Menaechmus. Whom is it meant to be?"

For a moment, he thought the sculptor would not reply. But he became uneasy when he saw that Menaechmus was smiling.

"It's called *The Translator.* The man who tries to decipher the mystery of a text written in a foreign language, not realizing that words simply lead to other words, and thoughts to other thoughts, while the truth remains unattainable. Is it not a good metaphor for what we all do?"

Diagoras was unsure what the sculptor meant, but not wishing to be at a disadvantage, he remarked, "A strange figure. What form of dress is that? It doesn't look Greek."

Menaechmus said nothing. He stared at his work and smiled.

"Could I take a closer look?"

"Yes," said Menaechmus.

The philosopher mounted the podium. His steps resounded on the dirty wooden boards. He approached the statue and observed its profile.

Hunched over the table, the man of marble held a fine quill between forefinger and thumb. He was surrounded by scrolls. What form of dress is that? Diagoras wondered. A sort of highly fitted cloak. Clothing from foreign parts, evidently. He peered at the bent neck, with the top vertebrae protruding (he had to admit it was skillfully executed), the thick hair, the ears with almost obscenely thick lobes.

Diagoras couldn't see the face, as the figure's head was bowed. He bent over a little and saw a receding hairline. And he couldn't help admiring the hands—veined, slender, the right gripping the quill, the left palm down, holding open the scroll on which he was writing. The middle finger bore a large signet ring engraved with a circle. A second roll of papyrus lay to one side—the original work, no doubt. The man was writing out his translation on the parchment. Even the letters on it had been skillfully and meticulously engraved! Intrigued, Diagoras leaned over the statue's shoulder and read the words that the figure had, supposedly, just translated. He didn't understand them. They said:

He didn't understand them. They said

He still hadn't seen the statue's face. He leaned over a little farther and looke[6]

6. I can't go on. My hands are shaking.—TRANS.

I'm coming back to the translation after two anxious days. I still don't know whether I'm going to go on or not. I may not have the courage. But at least I've managed to sit at my desk and look at my papers. Yesterday, when I was talking to Helena, I felt I would never be able to do so again. I acted a little impulsively with Helena, I admit. I asked her the day before to come and keep me company—I didn't feel I could stay in the house alone at night—and, though I didn't tell her the real reason for my request, she must have sensed something, because she agreed immediately. I tried not to talk about work. I was friendly, polite, and shy. And I continued to be so even when we made love. I made love to her hoping secretly that she would *make love* to me. I felt her body beneath the sheets, breathed in the acrid smell of pleasure, heard her moan, but it didn't help. I sought—at least I think I did—to feel *in her* what she could feel *of me.* I wanted—longed—for her hands to explore me, feel me, *come up against me,* give me a shape in the darkness. . . . No, not a *shape.* I wanted simply to feel that I was matter, a solid remainder, something that was there, occupying a space, not just an outline, a figure with features and an identity. I didn't want her to talk to me,

But he still hadn't seen the statue's face. He leaned over a little farther and looked at it.

I didn't want to hear words—especially not my name—or empty sentences relating to me. I now have some understanding of what happened: I think it was due to the panic induced by translating, to a horrible feeling of *porousness,* as if my existence was suddenly revealed to be much more fragile than the text I'm translating and which manifests itself through me in the *upper* part of these pages. It's made me feel that I need to augment these footnotes, as a counterbalance to the huge weight of the *main* text. *If only I could write,* I thought, not for the first time, but more longingly than ever. *If only I could create something of my own. . . .* My encounter with Helena—her body, her firm breasts, her smooth muscles, her youth—didn't help much; it served perhaps only to make me recognize myself (I desperately needed her body as a mirror in which to see myself without having to *look at myself*). But this brief reunion, this *anagnorisis,* only served to help me sleep and, therefore, to disappear again. The following day, as dawn broke over the hills, I stood naked at the bedroom window. I heard a rustling of sheets and Helena's sleepy voice as she lay there naked, and I decided to tell her everything. I spoke calmly, my eyes fixed upon the fire growing on the horizon.

"*I'm in the text,* Helena. I don't know how or why, but it's me. I'm the statue, carved by one of the characters, called *The Translator,* sitting at a desk translating just like I do. It all matches: a receding hairline, delicate ears with thick lobes, slender, veined hands. . . . It's me. I don't dare go on with the translation. I couldn't bear to read a description of my own *face.*"

She protested. She sat up in bed, asked lots of questions, became angry. Still naked, I went to the sitting room and returned with the pages of my translation. I handed them to her. We were a comical sight: both of us naked—her sitting, me standing—colleagues once more. Her breasts—quivering, pink—rising with each breath, she furrowed her teacher's brow. I stood in silence at the window, my member pathetically shriveled by anxiety and cold.

"It's ridiculous," she said as she finished reading. "Absolutely ridiculous."

She protested again. She berated me. She said I was becoming obsessed, that the description was very vague—it could have been anybody. Then she added, "And the signet ring the statue is wearing is engraved with a circle. A *circle*! Not a *swan,* like yours!"

That was the most awful part. And she knew it.

"You know very well that in Greek *kuklos* is the word for 'circle' and *kuknos* that for 'swan,'" I said calmly. "Only one letter's difference. If that *l,* that lambda, is an *n,* then there's absolutely no doubt: It's me." I stared at the ring on the middle finger of my left hand, engraved with the outline of a swan. It was a gift from my father, and I never take it off.

"But in the text it's *kuklos,* not—"

"Montalo said in one of his notes that the word was hard to make out. He took

The features were[7]

"A shrewd man," said Heracles as they left the workshop. "He doesn't finish his sentences, or his sculptures. He affects a repulsive personality to make us back away holding our noses, but I'm sure he's utterly charming with his followers."

"Do you think he—" began Diagoras.

"Let's not be too hasty. The truth may be far away, but it will await

---

it to be *kuklos,* but he stated that the fourth letter was unclear. Do you understand, Helena? The fourth letter." My voice was flat, almost offhand. "My sanity depends on Montalo's opinion as a philologist about *a single letter.*"

"But that's absurd!" she said, exasperated. "What are you doing . . . in here?" She thumped the papers. "This book was written thousands of years ago! How . . ." She pulled off the sheets, uncovering her long legs. She smoothed down her red hair. She went, naked and barefoot, to the door. "Come on. I want to read the original text." Her voice was firm now, determined.

Horrified, I begged her not to.

"We're going to read Montalo's text together," she said, standing at the door. "I don't care if afterward you decide not to go on with the translation. I just want you to get this mad notion out of your head."

We went to the sitting room, both still naked and barefoot. I remember having a ridiculous thought as I followed her. We want to make sure that we're human beings, physical bodies, flesh, organs, not just characters in a novel or readers. We're going to find out. We have to. It was cold in the sitting room, but it didn't bother us. Helena got to the desk first and leaned over the papers. I couldn't bring myself to go any closer. I stood behind her, admiring her smooth back, the gentle curve of her spine, the soft buttocks. There was a silence. I remember thinking, She's reading my face. I heard her moan. I closed my eyes. She said, "Oh."

She put her arms around me. I was horrified by her tenderness. She said, "Oh . . . oh . . ."

I couldn't bring myself to ask, didn't want to know what she had read. I clung to her warm body. Then I heard laughter—gentle, becoming louder, growing in her belly like a new life.

"Oh . . . oh . . . oh . . ." She continued laughing.

Later, much later, when I read what she had read, I understood why she had laughed.

I've decided to go on with the translation. I'm starting from the sentence: "But he still hadn't seen the statue's face."—TRANS.

7. There's a gap in the text at this point. Montalo stated that the following five lines were illegible.—TRANS.

our arrival with infinite patience. For the moment, I'd like another opportunity to talk to Antisus."

"Unless I'm much mistaken, we'll find him at the Academy. There is to be a dinner there this evening in honor of a guest of Plato's, and Antisus is one of the cupbearers."

"Very well, Diagoras." Heracles Pontor smiled. "I believe the time has come for me to see this Academy of yours."[8]

8. I've just made an amazing discovery! If I'm right—and I'm pretty sure I am—all the strange enigmas surrounding this novel will start to make sense . . . even if still strange and, as far as I am personally concerned, far more worrying. I made my discovery—as is so often the case—quite by chance. This evening, I was looking over the last part of chapter 6 in Montalo's edition, which I hadn't yet finished translating, when I noticed irritably that the edges of the pages were stubbornly sticking together (it's happened before, but I've simply ignored it). I peered at them more closely. They looked normal, but the substance with which they were stuck together was *still fresh*. I frowned, increasingly anxious. I examined chapter 6 page by page, and became convinced that, without a shadow of a doubt, the last few pages had been added *recently*. A storm of possible explanations swirled in my brain. I went back to the text and found that the "new" pages contained the *detailed description of Menaechmus's statue*. My heart started pounding. What on earth could it mean?

I put off any more theorizing till later and finished translating the chapter. Then, suddenly, as I looked out of the window (it was night by then) at the row of apple trees marking the boundary of my garden, I remembered the man who had been watching me and who ran off when I saw him . . . and my feeling, the following night, that someone *was in the house*. I jumped up. My forehead was clammy and my temples were throbbing.

The answer seems obvious: *Someone has been sitting at my desk, swapping some of the pages of Montalo's text, and has done so very recently.* Could it be someone who *knows me,* or at least knows what I look like, and who was therefore able to add such accurate details to the description of the sculpture? But if so, who would be capable of ripping out pages from an original work and replacing them with other pages, for the sole purpose of tormenting the translator?

Whatever the truth, I can obviously no longer sleep peacefully at night. Or work peacefully, because I can't be sure *whose words* I'm translating. Worse still, will I be able to go on without stopping to wonder if any—or all—of the sentences constitute messages addressed directly to *me* by the mysterious intruder? Now that I've begun to have doubts, how can I be sure that other paragraphs, in previous chapters, don't have anything to do *with me*? The fantasy of literature is so full of ambiguity that the rules of the game don't even have to be broken: The mere *suspicion* that someone might have broken them changes everything, puts a terrible spin on everything. Let's be frank, dear reader, have you never had the mad

---

feeling that a novel—the one you're reading right now, for instance—*is addressed to you personally*? And once you believe this, do you shake your head, blinking, and think, That's ridiculous. Better to forget it and go on reading? So imagine my terror at knowing with absolute certainty that part of this book *concerns me*! And I mean *terror.* I've been used to looking at novels from a distance . . . and now suddenly to find myself in one!

I have to do something.

I'm stopping work on the translation until this is resolved. And I'm going to try to catch my mysterious visitor.—TRANS.

THE ROAD to the Academy of Philosophy starts as little more than a narrow path branching off the Sacred Way just outside the Dipylon Gate. There is nothing special about this path: It enters a forest of tall pines and twists and sharpens to a point, like a tooth, so that one feels that it might at any moment end in an impenetrable thicket. But once the early bends in the path are left behind, one glimpses, beyond a brief, though dense, expanse of stones and greenery with leaves as curved as eyeteeth, the smooth facade of the main building, a marble cube placed carefully on a small hill. The path then broadens proudly. There is a portico at the entrance, with busts the color of tooth ivory standing in niches on either side, observing in symmetrical silence as travelers approach. It is not known for certain whom the sculptor wished the busts to represent. Some say the True and the False, others the Beautiful and the Good, but the less wise (or possibly the wisest?) say they represent nothing and that they are merely decorations—after all, something had to be placed in those niches. In the center, an inscription, engraved in twisting letters: MAY NO ONE ENTER WITHOUT KNOWLEDGE OF GEOMETRY. And beyond, the beautiful gardens of the Academy, laid out with curving paths. At the center of a small square, a statue of the hero seems to demand respect from the visitor—left hand outstretched, with index finger pointing down, a lance in the other, gaze framed by a helmet with bristling horsehair topped with toothlike points. And standing in the leafy glade, the sober marble architecture of the school. There are open spaces surrounded by white colonnades with red serrated roofs for classes in summer, while an indoor area affords protection to students and tutors when the cold bares its teeth. The gymnasium has all the necessary equipment, but is smaller than the one at the lyceum. More modest buildings serve as dwellings for some of the tutors and as Plato's place of work.

By the time Heracles and Diagoras arrived, twilight had unleashed a harsh Boreas that shook the twisted branches of the tallest trees. No sooner had they entered the white portico than the Decipherer noticed Diagoras's mood and demeanor change. He became like a hunting dog sniffing for prey: head up, frequently licking his lips, his usually neat beard bristling. He barely listened to Heracles (although the Decipherer spoke little, as was his custom), didn't look at him, and merely nodded and muttered "Yes" to any remark, or "Wait a moment" in answer to his questions. Heracles sensed that Diagoras wished to make him see that this was the most perfect place in the world, and that the mere thought of something going wrong was unbearably distressing to him.

The small square was empty and the school building appeared deserted, but Diagoras seemed unconcerned. "They often take a brief walk around the garden before dinner," he said.

Heracles suddenly felt his cloak being twisted by a violent tug.

"Here they come." The philosopher gestured toward the dark gardens, adding ecstatically, "And there's Plato!"

A group of men was approaching along the confusion of paths. They all wore dark himations covering both shoulders, with neither tunics nor chitons underneath. They appeared to have learned the art of walking like ducks in single file, ranging from the tallest to the shortest. They were conversing. It was wonderful to watch them talking and walking in single file at the same time. Heracles suspected they had some mathematical formula that determined whose turn it was to speak and whose to answer. They never interrupted one another: Number two stopped talking, and *at that precise moment,* number four answered; number five seemed to sense exactly when number four would finish, and he then proceeded to make a comment. Their laughter sounded choral. And Heracles sensed something else: While number one—Plato—remained silent, all the others seemed to address their remarks to him, though never directly. To that end, the pitch rose gradually and melodically from the deepest voice—that of number two—to the highest—that of number six, who not only was the shortest in stature but shrieked his remarks, as if to ensure that number one would hear. The overall impression was of a lyre on the move.

The group wound its way through the garden, drawing closer with every turn. By a strange coincidence, several youths emerged from the gymnasium, some quite naked, others in short tunics, and they immediately reined in their disorderly chatter on glimpsing the line of philosophers. The two groups came together in the small square. Heracles wondered for a moment what it would look like to a hypothetical observer in the sky: the line of youths and the line of philosophers moving toward each other until they joined at the vertex. Perhaps, if one included the straight hedge, a perfect letter delta?

Diagoras waved for the group to approach.

"Master Plato," he said reverentially, pushing past Heracles to get to the great philosopher, "Master Plato, this is Heracles, of the deme of Pontor. He wished to see the school, so I took the liberty of inviting him to dinner this evening."

"You did right, Diagoras, unless Heracles believes otherwise," rejoined Plato affably, in a beautiful deep voice. He turned to the Decipherer, raising a hand in greeting. "Welcome, Heracles Pontor."

"I am grateful to you, Plato."

Like many others, Heracles had to look up when addressing Plato. He was a huge figure of a man, enclosed between sturdy shoulders, with a powerful torso, from which welled the silver torrent of his voice. But there was something in the famous philosopher's bearing that made him resemble a child locked in a fortress. Perhaps it was the rather endearing look of almost constant amazement. When spoken to, or when addressing someone, or when simply reflecting, Plato would either open his enormous curly-lashed gray eyes very wide and raise his eyebrows so high as to be almost comical or frown like a bristly-browed satyr. It made him look like a man who has just, unexpectedly, been bitten on the bottom. Those who knew him claimed that his amazement was not genuine—the more amazed by something he appeared, the less important he considered it.

As he was introduced to Heracles Pontor, Plato's face expressed utter amazement.

The philosophers began filing into the school. The students awaited their turn. Diagoras held Heracles back and said, "I can't see Antisus. He must still be in the gymnasium." Then suddenly, without transition, he muttered, "Oh Zeus . . ."

The Decipherer followed the direction of his gaze.

A man was walking up the path. His appearance was no less imposing than Plato's but, unlike the philosopher, there was a wild quality about him. In his enormous arms, he cradled a white dog with a deformed head.

"I decided to accept your invitation after all, Diagoras," said Crantor, smiling good-naturedly. "We are sure to have an entertaining evening."[1]

1. I've managed to calm down over the past few hours. This is due, mainly, to the fact that I've had a rest between every paragraph. I stretch my legs and take brief turns about my cell. I now know every inch of the reduced world in which I'm now living: a rectangular room four paces by three, with a hard old bed in one corner, and a table and chair against the opposite wall. On the table, my translation and Montalo's edition of *The Athenian Murders.* There is also—oh wondrous luxury—a small hole dug in the ground for me to relieve myself. A solid wooden door reinforced with iron strips stands between me and freedom. Both the bed and the door—not to mention the hole—are somewhat coarse, but the table and chair look like expensive pieces of furniture. I also have at my disposal a plentiful supply of writing materials. It is all part of the ploy to keep me occupied. The only light my jailer allows me is the miserable, temperamental lamp that I'm gazing at now, on the table. So however much I try to resist, I always end up sitting down and carrying on with the translation, just to keep sane, among other things. I know that this is exactly what he wants—whoever *he* is. "Keep translating!" he commanded through the door about—how long ago? Ah, I can hear something. He must be bringing my food. At last.—TRANS.

"Philotextus offers his greetings, Master Plato, and remains at your disposal," said Eudoxus. "He has traveled as widely as you, and I am sure none of his conversation will go to waste."

"Like the meat we ate earlier," rejoined Policletus.

There was laughter, but they all knew that the trivial or private remarks that had so far been the essence of the gathering must now give way, as in any good symposium, to thoughtful discussion and the fruitful exchange of opinions. The guests reclined on comfortable couches arranged in a circle, and students waited on them like perfect slaves. No one took much interest in the silent, though well-known, figure of the Decipherer of Enigmas; his was a renowned profession, but most of them considered it vulgar. Instead, there was a growing flurry around Philotextus of Chersonnese, a mysterious little old man whose face was veiled by shadows, who was a friend of the tutor Eudoxus, and the philosopher Crantor, of the deme of Pontor, a "friend of the tutor Diagoras," as he himself had put it, recently arrived in Athens after lengthy travels, of which all were impatient to hear tales. Now, as the guests tirelessly exercised their tongues, twisting them inside their mouths to remove remnants of meat from their sharp teeth—remnants that would be washed down with aromatic wine that made the palate bristle—the moment had arrived for the curiosity aroused by the two guests to be satisfied.

"Philotextus is a writer," continued Eudoxus. "He has read and admires your dialogues. In addition, he seems to have been invested by Apollo with the power of the Delphic oracle. He has visions. He claims that he has seen the world of the future and that, in some respects, it is consistent with your theories. Regarding the equality you advocate for the labor of men and women, for instance."

"By Cronius Zeus," put in Policletus once again, feigning anxiety, "let me have a few more cups of wine, Eudoxus, before women are trained as soldiers."

Expecting Crantor to explode at any moment, Diagoras alone took no part in the general cordiality. He wanted to whisper something to Heracles to that effect, but he saw that the Decipherer, in his own way, was not joining in, either—motionless on his couch, he held a goblet in his pudgy hand, neither replacing it on the table nor taking it to his lips. He looked like the reclining statue of a fat old tyrant. But his gray eyes were alive. What was he looking at?

Diagoras saw that the Decipherer did not let Antisus out of his sight.

The youth, dressed in a blue chiton mischievously open at the sides, had been appointed chief cupbearer. As was the custom, he wore a bristling crown of ivy in his blond curls and a *hipothymides,* or garland of flowers, around his marble shoulders. At that moment, he was serving Eudoxus; he would then move on to Harpocrates, attending to all the guests in strict order of precedence.

"And what is it that you write, Philotextus?" asked Plato.

"All sorts," replied the old man from the shadows. "Poetry, tragedy, comedy, prose, epics, and many other things. The Muses have been kind, placing few obstacles in my way. On the other hand, though Eudoxus referred to my having 'visions,' even comparing me to the oracle of Delphi, I must make it clear, Plato, that I do not 'see' the future: I invent it. I write it, and that, for me, is equivalent to inventing it. Simply for pleasure, I conceive worlds that differ from this one, voices that speak from other times, past or future. When I have completed my creations, I read them, to judge if they're good. If they're bad, as is sometimes the case, I throw them away and start again." Following the brief laughter that greeted these last sentences, he added, "On occasion, Apollo has allowed me to *deduce* what the future *might* be like, and I feel that men and women will eventually practice the same professions, as you suggest in your dialogues. On the other hand, I don't believe there will ever be wonderful governments or 'golden' rulers working for the city."

"Why not?" asked Plato, sincerely curious. "True, it would be difficult for such governments to exist in our times. But, in the distant future, in hundreds or thousands of years' time, why not?"

"Because men never change, Plato," replied Philotextus. "Though it may pain us to admit it, human beings are guided not by invisible, perfect ideas, or even logical arguments, but by impulses and irrational desires."

This gave rise to a sudden controversy, with guests interrupting one another in their eagerness to be heard. But a voice with a twisted, bristling accent rose above the rest: "I agree."

All faces turned toward Crantor.

"What do you mean, Crantor?" asked Speusippus. He was one of the most respected tutors, for everyone assumed he would become head of the Academy upon Plato's death.

"I mean that I agree."

"With what? With what Philotextus said?"

"Yes."

Diagoras closed his eyes and recited a silent prayer.

"So you believe that men are guided not by the obvious presence of ideas but by irrational impulses?"

Instead of answering the question, Crantor said, "Since you are so fond of Socratic questions, Speusippus, I will put one to you. Had you to discuss the art of sculpture, what would you take as an example: a beautiful figure of a youth painted on an amphora, or an ugly, damaged clay figure of a dying beggar?"

"With your dilemma, Crantor," Speusippus replied, not even attempting to hide his distaste for the question, "you leave me no choice but to choose the clay figure, since the other is a painting, not a sculpture."

"Then let us speak of clay figures, not beautiful paintings." Crantor smiled.

The sturdy philosopher seemed quite oblivious to the sense of expectancy he had caused, occupied as he was with taking large drafts of wine. At the foot of his couch, Cerberus, the deformed white dog, was finishing off the remains of his master's meal, to the sound of tireless gnawing.

"I don't really understand what you mean," said Speusippus.

"I don't mean anything."

Diagoras bit his lip so as not to intervene. He knew that if he spoke, the harmony at the symposium would crumble like a honey cake beneath sharp teeth.

"I think what Crantor means is that we human beings are merely clay figures," interjected the tutor Harpocrates.

"Do you really believe that?" asked Speusippus.

Crantor shrugged.

"Strange," said Speusippus. "So many years traveling through distant lands, and you're still locked in your cave. I assume you know our legend about the cave? A prisoner who has spent all his life in a cave, watching the shadows of real objects and beings, is suddenly freed and emerges into the light of day. He realizes that he has seen nothing but shapes until then, and that reality is much more beautiful and complex than he had ever imagined. Oh, Crantor, I feel sorry for you! You are still a prisoner, blind to the luminous world of ideas."[2]

Without warning, Crantor rose from his couch, as if he had suddenly grown weary, of the other guests perhaps, or the conversation, or simply of having to maintain the same position. He moved so abruptly that Hypsipylus—with his round, fat body, the tutor who most resembled Heracles Pontor—awoke from the deep sleep that he had been struggling against since the start of the libations, and almost spilled his wine over the immaculate Speusippus. And where is Heracles Pontor, wondered Diagoras fleetingly. His couch was empty, but he hadn't noticed him leave.

"You're all very good at talking," said Crantor, a twisted smile tensing his bristly black beard.

2. I, too, see shadows in my cell-cave: Greek words dance before my eyes. How long is it since I've seen the light of the sun—the light of the Good, from which everything comes? Two days? Three? But behind the letters' frenetic dance, I perceive the "twisted teeth" and "bristly," "rough" coat of the idea of a boar, relating to the third labor of Hercules, the capture of the Erymanthian boar. And if, though the word *boar* is never mentioned, I can still *see* one—I think I can even hear it: its snorting, its stamping in the dust, and the unsettling cracking of branches beneath its hooves—then the idea of a boar *exists,* is as real as I am. Was Montalo interested in this book because he thought it provided definite *proof* of Plato's Theory of Ideas? And what about Whoever He Is? Why did he first play games with me, inserting bogus pages into the original, then kidnap me? I want to shout, but I think the idea of a shout would provide more relief.—TRANS.

He started pacing around the circle of guests, occasionally shaking his head and giving a short little laugh, as if the whole situation were terribly amusing. He said, "Unlike the tasty meat you have served us this evening, your words are inexhaustible. I have forgotten the art of oratory, because I have lived in places where it was not needed. I have known many philosophers who found emotion far more persuasive than speeches, and others who could not be persuaded, because their opinions could not be expressed, understood, demonstrated, or refuted with words—they simply pointed to the night sky, indicating that they had not become mute, but were engaged in a dialogue, like the stars above our heads."

He continued walking slowly around the table, his tone becoming gloomier.

"Words . . . You talk. I talk. We read. We decipher the alphabet. And we chew at the same time. We're hungry, aren't we?[3] Our stomachs receive food. We grunt and snort. We sink our teeth into twisted lumps of meat."

He stopped suddenly and, stressing every word, said, "Note that I said 'teeth' and 'twisted'!"[4]

Nobody was sure quite whom Crantor had addressed. After a pause, he resumed his pacing and his speech: "I repeat, we sink our teeth into twisted lumps of meat; and our hands raise the wine to our lips; and the hair on our skin bristles when the wind blows; and our members stand erect when they sense beauty; and sometimes our intestines are lazy, which is a problem, isn't it? Admit it."[5]

"You're telling me!" Hypsipylus felt this was addressed to him. "I haven't had a good bowel movement since the last Thesmopho."

Indignantly, some of the other tutors told him to be quiet. Crantor

3. Yes, Crantor, very hungry. As I translate your words, I'm eating the filth with which Whoever He Is has seen fit to fill my bowl today. Would you like to try some?—TRANS.

4. This chapter's eidetic words, yes, I had noticed. Thanks anyway, Crantor. —TRANS.

5. Yes, that's true. You've guessed everything, Crantor. Since I've been locked in here, one of my biggest problems has been constipation.—TRANS.

went on: "We have sensations, sometimes impossible to define. But how many words we bury them beneath! How we change them for images, ideas, emotions, facts! This world is a torrent of words and we flow along it! Your precious legend of the cave . . . mere words. I will tell you something, and I will tell it in words, but then I will resume my silence: Everything we have thought, and will think, everything we already know and will know in the future, absolutely everything, makes up a beautiful *book* that we are all writing and reading together! But what of our body while we attempt to decipher and compose the text? It makes demands, grows tired, dries up, and eventually crumbles to dust." Pausing, he smiled, his large face an Aristophanic mask. "But oh, what an interesting book! How entertaining, and containing so many words! Isn't that so?"

There was a deep silence when Crantor finished.[6]

Cerberus, who had been following his master, now stood at his feet, barking furiously, his stump of a tail bristling, baring his sharp teeth, as if inquiring what Crantor intended to do next. Like a parent in conversation with other adults patiently dealing with a child's interruption, Crantor bent down affectionately and gathered up the dog in his huge arms. He then carried it like a little white knapsack, full at one end and almost empty at the other, to the couch. After that, he began playing with the dog, appearing to take no interest in what was going on around him.

"Crantor uses words only to criticize them," said Speusippus. "As you see, he contradicts himself as he speaks."

"Well, I rather like the idea of a book bringing together all our thoughts," remarked Philotextus from the shadows. "Would it be possible to create such a book?"

6. I must be insane—I've been talking to a character in a book! I suddenly felt he was addressing me, and I *answered* him in my notes. It must be because I've been locked in this cell all this time, with no one to talk to. But Crantor does always stand on the dividing line between fiction and reality. Or rather, the dividing line between the literary and the nonliterary. And he doesn't care whether he's believable or not; he even enjoys drawing attention to the verbal artifice that surrounds him, as when he stresses the eidetic words.—TRANS.

Plato burst out laughing. "It's obvious you're a writer and not a philosopher! I, too, wrote once. That's why I make a clear distinction between the two."

"Perhaps they are the same," said Philotextus. "I invent characters; you invent truths. But I want to keep to the subject. I was talking about a book that would reflect our way of thinking, our knowledge of things and beings. Could such a book be written?"

Just then, Callicles, a young geometrician whose only, though highly visible, fault was his ungainly way of moving—as if his extremities were dislocated—excused himself, rose, and shifted the collection of bones that was his body into the shadows. Diagoras thought Antisus's absence conspicuous, as he was principal cupbearer. Where could he be? Heracles had not returned, either.

After a pause, Plato declared, "The book of which you speak, Philotextus, cannot be written."

"Why not?"

"It would be impossible," replied Plato calmly.

"Please explain," said Philotextus.

Slowly stroking his gray beard, Plato said, "For some time now, we members of the Academy have known that knowledge of any thing has five levels or elements: the name of the thing, the definition, the image, intelligence or knowledge of the thing, and then the thing itself, which is the true aim of knowledge. But writing can give us only the first two: the name and the definition. The written word is not an image, thus precluding the third element. And the written word does not think, and so cannot have intelligence or knowledge. And of course, the last one of all, the idea itself, is truly beyond its reach. It would thus be impossible to write a book describing our knowledge of things."

Philotextus remained thoughtful a moment before saying, "Would you be so kind as to give me an example of each of these elements, so that I may understand them?"

Speusippus stepped in quickly, as if it were beneath Plato to provide examples.

"It's very simple, Philotextus. The first element is the 'name,' and it could be any name—'book,' or 'house,' or 'cenacle.' The second element is the 'definition,' which consists of sentences relating to those names. In the case of 'book,' one definition would be: 'A book consists of writing on a papyrus that comprises a complete text.' Literature, obviously, can only include names and definitions. The third element is the 'image,' the vision that each of us forms in his head when he thinks of a thing. For instance, when I think of a book, I see a papyrus scroll spread out on a table. The fourth element, 'intelligence,' covers precisely what we're doing now: discussing a subject, using our intelligence. In our case, this consists of talking about the book, its origins, its purpose. The fifth and final element is the 'idea itself'—in other words, the true aim of knowledge. In the case of the book, this would be the book itself, the ideal book, which was superior to all other books."

"That's why we believe the written word is imperfect, Philotextus," said Plato. "But by that, we certainly don't mean any disrespect to writers." There was discreet laughter. Plato added, "In any case, I'm sure you now understand why it would be impossible to create such a book."

Philotextus looked thoughtful. After a pause, he said in his thin, trembling voice, "What shall we wager?"

The laughter was louder now.

Diagoras was starting to find the discussion rather silly. He shifted uneasily on his couch and wondered where Heracles and Antisus could have gotten to. At last, to his great relief, he saw the Decipherer's obese figure returning from the kitchens. His face, as always, was expressionless. What could have happened?

Heracles didn't return to his couch. He expressed his thanks for the meal, and claimed that he had business to attend to back in Athens. The tutors bade him farewell quickly but cordially, and Diagoras accompanied him to the door.

"Where have you been?" he asked once he was sure no one else could hear.

"My investigation is almost at an end. There is one last, important step. But we've got him."

"Who? Menaechmus?" Agitated, Diagoras realized he was still holding his goblet. "Is it him? Can I accuse him publicly?"

"Not yet. Everything will become clear tomorrow."

"What about Antisus?"

"He has left. But don't worry: I will have him watched tonight." Heracles smiled. "I have to leave now. But rest assured, good Diagoras, you'll find out the truth tomorrow."[7]

7. I've realized that I haven't yet recounted how I ended up in this cell. If these notes are to help me stay sane, it may do me good to relate everything that I can remember about what happened, as if I were addressing a future (unlikely) reader. So, dear reader, allow me yet another interruption. I know you would much rather carry on reading the book than listen to my woes, but remember that however marginal I may seem down here, you owe me a little attention—were it not for my labors, you wouldn't be enjoying said book. So read me patiently.

You may remember that the evening I finished translating the previous chapter, I decided to catch the mysterious intruder who had been adding bogus passages in the text. To that end, I turned out all the lights and pretended to go to bed. In fact, I hid behind the sitting room door, awaiting his "visit." I had almost convinced myself that he wouldn't turn up that night, when I heard a noise. I peeped around the door, and only just had time to see a shadow bearing down on me. I came to with a bad headache, and found myself locked up within these four walls. (I've already described the cell, so I refer the interested reader to my earlier footnote on the subject.) Montalo's text and my translation, up to chapter 6, were lying on the table. On top of my translation, there was a note written in a fine hand: "My identity doesn't concern you. Call me 'Whoever He Is.' If you really want to get out of here, carry on with the translation. You'll be set free once you've finished." This is the only contact I've had so far with my anonymous kidnapper. Well, that and his genderless voice, which I hear from time to time through the door of my cell, ordering me, "Translate!" So that's what I do.—TRANS.

I HAD FALLEN ASLEEP at the desk (not for the first time since I've been in here), but woke up immediately when I heard the sound. I sat up slowly, thick with sleep, prodding my right cheek, which was numb from having borne the entire weight of my head. I moved the muscles of my face. I wiped away a faint trail of saliva. I lifted my elbows, knocking the translation of the end of chapter 7 off the desk. I rubbed my eyes and looked around: Nothing had changed. I was in the same room, sitting at the desk, alone in a pool of lamplight. I was hungry, and that, too, was nothing new. Then I peered into the shadows and realized that *something was different*.

Heracles Pontor stood in the darkness, watching me with his placid gray eyes.

"What are you doing here?" I whispered.

"You're in quite a mess," he said. His voice was just as I'd imagined, though that only occurred to me later.

"You're a character in the book," I complained.

"This *is* the book," the Decipherer of Enigmas replied. "You're obviously part of it. And you need help, which is why I'm here. Let's reason it out: You've been locked up while you translate *The Athenian*

Murders, but there's no guarantee you'll be released once you've finished. Now, don't forget, your jailer is very keen to get the translation. You just have to find out why. Once you know that, you can offer him a deal—you want your freedom; he wants *something.* You can both get what you want, can't you?"

"He doesn't want anything!" I moaned. "He's insane!"

Heracles shook his stout head.

"What does it matter? Concern yourself not with his sanity, but his interests. Why is it *so* important to him that you translate this book?"

I pondered a moment.

"It contains a secret."

I could see from his face that this wasn't the answer he'd expected. But he said, "Very good! That's one obvious reason. An obvious question must have an obvious answer. *Because it contains a secret.* So if you found out *what* that secret was, you'd be in a position to make a deal, wouldn't you? 'I know what the secret is,' you'd say, 'but I won't talk unless you let me out of here.' It's a good idea."

He was trying to sound encouraging, to give me hope, but I could tell he didn't think it such a good idea.

"Actually," I said, "I have discovered something—the labors of Hercules, and a girl with a lily who—"

He interrupted impatiently. "They mean nothing. They're just images! To you, they may be the labors of Hercules or a girl with a lily, but to another reader, they might be something quite different. Don't you see? Images change—they're imperfect! You have to find a final idea that's *the same* for all readers! You have to ask yourself what the key is. There must be a hidden meaning!"

I stammered a few clumsy words. Heracles observed me, coldly curious, before saying, "Pah! Why are you crying? You should be getting down to work, not giving up! Look for the central idea. Use my method of logic: You know me; you know how I work. Delve into the words! There must be something! *Something!*"

I leaned over the papers, my eyes still wet. But it suddenly seemed terribly important to ask him how he'd managed to get out of the novel and to appear in my cell. He interrupted imperiously, "The end of the chapter," he said.[1]

1. I've resisted a strong urge to destroy this bogus chapter 8, no doubt added to the book by my kidnapper. The only thing the bastard has succeeded in doing is making me cry—something I seem to be doing all the time lately. It's one of the ways I measure time. But Whoever He Is is quite wrong if he thinks these interpolated pages are going to make me lose my mind. I now know what he's up to—they're messages, instructions, orders, threats. He no longer even tries to disguise the fact that they're fake. *Reading myself* in the first person made me feel quite sick. To dispel the feeling, I tried to think of what *I really would have said.* I don't think I would have "moaned," as he put it in the text. I'm sure I would have asked a lot more questions than the pathetic creature that was supposed to be me. He got it completely right about the crying, though. I'm now starting on what I assume to be the real chapter 8.—TRANS.

THE FINAL DAYS of the Lenaea slowed the usual rhythm of the city.

That sunny morning, a dense line of merchants' carts was blocking the Dipylon Gate; insults and orders filled the air, but movements remained heavy and clumsy. By the Peiraic Gate, the pace was even slower, and a complete turn of a cart's wheel could take a quarter of a clepsydra. Slaves carrying amphorae, messages, bundles of firewood, and sacks of wheat through the streets shouted at one another to clear the way. People rose late. The Assembly at the Theater of Dionysus Eleuthereus was behind schedule. Since many of the *prytaneis* were absent, votes could not be held. Speeches flagged, and the few spectators dozed on the tiers. Let us now listen to the magnificent Janocrates. Owner of large estates on the outskirts of the city, Janocrates went with a shambling gait to the speaker's podium and began slowly declaiming, to general indifference. In the temples, sacrifices were delayed because the priests were busy preparing the last few processions. At the monument to the eponymous heroes, heads bowed reluctantly over edicts and new reg-

1. I'm working very slowly! Very, very *slowly*! I've got to work faster if I want to get out of here.—TRANS.

ulations. The situation in Thebes was stable. The return of Pelopidas, the exiled Cadmean general, was expected. Agesilaus, king of Sparta, was opposed by almost all Hellas. "Citizens, our support for Thebes is crucial to the stability of . . ." But judging by the tired faces of those reading, nobody seemed to feel anything was "crucial" just then.

Two men stood peering at a tablet and exchanging leisurely words.

"Look, Amphicus, it says here that more volunteers are needed for a patrol to exterminate the wolves on Lycabettus."

"We're so much slower and clumsier than the Spartans."

"Peace has made us soft—we won't even sign up to kill wolves."

Another man was gazing at the tablets with the same torpid interest as the rest. From the blank look on his face—set into a spherical bald head—one might have thought that his mind was clumsy and slow. In fact, he had hardly slept the previous night. Time to go and see the Decipherer, he thought. He walked away from the monument, directing his slow steps toward the district of Scambonidai.

What is wrong with the day? Diagoras wondered. Why did everything around him seem to be sliding clumsily, slowly, like honey?[2] The sun's chariot stood motionless in its furrow in the sky; time was thick as mead. It was as if the goddesses of Night, Dawn, and Morning refused to move and remained still, united, fusing darkness and light into a stagnant gray color. Diagoras felt slow and confused, but his anxiety kept him going: It was like a weight in his stomach; it emanated slowly as sweat on his palms. It plagued him like a horsefly, drove him on despite his lethargy.

The journey to Heracles Pontor's house seemed as endless as the distance from Marathon. The garden was quiet, the silence embellished only by the slowly repetitive chant of a cuckoo. He knocked hard at the door and waited. He heard steps. The door opened, and he said, "I've come to see Heracles Po—"

The young woman was not Ponsica. Her untidy curly hair floated

2. It's eidesis, idiot, eidesis, *eidesis*! It changes everything, gets into everything, influences everything. Now we have the idea of "slowness," which, in turn, hides another idea.—TRANS.

freely, framing an angular face. While not exactly beautiful, she was strange, mysterious, as challenging as a hieroglyph carved in stone—unblinking eyes as clear as quartz, thick lips, a slender neck. Her prominent bosom filled her peplos and . . . By Zeus, now he remembered who she was!

"Come in, come in, Diagoras," said Heracles Pontor, poking his head over the girl's shoulder. "I was expecting someone else, so that's why—"

"I don't wish to disturb you . . . if you're busy." Diagoras's eyes went from Heracles to the girl and back again, as if seeking an answer from either. "You're not disturbing me. Come in." There was a slow, clumsy moment as the girl moved aside in silence. Heracles gestured toward her: "You've met Yasintra. Come on. We'll be more comfortable on the terrace in the orchard."

Diagoras followed the Decipherer down a dark corridor. *He sensed*—he didn't want to look around—that *she* wasn't behind them, and he breathed a sigh of relief. Outside, the light of the sun was powerful, blinding. It was hot, but not uncomfortably so. Among the apple trees, Ponsica was leaning over the parapet of a white stone well, struggling to draw water with a heavy bucket; her grunts of effort echoed faintly through the mask. Heracles invited Diagoras to be seated. The Decipherer seemed pleased, delighted even. He smiled, rubbing his fat hands together, his pudgy cheeks flushed (*flushed!*). There was a new mischievous twinkle in his eyes, which took the philosopher aback.

"You may not believe it, but that young woman has helped me a great deal!"

"Of course I believe it."

Surprised, Heracles suddenly understood Diagoras's suspicions.

"Please, it's not what you think, good Diagoras. Allow me to recount what happened last night, when I returned home after satisfactorily completing my task."

By the time Heracles arrived home, Selene's gleaming sandals had trodden more than half of the celestial furrow that she plowed each night. He entered the familiar darkness of his garden. The thick foliage of the trees, silvered by the cold emanations of the moon, waved soundlessly, without disturbing the light sleep of the cold little birds dozing on the heavy branches, densely packed into their nests.[3]

Then he saw it: thrown into relief by the moon, a shadow among the trees. It stopped suddenly. He regretted not carrying a dagger beneath his cloak—in his profession, it was sometimes needed.

But the shape—a dark pyramid with a wide base and rounded apex topped by silver-streaked hair—was still motionless.

"Who is it?" he asked.

"Me."

A young man's voice, possibly an ephebe's . . . But there was something. . . . He was sure he'd heard it before. The figure stepped toward him.

"Who's 'me'?"

"Me."

"Whom are you looking for?"

"You."

"Come closer. Let me see you."

"No."

He felt uneasy. The stranger seemed afraid, yet not afraid; dangerous, yet harmless. It occurred to him suddenly that such opposing qualities were characteristic of a woman. Who could she be? Out of the corner of his eye, he glimpsed torches and heard dissonant singing. Perhaps the survivors of one of the last processions of the Lenaea, returning home inspired by the songs heard or sung during the ritual, driven by the anarchic will of the wine.

"Do I know you?"

"Yes. No," said the figure.

3. I'm sorry, but I can't stand it. Eidesis has now slipped into the descriptions, and Heracles' meeting with Yasintra is being recounted at an exasperatingly slow pace. In an attempt to speed things up, I'm going to take advantage of my position as translator and condense the text, including only the essentials.—TRANS.

Paradoxically, it was the enigmatic answer that yielded her identity at last.

"Yasintra?"

The figure didn't answer immediately. The torches approached, yet they didn't seem to move.

"Yes."

"What do you want?"

"Help."

Heracles decided to go nearer, and his right foot took a step forward. The song of the crickets seemed to subside. The torch flames waved sluggishly, like heavy curtains drawn by an old man with trembling hand. Heracles' left foot advanced by another Eleatic segment. The crickets resumed their chirruping. The torch flames changed shape imperceptibly, like clouds. Heracles raised his right foot. The crickets fell silent. The flames reared, petrified. The foot descended. Sounds no longer existed. The flames did not move. The foot paused on the grass.[4]

Diagoras felt as if he'd been listening to Heracles for a very long time.

"I've offered her my hospitality and have promised to help her," Heracles was explaining. "She's just been threatened and she's very frightened. She didn't know whom to turn to—our laws aren't kind to women like her, as you know."

"Who has threatened her?"

4. I can't go on. The rest of this lengthy paragraph consists of an agonizingly slow description of each step Heracles takes toward Yasintra, though, paradoxically, he never reaches her—putting one in mind of Zeno of Elea's paradox of Achilles and the tortoise (which is where we get the term *Eleatic segment*). All this, and the frequent repetition of the words *slow, heavy,* and *clumsy,* together with all the "plowing" metaphors, suggests the labor of the oxen of Geryon, the cattle Hercules has to steal from the monster Geryon. The "shambling gait" mentioned hereafter is from Homer for, according to the author of the *Iliad,* oxen are animals of "shambling gait." And talking of heavy and slow, I must just mention that I've managed to empty my bowels at last, and it's put me in a good mood. The end of my constipation may be a good omen, a sign that I'm going to speed up and achieve my goals.—TRANS.

"The same people who threatened her before we found her. That's why she ran away when she saw us. Please don't get impatient. I'll explain everything. We have plenty of time. We now simply have to wait for news. Ah, the final moments in the solving of an enigma are particularly enjoyable! Would you like a cup of undiluted wine?"

"Yes, today I would," muttered Diagoras.

Once Ponsica had left, having placed a heavy tray with two cups and a krater of undiluted wine beside him, Heracles said, "Listen, and please don't interrupt, Diagoras. My explanation will take longer if you distract me."

He began pacing up and down with a slow, shambling gait, addressing now the walls, now the gleaming orchard, as if practicing a speech to the Assembly. He accompanied the words with leisurely gestures of his fat hands.[5]

Tramachus, Antisus, and Euneos meet Menaechmus. When? Where? Who knows? It doesn't matter. The fact is, Menaechmus suggests they pose for him and perform in his plays. He falls in love with them and invites them to his licentious gatherings, together with other ephebes.[6] But he lavishes more attention on Antisus than on the other two, and they grow jealous. Tramachus threatens to reveal everything unless Menaechmus spreads his affections more fairly.[7] Menaechmus gets scared, and he arranges to meet Tramachus in the forest. Tramachus pretends he is going hunting, but in fact, he goes to the agreed-upon meeting place. He and Menaechmus argue. Either premeditatedly or in a moment of blind rage, Menaechmus beats him and

5. Heracles Pontor's dense explanation of the mystery serves to emphasize the eidesis yet again. Usually so laconic, the Decipherer here goes off on long, bizarre digressions that move forward as slowly as Geryon's oxen. I've decided to summarize the passage, noting some of his original remarks when appropriate.—TRANS.

6. "We can imagine their laughter in the night, the subtle swaying of hips before Menaechmus's slow chisel," says Heracles. "Playful, unhurried love, nubile bodies glowing red in the torchlight."—TRANS.

7. "After the enthralling wine of pleasure come the bitter dregs of strife," remarks Heracles.—TRANS.

leaves him dead or unconscious, to be devoured by wild animals. Antisus and Euneos are terrified when they hear what has happened. One night, they confront Menaechmus and demand an explanation. Menaechmus coldly confesses to the crime, possibly in order to intimidate them. Antisus decides to flee Athens, under the pretext of joining the army, but Euneos can't break Menaechmus's hold over him. Frightened, he wants to denounce Menaechmus, but the sculptor beats him to death. Antisus witnesses the crime. Menaechmus decides to stab Euneos savagely, pour wine over him, and dress him in women's clothing, to make it look like an act of madness by a drunken youth.[8] And that's all.[9]

"And this, good Diagoras, is what I had deduced by the end of our meeting with Menaechmus. I was almost certain he was guilty, but how to be absolutely sure? So I thought of Antisus. He was the weakest point of the branch, likely to snap at the slightest pressure. I devised a simple plan: During dinner at the Academy, while you were all wasting time discussing poetic philosophy, I kept an eye on our handsome cupbearer. Now, as you know, cupbearers serve the guests in strict order. So when Antisus was about to approach my couch, I took a small piece of papyrus from under my cloak and handed it to him, without a word, but with a meaningful look. It said, 'I know all about Euneos's death. If you want me to keep quiet, don't return from the kitchen to serve the next guest. Wait for me there, alone.' "

8. "See how cunning Menaechmus is!" says Heracles. "He's not an artist for nothing—he knows that impressions, appearances, can be a potent liqueur. When we found Euneos stinking of wine and dressed in women's clothes, our first thought was, A young man who gets drunk and dresses up like this is capable of anything. And therein lay the trap: The habits of our moral judgment negate the processes of our rational judgment entirely!"—TRANS.

9. "But what about the lily?" Diagoras asks. Annoyed at the interruption, Heracles declares, "A poetical detail, no more. Menaechmus is an artist." But what Heracles doesn't know is that the lily isn't "poetical," but eidetic, and is, therefore, inaccessible to him and his reasoning. The lily is a clue for the reader, not for Heracles. I'll proceed with the normal dialogue now.—TRANS.

"How could you be so sure that Antisus had witnessed Euneos's murder?"

Heracles looked delighted, as if he'd been hoping for this question. He smiled, narrowing his eyes, and said, "I wasn't sure! My message was the bait, and Antisus took it. When I saw that he was late serving the next guest—that colleague of yours who moves as if his bones were reeds in a river—"

"Callicles," said Diagoras. "Yes, now I remember—he was away for a few minutes."

"Yes. He came to the kitchen to find out why Antisus hadn't served him. He almost caught us, but luckily we had finished our conversation. So, as I was saying, when I noticed that Antisus hadn't returned to serve the next guest, I got up and went to the kitchen."

Heracles slowly rubbed his hands with relish. He raised a grizzled eyebrow.

"Ah, Diagoras! What can I say about that beautiful, cunning creature? I assure you, your student could teach us both a thing or two! He was waiting for me in a corner, trembling, with wide, shining eyes. His garland of flowers shook with the heaving of his chest. He motioned quickly for me to follow him, then led me to a small pantry where we could talk undisturbed. The first thing he said was, 'I swear by all the sacred household gods, I didn't do it! I didn't kill Euneos! It was him!' I got him to tell me everything, implying that I knew it all already. And it was as I had thought—his answers confirmed my theories point by point. When he finished, he asked—begged me, with tears in his eyes—not to reveal anything. He didn't care what happened to Menaechmus, but he didn't want his involvement to become known—he had to think of his family, and the Academy—it would be terrible. I said I didn't know if I could do as he asked. Breathless, eyes lowered, he came seductively close and whispered to me, deliberately slowing his words, his sentences. He promised me many favors, for, he said, he knew how to be agreeable to men. I smiled calmly and said, 'Antisus, you don't have to do this.' His only answer was to tear the fibulae from his chiton in two quick movements, so that the garment dropped to the floor. I said 'quick' movements, but they seemed very slow. I suddenly understood how he could unleash passions and make even the most sensible lose his head. I felt his perfumed breath on my face and moved away. I said, 'Antisus, as I see it, we have here two quite distinct matters: On one hand, your incredible beauty; and on the other, my duty to ensure that justice is done. Reason dictates that I admire the former and comply with the latter, not the other way around. So please don't make me confuse your admirable beauty with my duty.' He said and did nothing, simply stared. I don't how long he stood looking at me like that, motionless, silent, wearing nothing but his crown of ivy and garland of flowers. The pantry was dimly lighted, but I could see mockery in his lovely face. I think he wanted to show that he was aware of his power over me, despite my rejection. That boy holds men in thrall, and he knows it. Suddenly, someone called his name—it was your fellow tutor. Antisus dressed unhurriedly, as if he relished the prospect of being caught in that state, and left. I then returned to the dining hall myself."

Heracles sipped his wine. His face was slightly flushed. Diagoras's, by contrast, was as pale as quartz. The Decipherer said dispassionately, "Don't blame yourself. Doubtless, it was Menaechmus who corrupted them."

Diagoras replied in a flat voice, "I don't think it wrong that Antisus should offer himself to you, or even to Menaechmus, or any other man. After all, what could be more delightful than the love of an ephebe? It's the motives for love, rather than love itself, that are evil. Love merely for the purpose of physical pleasure is detestable; and using love to ensure your silence is a crime."

His eyes filled with tears. His voice as languid as a late afternoon, he added, "The true lover does not even need to touch his beloved; he is happy simply to gaze at him and appreciate the wisdom and perfection of his soul. I feel sorry for Antisus and Menaechmus. They don't know the incomparable beauty of true love." He sighed and added, "But let us change the subject. What do we do now?"

Heracles stared at the philosopher curiously for a moment before answering. "As jacks players say, 'From now on, every throw must be a good one.' We have the culprits, Diagoras, but it would be a mistake to rush in. How do we know that Antisus was telling the whole truth? I assure you, that beguiling young man is as cunning as Menaechmus, if not more so. And we still need a public confession or other proof before we can openly accuse Menaechmus, or both of them. But we've taken an important step forward: Antisus is scared now, and that's to our advantage. What will he do? The most logical thing would be to warn his friend so that he can escape. I'm sure Menaechmus would rather live in exile than be sentenced to death. But if Menaechmus leaves the city, publicly accusing Antisus will be futile."

"But then Menaechmus will get away!"

Heracles shook his head slowly and smiled astutely. "No, good Diagoras: I'm having Antisus watched. Eumarchus, his old pedagogue, follows him every night on my orders. Last night, after I left the Academy, I went to give Eumarchus his instructions. If Antisus goes to see Menaechmus, we'll know about it. And if necessary, I'll arrange for another slave to keep an eye on the workshop. Neither Menaechmus nor Antisus will be able to make a move without us knowing. I want them to feel cornered, to panic. Should one of the two decide to accuse the other publicly in order to save himself, the problem would be resolved in a most convenient manner. If not . . ."

He slowly pointed a thick index finger at the house. "If they don't give themselves away, we can use the hetaera."

"Yasintra? How?"

Heracles shook the same finger to emphasize his words. "The hetaera was Menaechmus's other *big mistake*! Tramachus fell in love with her and told her about his relationship with the sculptor, admitting that he felt both attracted and repulsed by him. Just before his death, your student confessed to her that he would do anything, even tell his family and his tutors about the wild gatherings at the workshop, to free himself of Menaechmus's harmful influence. But he also said he feared the sculptor—Menaechmus had said he'd *kill* Antisus if he talked. We don't know how Menaechmus found out about Yasintra, but we can conjecture that Tramachus told him in a moment of spite. The sculptor realized immediately that she might cause problems and sent a couple of slaves to Piraeus to threaten her, just in case she thought of talking. But our visit made Menaechmus nervous—he thought the hetaera must have betrayed him, so again he threatened to kill her. That was when Yasintra found out about me. And last night, terrified, she came to ask for help."

"So she's our only proof."

Heracles nodded, eyes wide, as if Diagoras had said something quite astounding. "That's right. If our two cunning criminals won't talk, we can make a public accusation based on Yasintra's testimony. I realize that a courtesan's word is worth nothing against a free citizen's, but the accusation might prompt a confession from Antisus, or even from Menaechmus."

Blinking, Diagoras looked out at the brilliantly sunny orchard. An enormous docile white cow was grazing lazily by the well.[10] Heracles said cheerfully, "Eumarchus will bring news at any moment. Then we'll know what our two rogues intend to do and we can act accordingly."

He took another sip of wine, savoring it slowly. Possibly uncomfortable on sensing that Diagoras didn't share his optimism, he went on a little abruptly: "So, what do you think? Your Decipherer has solved the enigma!"

Still gazing at the orchard beyond the placidly ruminating cow, Diagoras said, "No."

"What?"

Diagoras shook his head in the direction of the orchard and appeared to address the cow: "No, Decipherer, no. I remember clearly what I saw in Tramachus's eyes. He was more than worried; he was *terrified*. You want me to believe that he was going to tell me about his licentious games with Menaechmus, but—No. The secret was far more horrifying."

Heracles shook his head lazily, as if summoning the patience to explain something to a small child, and said, "Tramachus was afraid of

10. As in previous chapters, the eidesis is emphasized, this time in order to underline the image of the oxen of Geryon.—TRANS.

Menaechmus! He believed the sculptor would kill him if he denounced him! That's what you saw in his eyes!"

"No," retorted Diagoras quite calmly, as if the wine or the languid day was making him drowsy.

Very slowly, as if speaking a foreign language and pronouncing every word carefully for it to be translated, he went on: "Tramachus was *terrified,* but his fear was beyond understanding. It was terror itself, the idea of terror. Something that your reason, Heracles, cannot grasp, because you didn't look into his eyes as I did. Tramachus wasn't afraid of what Menaechmus might do to him, but of something much more terrifying. I know it." And he added, "I'm not quite sure why I know. But I do."

Heracles asked disdainfully, "Are you trying to tell me that my explanation is wrong?"

"Your explanation is entirely reasonable." Diagoras was still gazing at the orchard and the grazing cow. He breathed in deeply. "But I don't think it's the truth."

"It's reasonable but it isn't true? What on earth do you mean, Diagoras of Mardontes?"

"I don't know. My logic tells me, Heracles is right, but— Maybe your friend Crantor could explain it better. Last night at the Academy, we discussed it at length. Perhaps reason cannot be applied to the truth. I mean, if I were to say something ridiculous now, such as 'There's a cow grazing in your orchard, Heracles,' you'd think I was mad. But for someone other than you or me, might such a statement not be *true*?" Diagoras went on before Heracles could reply. "I know it's not *rational* to say there's a cow in your orchard, because there isn't one, nor could there be. But why does the *truth* have to be *rational,* Heracles? Might there not exist . . . irrational truths?"[11]

"Is that what Crantor told you all yesterday?" Heracles could

11. The "cow in the orchard" is, of course, like the "savage beast" in chapter 4 and the snakes in chapter 2, purely eidetic, and therefore invisible to the characters. The author used it to underline Diagoras's doubts. Indeed, to the *reader,* the cow is *real.* My hands are trembling. Maybe it's because I'm so tired.—TRANS.

scarcely contain his anger. "Philosophy will drive you insane, Diagoras! I'm talking about logical, coherent things, while you— The enigma surrounding your student isn't a philosophical theory; it's a rational chain of events that—"

He broke off, for Diagoras, still looking out at the empty orchard,[12] was shaking his head. Diagoras said, "I remember you saying, 'There are strange places where you and I have never been.' It's true. We live in a strange world, Heracles. A world where nothing can be entirely rationalized or understood. A world that doesn't always behave according to the laws of logic, but to those of dreams or literature. Socrates was a great reasoner, but he claimed that a daemon, a spirit, inspired him with the most profound truths. And Plato believes that madness is, in some ways, an arcane method of attaining knowledge. This is what is happening now: My daemon, or my madness, is telling me that your explanation is wrong."

"My explanation is logical!"

"But wrong."

"If my explanation is wrong, then *everything is wrong*!"

"That's possible," said Diagoras bitterly. "Yes, who knows."

"Very well," grunted Heracles. "As far as I'm concerned, Diagoras, you're welcome to wallow in the swamp of your philosophical pessimism! I'm going to prove to you that— Ah, a knock at the door. That must be Eumarchus. You stay there, contemplating the world of ideas, my dear Diagoras! I'll bring you Menaechmus's head on a tray, and you will pay me for my work! Ponsica, answer the door!"

But Ponsica had already done so, and the visitor came out onto the terrace.

It was Crantor.

"Heracles Pontor, O Decipherer of Enigmas. And you, Diagoras, from the deme of Mardontes. Athens has been rocked to its very foundations! All citizens who yet possess the strength to cry out are clamoring for your presence."

12. Having fulfilled its eidetic purpose, the cow disappears, even for the reader, and the orchard is now "empty." This isn't magic, just literature.—TRANS.

He tried to calm Cerberus, who was squirming furiously in his arms. Smiling, as if about to announce good news, he added, "Something horrible has happened."

The dignified, imposing figure of Praxinoe seemed to reflect the light that poured in thick waves through the windows of the workshop. Gently, he pushed aside one of his companions, while motioning for help to another. He knelt. He remained thus for what seemed like an eternity. Onlookers imagined expressions for his face—anguish, grief, wrath, fury. But Praxinoe's immobile features disappointed them all. His countenance bore the traces of memories, almost all of them good; symmetrical black eyebrows contrasted with a snow white beard. There was nothing to indicate that he was looking at his son's mutilated body. Save for one detail: He blinked, incredibly slowly. He fixed his gaze on a point between the two corpses, and his eyes seemed to sink into their sockets, as slowly as the setting sun, until they were two waning moons behind his lashes. Then he opened his eyes again. That was all. Helped by those around him, he got to his feet and said, "The gods have called you to them before me, my son. Hungry for your beauty, they will keep you with them and make you immortal."

A murmur of admiration greeted his noble, virtuous words. More men arrived: several soldiers, and a man who appeared to be a doctor. Praxinoe looked up, and Time, which had halted out of respect, now moved on.

"Who did this?" His voice was less firm now. Soon, with no one looking, perhaps he would weep. Emotion was taking a long time to appear on his face.

There was a pause—the kind of moment at which looks are exchanged to see who will speak first. One of the men accompanying Praxinoe said, "The neighbors heard shouting in the workshop in the early hours, but they thought it was another of Menaechmus's parties."

"We saw Menaechmus running away!" said someone else, his voice and unkempt appearance contrasting with the dignified respectability of Praxinoe's men.

"You saw him?" asked Praxinoe.

"Yes! And others did, too! We called the servants of the *astynomi*!"

The man seemed to expect a reward for his statement but, ignoring him, Praxinoe asked, "Can anyone tell me who did this?"

He pronounced the word *this* as if referring to an unimaginable sacrilege, a godless act worthy of hounding by the Furies. All those present looked down. There was total silence in the workshop; even the flies slowly circling in the glare of the open windows made not a sound. Almost all unfinished, the statues gazed upon Praxinoe with rigid compassion.

The doctor—a thin, gangly man, even paler than the corpses—was kneeling, examining the bodies in turn, touching first the old man, then immediately touching the young, as if to compare them, and whispering his findings with the slow perseverance of a child reciting the alphabet. Beside him, an *astynomos* listened respectfully, nodding in approval.

The corpses lay facing each other on their sides, in a majestic lake of blood. They resembled figures of dancers painted on a vase. The old man wore a shabby gray cloak. His right arm was bent; his left was stretched above his head. The young man's position was a mirror image of the old man's, but he was naked. Otherwise, old and young, slave and freeman, were equals when it came to their wounds: The eyes had been torn out, the faces ravaged, and the skin scored with deep cuts; between their legs, the amputation had been impartial. There was one other difference: Two eyeballs were gripped in the old man's stiffened right hand.

"Blue," declared the doctor, as if entering them in an inventory.

And, incongruously, after these words, he sneezed. Then he went on: "They belong to the young one."

"The servant of the Eleven!" someone announced, breaking the ghastly silence.

But though all eyes searched the group of onlookers at the door, none could identify the official. Suddenly, a voice full of feeling drew everyone's attention: "O Praxinoe, noblest of men!"

It was Diagoras of Mardontes. He had arrived at the workshop just before Praxinoe, accompanied by a short, fat man, and a second, huge, strange-looking man carrying a small dog. The fat man appeared to have vanished, but Diagoras had been attracting notice for some time as he knelt beside the corpses, weeping bitterly. Now, however, his manner was resolute. He seemed to have gathered all his energy in his throat, no doubt for the words to issue with the necessary force. His eyes were red, his face deathly pale.

"I am Diagoras of Mardontes, Antisus's tutor at the Academy."

"I know who you are," Praxinoe said without gentleness. "Speak."

Diagoras licked his parched lips and took a breath. "I wish to act as a sycophant and publicly accuse the sculptor Menaechmus of these crimes," he said.

There were lazy murmurs. After a slow battle, emotion had taken over Praxinoe's face—flushed, he raised a black eyebrow, slowly pulling at the strings of his eye and eyelid; his breathing was audible. He said, "You seem sure of what you say, Diagoras."

"I am, noble Praxinoe."

With a foreign accent, another voice said, "What has happened here?"

It was, at last—it could be no one else—the servant of the Eleven, the eleven judges who constituted the supreme authority in criminal cases. He was well built, and dressed in the barbarian manner in animal skins, with an ox-hide whip wound around his waist. He looked menacing, if dim-witted. He was panting loudly, as if he had run, and, judging by the expression on his face, he was disappointed to see that anything interesting had happened before his arrival. Several men (there are always some on such occasions) came forward to explain what they knew, or thought they knew. Most, though, stood listening to Praxinoe, who said, "Diagoras, why do you believe Menaechmus did . . . this . . . to my son and to his old pedagogue, Eumarchus?"

Diagoras licked his lips again.

"He himself will tell us, noble Praxinoe, under torture, if necessary. But do not doubt his guilt. It would be like doubting the light of the sun."

With different pronunciations, different intonations, Menaechmus's name was on everybody's lips. His face, his entire appearance, was called to mind. Someone shouted, but he was immediately ordered to be quiet. At last, Praxinoe loosed the reins of the respectful silence, saying, "Find Menaechmus."

As if this were the long-awaited signal, Anger raised heads and arms. Some demanded vengeance; others swore by the gods. Some, who didn't know Menaechmus even by sight, called for him to suffer appalling torment. Those who knew him shook their heads and stroked their beards, thinking, perhaps, Who would have thought it? The servant of the Eleven appeared to be the only one who didn't understand what was happening, asking those around him what they were talking about, and who was the mutilated old man lying beside young Antisus, and who was it who had accused the sculptor Menaechmus, and what were they shouting, and who, and what.

"Where is Heracles?" Diagoras asked Crantor, tugging at his cloak. There was great confusion.

"I don't know." Crantor shrugged his huge shoulders. "He was here a moment ago, sniffing around the corpses. But now—"

It seemed to Diagoras that there were two kinds of statues in the workshop: some still, others moving only a little. Clumsily, he tried to make his way through them; he was jostled. In the tumult, he heard someone call his name; his cloak was being pulled. He turned and saw the approaching face of one of Praxinoe's men, who was moving his lips.

"You must speak to the archon if you wish to file an accusation."

"I will," said Diagoras, not really understanding what the man was saying.

He freed himself of all hindrances, tore himself from the crowd, made his way to the door. Outside, the day was beautiful. Slaves and freemen stood petrified under the portico, seemingly envious of the statues inside. The presence of the crowd was a slab of stone pressing on Diagoras's chest, but he breathed freely once he had left the building behind. He stopped and looked around. In desperation, he chose a street. To his immense relief, he glimpsed the Decipherer's shambling gait as he made his plodding, meditative way up the hill. He called out.

"I want to thank you," Diagoras said, catching up. There was a strange insistence in his tone, like a cart driver urging on his oxen without raising his voice. "You've done your job well. I no longer need you. I will pay you the agreed-upon sum this very afternoon." As if uncomfortable at the Decipherer's silence, he added, "In the end, all was as you thought. You were right, and I was wrong."

Heracles muttered. Though the words came out very slowly, Diagoras had to lean toward him to understand.

"Why did he do it, the fool? Fear, or madness, obviously got the better of him. But—both bodies mutilated! It's absurd!"

Strangely, fiercely joyful, Diagoras replied, "He will tell us his motives himself, good Heracles. Torture will make him talk!"

They walked in silence along the sun-filled street. Heracles scratched his pointed head.

"I'm sorry, Diagoras. I was wrong about Menaechmus. I was sure he'd try to escape, not—"

"It no longer matters." Diagoras sounded like a man resting after a long, slow journey through a wilderness. "I was wrong. I see that now. I put the honor of the Academy before the lives of those poor boys. But it no longer matters. I will speak and make my accusation! I will also accuse myself as their tutor, because . . ." He rubbed his temples, as if immersed in a complex mathematical problem. He went on: "Because if something drove them to seek the guidance of that criminal, I must answer for it."

Heracles was about to interrupt, but he thought better of it and waited.

"I must answer for it," repeated Diagoras, as if learning the sentence by heart. "I must answer! Menaechmus is just a furious madman, but I . . . What am I?"

Something strange happened, though neither noticed at first: They both started speaking at once, not listening to each other, dragging out their sentences, one sounding impassioned, the other cold.

"I'm responsible; I'm the true culprit!"

"Menaechmus catches Eumarchus, gets scared, and—"

"Now, let's see, what does it mean to be a tutor? Tell me!"

"Eumarchus threatens him. And then—"

"It means to teach. It is a sacred duty!"

"They fight, and Eumarchus falls, of course."

"To teach means to mold souls!"

"Perhaps Antisus tries to protect Eumarchus."

"A good tutor knows his students!"

"Very well, but then, why mutilate them?"

"If not, then why teach?"

"I've made a mistake."

"I've made a mistake!"

They stopped. Anxious, disconcerted, they looked at each other for a moment, as if each was what the other needed most urgently at that moment. Heracles seemed to have aged. He said, incredibly slowly, "Diagoras . . . I confess that I've been as clumsy as a cow in this entire matter. My mind has never felt so heavy or awkward. What I find most surprising is that events possessed a certain logic, and my explanation was, on the whole, satisfactory, but certain details—very few, admittedly . . . But I'd like some time to ponder things. I won't charge you for my time."

Diagoras placed his hands on the Decipherer's sturdy shoulders. Looking straight into his eyes, he said, "Heracles, we've reached the end." He paused, then repeated slowly, as if to a child, "We've reached the end. It's been a long and difficult journey. But here we are. Give your brain a rest. I, for my part, will try to ensure that my soul finds tranquility."

The Decipherer jerked away from Diagoras and set off up the street. Then he seemed to remember something and turned back to the philosopher. "I'm going to shut myself away at home to think," he said. "I'll let you know if I have any news."

And before Diagoras could stop him, he slipped into the furrows of the slow, heavy crowd moving along the street, drawn by the tragedy.

Some said it happened too fast. But most felt it had all been very slow. Perhaps it was the slowness of the fast, which is how things seem when wished for fervently, but nobody said so.

It happened before the evening shadows showed themselves, well before the metic merchants closed their shops and the priests in the temples raised their knives for the final sacrifices. Nobody noticed the exact time, but general opinion held that it took place in the hours after midday when, heavy with light, the sun begins its descent. Soldiers were mounting guard at the gates, but it didn't happen there. Or in the outbuildings, where some searched, thinking they might find him, crouched trembling in a corner like a hungry rat. In fact, events unfolded in an orderly manner, in a busy street lined with new potters' workshops.

A question was making its way down the street, clumsily but inexorably, with slow resolve, from mouth to mouth: "Have you seen Menaechmus, the sculptor from the Ceramicus?"

Like the most fleeting of religions, the question drew recruits, who, once converted, carried it proudly. Some—those who thought they knew where the answer might be—stopped along the way. "Wait, we haven't looked in this house!" "Let's stop and ask this old man!" "I won't be long; I'm just going to see if I'm right!" More skeptical, others wouldn't join the new faith; they thought the question would be better phrased as: "Have you seen the man whom you've never seen and will never see, for as we speak, he's already far away?" And they slowly shook their heads and smiled, thinking, You're a fool if you think Menaechmus is simply waiting to be—

And yet, the question moved forward.

Just then, its shambling, devastating path took it to the tiny shop of a metic potter.

"Of course I've seen Menaechmus," said a man absentmindedly, surveying the potter's wares.

By now accustomed to hearing the same answer, the man who had asked the question was going to ignore him, but then he suddenly seemed to bump into an invisible wall. He turned and saw a weather-beaten, placidly furrowed face, a sparse, untidy beard, and locks of gray hair.

"You say you've seen Menaechmus?" he asked eagerly. "Where?"

The man replied, "I am Menaechmus."

"They say he was smiling."

"No, he wasn't."

"I swear by owl-eyed Athena, Harpalus, he was smiling!"

"And I swear by the black river Styx that he wasn't!"

"Were you near him?"

"As near as I am to you now, and he wasn't smilling—he was making a face!"

"He was smiling; I saw him, too. When several of you grabbed him by the arms, he was smiling. I swear by—"

"It was a grimace, you fool; he did this with his mouth! Do I look like I'm smiling?"

"You look like an idiot."

"But by the god of truth, how could he possibly smile, knowing what awaits him?"

"If he knows, why did he give himself up instead of fleeing the city?"

The question had spawned many young, all of them deformed, dying, dead by nightfall.

The Decipherer of Enigmas sat at his desk, resting his fat cheek on his hand, deep in thought.[13]

Yasintra entered without a sound. He looked up and found her standing in the doorway, surrounded by shadows. She wore a long peplos pinned on her right shoulder with a fibula. Her left breast, brushed lightly by the edge of the cloth, was almost entirely bared.[14]

"Please carry on. I don't want to disturb you," said Yasintra in her manly voice.

13. This is how I like to sit. In fact, I've only just changed position, in order to start work. The parallel is appropriate here, I feel, because in this chapter things seems to happen twice, occurring simultaneously to different characters. This must be a subtle way of emphasizing the eidesis—oxen walk along side by side, yoked together. —TRANS.

14. I'm now convinced that my jailer is completely insane. I was about to translate this paragraph, when I looked up and found him standing there, just as Heracles does Yasintra. He'd come in without making a sound. He looked quite ridiculous: He was wearing a long black cloak, a mask, and a straggly wig. The mask was female, but

Heracles didn't seem disturbed. "What do you want?" he asked.[15]

"Don't stop working. It looks so important."

Heracles didn't know if she was making fun of him (he found it difficult to tell—to him, all women were masks). He watched her as she slowly came toward him, at ease in the darkness.

"What do you want?" he repeated.[16]

She shrugged. Slowly, almost reluctantly, she moved her body close to his.

"How can you sit for so long in the dark?" she asked curiously.

"I'm thinking," said Heracles. "The darkness helps me think."[17]

"Would you like me to give you a massage?" she whispered.

Heracles stared at her and said nothing.[18]

She held out her hands.

"Leave me alone," said Heracles.[19]

"I just want to give you a massage," she whispered playfully.

"No. Leave me alone."[20]

Yasintra stopped.

"I want to give you pleasure," she murmured.

"Why?" asked Heracles.[21]

"I owe you a favor," she said. "I'd like to repay you."

"Please, it's not necessary."[22]

"I'm lonely, too. But I can make you happy; I can assure you."

---

the voice and hands were those of an old man. And, as I found when I proceeded with the translation, he said and did *exactly the same* as Yasintra in this section (he spoke in the same language as I, his words a precise translation of hers). I'll note down only my answers, therefore, after Heracles'.—TRANS.

15. "Who are you?" I asked.—TRANS.

16. I don't think I said anything at this point.—TRANS.

17. "But I don't want to be in the dark!" I cried. "And you're the one who's locked me in here!"—TRANS.

18. "A . . . massage? Are you mad?"—TRANS.

19. "Get away from me!" I shrieked, jumping up.—TRANS.

20. "Don't touch me!" I think I said this here; I'm not sure.—TRANS.

21. "You're . . . completely insane," I said, horrified.—TRANS.

22. "Favor? What favor? Translating the book?"—TRANS.

Heracles stared at her. Her face was expressionless. "If you want to make me happy, leave me alone," he said.[23]

She sighed and shrugged again. "Would you like something to eat? Or drink?" she asked.

"I don't want anything."[24]

Yasintra turned to leave, but she stopped in the doorway. "Call me if you need anything," she said.

"I will. Now go away."[25]

"You just have to call, and I'll come."

"Go away!"[26]

The door closed. The room was in darkness once more.[27]

23. "If you want to make me happy, let me out!"—TRANS.

24. "Yes! I'm hungry! And thirsty!"—TRANS.

25. "Wait, please, don't go!" I cried, suddenly anxious.—TRANS.

26. "*Don't go!*"—TRANS.

27. "No!!" I yelled, and started crying.

I've calmed down now. I've been wondering what on earth my kidnapper thought he was doing. Showing me how well he knows the novel? Letting me know that he's keeping tabs on the progress of the translation? I know one thing for sure—I'm in the hands of an old *madman*! Protect me, O Greek gods!—TRANS.

AS THE CRIMES ATTRIBUTED TO MENAECHMUS, son of Lacos, of the deme of Carisio, were crimes of blood—of "flesh," some called them—the trial was held at the Areopagus, the court on the Hill of Ares, one of the most venerable institutions in the city. Once, the sumptuous decisions of government had been prepared within its marble structure, but with Solon's and Cleisthenes' reforms, it was reduced to a simple tribunal for murder cases, offering its customers only the death sentence, loss of rights, or ostracism. Athenians, therefore, felt no pride at the sight of the white tiers, severe columns, and the archons' high podium, facing an incense burner as round as a plate, containing fragrant herbs burning in honor of Athena, their scent, some claimed, vaguely reminiscent of roasted human flesh. Modest banquets were, however, sometimes held there at the expense of high-ranking defendants.

The trial of Menaechmus, son of Lacos, of the deme of Carisio, had aroused great interest. This was because of the noble birth of the victims and the sordid nature of the crimes, rather than Menaechmus himself, who was, after all, just one more heir of Phidias and Praxiteles earning a living by selling his work, as one sells meat, to aristocratic patrons.

Soon, following the herald's strident announcement, not a single empty seat remained on the historical tiers. Most of the hungry crowd consisted of metics and Athenians belonging to the guild of sculptors and potters, together with poets and soldiers, though there were, too, fair numbers of the merely curious.

Eyes grew as wide as saucers and there were murmurs of approval as the soldiers brought in the accused with his wrists bound. Lean but robust, solid, Menaechmus, son of Lacos, of the deme of Carisio, puffed out his chest and held his grizzled head high, as if about to receive not a sentence but a military honor. He listened calmly to the succulent list of accusations, and, as was his right, remained silent when the speaker archon called upon him to correct the charges against him as he thought appropriate. "Will you speak, Menaechmus? . . . Nothing, not even a 'Yes' or a 'No'?" He continued to puff out his chest, as obstinately proud as a peacock. Would he plead guilty? Not guilty? Did he have some terrible secret that he intended to reveal at the end?

Witnesses filed past. His neighbors offered a tasty preamble by describing the youths, mostly vagabonds and slaves, who frequented the workshop under the pretext of posing for his statues. They referred to his nighttime activities—the piquant cries, the greedy grunts, the bittersweet smell of the orgies, the daily half dozen ephebes as naked and white as cream cakes. Many stomachs clenched on hearing such statements. Several poets then declared that Menaechmus was a good citizen and an even better writer, who had tried painstakingly to revive the ancient formula for Greek theater. But since they were as dull artists as the man they praised, the archons ignored their testimony.

It was now time to hear of the butchery—attention was drawn to the bloody trimmings, the sliced flesh, the deliquescing viscera, the crude reality of the bodies. The captain of the border guard, who had found Tramachus, spoke; the *astynomi* who had discovered Euneos's and Antisus's bodies gave their opinion. Questioning revealed an array of remains; imagination seasoned a corpse with chunks of limbs, faces, hands, tongues, loins, and bellies. At last, at midday, beneath the roasting dominions of the sun's steeds, the dark figure of Diagoras, son of

Iampsachus, of the deme of Mardontes, climbed the stairs to the podium. There was deep silence—all were waiting with ravenous impatience for what they knew would be the principal testimony for the prosecution. Diagoras, son of Iampsachus, of the deme of Mardontes, did not disappoint them: His answers were firm, his diction impeccable, his exposition of the facts honest; his assessment of those facts was cautious, with a slightly bitter aftertaste, a little harsh at times, but in general satisfactory. As he spoke, he looked up not at the tiers, where Plato and some of his colleagues sat, but at the archons' podium. The judges, however, seemed to be paying little attention, as if they had already decided upon a verdict and Diagoras's testimony were merely an appetizer.

At the hour when hunger begins to importune the flesh, the king archon decided that the court had heard enough. With the courteous indifference of a horse, he turned his limpid blue gaze toward the accused.

"Menaechmus, son of Lacos, of the deme of Carisio, this court grants you the right to defend yourself, if you so wish."

And suddenly, in the circular Areopagus, with its columns, burner of fragrant incense, and podium, there was a single point of focus upon which the gluttonous gazes of the spectators converged: the sculptor's roughly drawn face, his dark flesh scored by age, his blinking eyes, and his head sprinkled with gray hair.

In the hungry silence, as during a libation before a banquet, Menaechmus, son of Lacos, of the deme of Carisio, opened his mouth and slowly licked his dry lips.

And he smiled.[1]

It was a woman's mouth—her teeth, her burning breath. He knew that the mouth could bite, eat, devour, but what worried him just

1. And the spectators ate him. The description of Menaechmus's trial bears the eidetic overlay of a banquet, at which the sculptor is the main course. I'm not sure yet to which labor it refers, but I have my suspicions. The fact is the eidesis is making my mouth water.—TRANS.

then was the beating heart grasped by an unknown hand. He wasn't bothered by the slowly searching female lips (for it was a female, rather than a woman), her teeth running over his skin, for part of him (only part) found such caresses pleasant. But the heart—the throbbing moist flesh gripped by strong fingers—he had to find out what was beyond it, and to whom the thick shadow lurking at the edge of his vision belonged. Because the arm wasn't floating in midair; he knew that now. The arm was attached to a figure that appeared and disappeared, like the body of the moon in its different phases. Now . . . a little . . . he could almost see an entire shoulder, a . . . A soldier, in the distance, was issuing orders, or clarifying something. The voice was familiar, but he couldn't quite make out the words. Yet they were so important! Something else was bothering him: Flying caused a pressure on the chest. He must remember that for future investigations. Pressure, yes, and a pleasurable feeling in the most sensitive places. Flying was enjoyable, despite the gently nibbling mouth, the relaxing of one's flesh. . . .

He woke up. The shadow was sitting on top of him. He thrust it aside furiously. He remembered that in some cultures a nightmare was a monster with a mare's head and woman's body and that it rested its naked buttocks on the sleeper's chest, whispering bitter words into his ear before devouring him. There was a confusion of bedclothes, taut flesh, intertwined limbs, moans. It was so dark! So dark!

"No, no, calm down."

"What . . . Who . . ."

"Hush. It was a dream."

"Hagesikora?"

"No."

He was shaking. He recognized his own body, lying on its back in his own bed in what was still (he knew it now) his own bedroom. Everything was as it should be, except for the naked warm flesh moving beside him like a strong, restless colt. He yawned. His reason lighted a candle in his head and, with a jolt, he began a new day.

"Yasintra?" he asked.

"Yes."

Heracles sat up, the bands of muscle round his belly tense, as if he had just finished eating, and rubbed his eyes.

"What are you doing here?"

She didn't answer. He felt her move, warm and moist, as if her flesh were exuding juices. Suddenly, the bed dipped in several places and he lost his balance. He heard thuds and the unmistakable slap of bare feet upon the floor.

"Where are you going?" he asked.

"Don't you want me to light a lamp?"

He heard scratches as the flint was struck. She knows where I leave the lamp at night and where to find the flint, he thought, storing the information somewhere in his vast mental library. Soon after, her body appeared before him, half of the flesh smeared with honey in the lamplight. He would hesitate to describe her as naked. He had, in fact, never seen a woman so utterly naked—without makeup, or jewels, or the protection of dressed hair, stripped even of the fragile, but effective, tunic of modesty. Quite naked. Raw even, he thought, like a piece of meat thrown on the floor.

"Forgive me, I beg you," said Yasintra. There was not a trace of anxiety in her boyish voice at the possibility that he might not forgive her. "I heard you moaning from my room. You seemed to be suffering. I simply wanted to wake you."

"It was a bad dream," said Heracles. "A nightmare I've been having recently."

"The gods speak to us through recurring dreams."

"I don't believe that. It's illogical. Dreams can't be explained. They're simply random images that we create ourselves."

She said nothing.

Heracles thought of calling Ponsica, then remembered that she had requested permission the previous evening to go to Eleusis for a meeting of worshipers of the Sacred Mysteries. So he was alone in the house with the hetaera.

"Would you like to wash?" she asked. "Shall I bring you a bowl?"

"No."

Suddenly, Yasintra asked, "Who is Hagesikora?"

For a moment, Heracles stared at her blankly. Then he said, "Did I call out her name in my sleep?"

"Yes. And the name Itys. You thought I was both of them."

"Hagesikora was my wife," said Heracles. "She fell ill and died some time ago. We had no children."

He paused, then added in the same didactic tone, as if reciting a boring lesson, "Itys is an old friend. Strange that I called out both names. But, as I said, dreams have no meaning."

There was a silence. The girl was now lighted from below, the lamp disguising her nakedness—a wavering black harness covered her breasts and pubis; fine straps ran over her lips, brows, and eyelids. Heracles scrutinized the hetaera avidly for a moment, trying to find what lay beneath the surface, other than blood and muscles. How different she was from his lamented Hagesikora!

Yasintra said, "I'll go now, unless there's anything you want."

"Is there long to go before dawn?" he asked.

"No. The color of the night is gray."

"The color of the night is gray," Heracles repeated to himself. "A remark worthy of the creature."

"Leave the lamp on, then," he said.

"Very well. May the gods grant you rest."

He thought, Yesterday she said, "I owe you a favor." But why is she forcing such payment on me? Did I really feel her *mouth* on . . . Or did I dream it?

"Yasintra."

"What?"

There was not the slightest trace of hope or longing in her voice, and—oh, the all-consuming pride of men!—he felt pained. And it pained him that he was pained. She had simply stopped and looked around, turning her naked gaze upon him as she said, "What?"

"Menaechmus has been arrested for the murder of another ephebe. His trial is taking place today at the Areopagus. You no longer have anything to fear from him." And, after a pause, he added, "I thought you'd like to know."

"Yes," she said.

The door creaked as it closed behind her, echoing the sound: "Yes."

He remained in bed all morning. In the afternoon, he rose, dressed, devoured an entire bowl of figs, and decided to go for a walk. He didn't even bother to find out whether Yasintra was still in the small guest room, or whether she had already left, without saying good-bye. Her door was closed and, anyway, Heracles didn't mind leaving her alone in the house, for he didn't believe her to be a thief, or even a bad woman. He walked unhurriedly to the Agora and, once there, came across several men he knew and many more he did not. He preferred to inquire of the latter.

"The sculptor's trial?" said a man with tanned skin and the look of a satyr spying upon nymphs. "By Zeus! Don't you know? In the entire city, there's talk of nothing else!"

Heracles shrugged apologetically. The man added, baring huge teeth, "He's been condemned to the *barathrum*. He confessed."

"He confessed?" repeated Heracles.

"He did."

"To all the crimes?"

"Yes. It was just as noble Diagoras said. He's guilty of the murders of the three youths and the old pedagogue. And he confessed before everyone, with a smile: 'I'm guilty!' or something smiliar. The crowd was astounded by his audacity, and with reason!" The man's faunlike face grew darker still as he added, "By Apollo, the *barathrum* is too good for the scoundrel! For once, I agree with what the women are calling for!"

"What are they calling for?"

"A delegation of wives of the *prytaneis* has requested that the archon have Menaechmus tortured before he is killed."

"Flesh. They want flesh," said the man with whom the faun had been talking before Heracles interrupted. He was short and sturdy, with broad shoulders, his head and chin lightly seasoned with blond hair.[2]

The faun nodded and again bared horselike teeth.

"I'd give them what they want, if only this once! Those poor innocent ephebes! Don't you think . . ." He turned toward Heracles but found only empty space.

The Decipherer was walking away, clumsily avoiding the people who stood chatting in the square. He felt dazed, almost dizzy, as if he'd been asleep for a long time and had awakened in a city he didn't know. But as his thoughts raced on, the charioteer in his brain kept a tight grip on the reins. What was going on? He was beginning to see something illogical in all this. Or maybe it had never been logical, and only now was the mistake becoming apparent.

He thought of Menaechmus. He saw him in the forest, beating Tramachus until he was dead or unconscious, leaving him to be devoured by wild beasts. He saw him murdering Euneos and, out of fear or prudence, mutilating and disguising the corpse to hide his crime. He saw him savagely stabbing Antisus and the slave Eumarchus, whom he'd no doubt caught spying on them. He saw him at the trial, smiling, admitting to *all* the murders. Here I am, Menaechmus of Carisio. I did everything I could to avoid being caught, but now . . . what does it matter? I am guilty. I killed Tramachus, Euneos, Antisus, and Eumarchus. I fled, but then I handed myself in. Sentence me. I am guilty.

Antisus and Yasintra had accused Menaechmus. . . . But now Menaechmus was delivering himself into the hands of death! He must have lost his mind. . . . But if so, it had happened only recently. He hadn't behaved like a madman when he arranged to meet Tramachus in the forest, far from the city. Or when he contrived Euneos's "suicide." He'd shown great cunning in both cases and been an opponent

2. The frequent culinary metaphors, and metaphors relating to horses, allude eidetically to the labor of the mares of Diomedes. As everyone knows, they ate human flesh and devoured their own master. I'm not sure whether the "wives of the *prytaneis*" who "want flesh" are meant to represent the mares. It's a rather irreverent comparison if they are.—TRANS.

worthy of a decipherer. But now . . . now it seemed as if nothing mattered to him! Why?

There was something wrong with his meticulously constructed theory. And that something was . . . everything. The great edifice of reasoning, the structure of inferences, the harmonious framework of causes and effects . . . He was wrong, he had been from the start. But what tormented him was the certainty that he had reasoned it out *correctly,* that he hadn't overlooked any important details, that he had followed every single clue. . . . And this was the cause of the anxiety that was devouring him! If his reasoning was *correct,* why was he wrong? Could it be, as his client Diagoras claimed, that *irrational* truths really did exist?

This last thought interested him much more than the previous ones. He stopped and looked up at the symmetrical summit of the Acropolis, gleaming white in the afternoon sun. He observed the wonder of the Parthenon, the slender, precise marble structure, the beautiful purity of its lines—the tribute of an entire people to the rules of logic. Might there be truths that opposed its concise, definitive beauty? Erratic, deformed, absurd truths that shone from within? Truths as dark as caves, as sudden as lightning, as unyielding as wild horses? Truths that eyes could not see, that were neither written words nor images, truths that could not be understood, expressed, translated, or even sensed, other than through dreams or madness? A cold feeling of vertigo seized him and he staggered, bewildered, like a man who suddenly finds that he no longer understands his native language. For one terrible moment, he felt exiled from himself. But then he grasped the reins of his mind, the sweat on his skin dried, the beating of his heart slowed, and his Greek integrity returned to his person. He was Heracles Pontor, Decipherer of Enigmas, once more.

A commotion in the square drew his attention. Several men were shouting in unison, but they restrained their cries when one of them, mounting a pile of stones, declared that enough was enough, that they could bear it no longer.

"The archon will help the peasants even if the Assembly won't!" declared the man.

"What's going on?" Heracles asked the person nearest to him, an old man wearing a combination of rags and skins and smelling of horses. His slovenly appearance was finished off with a cloudy eye and several missing teeth.

" 'What's going on?' " the old man spat back at him. "If the archon won't protect the peasants of Attica, no one will!"

"The Athenian people definitely won't!" put in a similar-looking but slightly younger man.

"Peasants killed by wolves!" added the first man, fixing his healthy eye on Heracles. "That's already four this moon! And the soldiers won't do a thing! We've come to the city to speak to the archon and request his protection!"

"One of them was my friend," said a third man. This one was thin and devoured by mange. "His name was Mopsus. I found his body! Wolves had eaten his heart!"

The three men continued shouting at Heracles, as if he were responsible for their misfortunes, but he was no longer listening.

Something—an idea—was beginning to take shape in his mind.

And suddenly, the truth seemed to reveal itself to him at last. And he was overcome with horror.[3]

Just before dusk, Diagoras decided to go to the Academy, even though classes had been canceled. He needed to soothe his spirits, to take refuge in the precise calm of his beloved school. He knew, too, that

3. The truth? What is the truth? Oh, Heracles Pontor, Decipherer of Enigmas, tell it to me! I'm going blind from deciphering your thoughts, trying to find some truth, however small, but I find nothing but eidetic images, horses that eat human flesh, oxen with a shambling gait, a poor young girl with a lily who disappeared pages ago, and a translator who comes and goes, who's as inscrutable and enigmatic as the madman who's locked me in here. You, at least, Heracles, have discovered something, but I—what have I found out? What was the cause of Montalo's death? Why have I been kidnapped? What is the secret hidden inside this book? I haven't worked any of it out! All I do, apart from translate, is cry, hanker after my freedom, think about food . . . and defecate. At least I'm having good bowel movements now. That keeps my spirits up.—TRANS.

if he remained in the city, he would become the target of questions and idle remarks, and it was what he least wanted just then. As soon as he set off, he was glad of his decision—simply getting out of Athens made him feel better. It was a beautiful evening, the air was cooling as the winter sun set, and the birds offered him their song without even requiring that he stop to listen. As he entered the forest, he filled his lungs with air and managed to smile . . . in spite of everything.

His thoughts returned again and again to the harsh test he'd just endured. The crowd had been lenient with his testimony, but what had Plato and his colleagues thought? Diagoras hadn't asked. In fact, he'd hardly spoken to them after the trial. He'd left hurriedly, not even daring to look questioningly into their eyes. He didn't need to. Deep down, he already knew what they thought. He'd failed in his duty as a teacher. He'd allowed three colts to get away. What's more, he'd privately engaged the Decipherer and kept his findings to himself. He'd actually lied! He'd risked gravely damaging a family's reputation in order to protect the Academy. Oh by Zeus! How could it have happened? What had driven him to declare so shamelessly that poor Euneos had mutilated himself? The burning memory of his calumny devoured his peace of mind.

He stopped upon reaching the white portico with the two niches and unknown busts. MAY NO ONE ENTER WITHOUT KNOWLEDGE OF GEOMETRY ran the legend carved in stone. May no one enter lest he loves the truth, thought Diagoras in torment. May no one enter who is capable of vile lies that harm others. Would he dare enter, or would he turn back? Was he worthy of crossing that threshold? A warm trail ran slowly down his flushed cheek. He closed his eyes and clenched his teeth furiously, like a horse taking the bit in its teeth to wrest control from the charioteer. No, I'm not worthy, he thought.

Suddenly, he heard someone call him: "Diagoras, wait!"

It was Plato, approaching the portico. It would seem he had followed him the entire way. The director of the school strode up to Diagoras and put a sturdy arm around his shoulders. They went through the portico together and into the garden. Among the olive trees, a jet black mare and two dozen emerald green flies were fighting over some rotting pieces of meat.[4]

"Is the trial over?" Plato asked.

Diagoras thought Plato was making fun of him.

"You know it is, for you were in the crowd," he said.

Plato laughed quietly, though, with his huge body, it came out at normal volume.

"I don't mean Menaechmus's trial; I mean Diagoras's. Is it over yet?"

Diagoras understood, and he appreciated Plato's perceptiveness. Attempting to smile, he replied, "I think so, Plato, but I fear the judges are inclined to condemn the accused."

"The judges are too harsh. You did what you thought right, which is all a wise man can do."

"But I kept what I knew secret for far too long . . . and Antisus suffered the consequences. And Euneos's family will never forgive me for besmirching their son's *arete,* his virtue."

Plato narrowed his big gray eyes and said, "Sometimes, something useful and worthwhile comes of evil, Diagoras. I'm sure that Menaechmus would not have been caught had he not committed his last, horrifying crime. Euneos and his family have recovered all their *arete,* and have even risen higher in people's eyes, for we now know that our student was not guilty, but only a victim."

4. The absurd image—a mare eating rotting flesh, and in the gardens of the Academy!—is there to emphasize the eidesis. It made me laugh so hard that I scared myself, but then that made me laugh, too. I threw the papers on the floor, gripped my belly with both hands, and laughed louder and louder. Meanwhile, the mirror in my mind showed me the reflection of a middle-aged man with thinning black hair laughing his head off, alone in a locked and darkened room. By now, I was *crying,* not laughing, but then there is a strange point at which the distinction blurs. A carnivorous mare in Plato's Academy! Isn't that funny? And of course neither Plato nor Diagoras can *see* it! There is something perversely irreverent about the eidesis. Montalo said, "The presence of the animal is disconcerting. Historical sources make no mention of carnivorous mares in the gardens of the Academy. An error, like many committed by Herodotus?" Herodotus! Please! I must stop laughing—uncontrollable laughter is said to be a sign of incipient madness.—TRANS.

He paused and expanded his chest as if about to shout. Gazing at the clear gold sunset, he added, "It is right, however, that you should listen to the complaints of your soul, Diagoras. After all, you lied; you concealed the truth. Both have had beneficial consequences in the end, but we mustn't forget that they were bad intrinsically, in themselves."

"I know, Plato. That is why I no longer consider myself worthy of seeking virtue in this sacred place."

"On the contrary. You are now better qualified to seek it than any of us, for you have found new paths to lead you there. Error is a form of wisdom, Diagoras. Wrong decisions are solemn teachers that influence future decisions. Warning against doing wrong is far more important than tersely advising as to what is right. And who better to learn what he should not do than the man who has tasted the bitter consequences of having done so?"

Diagoras stopped and filled his lungs with the fragrant air of the garden. He felt calmer, less guilty, for the words of the founder of the Academy were balm to his wounds. Two paces away, the mare seemed to smile at him as she tore carnivorously into the meat.

He didn't know why, but he suddenly remembered the chilling smile on Menaechmus's lips as he pleaded guilty at the trial.[5] And out of curiosity, and a desire to change the subject, he asked, "What drives men to behave as Menaechmus did, Plato? What reduces us to the level of beasts?"

The mare snorted and attacked the last bloody pieces of meat.

"Our passions leave us bewildered," said Plato after a moment's thought. "Virtue requires an effort which is pleasant and rewarding over the long term, but passions are immediate desire. They blind us; they stop us thinking clearly. Men who, like Menaechmus, allow themselves to be swept along by instant pleasures don't see that virtue provides a much more lasting and useful form of gratification. Evil is

5. He doesn't know why? This makes me want to laugh again! The eidetic images clearly often seep into Diagoras's mind (though, strangely, never into Heracles'; he sees only what his eyes see). The mare's smile has become the memory of Menaechmus's smile.—TRANS.

nothing but ignorance. Ignorance, pure and simple. If we were all aware of the benefits of virtue and could use our reason in time, we would never voluntarily choose evil."

The mare snorted again, spraying blood. She appeared to roar with laughter, her thick red lips shaking.

Diagoras said pensively, "I sometimes think that evil is making fun of us, Plato. I lose hope, and end up believing that wickedness will defeat us, laughing at our efforts. It will be waiting for us at the end and have the last word."

Huii, huii, went the mare.

"What was that?" asked Plato.

"There." Diagoras pointed. "A blackbird."

Huii, huii, went the blackbird again, and flew away.[6]

Diagoras and Plato exchanged a few more words before bidding each other farewell in a most friendly manner. Plato went to his modest dwelling by the gymnasium, while Diagoras headed toward the school building. He felt satisfied yet anxious, as always after a talk with Plato. He was burning with the desire to put into practice all that he felt he had learned. He felt that life would start afresh the following day. The experience would teach him not to neglect any of his students, to speak up when necessary, to act as a confidant, certainly, but also as a teacher and adviser. Tramachus, Euneos, and Antisus were three serious mistakes that he would never repeat!

As he entered the cool, dark hallway, he heard a sound in the library and frowned.

The Academy library was a large-windowed room. A short corridor, to the right of the main entrance, led into it. The door was open, which was surprising, because classes had been canceled and students didn't usually spend holidays consulting texts. Perhaps some tutor . . .

He approached confidently and peered around the door.

Scraps of light from the sun's evening banquet came through the

6. The metamorphosis of the eidetic mare into a real blackbird (I mean a blackbird belonging to the reality of the novel) underlines the mysterious message of this scene. Is evil mocking the philosophers? It must be remembered that blackbirds are black.—TRANS.

windows. The tables by the door were empty, the next ones, too, and at the back . . . one of the tables was covered with scrolls, but the chair was empty. And nothing seemed to have been moved from the shelves where the philosophical texts (among them, several copies of Plato's dialogues), together with works of poetry and drama, were carefully stored. Wait—what about over there, on the left?

There was a man in the corner. He was crouching, searching the lower shelves, which was why Diagoras hadn't noticed him at first. The man stood up suddenly, holding a papyrus, and Diagoras recognized him before he looked around.

"Heracles!"

The Decipherer turned with unusual speed, like a horse lashed by a whip.

"Oh, it's you, Diagoras! When you invited me here for dinner, I made the acquaintance of a couple of slaves, and they let me into the library today. Don't be angry with them . . . or with me, of course."

The philosopher thought Heracles must be unwell, such was his extreme pallor.

"But why—"

"By Zeus's sacred aegis," declared Heracles, shaking. "We face a strange and powerful evil, Diagoras. An evil as unfathomable as the gorges of Pontus, one that grows darker the deeper into it we fall. We've been deceived!"

And just as charioteers are said to talk to their horses during races, Heracles spoke very fast, busying himself all the while, unrolling and rolling up scrolls, putting them back on the shelves. His fat hands and his voice were trembling. He went on angrily: "We've been used, Diagoras, both of us, to stage a horrifying farce. A Lenaean comedy, but with a tragic ending!"

"What are you talking about?"

"About Menaechmus, and Tramachus's death, and the wolves of Lycabettus—that's what I'm talking about!"

"You surely don't mean that Menaechmus is innocent?"

"Oh, no, no, he's guilty, more guilty than destructive desire! But . . . but . . ."

He stopped and put his fist to his mouth, then added, "I'll explain everything in due course. But I have to go somewhere tonight. I'd like you to accompany me, but I warn you, what we'll see there will not be pleasant!"

"I'll go with you," said Diagoras. "I'd cross the Styx if it would help to find the source of the deception of which you speak. Just tell me this: It has to do with Menaechmus, has it not? He was smiling as he confessed his guilt. It must mean he intends to escape!"

"No," retorted Heracles. "Menaechmus smiled as he confessed because he does *not* intend to get away."

And at Diagoras's look of amazement, he added, "That's how we've been deceived!"[7]

7. He entered wearing a different mask (a smiling male face this time). I got up from the desk.

"Have you found the final key yet?" His voice sounded muffled behind the mocking face.

"Who are you?"

"I'm the question," answered my jailer. And he said again, "Have you found the final key yet?"

"Let me out of here."

"When you find the key. Have you found it yet?"

"No!" I shouted, losing my temper, the eidetic reins of my equanimity. "The eidesis refers to the labors of Hercules . . . and a girl with a lily, and a translator . . . but I don't know what any of it means! I—"

He interrupted, with mock seriousness: "Perhaps the eidetic images are only part of the key. What's the novel about?"

"A murder investigation . . ." I stammered. "The central character thought he'd found the murderer, but now . . . now, new problems have emerged. . . . I don't know what they are yet."

My kidnapper seemed to give a little laugh. I say "seemed" because the mask made it difficult to tell. He said, "Isn't it possible that there might not be a final key?"

"I don't think so," I answered immediately.

"Why not?"

"Because if there was no key, I wouldn't be locked up in here."

"Oh, that's very good." He seemed amused. "So, to you, I'm *proof* that there is a key! Or should I say, I'm the *most important* proof."

I thumped the table and shouted, "That's enough! You know the novel! You've even changed it, mixing bogus pages in with the originals! You're perfectly familiar with the language and the style! Why do you need me?"

He seemed thoughtful for a moment, although the mask was still smiling. Then he said, "I haven't made any changes. There are no bogus pages. The thing is, you've swallowed the eidetic bait."

"What do you mean?"

"When there's a very strong element of eidesis in a text, as here, the reader becomes so obsessed with the images that he feels as if he's in the novel. You can't become obsessed with something without feeling you're part of it. In your beloved's eyes, you think you see her love for you, and in the pages of an eidetic book, you think you see yourself."

Annoyed, I rummaged through my papers.

"What about this?" I showed him a page. "Is that the case here, in the bogus chapter eight when Heracles Pontor talks to a translator who's supposedly been kidnapped? Have I swallowed the 'eidetic bait' here, too?"

"Yes," he replied calmly. "Throughout the novel, there is mention of the Translator, whom Crantor sometimes addresses in the second person, and with whom Heracles talks in your 'bogus' chapter. But that doesn't mean *he's you*!"

I didn't know what to say; his logic was devastating. Suddenly, I heard him tittering behind the mask.

"Ah, literature!" he said. "Reading isn't thinking by oneself, my friend—it's a dialogue! But the dialogue in question is a Platonic dialogue: Your interlocutor is an idea. Though not an immutable idea. As you converse with it, you alter it, you make it yours; you come to believe it exists independently. Eidetic novels make the most of this, setting cunning traps . . . that can drive you insane." And he added after a silence, "Which is what happened to Montalo, your predecessor."

"Montalo?" I felt cold inside. "Montalo was here?"

There was a pause. Then the masked figure burst out laughing and said, "For a long time! In fact, like you, I came across *The Athenian Murders* thanks to Montalo's edition. But I *knew* that there was a hidden key to it, so I locked him up and made him find it. He failed."

He said it as if failing were exactly what he expected his victims to do. He paused and the mask's smile seemed to widen. He went on: "But I lost patience, and let my dogs feast on him. Then I dumped his body in the forest. The police thought he'd been attacked by wolves."

After another pause, he added, "But don't worry, I won't get fed up with you for some time."

My fear turned to rage.

"You're . . . a vile, ruthless—" I stopped, searching for the appropriate word. Murderer? Criminal? Executioner? In the end, in desperation, realizing that my disgust could not be translated into words, I spat out, "Twaddle!" And I went on defiantly: "You think you frighten me? You're the one who's scared, hiding your face like that!"

"Would you like me to remove my mask?" he asked.

There was a deep silence. I said, "No."

"Why not?"

"Because I know that if I see your face, I'll never get out of here alive."

I heard his odious little laugh again.

"So, my mask ensures *your safety,* and your presence ensures *mine*! That means we have to stay together!" He went out, slamming the door before I could reach it. His voice came through the cracks in the door: "Carry on with the translation. And remember, if there is a key, and you find it, you'll get out of here. If there isn't, you'll never get out. So it's in your interest to see that there is one, isn't it?"—TRANS.

10[1]

"WOULD YOU LIKE ME to remove my mask?"

"No. . . . Because I know that if I see your face, I'll never get out of here alive."[2]

A dark mouth was dug into the rock. Together, the gently curving frieze and threshold formed a huge pair of women's lips. But, above the frieze, the unknown sculptor had carved an androgynous mustache, decorated with aggressive naked male figures. It was the entrance to a small temple dedicated to Aphrodite on the northern slope of the Pnyx but, inside, one had the feeling of descending into a deep chasm, a cavern in Hephaestus's kingdom.

"On specific nights every moon," Heracles explained to Diagoras on the way there, "secret doors are opened, leading to a honeycomb of galleries on this side of the hill. At the entrance, there is a guard in a mask and dark cloak, who could be a man or a woman. It's impor-

1. "The penetrating scent of a woman. And the feel—oh, firm and velvety!—has something of the toughness of an athlete's arm and the smoothness of a young girl's breast." This is Montalo's absurd description of the texture of the papyrus for chapter 10.—TRANS.

2. This password (we'll find out it's a password in a moment) is a strangely exact repetition of part of the conversation I had with my kidnapper only a few hours ago. Another piece of "eidetic bait"?—TRANS.

tant to give the right answer to the question, or we won't be allowed in. Luckily, I know the password for tonight."

The steps were wide, and Heracles and Diagoras's descent was further aided by torches placed at irregular intervals. The smell of smoke and spices grew stronger with every step. The mellifluous, inquiring tones of an oboe and the virile response of a cymbal reached their ears, disguised by echoes, together with the voice of a rhapsode of indeterminate sex. Rounding a bend at the bottom of the stairs, they came to a small room. There appeared to be two exits: a dark, narrow tunnel to the left, and another on the right, through a pair of curtains nailed to the rock. The air was almost unbreathable. A figure stood by the curtains, in a mask frozen in an expression of terror. It wore a small, almost indecent chiton, but, since much of its nudity was clothed in shadows, it was impossible to tell whether it was a particularly slim young man or a small-breasted girl. On seeing the new arrivals, it took something from a shelf on the wall and held it out to them like an offering. It said, the voice young, ambiguous, "Your masks. Sacred Dionysus Bromios. Sacred Dionysus Bromios."

Diagoras glanced at his mask. It was very much like those worn by the chorus in tragedies, with a handle made of the same clay as the rest, and a happy or insane expression. He couldn't tell if it was a male or female face. It felt very heavy. Gripping it by the handle, he held it up and observed everything through the mysterious eye slits. As he breathed, his view misted over.

It (the creature that had handed them the masks and whose identity, Diagoras found, wavered disturbingly with each word and gesture between one gender and the other) parted the curtains and let them through.

"Careful. There's another step," said Heracles.

They were in an underground room as closed as the chamber where life itself begins. The walls exuded red droplets, and the penetrating smell of smoke and spices filled one's nose. The rhapsode and musicians stood on a smallish wooden stage erected at the far end. The audience was crowded into a small area—indistinct shadows, heads swaying, one hand resting on a neighbor's shoulder, the other holding up a mask. A golden bowl on a tripod stood in the middle of the room. Heracles and Diagoras went to stand in the back row, and waited. The philosopher guessed that the incense burners hanging from the ceiling and the rags tied around the torches must contain coloring herbs, for they produced strange blue-red tongues of flame.

"What is this place?" he asked. "Another clandestine theater?"

"No. These are rituals," replied Heracles through his mask. "Not the Sacred Mysteries, something else. Athens is full of them."

Suddenly, a hand appeared in the field of vision allowed by Diagoras's eye slits. It held out a small krater filled with dark liquid. Diagoras swiveled his mask and found another mask facing him. In the red light, he could not tell its color, but he could see that it was hideous, with a long nose like that of an old witch; hair spilled abundantly around the edges. The figure—man or woman—was dressed in a diaphanous tunic, like those worn by courtesans to arouse guests at licentious banquets, but, once again, its sex was skillfully concealed.

Diagoras felt Heracles nudge his elbow.

"Take what you're offered."

Diagoras took the krater. The figure vanished through the doorway, affording a lightning glimpse of its true nature, for the tunic was open at the sides. But in the bloodred light the questions remained unanswered: What was that hanging there? A high belly? Low breasts? The Decipherer, in turn, accepted a krater.

"When the time comes," he whispered to Diagoras, "pretend to drink. But don't even think of actually doing so."

The music stopped abruptly and the audience divided into two groups, standing against the side walls and clearing a central aisle. There was coughing, hoarse laughter, and whispered shreds of words. The musicians had withdrawn and only the rhapsode's red figure remained on the stage. A fetid smell rose like a corpse revived by sorcery, and Diagoras had to suppress a sudden urge to flee from the room in search of fresh air. He sensed confusedly that the stench came from the bowl, and the lumpy matter it contained. As the crowd around it had parted, the putrid odor had spread unhindered.

A crowd of improbable figures now came through the curtains.

One was conscious first of their complete nakedness. Then the bulging forms were suggestive of women. They crawled in, outlandish masks hiding their faces. On some, breasts swung more freely than on others. Some bodies complied with the canon for ephebes more closely than others. Some were slender, lively, agile; others were fat and clumsy. Their backs and buttocks, the most visible parts of their bodies, displayed varying nuances of beauty, age, health. But they were all naked, rooting around on all fours, grunting like sows in heat. The audience urged them on loudly. Diagoras wondered where they had come from, but then he remembered the tunnel leading off the small room at the entrance.

They advanced in rows of increasing size: one at the head, two behind, then three, then four—this was the largest number that the central aisle could accommodate—so that the front of the strange herd resembled a living spear tip. As it came level with the tripod, the naked torrent broke up and engulfed it.

The ones at the front mounted the stage, flinging themselves at the rhapsode. More kept arriving, the ones at the back having to stop. While they waited, they teased one another, pressing their masks into the backsides and thighs of the ones in front. As they reached the stage, they collapsed, panting frenziedly, in a soft disordered heap of writhing bodies, a jumble of pubescent flesh.

Astounded, gripped by dismay and revulsion, Diagoras again felt Heracles nudge his arm.

"Pretend to drink!"

Diagoras looked around at the crowd—heads were thrown back, tunics stained with dark fluids. He moved his mask aside and raised the krater to his lips. The liquid smelled like nothing he had encountered before—a dense mixture of ink and spices.

The aisle was almost empty, while the stage creaked beneath the weight of bodies. What was happening? What were they doing? The noisy, naked, shifting mass blocked his view.

Suddenly, an object flew off the stage, landing by the tripod. It was the rhapsode's right arm, easily identifiable by the piece of black cloth from the tunic attached to the shoulder. Its appearance was greeted with joyful cries. The same fate befell the left arm. It hit the floor with a thud, like a dead branch, and came to a stop at Diagoras's feet, the hand open like a white five-petaled flower. The philosopher screamed, but, luckily, nobody heard. As if the act of dismemberment were an agreed-upon signal, the audience rushed toward the bowl in the center like joyful young girls frolicking in the sun.[3]

"It's a dummy," said Heracles to his horrified companion.

A leg struck one of the spectators before falling to the ground; the other leg, flung too hard, crashed against the opposite wall. The women were now vying with one another to see who could rip the head from the mutilated dummy. Some pulled one way, while others pulled the other way, some tearing at it with their teeth, others with their hands. The winner crawled to the middle of the stage and raised her trophy in the air with a howl, spreading her legs shamelessly, displaying athletic muscles, unbecoming an Athenian maiden, and flaunting her breasts. The torchlight branded her ribs with red. She began stamping a bare foot on the wooden stage, raising ghosts of dust. Panting but more subdued, her companions watched with reverence.

Chaos reigned over the audience. What was happening? They were crowding around the bowl. Stunned, jostled, Diagoras moved closer. An old man in front of him was shaking his thick gray hair, as if in a private, ecstatic dance. There was something hanging from his mouth. He looked as if he had been slapped in the face until his lips split, but the shreds of flesh dangling from the corners of his mouth were not his.

"I have to get out," moaned Diagoras.

The women had begun chanting, shrieking, "*La, la, Bromios, evohe, evohe!*"

"By the gods of friendship, Heracles, what was that? Definitely not Athens!"

3. "Young girls" and white petals remind me of the image of my girl with the lily. I can picture her running under the strong Greek sun, holding a lily, happy, trusting. . . . And all of it in this horrible paragraph! Damn this eidetic novel!—TRANS.

They were in the cool peace of an empty street, sitting on the ground, with their backs against a wall, breathless. Diagoras's insides felt much improved after the violent purge they had just undergone. Frowning, Heracles replied, "I fear that it was Athens much more than your Academy, Diagoras. It was a Dionysian ritual. Dozens of them are celebrated in and around the city every moon, all differing in small details, yet similar overall. I knew of these rituals, of course, but, until now, I'd never seen one, although I'd wanted to."

"Why?"

The Decipherer scratched his short silver beard for a moment.

"According to legend, Dionysus's body was destroyed by the Titans, just as Orpheus's was by the women of Thrace. Zeus brought him back to life from his heart. Tearing out the heart and devouring it is one of the most important parts of Dionysian rites."

"The bowl," murmured Diagoras.

Heracles nodded.

"It probably contained chunks of rotting hearts torn from animals."

"And those women . . ."

"Women and men, slaves and freemen, Athenians and metics—the rites acknowledge no difference. Madness and frenzy unite people. One of those naked women you saw on all fours could have been the daughter of an archon, and that may have been a slave girl from Corinth or a hetaera from Argos crawling beside her. It's madness, Diagoras. We can't explain it."

Diagoras shook his head, stunned.

"But what does it all have to do with—" Suddenly, he opened his eyes wide and exclaimed, "The torn-out heart! Tramachus!"

Heracles nodded again.

"The sect we saw tonight is more or less legal, known and accepted by the archons, but there are others that operate clandestinely, due to the nature of their rites. You set out the problem clearly at my house. Do you remember? We wouldn't reach the truth by applying reason. I didn't believe you, but now I have to admit that you were right. What I felt in the Agora today as I listened to Attic peasants mourning the death of their friends attacked by wolves was not the logical consequence of a . . . reasoned argument, shall we say . . . but . . . something I can't define. Perhaps it was a flash of inspiration from my Socratic daemon, or the intuition women are said to possess. It happened when one of them mentioned that his friend's heart had been devoured. Suddenly, it came to me: It was a ritual, and we didn't suspect. The victims are mainly peasants whose deaths have gone unnoticed until now. But I'm sure they've been active in Attica for years."

The Decipherer got to his feet wearily. Diagoras did likewise, murmuring anxiously, "Wait. That's not how Euneos and Antisus died! Their . . . their hearts were not torn out!"

"Don't you see? Euneos and Antisus were murdered in order to *mislead* us. It was Tramachus's death they wished to cover up. When they found out you had engaged the Decipherer of Enigmas to investigate Tramachus's death, they were so scared, they devised this horrific comedy."

Diagoras ran his hand over his face, as if trying to erase his look of disbelief.

"It's not possible. . . . They devoured . . . Tramachus's heart? When? Before or after the wolves—" He stopped when he saw the Decipherer staring back at him.

"*There never were any wolves,* Diagoras. That was what they tried to hide from us by all possible means. The tears, the bites—*it wasn't* a wolf attack. Some sects—"

There was a shadow and a sound at the same time. The shadow was an irregular, elongated shape that detached itself from the bend in the road closest to where they stood, and headed swiftly away, outlined by the moonlight. The sound was, first, panting, then hurried steps.

"Who . . ." asked Diagoras.

Heracles was the first to realize what had happened.

"Somebody was watching us!" he shouted.

He set his fat body in motion, forcing himself to run. Diagoras quickly overtook him. The figure—man or woman—seemed to roll down the street and disappear into the darkness. Snorting and puffing, the Decipherer stopped.

"Pah, it's no use!"

They came level with each other. Diagoras's cheeks were flushed and his girlish lips looked painted; he delicately rearranged his hair, raised his prominent bust as he breathed in, and said in a sweet nymphlike voice,[4] "He's gotten away. Who could it have been?"

Heracles replied gravely, "If it was one of them, and I believe it was, our lives won't be worth an obol come daybreak. The members of this cult are cunning and quite unscrupulous. I told you: They didn't hesitate to use Antisus and Euneos as a distraction. I'm certain they were both members of the sect, like Tramachus. I understand everything now. The fear I saw in Antisus's face was due not to Menaechmus but to *us.* His superiors must have told him to get an army posting away from Athens so that we wouldn't be able to question him. But as we proceeded with our investigation, the sect decided to sacrifice him anyway, to divert our attention toward Menaechmus. I can still see Antisus's expression as he stood naked in the pantry the other night. How that wretched young man deceived me! As for Eumarchus, I don't believe he was one of them. Perhaps he witnessed Antisus's murder, and when he tried to stop them, they killed him, too."

"But then Menaechmus—"

"A cult member of some importance. He played the part of the guilty man to perfection when we went to see him." Heracles frowned. "And I've no doubt he recruited your students."

4. I would ask the reader to ignore Diagoras's sudden hermaphroditism, since it is purely eidetic. The sexual ambiguity dominating the descriptions of secondary characters in this chapter is now affecting one of the protagonists. It would seem to hint at the ninth labor, the girdle of Hippolyta, in which the hero must face the Amazons (warrior maidens—in other words, women-men) and steal Queen Hippolyta's girdle. Still, I think the author allowed himself a rather malicious joke at the expense of one of the most "serious" characters in the novel (picturing Diagoras in such a guise made me start laughing again). In many ways, his bizarre sense of humor resembles my masked jailer's.—TRANS.

"But Menaechmus has been condemned to death! He's going to be thrown into the *barathrum*!"

Heracles nodded gloomily.

"I know. It's what he *wanted*. Oh, don't think I understand it, Diagoras! You should read some of the texts I found in your library. The members of some Dionysian cults long to be tortured or to die dismembered. They rush eagerly to the sacrifice, like a maiden into the arms of her husband on her wedding night. Do you remember what I said about Tramachus? His arms were unscathed! He didn't defend himself! That must have been what you saw in his eyes that day. You thought it was terror, but it was *pleasure*! The terror was in *your* eyes, Diagoras!"

"No!" Diagoras shouted, shrieked almost. "That's not what pleasure looks like!"

"Maybe *this* kind of pleasure does. What do you know? Have you ever felt it? Don't look at me like that. I don't understand, either! Why did those taking part in the ritual tonight eat chunks of rotting viscera? I don't know, Diagoras! I can't understand it! Perhaps the entire city has gone mad without us knowing!"

Heracles almost jumped when he saw his companion's face—a combination of horror, anger, and shame distorting his muscles in a grotesque manner. The Decipherer had never seen him look like that. When Diagoras spoke, his voice suited the mask he now wore.

"Heracles Pontor, you're talking about a student at the Academy! About *my* students! I knew them to the very depths of their souls! I—"

Heracles, usually so calm, suddenly felt overcome with rage.

"What does your damned Academy matter now? What did it ever matter?"

The philosopher stared at him bitterly. Heracles went on more gently, recovering his composure: "We have to accept that people find your Academy a very boring place, Diagoras. They go there, listen to your lectures, and then—then they go off and eat one another. That's all."

He'll accept it eventually, he thought, moved by the look on the tutor's haggard face, visible in the moonlight. After an uncomfortable silence, Diagoras said, "There has to be an explanation. A key. If what you say is true, there must be some final key that we still haven't found."

"Perhaps there is a key to this strange text," agreed Heracles, "but I'm not the right translator for it. Maybe we need to see things from a distance to understand them better.[5] Anyway, let's proceed cautiously. If they've been watching us, and I suspect they have, they'll know what we've discovered. And that's what they least like. We have to move quickly."

"What are we going to do?"

"We need proof. All the cult members we know of have been killed, or are about to be: Tramachus, Euneos, Antisus, Menaechmus. Their plan was very clever. But we may have a chance. If only we could get Menaechmus to confess!"

"I could try to talk to him," suggested Diagoras.

Heracles thought a moment. "Very well. Go and see Menaechmus tomorrow. I'm going to see what information I can get from a certain other person."

"Who?"

"The person who may constitute the only mistake they've made! I'll see you tomorrow, good Diagoras. Be prudent!"

The moon was a woman's breast, with a finger of cloud approaching its nipple. The moon was a vulva, which the pointed cloud tried to penetrate.[6]

5. From what kind of distance? From down here?—TRANS.

6. I've been locked up in here for too long. For a moment, I thought these two sentences could perhaps be rendered less crudely: "The moon was a breast lightly brushed by the finger of cloud. The moon was a hollow in which a cloud of pointed outline sought refuge," or something. Something much more poetic than what I've produced anyway. It's just that . . . Oh, Helena, I need you and miss you! I've always believed that physical desires were merely servants of our noble intellect, but now . . . What I wouldn't give for a good tumble! (I put it like that, without beating around the bush, because—let's be honest—*who's going to read this*?) Oh, translating, translating, a mindless labor of Hercules imposed by a mad Eurystheus! So be it! Here in this dark cubbyhole, am I not the master of what I write? Well then, that is my version of the sentences, however shocking!—TRANS.

But Heracles Pontor was not watching all this celestial activity. He crossed the garden, laid out beneath Selene's watchful gaze, and opened his front door. The dark, silent hollow of the hall resembled a watchful eye. Heracles watched out in case his slave Ponsica had left a lamp on a shelf by the door, but Ponsica had obviously not watched out for such a possibility.[7] So he entered the dark house, like a knife cutting into flesh, and closed the door.

"Yasintra?" he called. There was no answer.

His gaze stabbed the darkness, to no avail. He made slowly for the rooms at the center of the house. His feet seemed to step on the points of knives. The icy cold of the dark house pierced his cloak like a knife.

"Yasintra?" he called again.

"Here," came the reply, cutting through the silence.[8]

He went to the bedroom. She had her back to him in the darkness. She turned.

"What are you doing here . . . in the dark?" asked Heracles.

"Waiting for you."

Yasintra hurried to light the lamp. He observed her back as she did so. The brightness grew, hesitantly, and spread up the wall. Yasintra didn't turn around immediately, and Heracles continued to observe the strong lines of her back. She wore a smooth floor-length peplos, pinned with a fibula at each shoulder, forming folds down her back.

"Where is my slave woman?"

"She hasn't returned from Eleusis," she replied, still with her back to him.[9]

Then she turned. Her face was beautifully painted—eyes outlined with pigments, cheeks whitened with ceruse, and lips stained very red;

7. What's going on? The infinitive *to watch* is springing up eidetically all over the place, but what does it mean? Is somebody "watching" Heracles?—TRANS.

8. Knives! The eidesis is spreading like poison ivy! What image is being conjured up here? "Watchfulness" . . . "Knife" . . . Oh, Heracles, Heracles, look out. You're in *danger*!—TRANS.

9. And now the word *back*! It's a warning! Maybe: "*Watch* your *back,* because . . . there's a *knife*." Oh, Heracles, Heracles! How can I warn you? How? Keep away from her!—TRANS.

her breasts hung freely beneath the blue peplos; a gold link belt cinched her already narrow waist; her toenails were painted two different colors, as was the custom of Egyptian women. As she turned, a light perfumed dew spread through the air.

"Why are you dressed like that?" asked Heracles.

"I thought you'd like it," she said, eyes watchful. From each small earlobe hung an earring—as sharp as a knife—shaped like a naked woman with her back turned.[10]

The Decipherer said nothing. Yasintra stood still, surrounded by a halo of lamplight. A twisted column of shadow stretched from her forehead to the pubic confluence of the folds of her peplos, neatly dividing her body in half. She said, "I've prepared some food."

"I'm not hungry."

"Are you going to bed?"

"Yes." Heracles rubbed his eyes. "I'm exhausted."

She went to the door. Her bracelets jangled as she moved. Watching her, Heracles said, "Yasintra." She stopped and turned. "I need to talk to you." She nodded in silence and came to stand in front of him. "You told me that some slaves, claiming to have been sent by Menaechmus, threatened to kill you." She nodded again, more quickly this time. "Have you seen them again?"

"No."

"What did they look like?"

Yasintra hesitated a moment.

"They were very tall. With Athenian accents."

"What exactly did they say?"

"What I told you."

"Remind me."

Yasintra blinked. Her pale, almost limpid eyes avoided Heracles'. The pink tip of her tongue slowly ran over her red lips.

"They said that I should tell no one of my relations with Tramachus, or I'd be sorry. And they swore by the Styx and by all the gods."

10. The repetition, in this paragraph, of the three eidetic words emphazises the image. Watch your back, Heracles. She's got a knife!—TRANS.

"I understand. . . ."

Heracles stroked his silver beard. He began pacing quickly to and fro in front of Yasintra: left, right, left, right.[11] He murmured, thinking aloud, "I'm sure they, too, must have been members of . . ."

He turned his back to the girl.[12] On the wall in front of him, Yasintra's shadow appeared to grow. A sudden thought made Heracles turn back to the hetaera. She seemed to have moved a few steps closer, but he thought nothing of it.

"Wait. Do you remember if there was anything distinctive about them? I mean, such as tattoos, bracelets. . . ."

Yasintra frowned and averted her gaze.

"No."

"But they were definitely grown men, not boys. You're sure of that?"

She nodded and said, "What is it, Heracles? You told me I no longer had anything to fear from Menaechmus."

"You don't," he reassured her. "But I'd like to catch those two men. Would you recognize them if you saw them again?"

"I think so."

"Good." Heracles suddenly felt tired. He glanced at the tempting prospect of his bed and sighed. "I'm going to rest now. It's been a difficult day. If you can, call me at daybreak."

"I will."

He dismissed her with indifference and laid his large back on the bed. Gradually, his watchful mind closed its eyes and sleep cut through his consciousness like a knife.[13]

The fingers gripped the beating heart. There were shadows all around, and Heracles could hear a voice. He turned to look at the soldier—he was speaking. What was he saying? He must find out! Enclosed in a

11. Don't turn your *back* to her!—TRANS.

12. *No, damn it, no!*—TRANS.

13. The danger isn't past—the three words recur like eidetic warnings!—TRANS.

trembling gray cloud, the soldier was moving his lips, but the booming heartbeats drowned out his words. Heracles could see him clearly—he was wearing a cuirass, skirt, greaves, and a helmet with a brightly colored plume. He could tell his rank. He thought he understood a few words. The heartbeats grew louder; they sounded like approaching footsteps. Naked women crawled from the tunnel. Menaechmus was there, smiling, of course. But the most important thing was to remember what he had just forgotten. Only then—

"No!" he moaned.

"Was it the same dream as before?" asked the shadow leaning over him.

The bedroom was dimly lighted. Fully dressed and with painted face, Yasintra lay down beside him, watching him tensely.

"Yes," said Heracles. He ran his hand over his damp forehead. "What are you doing here?"

"I heard you, like last time. You were talking in your sleep, moaning. I couldn't bear it, so I came to wake you. The gods have sent you the dream; I'm sure of it."

"I don't know. . . ." Heracles licked his dry lips. "I think it's a message."

"A prophecy."

"No, a message from the past. Something I have to remember."

Softening her mannish voice, she replied, "You haven't attained peace. You do too much thinking. You don't give yourself up to sensations. When my mother taught me to dance, she said, 'Yasintra, don't think. Don't use your body. Let it use you. Your body belongs not to you but to the gods. They manifest themselves through your movements. Let your body give the orders—its voice is desire; its language is gesture. Don't translate the language. Listen to it. Don't translate. Don't translate. Don't translate.' "[14]

"Your mother may have been right," said Heracles. "But I feel I cannot stop thinking." And he added proudly, "I'm a decipherer in the purest sense."

14. These hypnotic words make my eyes close.—TRANS.

"Maybe I can help you."

And with that, she lifted the sheet, leaned over meekly, and placed her mouth over the area of tunic covering Heracles' flaccid member.

He was dumbfounded. He sat up abruptly. Barely parting her thick lips, Yasintra said, "Let me."

She kissed and kneaded the docile, malleable thing beneath his tunic, the long, soft bulge of which he'd hardly been aware since Hagesikora's death. But then, during her meticulous exploration, her mouth found a small rim. He felt it, as if his flesh had cried out, perceived it suddenly, piercingly. He moaned with pleasure, fell back on the bed, and closed his eyes.

The feeling spread to cover a patch of his lower abdomen. It grew in breadth, volume, intensity, until it was no longer merely an area of his body, but a rebellion. Heracles couldn't tell from where in the pleasurable mystery of his member it proceeded. The rebellion was now a movement of tacit disobedience that had become a separate entity with a form and will of its own. And all she'd used was her mouth! He moaned again.

Without warning, the feeling stopped. He was left with a stinging emptiness, as if he'd been slapped. He realized that the girl's caresses had ceased. He opened his eyes and saw her lift her peplos and sit astride his legs. Her firm dancer's belly pressed against the rigid sculpture she had created, which now stood up urgently. He questioned her with his moans. She began moving her hips. . . . No, not exactly; she was dancing, using only her torso. Her thighs gripped Heracles' fat legs and her hands rested on the bed, but her torso moved in time to the music of the flesh.

A shoulder appeared; then, slowly, deliberately, the peplos began to slide over its shapely edge, down her arm. Yasintra turned her head and freed the other shoulder. The cloth clung to it a little longer, and Heracles thought this might even have been calculated. In a single, practiced move, the hetaera drew in her arms and freed them from the tunic. It slipped down and hung from her erect breasts.

Undressing without using your hands must be tricky, Heracles reflected, and this slow difficulty was one of the pleasures that she was offering him; the other—more unruly, less immediate—was the continuous, increasing pressure of her pubis on his reddened shaft.

With a precise sway of her torso, Yasintra made the tunic slide like oil down over the convex surface of one of her breasts, and, clearing the obstacle of her nipple, it floated as lightly as a feather down her stomach. Heracles gazed at the newly bared breast: dark-skinned, round, within reach of his hand. He felt the urge to squeeze the hard, dark embellishment trembling atop the hemisphere of flesh, but he held back. The peplos began to spill down the other breast.

Heracles' slim body tensed; his forehead, with its sharply receding hairline, was damp with sweat; his black eyes blinked; his mouth, surrounded by a neat black beard, issued a moan; his entire face was flushed; even the small scar on his prominent right cheekbone (a memento from a childhood fight) looked darker.[15]

Trapped by the metal link belt, the peplos ceased its ecstatic descent. Yasintra used her hands for the first time, and the belt yielded with a gentle click. Full of resolve, her body made its way toward nudity. Free at last, the flesh appeared, to Heracles' eyes, beautifully muscular; the memory of movement was apparent in every area of skin.

Grunting, Heracles sat up. Acquiescing to his initiative, she allowed him to push her down onto the bed. He couldn't look at her face. Turning, he flung himself on top of her. He felt capable of causing pain—he parted her legs and, gently, roughly, thrust inside her. He wanted to believe that he made her moan. He felt Yasintra's face with his hand, and she cried out as he nicked her with the ring on his middle finger. Their movements were now questions and answers, orders and acts of obedience, an instinctive ritual.[16] Yasintra stroked his wide

15. It's me. This is a description of my body, not Heracles'. It's me lying with Yasintra!—TRANS.

16. It's appalling to see myself here, described during the sexual act. Perhaps all readers picture themselves when they read scenes such as these: He thinks he is him, and she, her. I'm aroused, despite myself. As I read and write, I sense *the arrival of a strange and overwhelming pleasure.*—TRANS.

back with nails as sharp as knives, and he closed his watchful eyes.[17]

He kissed the gentle curves of her neck and her shoulder, biting her gently, placing modest cries here and there, until he sensed *the arrival of a strange and overwhelming pleasure.*[18] He cried out for the last time, his voice echoing—thick, torrential—inside her.

As this was happening, belying her apparent ecstasy, the hetaera slowly raised the object she had picked up earlier—Heracles saw it, but he couldn't move, not just *then*—and plunged it into his back.[19]

He felt a sting in his spine.

A moment later, he jerked away from her, raising his hand and bringing it down on her jaw as if it were a sword handle. She tried to move aside, but she was pinned to the bed by the weight of his body. He sat up straighter and pushed her. She rolled, like a flayed animal, and fell to the floor with a strangely gentle thud. But she let go of the long, sharp knife and it bounced with a clink that seemed quite absurd amid so many smooth sounds. Clumsily, wearily, Heracles got off the bed. He pulled Yasintra up by the hair and dragged her to the nearest wall, slamming her head against it.

He started thinking again, and his first thought was, She didn't hurt me. She could have stabbed me, but she didn't. His rage was unabated, however. Still gripping her hair, he banged her head against the adobe wall.

"What else were you to do, other than kill me?" he asked hoarsely.

As she spoke, two red trails ran from her nose, avoiding her thick lips. "I wasn't ordered to kill you. I could have done so if I'd wanted to. They just said that when you reached the peak of pleasure, and

17. The three eidetic words of warning: *back, knife,* and *watch*! It's a TRAP! I must . . . I mean, Heracles must . . .—TRANS.

18. My own words! The ones I've written in a previous note! (I've italicized them in the text and in my note so that the reader can check.) Of course I wrote them *before* I translated the sentence. Isn't this almost a *fusion,* an act of love? What is making love if not the merging of fantasy and reality? Oh, the pleasure of the text—stroking it, enjoying it, rubbing my pen against it! I don't care if it is a coincidence—there can no longer be any doubt: *I am him.* I am *there, with her.*—TRANS.

19. Heracles doesn't react. Nor do I. He continues. I continue. And so on, to the end. We've both chosen to continue.—TRANS.

only then, not before or after, I was to place the point of the dagger against your flesh, without harming you."

Heracles still held her by the hair. They were both panting, and her naked breasts were pressing against his tunic. Shaking with fury, the Decipherer changed hands, now gripping her hair in his left. With the right, he hit her twice, extremely hard. Afterward, the girl simply ran her tongue over her split lip, staring at him, showing neither pain nor fear. Heracles said, "There never were any 'tall men with Athenian accents,' were there?"

Yasintra replied, "Yes, there were. But they wore masks. The first time they threatened me was just after Tramachus's death. And they came back after you and your friend spoke to me. Their threats were terrifying. They told me what to do. I was to tell you that it was Menaechmus who threatened me. I was to go to your house and ask for protection. And tempt you and let you enjoy me." He raised his hand again. She said, "Kill me. I'm not afraid of death, Decipherer."

"But you are afraid of them," murmured Heracles. He didn't strike her this time.

"They're very powerful." Yasintra smiled, despite the split lip. "You can't imagine what they said they'd do if I didn't obey. Sometimes death comes as a relief. They promise infinite pain, not death. They soon convince anyone they wish. Neither you nor your friend stands the slightest chance against them."

"Did they tell you to say that, too?"

"No. I just know it."

"How do you contact them? Where can I find them?"

"They find you."

"Have they been here?"

"Yes," she said, and Heracles noticed that she hesitated. He pressed her *back* more firmly against the wall, digging his elbow into her shoulder as if it were a *knife* and *watching out* for any move she might make.[20]

20. Why have the four eidetic words (I've italicized them) reappeared, when Heracles would no longer seem to be in danger? What's going on?—TRANS.

Yasintra added, "*They're here now.*"

"Here? What do you mean?"[21]

Yasintra paused. She glanced around the room. Strangely slowly, she said, "They also said that . . . after lying with you, I should talk . . . and distract you."

Heracles saw her eyes dart from side to side.[22]

Suddenly he seemed to hear a voice inside him, shouting, Turn around! He did so just in time.

The figure wore a mask and heavy black cloak. Its right arm had just described a silent, deadly arc, when the unexpected obstacle of Heracles' forearm knocked it off course and the blade stabbed the air harmlessly. The Decipherer turned around and caught his attacker by the wrist. There was a struggle. Heracles looked into the masked face and felt his strength fail—he recognized the blank features, the artificial countenance, the dark unease seeping from the eye holes, now flashing with hatred. Making the most of Heracles' momentary confusion, Ponsica forced the point of the dagger closer to his soft, fleshy neck. Heracles stumbled backward against the wall. He reflected—a fleeting thought, like a glimpse out of the corner of one's eye—that at least Yasintra wasn't attacking him, though he couldn't imagine what else she was doing. So he was facing a single opponent, a woman (if extremely strong, as he had just discovered). He decided to risk allowing the blade a little closer while he summoned the strength to raise his right fist and strike the mask. He heard a moan so low, it might have come from the depths of a well. He struck another blow. Again, a moan, then nothing. But in concentrating on his fist, he had forgotten the dagger, which was moving ever closer to his throbbing neck, to the fragile branching veins and docile trembling muscles. He stopped and did something that must have taken his frenzied opponent by surprise: He unclenched his fist and began tenderly stroking the outline of the mask, the ridge of the nose, the sides of the cheeks, like a blind man trying to recognize an old friend by touch.

21. Now I understand! Heracles, watch your *back*!—TRANS.

22. *Turn around!*—TRANS.

Too late, Ponsica realized what he was going to do.

Two thick battering rams, two huge pistons, were thrust suddenly through the eye holes, sinking easily into a strange viscous substance protected by a slender membrane. The dagger immediately fell away from Heracles' neck, and moans, roars came from behind the mask. The Decipherer withdrew his fingers—moist to the second joint—and moved away from her. Ponsica howled. The mask remained patient, neutral. She stepped back, stumbling.

As she fell to the floor, Heracles flung himself on top of her. He managed with difficulty to restrain the almost irresistible urge to use his own dagger. Instead, after removing her weapon, he kicked her with his bare feet in several places left vulnerable by her blindness. He dug his heel in, as if squashing an enormous insect.

When it was over, panting, confused, he saw that Yasintra was still standing, motionless and naked, against the wall, just as he had left her; she seemed only to have wiped a little of the blood from her face. Heracles felt almost disappointed that she hadn't attacked him, too; he could have vented his rage at both of them, in a single fight, one long storm of blows. Now there was nothing but the air and the objects around him for him to tear up, destroy, annihilate. When he had recovered his voice, he said, "When did they recruit her?"

"I don't know. When they sent me here, they told me to obey her instructions. She can't speak, but her hand movements are easy to understand. And I already knew what the orders were."

"The Sacred Mysteries!" Heracles said contemptuously. Yasintra stared at him blankly. "Ponsica, like Menaechmus, told me she worshiped the Sacred Mysteries. They were both lying."

"Maybe not." The dancer smiled. "They didn't say *what kind* of Sacred Mystery they worshiped."

Heracles looked at her, one eyebrow raised. He said, "Go. Get out."

She gathered up her peplos and belt, then obediently crossed the room. She turned at the door.

"Your slave woman was meant to kill you, not I. They do things their own way, Decipherer, and neither you nor anyone else can understand them. That's why they're so dangerous."

"Get out," he said again, panting, gasping for breath.

But she added, "Flee the city, Heracles. You won't live beyond daybreak."

When Yasintra had gone, Heracles leaned against the wall and rubbed his eyes, no longer concealing his weariness. He needed to recover the peace of his thoughts, to clean the intellectual tools of his trade and start all over again, calmly.

A noise startled him. Ponsica was trying to get up. As she turned, two thick lines of blood ran from the eye openings of the mask. The white artificial face striped with red was terrifying. It can't be, thought Heracles. I broke several of her ribs. She must be dying. She shouldn't be moving. He recalled the fable of the merciless automatons created by the inventor Daedalus. Ponsica's movements reminded him of a broken mechanical device—she would rest on one hand, sit up, fall over again, lean on her hand again, in a jerking pantomime. At last, perhaps realizing the futility of her attempts, she grabbed the dagger and began dragging herself with relentless determination toward Heracles. Parallel trails of humors spewed from her eyes.

"Why do you hate me so much, Ponsica?" asked Heracles.

She stopped at his feet, her breath seething in her chest, and raised the dagger, trembling, in one last, hopeless attempt. Her strength failed and the knife fell to the floor with a clatter. She gave a deep sigh that ended in a furious grunt, and lay there, even her breathing seeming to express rage, still refusing to admit defeat. Heracles gazed at her in wonder. Cautiously, he moved closer, like a hunter uncertain that his prey is dead. Before ending her life, he wanted to understand. He bent down and removed the mask. He examined the face, marbled with scars, and the conspicuously ravaged eyes. She was opening and closing her mouth like a fish.

"When did you start hating me?"

It was like asking when she had decided to become a human being, a free woman, because it struck him suddenly that her hatred had, like the will of a powerful king, released her from slavery. He remembered the day he had seen her in the market, alone, ignored by buyers; and the years of efficient service, the silent gestures, the docile behavior, her compliance when he'd requested—ordered—that she wear a mask. He could find no hint, no moment in all that time that might explain it, or have led him to suspect.

"Ponsica," he whispered in her ear. "Tell me why. You can still move your hands."

She was struggling for breath. The devastated face, in profile, eyes like embryonic birds or snakes crushed in their shells, was horrifying. But Heracles was watching only for a reply. He worried that she might die without answering. He saw that her left hand was scratching at the floor, but there were no words. He looked at the other hand, now no longer holding the dagger. There were no words.

During the terrible silence, he thought, When was it? When were you granted your freedom, or when did you find it yourself? Perhaps you really went to Eleusis, like so many others, and came across them there. He leaned over a little farther and noticed the same smell he had found on the corpses of Eumarchus and Antisus, though not on Euneos's. Of course, he mused, Euneos stank of wine.

Suddenly, he heard the beating of a heart. His own? Hers? Perhaps hers, as she was dying. Her suffering must be atrocious, but she doesn't seem to care. He moved away from the heartbeats. The memory of his recurring nightmare overcame him once more, but this time it gripped his troubled mind as if a waking state were the light needed to end the deep gloom. He saw the torn-out heart, the hand gripping it; he could make out the soldier, and he understood his words at last.

And he remembered what he had forgotten, the small detail that the dream had been screaming at him fiercely, incomprehensibly, from the start.

Thoughout Ponsica's long agony, Heracles stood motionless beside her, staring into space. By the time she died, the new day had dawned and rays of sun crossed the dimly lighted bedroom.

But still Heracles did not move.[23]

23. I've saved your life, Heracles Pontor, my old friend! I can't quite believe it, but I think I've saved your life, and I weep at the thought. As I translated, I wrote down my own cry of alarm, and you heard it. Of course, one might think that I read the text beforehand and then, when I came to translate it, wrote the word a line before it appeared, but I swear that's not what happened, at least, not consciously. . . . And now, what have you remembered? Why don't I remember it, too? I should have realized, like you, but . . .

Important things have happened. My jailer has just left. I was translating chapter 10 when he made his usual abrupt entrance, wearing the smiling mask and black cloak, as always. He paced one way, then the other before asking, "How is it going?"

"I've finished chapter ten. The eidesis refers to Hippolyta's girdle, and the women warriors, the Amazons. But," I added, "I'm in it, too."

"Really?"

"You know it better than anyone," I said.

The mask, with its permanent smile, stared at me.

"I've already told you; I haven't added any text to the novel," he insisted.

I breathed deeply and looked over my notes.

"When Heracles is lying with the dancer Yasintra, his body is described as 'slim.' But, as the reader knows, Heracles is very fat."

"So?"

"*I'm* slim."

His laughter, through the mask, sounded forced. When he stopped laughing, he said, "*Leptos* in Greek means 'slim' but also 'subtle,' as you know. And any reader would understand that what is referred to here is Heracles Pontor's subtle intelligence, not his girth. The sentence is, as I recall, literally: 'Subtle Heracles tensed his body.' He's called 'subtle Heracles' in the same way Homer described Ulysses as 'cunning.' He laughed again. "Of course it suits *you* to translate *leptos* as 'slim,' and I can imagine why! But don't worry, you're not the only one; each person reads what he wants to read. Words are just a set of symbols that adapt to suit us."

He similarly demolished the rest of my supposed evidence: Heracles, too, could have had a "receding hairline," and mention of a "black" beard (like mine), instead of a "silver" one, could have been due to an error on the copyist's part. The scar on the left cheek, memento of a "childhood fight," so like one I have, was probably a "coincidence," and the same went for the ring on the middle finger of the left hand.

"Thousands of people have scars and wear rings," he said. "The thing is, you admire the protagonist and want to be like him, no matter what, particularly at the most interesting times. All readers have the same arrogance; you all assume the text was written with you in mind, and when you read it, you imagine the scene in your own

---

way!" His voice suddenly matched the mask's expression. "I'm sure you *had a good time* while you were reading those paragraphs, didn't you? Don't look at me like that; it's not unusual!"

Making the most of my uncomfortable silence, he leaned over and read the note that I'd been writing when he arrived.

"What's this? You 'saved his life'?" he said incredulously, standing behind me. "These eidetic novels are really powerful! Strange, a work written so long ago . . . and yet it still arouses such strong feelings!"

But his laughter ceased abruptly when I said, "Perhaps it wasn't written *so long ago.*"

It felt good to strike back! For a moment, he peered at me inscrutably through the eye holes in the mask, before spitting out, "What do you mean?"

"According to Montalo, the papyrus on which this chapter was written smelled of a woman, and had the texture of a 'breast' and an 'athlete's arm.' In its way, the ridiculous note is eidetic, too; it represents the 'woman-man' or 'woman warrior' in the labor of the girdle of Hippolyta. Looking back, we find similar examples in the descriptions of the papyrus for each chapter."

"And what do you deduce from that?"

"That Montalo's role is *part of the text.*" I smiled at his silence. "His few footnotes have nothing to do with the style. They're eidetic; they reinforce the images in the book. It always surprised me that an erudite man like Montalo never noticed that *The Athenian Murders* was eidetic. But now I know that *he knew,* and he was playing with the eidesis *in the same way* the author does in the novel."

"I can see you've given this a lot of thought," he said. "Anything else?"

"*The Athenian Murders,* as we know it, is a *bogus* novel. Now I understand why nobody has ever heard of it. We only have Montalo's edition, not the original. Now, the book's written with a possible translator in mind, and is full of devices and traps that could only have been devised by another similarly gifted, or better, writer. The only explanation I can think of is . . . that Montalo *wrote it!*"

The masked figure said nothing. I went on, implacable: "The original of *The Athenian Murders* didn't disappear—Montalo's edition is the original!"

"And why would Montalo have written something like this?" my jailer asked neutrally.

"Because he went insane," I answered. "He was obsessed with eidetic novels. He

---

thought they could prove Plato's Theory of Ideas, and therefore demonstrate that the world, life, the universe are reasonable and just. But he failed. He went mad, and wrote an eidetic novel himself, using his knowledge of Greek and the techniques of eidesis. The work was intended for his colleagues. It was a way of saying, Look! Ideas exist! Here they are! Come on! Find the final key!"

"But Montalo didn't know what the key was," retorted my jailer. "I locked him up."

I stared into the black eye holes and said, "Enough lies, Montalo."

Heracles Pontor himself couldn't have done better!

"In spite of everything," I added, for he said nothing, "you've played an intelligent game. You passed off an old tramp as Montalo's corpse. I prefer to believe that you found him dead and dressed him in your ripped clothes, copying the trick you thought up for Euneos's murder. Once you'd officially been declared dead, you started operating in the shadows. You wrote the novel with a possible translator in mind. When you found out I'd been commissioned to translate it, you kept an eye on me. You added bogus pages in order to confuse me, to make me become obsessed with the text, since, as you yourself put it, 'you can't become obsessed with something without feeling you're part of it.' And finally, you kidnapped me and locked me in here. Maybe this is the cellar of your house, or the place you've been hiding since you faked your death. So what do you want from me? The same thing you've always wanted: to prove the existence of ideas! If I manage to find the images that *you've* hidden in *your* book, then that means ideas exist independently of whoever thinks them. Isn't that so?"

After an extremely long silence, during which my face, like his, was a smiling mask, he said, stressing every word, "Translator, *stay* in the *cave* of your footnotes. Don't try to ecape *up into the text*. You're not the Decipherer of Enigmas, however much you'd like to be. You're just a translator. So *carry on translating*!"

"Why should I restrict myself to being just a translator when you don't stick to being a *reader*?" I said defiantly. "Since you're the author of the novel, I'm free to imitate the characters!"

"I'm not the author of *The Athenian Murders*!" the masked man said, moaned almost.

And he left, slamming the door behind him.

I feel better. I think I've won this round.—TRANS.

THE MAN descended the steep stone steps to the place where death awaited. It was an underground chamber, illuminated by oil lamps, consisting of a small vestibule and a central corridor lined with cells. The smell pervading it was, however, not the smell of death, but that of the preceding moment—agony. The difference between the two was subtle, thought the man, but any dog could have distinguished between them. He found it logical that it should reek thus, for it was the jail where prisoners sentenced to death awaited execution.

It had remained untouched since Solon's time, as if successive governments had feared to alter it in any way. In the vestibule, the door-

1. I was awakened by the furious barking of dogs. I can still hear them; they sound quite close. I wonder if my jailer is trying to scare me, or whether it's just a coincidence (one thing is certain at least: He wasn't lying when he said he owned dogs). But there's a third, rather strange possibility: I've got two chapters left to translate, with a labor of Hercules in each; if they're in the right order, this one—chapter 11—should refer to the dog Cerberus, while the last one should be the golden apples of the Hesperides. In the labor of Cerberus, Hercules goes down to the Underworld to capture the many-headed *dog* fiercely guarding its gates. Surely my masked jailer isn't trying to create an eidesis with *reality*? Incidentally, Montalo noted that the papyrus was "torn and dirty and smells of dead dog."—TRANS.

men played dice to decide who would take night duty and shouted oaths after crucial throws: "The dog, Eumolpus! You have to pay, by Zeus!"[2] Beyond, a short flight of steps led to the deep gloom of the cells, where the prisoners languished, counting the time that remained to them before the final darkness. Though the cells lacked the most basic comforts, as was to be expected, there had been a few notable exceptions. Socrates, for instance, who was locked in the last cell but one on the right—though some of the doormen claimed it was the last on the left—had had a bed, lamp, small table, and several chairs, which were always occupied by his numerous visitors. "But that," the doormen explained, "was because he was here a long time before his sentence was carried out. The end of his trial fell during the Sacred Days, when, as you know, the shipful of pilgrims journeys to Delos and executions are forbidden. But he never complained about the delay. He was so patient, poor man!" Be that as it may, such cases were rare. And certainly no exception had been made for the only prisoner there now awaiting the fateful hour. He was to be executed that same day.

The doorman on duty was a young Melian slave named Amphius. The man reflected, not for the first time, that Amphius would have been handsome—for he had a slender body and manners far more refined than others of his station—had not a mischievous god, or goddess, tugged at the leash of his left eye at his birth and turned his face—where beard sprouted only patchily, due to a strange form of ringworm—into a disturbing enigma. Through which eye was Amphius really looking? The right? The left? To his discomfort, the man wondered about it every time he saw him.

They greeted each other. The man asked, "How is he?"

Amphius replied, "He doesn't complain. I think he converses with the gods, because sometimes I hear him talking."

The man—a servant of the Eleven, named Triptemes—announced, "I'm going to see him."

2. The "throw of the dog" was the lowest: three ones. But the author used it to stress the eidesis. The dogs are still barking outside, by the way.—TRANS.

Amphius said, "What's that you've got there, Triptemes?"

The man showed him the small sealed krater. "When we locked him up, he asked us to get him a little of the wine of Lesbos."

"Wait, Triptemes," said Amphius, "you know it's forbidden for prisoners to receive anything from outside."

Sighing, the man rejoined, "Come, Amphius, you do your job, and let me do mine. What are you afraid of? That he might get drunk on the day of his death?" They laughed. The man went on: "If he does, so much the better. As he falls into the *barathrum,* he'll think he's on his way home from a symposium at a friend's house and has stumbled in the street. *By blue-eyed Athena, the city's streets are in a terrible state!*" And they laughed all the more.

Amphius blushed, ashamed at having been so suspicious. "Go on in, Triptemes, and give him the wine, but don't let the masters know."

"I won't."

He's looking through his right eye; I'm sure of it now, he thought as he took a torch and prepared to descend into the darkness of the cells.[3]

We descend from the sky with a martial retinue of thunderbolts and, on the wings of the wind, are blown away from the symmetry of the temples toward the elegant Scambonidai. Beneath our feet, we make out a cracked gray line that cuts across the district—the main street. Yes, the blot now moving along it at a prudent pace, heading for one of the private gardens, is a man, so insignificant seen from this height. A slave, judging by his cloak. And young, judging by his agile step. A second man awaits him beneath the trees. Despite the shelter afforded by the branches, his cloak is shiny with moisture. The rain beats down, as does our gaze. We fall on the waiting man's face—large, greasy, with a neat little silver beard and gray eyes with pupils like ebony pins. He is visibly

3. The strange uncertainty between "right" and "left" in these paragraphs (Socrates' cell, the slave doorman's eye) may be an attempt to reflect eidetically Hercules' tortuous journey to the kingdom of the dead.—TRANS.

impatient: He looks one way, then the other. When at last he sees the slave, his face becomes more anxious still. What are his thoughts just then? Ah, but we cannot descend right into his head! We land in the tangle of gray hair, and there it all ends for us poor drops of water.[4]

"Master! Master!" shouted the young slave. "I've been to Diagoras's house, as you ordered, but found no one!"

"Are you sure?"

"Yes, master! I knocked on his door repeatedly!"

"Very well, this is what you must do now: Go into the house and wait for me there until midday. If I haven't returned by then, notify the servants of the Eleven. Tell them that my slave woman tried to murder me last night, and that I had to defend myself. If they know there's a corpse, they'll act with more haste. Hand them this scroll and request that they have their superiors read it, and then swear on your master's honor that grave danger is looming over the city. I'm not entirely certain that it is, but if you instill fear in them, they'll obey your instructions. Do you understand?"

Alarmed, the slave nodded. "Yes, master, I'll do as you say! But where are you going? Your words make me shudder!"

"Do as you're told," Heracles said, raising his voice as the rain grew stronger. "I'll be back by midday, if all goes well."

"Take care, master! This storm appears full of terrible portents!"

"If you obey my orders exactly, you have nothing to fear."

Heracles headed down the sloping street into the mortally pale abyss of the city.[5]

Dead fingers of rain woke Diagoras very early, drumming on the walls, scratching at the windows, knocking tirelessly at the door. He

4. The theme of descent, present since the beginning of the chapter, together with the "right and left" theme, evoke Hercules' journey to the Underworld. The image is emphasized in this last paragraph as the reader follows a drop of rain on its lengthy journey, which ends with it landing on Heracles Pontor's head.—TRANS.

5. The "fall" from the sky down to Heracles Pontor's worries continues.—TRANS.

rose from his bed and dressed quickly. Using his cloak as a hood, he went out.

His district, the Kolytos, was dead; some of the shops had even closed, as if it were a holiday. There were a few passersby in the busiest streets, but the rain had the dark alleys to itself. Diagoras reflected that he had to hurry if he wanted to get to see Menaechmus that morning. In fact, he felt that he would have to make haste if he wanted to see *anyone,* anywhere, for all of Athens seemed, to his eyes, to have become a rainy cemetery.

He walked down an unevenly sloping street until he came to a small square. Another street led off it downhill. He noticed the shadow of an old man sheltering beneath a cornice, no doubt waiting for the storm to abate. Diagoras was startled by his pale, gaunt face contrasting with the darkness ringing his eyes. A little later, he thought that the cheeks of a slave carrying two amphorae seemed far too pale. And a hetaera on a corner smiled at him like a starving dog, but the dissolving white lead on her face made him think of a disintegrating shroud. By the god of goodness, I've seen nothing but the faces of corpses since setting off! he thought. Maybe the rain is a premonition. Or perhaps the color of life in our cheeks becomes diluted with water.[6]

Deep in such thoughts, he noticed two hooded figures approaching down a side street. "Here we have another pair of spirits, by Zeus."

The figures stopped before him, and one of them said in a friendly voice, "O Diagoras of Mardontes, accompany us immediately. Something terrible is about to happen."

They stood in his path. Inside the darkness of their hoods, Diagoras could make out oddly similar white faces.

"Who are you?" he asked. "How do you know who I am?"

The hooded men looked at each other.

6. Neither one nor the other, of course. Diagoras, as usual, can "scent" the eidesis from a distance. Athens has, indeed, in this chapter become the kingdom of the dead.—TRANS.

"We are . . . the *terrible thing* that is about to happen if you don't come with us," said the other one.

Diagoras realized suddenly that his eyes had deceived him this time: The whiteness of their faces was artificial. They were wearing masks.

They may even have reached the king archon, thought Heracles with alarm. After all, *anyone* could belong to the sect. But a moment later, he reasoned more calmly: Logically, if they had gotten that far, they would be feeling safe. Instead, they're terrified of being found out. And he concluded, They may be as powerful as gods, but they fear the laws of men. He knocked at the door again. The slave boy appeared in the dark doorway.

"You again." He smiled. "It's a good thing you visit so often. Your visits mean rewards."

Heracles had two obols ready.

"The house is gloomy. You would get lost without me to guide you," said the boy, leading Heracles down the dark corridors. "Do you know what my friend, the old slave Iphimachus, says?"

"What does he say?"

The young guide stopped and lowered his voice.

"That a long time ago, someone got lost in here and died without ever finding his way out. And that sometimes, at night, you can see him in the corridors, whiter and colder than the marble of Chalcis, and he asks politely for the way out."

"Have you ever seen him?"

"No, but Iphimachus says he has."

They set off again as Heracles said, "Well, don't believe it until you've seen him for yourself. Anything you don't see with your own eyes is a matter of opinion."

"The truth is, I pretend to be frightened when he tells me the story," said the boy cheerfully, "because he likes it. But I'm not really. If I ever saw the dead man, I'd say, 'The way out is the second turning on the right!' "

Heracles laughed. "You're right not to be afraid. You're almost an ephebe now."

"Yes, I am," said the boy proudly.

They passed a man crawling with worms. He didn't look at them as he went by, because his eye sockets were empty. He walked past in silence, carrying with him the fetid smell of a thousand days in the cemetery.[7] When they came to the cenacle, the boy said, "Wait here. I'll call the mistress."

"Thank you."

They took leave of each other with a look of amused complicity. It struck Heracles suddenly that he was saying good-bye forever, not only to the boy but also to the dismal house and all its inhabitants, and even to his memories. It was as if the world had died and he were the only one to know. Strangely, the thing that most saddened him was leaving the boy; not even his own memories, whether fragile or lasting, valuable or trifling, seemed more important than the lovely, intelligent creature, the little man whose name, by some strange chance or amusing and continuing coincidence, he still didn't know.

As always, it was Itys's voice that announced her presence. "Too many visits in too short a time, Heracles Pontor, for it to be mere courtesy."

Heracles hadn't seen her enter. He bowed in greeting, and rejoined, "True, it is not courtesy. I promised I would return to tell you what I discovered about your son's death."

After the briefest pause, Itys waved to her slaves and they left the cenacle in silence. With her usual dignity, she motioned for Heracles to take one of the couches, while she reclined on the other. She was . . . Elegant? Beautiful? Heracles could not find a suitable epithet. He reflected that much of her mature beauty must be due to the gentle hint of ceruse on her cheeks, the pigment on her eyelids, the sparkle of brooches and bracelets, and the harmonious lines of her dark pep-

7. I don't need to point out that this walking corpse is eidetic and not an apparition—the boy and Heracles can't see it, just as they can't see the punctuation marks in the text that recounts their conversation.—TRANS.

los. But even without such help, her austere face and sinuous figure would retain all their power . . . or might acquire a new one.

"My slaves have not even offered you a dry cloak," she said. "I'll have them whipped."

"It doesn't matter. I arrived in a great hurry."

"Are you so anxious to tell me what you know?"

"Yes."

He averted his eyes from Itys's dark gaze. He heard her say, "Speak, then."

Staring at his hands resting before him, chubby fingers intertwined, Heracles said, "When I was last here, I mentioned that Tramachus had been in some kind of trouble. I wasn't wrong. Of course, at his age anything could have become a problem. The souls of the young are clay that we shape as we please. But they're never entirely immune to contradictions, doubts. . . . They need firm guidance."

"Which Tramachus had."

"Doubtless he did. But he was very young."

"He was a man."

"No, Itys. He might have *become* one, but the Moirai denied him the opportunity. He was still a child when he died."

There was a silence. Heracles slowly stroked his silver beard, then said, "Perhaps that was the trouble—that he wasn't to be allowed to become a man."

"I see." Itys sighed. "You're referring to the sculptor, Menaechmus. I am aware of all that happened between them, though, fortunately, I wasn't forced to attend his trial. Tramachus was free to choose, and he chose him. It was a question of personal responsibility."

"Perhaps," said Heracles.

"And I'm quite sure he was never afraid."

"Are you?" Heracles raised his eyebrows. "I don't know. Maybe he hid his terror from you, to spare you any suffering."

"What do you mean?"

He ignored the question, continuing as if he were thinking aloud: "Who knows? Perhaps his terror wasn't entirely unfamiliar to you. When Meragrus died, you endured great loneliness, didn't you? The onerous burden of two children to educate, living in a city that had closed its doors to you, in this dark house. . . . Your house is very dark, Itys. Your slaves say it's haunted. I wonder how many ghosts you and your children have seen here over the years. How much loneliness, how much darkness does it take to change a person? In the past, everything was different."

Unexpectedly gentle, Itys interrupted: "But you don't remember the past, Heracles."

"Not willingly, I admit, but you're wrong if you think the past has meant nothing to me."

Lowering his voice, he went on coldly, as if talking to himself: "The past looked like you. I now know, and can tell you. The past smiled at me with your face as a young girl. For a long time, my past was your smile. True, I had no control over it, but things are as they are, and it may be time to concede, to admit, that it is so. . . . I mean, for me to admit it to myself, even though it's too late for either of us to do anything about it."

He muttered all this quickly, eyes lowered, relentlessly filling the silence.

"But now . . . now I look at you and I'm not sure whether I can see any of that past in your face. I'm not sure I care. As I've said, things are as the gods wish; it's no use complaining. And anyway, I've never been much given to emotion, as you know. But I've suddenly discovered that I'm not immune to feelings, however rare or brief. That's all."

He paused and swallowed. The ghost of a blush colored his fleshy cheeks. She must be wondering why on earth I've told her all this, he thought. Raising his voice a little now, he went on casually: "I'd like to know something before I leave. It's very important to me, Itys. I assure you that it has nothing to do with my work as a decipherer. It's a purely personal matter."

"What do you want to know?"

Heracles raised his hand to his mouth, as if he had a sudden pain. After a pause, still not looking at Itys, he said, "I have to explain something first. Since I began investigating Tramachus's death, a terrifying dream has disturbed my nights. I'd see a hand gripping a recently torn-out heart and a soldier in the distance saying something I couldn't make out. I've never attached much importance to dreams; they've always seemed ridiculous, irrational, opposed to the laws of logic. But this one has made me think that—I have to admit that the truth sometimes manifests itself in strange ways. Because this dream was pointing out something that I had forgotten, a trifle that my mind had refused to recall all this time."

He licked his dry lips and went on: "The night they found Tramachus's body, the captain of the border guard claimed that all he'd told you was that your son was dead, without giving you any details. Those were the words that the soldier in my dream was repeating over and over again: 'She knows *only* that her son is dead.' When I visited you to offer my condolences, you said something like 'The gods smiled when *they tore out and devoured my son's heart.*' Now, Tramachus's heart was indeed ripped out; Aschilos confirmed it on examining the corpse. But how did you know, Itys?"

For the first time, Heracles looked into the woman's expressionless face. He went on without any sign of emotion, as if he were about to die: "A simple sentence, that was all—mere words. Rationally, there was no reason to suppose they were other than lamentation, metaphor, hyperbole. But we're talking not of reason, but of my dream, and my dream was telling me that your sentence was a mistake. It was, wasn't it? You tried to deceive me with your false cries of anguish, with your imprecations against the gods, but you made a mistake. That simple sentence remained inside me like a seed, which later germinated and grew into a terrifying dream. The dream was telling me the truth, but I couldn't make out who the hand gripping the heart belonged to, a hand that made me tremble and moan in my sleep. That slender hand, Itys—"

His voice cracked and he stopped. He looked down, then went on calmly: "The rest was easy. You claimed to worship the Sacred Mysteries, like your son, and Antisus, Euneos, and Menaechmus, and like the slave who tried to kill me last night. But you didn't mean the Sacred Mysteries of Eleusis, did you?" He raised his hand quickly, as if fearing an answer. "Oh, I don't care! I don't want to interfere in your religious beliefs. As I said, I just came to find out one thing, and then I'll leave."

He stared at the woman's face. Gently, almost tenderly, he added, "Tell me, Itys, for doubt torments my soul. If you are, as I think, one of *them,* tell me. Did you just *watch,* or did you—" He raised his hand quickly again, as if to stop her answering, though she had not made a single gesture, moved her lips, even blinked, or indicated in any other way that she might be about to speak. He went on, entreating: "By the gods, Itys, tell me you didn't harm your own son. Lie, if you have to. Please. Say, 'No, Heracles, I didn't take part.' That's all. Lying with words is easy. I need another sentence from you to relieve the anguish caused by your first. I swear by Zeus that I don't want to know which of them is the truth. Tell me that you didn't take part, and you have my word that I'll leave and never bother you again."

There was a brief silence.

"I didn't take part, Heracles, I assure you," said Itys, moved. "I couldn't hurt my own son."

Heracles tried to say something, but he found, strangely, that the words, though clearly formed in his mind, refused to issue from his lips. He blinked, confused and surprised by his unexpected[8]

"I need another sentence from you to relieve the anguish caused by your first. I swear by Zeus that I don't want to know which of them is the truth. Tell me that you didn't take part, and you have my word that I'll leave and never bother you again."

There was a brief silence.

8. I'm sorry, Heracles, old friend. What can I do to ease your distress? You needed a sentence and I, as omnipotent translator, had it in my power to provide one. . . . But no, I mustn't! The text is sacrosanct, Heracles. My work is sacred. You beg me, encouraging me to perpetuate the lie. It's easy to lie with words, you say. You're right, but I can't help you. I'm not a writer, just a translator. It's my duty to confess to the reader that I made up Itys's reply, and I apologize for it. I'll go back a few lines and, this time, set down the character's reply as it appears in the original. Forgive me, Heracles. Forgive me, reader.—TRANS.

"I was the first to sink my nails into his chest," said Itys in a flat voice.

Heracles tried to say something, but he found, strangely, that the words, though clearly formed in his mind, refused to issue from his lips. He blinked, confused and surprised by his unexpected muteness. He heard her voice, faint and terrible, like a painful memory.

"I don't care if you understand or not. How could you understand, Heracles Pontor? You've obeyed the rules since you were born. What do you know of freedom, of instinct, of . . . rage? How did you put it? 'You endured great loneliness.' What do you know of my loneliness? To you, it's just another word. For me, it's been a deadweight on my chest, an end to sleep, to rest. What do you know of all this?"

She has no right to abuse me, thought Heracles.

"We loved each other, you and I," continued Itys, "but you demeaned yourself when your father ordered, or advised you, if you prefer, to marry Hagesikora. She was more—how shall I put it? Suitable? She came from a noble family. And if that was your father's will, how were you to disobey? It would have been neither virtuous nor legal. Laws, Virtue . . . Behold the names of the heads of the dog that guards the kingdom of the dead that is Athens: Law, Virtue, Reason, Justice! Does it surprise you that some of us refuse to continue languishing in this beautiful tomb?" Her dark gaze seemed to become lost in a corner of the room as she went on: "My husband, your childhood friend, wanted to transform our absurd political system. He believed that the Spartans weren't hypocrites at least. They waged war and admitted to it, even boasted of it. Yes, he collaborated with the Thirty, but that wasn't his greatest mistake. It was having more faith in others than in himself, until the day came when a majority of 'others' at the Assembly condemned him to death." She pressed her lips together. "But perhaps he made an even graver error—believing that all of this, this kingdom of thinking dead, of corpses that ponder and discuss, could be transformed through mere political change." Her laughter sounded hollow, empty. "That naïve fool Plato believes the same! But many of us have learned that we can only change things if we ourselves change first! Yes, Heracles Pontor, I am proud of my faith! To minds like yours, a religion that pays homage to the most ancient gods through the ritual dismemberment of its followers is absurd, I know, and I won't try to convince you otherwise. But what religion is not absurd? Socrates, the great rationalist, reviled every one of them, and that's why you all condemned him! But a time will come when devouring someone you love will be considered an act of piety! Why not? Neither you nor I will live to see it, but our priests claim that, in the future, there will be religions that worship tortured, ravaged gods! Who knows? Perhaps *devouring the gods* may constitute the most sacred act of adoration!"[9]

This new tone was easier for Heracles to deal with. Her blank face, her apparent indifference had been like molten lead on his soul. But the awakening of her rage allowed him a certain detachment. He said calmly, "You mean devouring the gods *in the same way* you devoured your son's heart? Is that what you mean, Itys?"

She did not reply.

Suddenly, quite unexpectedly, the Decipherer felt vomit rise to his mouth. But, just as abruptly, he realized that it was, in fact, words that he had to spew out, making him lose his composure for a moment.

"And was all this what made you tear at his heart while he looked at you in agony? What did you feel as you *mutilated* your son, Itys?"

"Pleasure," she said.

For some reason, her simple answer didn't anger Heracles Pontor. She's admitted it, he thought. Ah well . . . She's been able to admit it! He even allowed himself to regain his serenity, but then growing anxiety made him rise from his couch. Itys rose, too, as if to indicate that the visit was at an end. Elea and several slave women were now in the room, though Heracles hadn't noticed them enter. It seemed like a family meeting. Elea approached her mother and embraced her, as if she wished to show that she supported her to the end. Still addressing Heracles, Itys said, "I know that it is difficult to understand what we

9. Itys's prophecy has obviously not come true: Fortunately, religious beliefs have taken a different path.—TRANS.

have done. Perhaps I can explain it to you thus: Tramachus was dearer to Elea and to me than life itself, for he was the only man we had. And *that* is the reason, because of our love for him, that we rejoiced when he was chosen for the ritual sacrifice. For it was Tramachus's greatest *wish*. And what greater joy could a poor widow hope for than to grant her only son's greatest wish?" She stopped, exultant. When she spoke again, her voice was soft, tender, almost musical, as if she were lulling a baby to sleep. "When the time came, we loved him more than ever. I swear, Heracles, I've never felt as close to him as when I sank my fingers into his chest. It was as beautiful and mysterious as giving birth." And she added, as if, having confided a most intimate secret, she had now decided to continue with a normal conversation. "I know you can't understand, because this is something that reason cannot comprehend. You have to feel it, Heracles, just as Elea and I do. You have to make an effort to feel it." She sounded suddenly as if she were begging. "Stop thinking for one moment and give yourself up to the *feeling*!"

"Which one?" asked Heracles. "The one you get from that potion you all drink?"

Itys smiled.

"*Kyon,* yes. I see you know everything. Actually, I never doubted your deductive powers. I knew you would find us out eventually. We do indeed drink *kyon,* but it's not a magic potion: It simply makes us become our true selves. We stop reasoning and become bodies that enjoy and feel. Bodies to which it makes no difference if they're killed or mutilated, that offer themselves for sacrifice with childlike joy."

He was falling. He was vaguely aware of falling.

The descent could not have been more perilous: His body willfully maintained a vertical trajectory, while the rock-strewn slope of the *barathrum*—the precipice near the Acropolis where prisoners condemned to death were thrown—was at an angle similar to the sides of a krater. Very soon, his body and the rocks would meet. It would happen *now,* as he was thinking it. He would smash into them and roll, and smash into them again. His hands would be of no use—they were tied behind his back. Perhaps he would crash against the rocks many times before reaching the cadaverously pale stones at the bottom. But what did it all matter as long as he experienced the *sacrifice*? A good friend, Triptemes, servant of the Eleven and cult member like himself, had brought him some *kyon* in prison, as agreed, and the sacred drink brought comfort to him now. He was the *sacrifice* and he would die for his brothers. He was the victim of the holocaust, one of the oxen of the hecatomb. He could see it: his life spilling over the ground, and, in appropriate symmetry, the brotherhood, the secret fraternity of free men and women to which he belonged, spreading throughout Hellas and welcoming new followers. He smiled joyfully at the thought!

The first impact snapped his right arm like a lily stem and crushed half of his face.

He went on falling.

When he reached the bottom, his small breasts were crushed against the rocks, the beautiful smile froze, the pretty blond hair was scattered like treasure, and the lovely little body resembled a broken doll.[10]

"Why don't you join us, Heracles?" There was barely concealed eagerness in Itys's voice. "You can't imagine the joy that liberating your instincts brings! It's an end to worry, fear, suffering. You become a god."

She stopped, then added more gently, "We could—who knows—start over, you and I."

Heracles said nothing. He stared at them all, one by one. There were six of them: two old slaves (perhaps one was Iphimachus), two young slave women, and Itys and Elea. He was reassured to see that the boy was not among them. He stopped at the pale face of Itys's

10. This is grotesque—as he dies, the repulsive Menaechmus turns into the girl with the lily. I find this cruel game with the eidetic images highly disturbing. —TRANS.

daughter and said, "You suffered greatly, didn't you, Elea? Unlike your mother's grief, your cries were sincere."

The girl did not reply. Her face, like Itys's, was expressionless. He now saw the strong resemblance between them. He went on, imperturbable: "No, you weren't pretending. Your pain was *real.* Once the drug had worn off, you remembered, didn't you? And you couldn't endure it."

The girl made as if to answer, but Itys intervened.

"Elea is very young. There are things she finds hard to understand. But she's happy now."

He looked at them both, mother and daughter. Their faces were white walls, empty of emotion, intelligence. He looked around: The slaves' faces were the same. It would be futile for him to try to break through the blank adobe of fixed stares. Such is religious faith, he said to himself. As with the simple-minded, anxiety or doubt is wiped from your face. He cleared his throat and asked, "Why did it have to be Tramachus?"

"It was his turn," said Itys. "One day, it will be mine, and Elea's."

"And the Attic peasants'," said Heracles.

For a moment, Itys looked like a mother patiently explaining something to a small child.

"Our victims are always willing, Heracles. We offer the peasants *kyon,* and they can agree to drink it or not. But most accept." And she added, with a faint smile, "One cannot be happy if one is ruled by thoughts alone."

Heracles retorted, "But remember, Itys, I would have been an unwilling victim."

"You found us out, and we couldn't allow it. The brotherhood must remain secret. Didn't you all do the same to my husband when you thought men like him threatened your wonderful democracy? But we want to give you one last chance. Join us, Heracles." And she added suddenly, as if pleading, "Be happy for once in your life!"

The Decipherer breathed deeply. He assumed that everything had been said, and that they now expected an answer. So he began, firmly and quietly: "I don't want to be dismembered. That's not my way of finding happiness. I'll tell you, Itys, what I intend to do, and you can tell your leader, whoever that might be. I'm going to bring you before the archon. All of you. I'm going to see that justice is done. You're an illegal sect. You've murdered a number of Athenian citizens, and numerous Attic peasants who don't share your ridiculous beliefs. You will be sentenced, and tortured to death. That will make me happy."

Once more, he looked around at the stony faces staring at him. He stopped at Itys's dark gaze and added, "After all, as you said yourself, it's a question of personal responsibility, isn't it?"

After a silence, she said, "Do you think the prospect of death or torture frightens us? You've understood nothing, Heracles. We've found a kind of happiness that goes beyond reason. What do we care about your threats? If necessary, we'll die smiling, and you'll never understand why."

Heracles had his back to the door of the cenacle. Suddenly, a new voice—thick and powerful, but with a hint of mockery, as if it didn't take itself seriously—came from the doorway.

"We've been found out! The archon has received a papyrus revealing everything about us, and your name is mentioned in it, Itys. Our good friend here took precautions before he came to see you."

Heracles turned and saw the deformed head of a dog. The dog was in the arms of a huge man.

"You asked a moment ago about our leader, didn't you, Heracles?" said Itys.

Just then, Heracles felt a sharp blow to his head.[11]

11. He's standing in front of me as I write this note. The truth is, I don't care; I've become almost used to his presence.

He came in, as usual, just as I was finishing the chapter and was about to rest. When I heard the door, I wondered what mask he would be wearing this time. But he wasn't wearing one. I recognized him immediately, of course, because his face is well known to those in the profession: white hair swept back and falling to his shoulders, deeply lined face, sparse beard.

"As you see, I want to be honest with you," said Montalo. "You were right, up to a point, so I'm not going to keep my identity from you any longer. I did indeed fake my own death and come here to hide, but I followed the trail of my book. I wanted to know who would be translating it. Once I'd found you, I kept an eye on you and then, at last, brought you here. It's also true that I pretended to threaten you so that you wouldn't lose interest in the novel—when I repeated Yasintra's words and gestures, for instance. It's all true. But you're wrong if you think I wrote *The Athenian Murders.*"

"Is that what you call being honest?" I asked.

He breathed deeply.

"I swear I'm not lying," he said. "Why would I kidnap you and get you to translate my own work?"

"Because you needed a reader," I answered calmly. "What is an author without a reader?"

Montalo seemed amused by my theory. He said, "Am I such a bad writer that I have to kidnap someone before they'll read my work?"

"No. But what is reading?" I replied. "An unseen activity. My father was a writer and he knew that when you write, you create images that will be illuminated by the eyes of others and take on forms that their creator could never have imagined. But you needed to know what the reader was thinking *day by day,* because you wanted this novel to prove the existence of ideas!"

Montalo smiled, nervously affable.

"It's true. For many years, I wanted to prove that Plato was right when he claimed that ideas existed," he admitted, "and that the world was therefore good, reasonable, and just. And I thought eidetic novels would provide that proof. I never succeeded, nor was I ever hugely disappointed . . . until I found the manuscript of *The Athenian Murders,* forgotten on the shelves of an old library. . . ." He paused, and his gaze became lost in the darkness of my cell. "I was terribly excited about it at first. Like you, I identified the subtle thread of images running through it—the labors of Hercules, the girl with the lily. . . . I became more and more convinced that at last I'd found the book I'd been searching for all my life!"

He turned his eyes to me, and I saw his deep desperation.

"But then I started to sense something strange. I found the image of the 'Translator' confusing. I wanted to believe that, like any novice, I'd taken the 'bait' and was allowing myself be swept along by the text. But as I read on, my mind was brimming with suspicions. No, it wasn't simply 'bait'; there was something else. And when I got to the last chapter, *I found out what it was.*"

He paused. He was terrifyingly pale, as if he had died the day before. He went on: "I suddenly discovered the key. And I understood that *The Athenian Murders* wasn't proof of the existence of Plato's good, reasonable, and just world, but of the *exact opposite.*" He suddenly exploded: "Yes, though you may not believe me, this novel proves that our universe, this ordered, luminous space full of causes and effects and governed by just, kind laws, *doesn't exist*!"

He was breathless, and his face had become a mask with trembling lips and a faraway look. I thought (and I don't care if Montalo reads this), He's completely insane. He appeared to recover his composure and added gravely, "Such was my horror at this discovery that I wanted to *die.* I shut myself away. I stopped working and refused to see anyone. There were rumors that I'd gone mad. And maybe I had—sometimes the truth can make you lose your mind! I even considered destroying the novel, but what would I gain by that, if I already *knew the work*? So I opted for something in between. As you suspected, I faked my death, appropriating the idea of the body ripped apart by wolves. I dressed the corpse of a poor old man in my clothes and disfigured him. Then I created my own version of *The Athenian Murders,* preserving the original text but emphasizing the eidesis, while not mentioning it explicitly."

"Why?" I asked.

He stared at me for a moment as if about to strike me.

"Because I wanted to see if a future reader would make the same discovery I had, without *my help*! Because there is still the hope, however faint, that I might be *wrong*!" His eyes grew moist as he added, "And if I am, and I pray that I am, the world—our world—will have been *saved.*"

I tried to smile, remembering that madmen should be treated gently.

"Please, Montalo, that's enough," I said. "The novel is a bit strange, admittedly, but it has nothing to do with the existence of the world, or the universe, or even us. It's just a book. However eidetic, and however obsessed with it we might both have become, we mustn't get carried away. I've read almost all of it and—"

"You still haven't read the final chapter," he said.

"No. But I've read almost all of it, and I don't—"

"You still haven't read the final chapter," he repeated.

I swallowed and looked at the book lying open on the desk, then back at Montalo.

"Fine," I said, "this is what we'll do: I'll finish the translation and I'll prove to you that . . . that it's just a fantasy, not too badly written, but—"

"Translate," he said.

I didn't want to make him angry, so I obeyed. He's still here, watching me. I'm now starting the final chapter.—TRANS.

THE CAVE, at first, was a gleam of gold hanging somewhere in the darkness. It became pure pain. It turned back into the gleam of gold. It went ceaselessly from one to the other. Then there were shapes—a brazier of hot coals that was, strangely, as pliable as water and contained irons resembling bodies of frightened snakes. And a yellow patch, a man whose outline was stretched at one end and shortened at the other, as if hanging by invisible ropes. And yes, there were noises, too: a faint metallic ring and, from time to time, the piercing torment of a dog barking. A wide variety of damp smells. And once again, everything closed up like a papyrus scroll and the pain returned. End of story.

He wasn't sure how many more similar stories unfolded before his mind began to understand. Just as a hanging object, when struck, swings violently and irregularly at first, then evenly, then terminally slowly, reverting gradually to its former stillness, the furious spinning stopped. His consciousness planed over a point of repose before managing at last to remain linear and motionless, in harmony with the surrounding reality. Now he could distinguish between what was his—the pain—and what was not—the images, noises, smells. Dismissing these, he focused on the pain, and wondered what was hurting—head, arms?—and why. He could only find out why by resorting to memory, so he tried to remember. Ah yes, I was at Itys's house when she said, "Pleasure." But no, afterward—

Just then, a moan issued from his mouth and his hands twisted.

"Oh, I was afraid we'd gone too far."

"Where am I?" asked Heracles, when what he really wanted to ask was, Who are you? But the man's response answered both questions.

"This is our meeting place," he said. And as he spoke, he motioned expansively with his muscular right arm, displaying a wrist ridged with scars.

Just as children playing at shaking rain-soaked trees are showered with the dense load of droplets hanging from the branches, the icy realization of what had happened fell upon Heracles.

It was a large cave. The golden gleam was a torch hanging from a hook fixed to the rock. It lighted a sinuous central corridor running between two walls; the torch hung on one; and Heracles, arms raised above his head, was bound by thick serpentine ropes to golden nails hammered into the other. To his left, the corridor formed a bend, which appeared to have a light of its own, though dimmer than the golden torchlight. The Decipherer deduced that it led to the cave entrance and that the greater part of the day must have elapsed. To his right, the corridor disappeared between sheer rock walls into complete darkness. In front of him stood a brazier with a poker protruding from its glowing bloodred embers. In the brazier, a bowl of golden liquid bubbled noisily. Cerberus was circling, barking equally at the brazier and Heracles' motionless body. Wrapped in a shabby gray cloak, his master was stirring the liquid in the bowl with a twig. He looked endearingly proud, like a cook admiring the push of a golden apple pie.[1]

1. "Apples," I complained. "How vulgar to mention them!"

"True," admitted Montalo. "It is in rather bad taste to specify the subject of the eidesis in a metaphor. The two most frequently repeated words, *hanging* and *golden,* should have been enough here."

"To evoke the apples of the Hesperides, which were made of gold and hung from trees," I said, "I know. That's why I think it's a vulgar metaphor. And I'm not sure that apple pies push—"

"Shut up and keep on translating."—TRANS.

Other objects that might have been of interest lay beyond the brazier, but Heracles couldn't see what they were.

Humming a tune, Crantor stopped stirring for a moment. He took a golden ladle that hung from the brazier, scooped up some of the liquid, and held it to his nose. The sinuous column of steam that enveloped his face seemed to issue from his own mouth.

"Hm. A little hot, but . . . Here. It'll make you feel better."

He held it to Heracles' lips, unleashing Cerberus's fury, for the dog seemed outraged that his master should offer something to the fat man before him. Reflecting that he had little choice and was thirsty anyway, Heracles took a sip. It tasted sickly sweet, with a hint of spiciness. Crantor tilted the ladle and most of the contents spilled down Heracles' beard and tunic.

"Come on, drink."

Heracles drank.[2]

"It's *kyon,* isn't it?" he said afterward, gasping.

Crantor nodded and returned to the brazier.

"It'll take effect soon. You'll feel it."

"My arms are as cold as snakes," complained Heracles. "Untie me."

"Once the *kyon* is working, you'll be able to free yourself. We possess incredible hidden strength, which our reason stops us using."

"What's happened to me?"

"I'm afraid we beat you and brought you here in a cart. By the way, some of us found it extremely difficult to get out of the city, because the soldiers had already been alerted by the archon." He raised his black gaze from the bowl and directed it at Heracles. "You've hurt us quite badly."

"You like being hurt," retorted the Decipherer contemptuously. "I take it you've all fled?"

2. "Can I have a drink?" I've just asked Montalo.

"Wait. I'll bring you some water. I'm thirsty, too. I'll be back in the time it takes you to write a note about this interruption, so don't for one second think you can escape."

The fact is, it hadn't occurred to me. He's kept his word: He's back now with a jug and two glasses.—TRANS.

"Oh yes, all of us. I've stayed behind to treat you to a *kyon* symposium and to have a little chat. The others have sought pastures new."

"Have you always been their leader?"

"I'm no one's leader." Crantor gently tapped the bowl with the twig, as if it had asked the question. "I'm an important sect member, that's all. I came forward when we found out that Tramachus's death was being investigated. We were surprised, because we didn't expect it to arouse suspicion. The fact that you were the principal investigator made my job trickier, if more pleasant. Actually, I agreed to deal with the matter *because I knew you.* My task consisted in trying to mislead you. To your credit, you made it very difficult."

He approached Heracles, holding the twig, like a schoolmaster swinging a cane to inspire respect in his pupils. He went on, "My problem was how to fool someone who notices *everything.* How to deceive a Decipherer of Enigmas like you, for whom the complexity of things holds no secrets. I came to the conclusion that your main advantage was also your biggest *fault.* You reason *everything* out, my friend. So I thought I would use this peculiarity of yours to distract you. I said to myself, If Heracles' mind can solve even the most complex problem, then why not stuff his mind full of them? If you'll excuse the vulgar expression."

Apparently amused by his own words, Crantor went back to stirring the liquid. He bent down occasionally to click his tongue at Cerberus, particularly when the shrill barking became more insistent than usual. The light from the bend in the corridor was growing ever dimmer.

"So I set out, quite simply, to make sure that *you never stopped reasoning.* It's easy to fool the mind by feeding it plenty of reasons—you all do it every day in the courts, at the Assembly, the Academy. The fact is, Heracles, I got a great deal of enjoyment out of it."

"And out of mutilating Euneos and Antisus."

The echoes of Crantor's noisy laughter seemed to hang from the walls of the cave and glow, golden, in the corners.

"You still don't understand, do you? I set you *false* puzzles! Euneos and Antisus weren't murdered—they just agreed to be sacrificed before their time. After all, their turn would have come sooner or later. All your investigation did was precipitate things."

"When did you recruit those poor boys?"

Crantor shook his head, smiling. "We never 'recruit' anyone, Heracles! People hear of our cult and want to know more. In this particular case, Tramachus's mother, Itys, found out about us at Eleusis shortly after her husband was executed. She attended secret meetings at the cave and in the forest, and took part in some of the first rituals that my companions held in Attica. Later on, as her children grew up, she made them followers of our faith. But, intelligent woman that she is, she knew she wouldn't want Tramachus to reproach her for not having given him the choice, so she didn't neglect his education. She encouraged him to attend Plato's school of philosophy and learn all that reason can teach, so that once he came of age, he could decide which path to follow. And Tramachus chose us. What's more, he got his friends Antisus and Euneos from the Academy to join in the rituals, too. They both came from ancient Athenian families, and it didn't take much to convince them. And Antisus knew Menaechmus, who, by happy coincidence, was also a member of our brotherhood. They found Menaechmus's 'teachings' much more useful than Plato's. They learned the pleasures of the body, the mystery of art, the enjoyment of ecstasy, the exaltation inspired by the gods."

Crantor did not look at Heracles as he spoke, keeping his gaze fixed on a vague point in the growing darkness. But now he turned suddenly toward the Decipherer and added, still smiling, "There was no jealousy between them! That was *your* idea! We happily used it to mislead you, making you suspect Menaechmus, who wanted to be sacrificed as soon as possible, as did Antisus and Euneos. It didn't take much to contrive a plan involving the three of them. Euneos stabbed himself in a most beautiful ritual at Menaechmus's workshop. Then we dressed him in a peplos slashed *in the wrong places,* so that you would think exactly as you did—that somebody had murdered him. Antisus did what he had to when his turn came. I did everything possible to make you think *they had been murdered,* don't you see? And, to that end, nothing better than making it *look* like suicides, which is what it really *was*. You would take care, later on, of *making up your own version* of the crime and catching the perpetrator." And, opening his arms, Crantor boomed, "Therein lies the weakness of your all-powerful reason, Heracles Pontor—it so easily imagines the problems that it believes it is solving!"

"And Eumarchus? Did he drink *kyon,* too?"

"Of course. The poor old slave was very keen to liberate his urges. He mutilated himself with his own hands. Incidentally, you suspected that we used a drug. Why?"

"I smelled it on Antisus's and Eumarchus's corpses and, later, on Ponsica's. And by the way, Crantor, could you clarify something? Was my slave a member of your sect before this all started?"

Despite the gloom, the look on Heracles' face must have been quite obvious, because Crantor raised his eyebrows and, looking into his eyes, replied, "Don't tell me you're surprised! Oh, by Zeus and Aphrodite, Heracles! Do you think it would have been hard to persuade her?"

There was even a little compassion in his voice. He moved closer to his enfeebled prisoner, adding, "My friend, for once in your life, try to see things as they are and not as your reason presents them to you! That poor girl, maimed as a child, then forced by you to endure the humiliation of that mask—do you think she needed anyone to unleash her *rage*? Heracles, Heracles! How long have you surrounded yourself with *masks* so that you don't have to see real, naked human beings?"

He paused and shrugged.

"In fact, Ponsica joined us soon after you bought her." He frowned and added with displeasure, "She should have killed you when I ordered her to. It would have saved us a lot of trouble."

"I assume using Yasintra was your idea, too."

"Yes. I thought of it when we heard you'd spoken to her. She doesn't belong to our sect, but we were keeping an eye on her. We threatened her when we found out that Tramachus had revealed some of our secrets, wishing to convert her to our faith. Getting her into your house was doubly useful: On one hand, it helped to distract and confuse you; on the other . . . Let's say it served an instructive purpose, proving to you in practice that physical pleasure, to which you believe yourself so indifferent, is more powerful than the will to live."

"By Athena, what a useful lesson," said Heracles sarcastically. "Tell me, Crantor, and make me laugh at least, is this how you spent your time away from Athens? Devising tricks to protect this sect of madmen?"

"I traveled for many years, as I told you," replied Crantor calmly. "But I returned to Greece much earlier than I said, and journeyed around Thrace and Macedonia, which is when I came into contact with the sect. It's known by different names, but the most common is Lykaion. I was so surprised to find such wild ideas on Greek soil that I immediately became a member. Cerberus . . . Cerberus, that's enough now. Stop barking. I assure you we're not madmen, Heracles. We don't do anyone any harm, unless our own safety is threatened. We perform rituals in the forest and drink *kyon*. We give ourselves up completely to an age-old force now known as Dionysus, but which isn't a god and cannot be represented in images or expressed in words. So what is it? We don't know ourselves! All we know is that it lies buried deep within men and causes rage, desire, pain, pleasure. Such is the power we worship, Heracles, and we sacrifice ourselves to it. Does that surprise you? Wars also demand sacrifices, yet no one is surprised. The difference is that we choose when, how, and why we sacrifice ourselves!"

He stirred the bowl of liquid vigorously and went on: "The brotherhood is Thracian in origin, but it now operates mainly in Macedonia. Did you know that Euripides, the celebrated poet, belonged to it in his final years?"

He glanced at Heracles, eyebrows raised, no doubt expecting him to show surprise, but the Decipherer gazed back impassively.

"Yes, Euripides himself! He came across our religion and embraced it. He drank *kyon* and was killed by other cult members. As you know, the legend goes that he was torn to pieces by dogs. But it's simply a symbolic way of describing a Lykaion sacrifice. And Heraclitus, the philosopher of Ephesus, who believed that violence and discord are not only necessary to man but desirable, was said to have been devoured by a pack of dogs. He, too, belonged to our sect!"

"Menaechmus mentioned both." Heracles nodded.

"Indeed, they were brothers of Lykaion."

Then as if some idea or related subject of conversation had come to him suddenly, Crantor added, "Euripides' was quite a strange case. All his life, he shied away, artistically and intellectually, from man's instinctive nature, writing insipid rationalist plays. In old age, during his voluntary exile to the court of King Archelaus of Macedonia, disillusioned with the hypocrisy of his Athenian homeland, he came across Lykaion. In those days, the brotherhood hadn't reached Attica, but it flourished in regions to the north. At Archelaus's court, Euripides witnessed the rites of Lykaion, and he was transformed. He wrote a play, a tragedy, quite unlike his previous work—*Bacchae,* in praise of fury, dance, and orgiastic pleasure. He intended it to repay his debt to primitive theater, which belongs to Dionysus. Poets still wonder how on earth the old master wrote such a thing at the end of his life. But they don't realize that it was his most heartfelt work!"[3]

"The drug makes you insane," said Heracles wearily. "Nobody in their right mind would want to be mutilated by others."

"So you think it's just the *kyon*?" Crantor gazed at the steaming liquid in the bowl. Tiny golden droplets hung from the rim. "I believe it's something we have inside us, all of us. The *kyon* enables us to feel it, certainly, but"—he tapped his chest—"it's here, Heracles. Inside you, too. It can't be translated into words. One can't philosophize about it. It's absurd, if you like, irrational, enraging . . . but *real.* That's the secret we're going to teach all men!"

He came closer to Heracles, and his face—a huge shadow—broke into a wide smile.

3. Montalo has just said, "Don't you think *Bacchae* could be an eidetic work? Blood, fury, madness—it's all there. Perhaps Euripides was describing a Lykaion ritual in eidesis."

"I can't believe Master Euripides went that insane!" I retorted.—TRANS.

"Anyway, you know I don't like discussions. We'll find out soon enough whether it's the *kyon,* won't we?"

Heracles tugged at the ropes tied to the golden nails. He felt stiff and weak, but he didn't think the drug had had any effect on him. He looked up at Crantor's craggy face and said, "You're wrong, Crantor. This isn't a secret that humanity wants to learn. I don't believe in prophecies or oracles, but if I were to predict one thing, I'd say that Athens will be the birthplace of a new kind of man. A man who fights with his eyes and mind, not his hands. A man who will translate the texts of his forebears, and learn from them."

Crantor listened with eyes wide, as if he were about to burst out laughing.

"The only violence I predict will be in the imagination," Heracles went on. "Both men and women will be able to read and write, and will form guilds of learned translators who will edit and decipher the works of our contemporaries. And, as they translate the writings left by others, they will find out about the world before the reign of reason. Neither you nor I will see it, Crantor, but man is advancing toward reason, not instinct."[4]

"No," said Crantor, smiling. "You're the one who's wrong."

With a strange look on his face, he seemed to be staring, not at Heracles but at somebody behind him, set into the rock, or perhaps beneath his feet, at invisible depths, though Heracles could not be sure in the growing darkness.

Crantor, in fact, was looking at you.[5]

He said, "These translators that you prophesy will discover nothing, because they won't exist, Heracles. Philosophy will never triumph over instinct." Raising his voice, he went on: "Heracles appears to defeat the monsters, but between the lines, in texts, in fine speeches, in logical reasoning, in the thoughts of men, *the Hydra raises its multiple*

4. Heracles' predictions have come true! Perhaps this is the key to the novel! Montalo stares at me in silence. "Carry on translating," he says.—TRANS.

5. "Strange," I note. "A change to the second person again."

"Carry on translating!" my kidnapper orders anxiously, as if we have come to a crucial point in the text.—TRANS.

heads, the terrifying lion roars, and the bronze hooves of the flesh-eating mares thunder. Human nature is not[6]

"Human nature is not a text to which a translator can find a final key, Heracles, or even a set of invisible ideas. So defeating the monsters is futile, for they lurk *within you.* The *kyon* will awaken them soon. Can you feel them shifting in your entrails yet?"

Heracles was about to make a sarcastic reply, when he heard a groan in the darkness beyond the brazier, coming from one of the

6. "What's the matter?" Montalo asks.
"These words of Crantor's . . ." I'm trembling.
"What about them?"
"My father . . . I remember . . ."
"Yes!" Montalo urges me on. "Yes! Your father, what?"
"He wrote a poem a long time ago."
Montalo urges me on again. I try to remember.
This is the first stanza of my father's poem, as I remember it:

> The Hydra raises its many heads,
> The terrifying lion roars, and the bronze hooves
> Of the flesh-eating mares thunder.

"It's the opening of one of my father's poems!" I declare, astounded. Montalo looks sad for a moment. He nods and murmurs, "I know the rest."

> The theories and ideas of men sometimes
> Seem like the exploits of Hercules,
> In a perpetual struggle with creatures
> That oppose his noble reason.
>
> But I sometimes picture my poor soul
> As a translator locked up by a madman,
> Forced to decipher an absurd text,
> Struggling to find meaning.
>
> And you, final Truth, Platonic Idea
> —In your beauty and fragility
> So like a lily in the hands of a young girl—
> How you cry for help once you realize
> That your own nonbeing will bury you!

vague shapes at the foot of the wall opposite. Although he couldn't see who it was, he recognized the voice immediately.

"Diagoras!" he said. "What have you done to him?"

"Nothing he hasn't done to himself," replied Crantor. "He drank *kyon,* and I assure you we were all surprised at how quickly it took effect!"

He raised his voice and added mockingly, "Oh, our noble Platonist philosopher! The great idealist! What rage against himself he had inside, by Zeus!"

Cerberus—a pale shape circling Crantor—provided a furious accompaniment to his master's words. His barks formed chains of echoes. Crantor bent down and stroked him affectionately.

"No, no. Calm down, Cerberus. It's all right."

Meanwhile, Heracles tugged sharply at the rope tied to one of the

---

Oh Hercules, how futile are your exploits,
For I know men who love monsters,
Who give themselves up with delight to the sacrifice,
Making of the bites their religion!

The bull roars amidst the blood,
The hound barks and spews flames,
The serpent still eagerly watches
Over the golden apples in the garden.

I've written out the whole poem. I'm rereading it. I remember it.

"It's one of my father's poems!"

Montalo looks down. What will he say? He says, "It's a poem by Philotextus of Chersonnese. Do you remember him?"

"The writer who appears in chapter seven, at the dinner with the tutors at the Academy?"

"That's right. Philotextus used his own poem as inspiration for the eidetic images contained in *The Athenian Murders*: the labors of Hercules, the girl with the lily, the Translator."

"But then—"

Montalo nods, his face inscrutable.

"Yes. *The Athenian Murders* was written by Philotextus of Chersonnese," he says. "Don't ask me how I know; the fact is, I just do. But please continue with your translation. There's still a little more before the end."—TRANS.

gold nails. It gave slightly. Encouraged, he pulled again and, soundlessly, the nail came out of the wall. Crantor was still attending to his dog. Heracles had to be quick now. But when he tried to move his free hand, he found that the fingers wouldn't obey him; they were frozen, filled from root to tip with an army of tiny snakes that had multiplied beneath the skin. So he pulled as hard as he could at the other gold nail.

As it gave way, Crantor turned around.

Heracles Pontor was a short, fat man. In addition, his aching arms now hung useless at his sides, like broken tools. He realized immediately that his only hope lay in using one of the nearby objects as a weapon. His eyes selected the poker protruding from the embers. But it was too far away, and Crantor, now bearing down upon him furiously, would block his path. So, in a heartbeat, or the blink of an eye, during which time stopped and thought ceased, the Decipherer realized, without even looking to check, that the golden nails were still hanging from the ropes tied to his wrists. When Crantor's shadow grew so large that it engulfed Heracles' entire body, he swiftly raised his right arm and described a quick violent semicircle in the air.

Perhaps Crantor expected the blow to come from Heracles' fist, for when he saw it pass without hitting him, he did not dodge and so received the nail full in the face. Heracles wasn't sure exactly where he'd struck, but he heard the pain. He lunged, eyes fixed on the poker, but a sharp kick to his chest winded him. He collapsed on his side and rolled like a ripe fruit that had fallen from a tree.

During the torment that followed, he recalled how he had competed in the pancratium in his youth. He even remembered the names of some of his opponents. Scenes, images of triumph and defeat, filled his memory. But his thoughts fragmented. Sentences lost coherence. They became loose words.

Cowering and shielding his head, he endured his punishment. When the rocks that were Crantor's feet ceased kicking him, he breathed in and smelled blood. The blows had swept him like a flabby piece of rubbish against one of the walls. Crantor was speaking, but Heracles couldn't make out what he was saying—a savage, terrifying child was shouting foreign words in his ear, dribbling sickening, bitter saliva over his face. He recognized Cerberus. He turned his head and half-opened his eyes. The dog, right beside his face, was a loud, wrinkled mask with empty sockets. He seemed like a ghost of himself. Beyond, across an infinite expanse of pain, Crantor stood with his back to him. Was he saying something? Heracles couldn't be sure, for Cerberus was a barrier of noise between him and all other sounds. Why was Crantor no longer kicking him? Why wasn't he finishing him off?

He thought of something. It wasn't a good plan, but by then, nothing was good. He grabbed the dog's puny body with both hands. Unused to being handled by strangers, it struggled, like a baby who appeared to consist predominantly of two rows of very sharp teeth. Heracles held his frantic prey well away as he lifted it. Crantor must have heard the change of tone in the dog's barking, for he turned and started shouting.

For a moment, Heracles allowed himself to recall that he hadn't been a bad discuss thrower.

Like a soft bundle tossed playfully by a child, Cerberus crashed into the brazier, knocking it and the bowl over. When the embers, spread over the ground like the slow juice from a volcano, came into contact with the animal's coat, the barking again changed. Smeared with flames, the dog rolled across the floor. Heracles hadn't thrown it very hard, but the added momentum came from the movements of the animal itself—it was a furious whirl of embers. Its howls, surrounded by echoes, pierced Heracles' ears like golden needles. As he had guessed, Crantor hesitated only a moment between attacking him again and rescuing the dog, and decided immediately to rescue the dog.

Bowl, brazier, poker—three distinct objects—scattered randomly on the ground. Heracles flopped painfully and obesely toward the poker. The unpredictable goddesses of luck had not cast it too far away.

"Cerberus!" shouted Crantor, crouching beside the dog. He was patting the little body, wiping away the ash. "Cerberus, it's all right. Let me—"

Heracles thought that a single blow, with the poker clasped in both hands, would be enough, but he underestimated the huge man's resilience. Crantor raised his hand to his head and tried to turn. Heracles struck him again. This time, Crantor fell on his back. But Heracles fell, too, collapsing on top of him, exhausted.

"Fat, Heracles," he heard Crantor gasp. "You should do . . . more exercise."

Heracles sat up slowly and painfully. His arms felt like heavy bronze shields. He leaned on the poker.

"Fat and weak." Crantor smiled from the floor.

The Decipherer managed to sit astride Crantor. They were both panting, as if they had just run an Olympic race. A dark, wet snake emerged from Crantor's head. It grew from a hatchling to a viper, then to a python, slithering over the ground. Crantor smiled again.

"Can you . . . feel the *kyon* yet?" he asked.

"No," said Heracles.

That's why he didn't kill me, Heracles thought. He was waiting for the drug to take effect on me.

"Strike me," murmured Crantor.

"No," said Heracles again. He struggled to his feet.

The snake now dwarfed the head that had engendered it. But it had lost its original form and now resembled a tree.[7]

"I'm going to tell you . . . a secret," said Crantor. "Nobody knows. Only a few . . . brothers. *Kyon* is . . . nothing but . . . water, honey, and"—he paused and licked his lips—"a little aromatic wine." His smile widened. Blood ran from the wound on his left cheek, caused by the nail. He added, "So what do you think, Heracles? The *kyon* is . . . *nothing*."

Heracles leaned against the wall. He said nothing, listening to Crantor's breathless whispers.

"They all believe that . . . it's a drug . . . so when they drink it,

7. "Snake" and "tree"—the blood pouring from Crantor's head becomes a beautiful eidetic image, evoking both the monster that guards the golden apples and the trees from which they hang. The thought that my father might have plagiarized a poem by Philotextus is still tormenting me! Montalo says, "Translate."—TRANS.

they're transformed. They become enraged. They lose their minds . . . and do . . . what we expect them to, as if they really had taken a drug. All except for you. Why?"

Because I only believe in what I can see, thought Heracles. But, too weak to speak, he didn't reply.

"Kill me," said Crantor.

"No."

"Cerberus, then. Please—I don't want him to suffer."

"No," said Heracles again.

He dragged himself to the other wall, where Diagoras lay. The philosopher's face was covered in bruises and he had a deep gash on his forehead, but he was alive. And his eyes were open and alert.

"Come on," said Heracles.

Diagoras didn't seem to recognize him, but he allowed himself to be guided by Heracles. They stumbled out of the cave into the night, and the sound of Crantor's dog barking in pain was buried at last.

The moon, round and golden, was hanging in the black sky when the patrol found them. A little earlier, leaning on Heracles for support, Diagoras had begun talking.

"They forced me to drink their concoction. I don't remember much after that, but it was as they predicted. It was—how can I describe it? I lost all control, Heracles. I felt a monster writhe inside me—a huge, raging serpent." He went on, panting, with reddened eyes, recalling his madness: "I started shouting and laughing. I cursed the gods. I think I even insulted Master Plato!"

"What did you say?"

After a pause, Diagoras replied with obvious effort, " 'Get away from me, satyr.' " He turned to Heracles, deeply unhappy. "Why did I call him a 'satyr'? How awful!"

The Decipherer said comfortingly that he should blame it all on the potion. Diagoras agreed, adding, "After that, I started dashing my head against the wall, until I lost consciousness."

Heracles thought of what Crantor had said about the *kyon*. Had he been lying? It was quite likely. But then, why had it had no effect on him? On the other hand, if the *kyon* really was no more than water, honey, and a little wine, why did it provoke such startling bouts of madness? Why had it made Eumarchus kill himself? Why had it affected Diagoras? And something else was troubling him: Should he tell the philosopher what Crantor had revealed?

He decided to remain silent.

They ran into the soldiers on the Sacred Way. Heracles saw the torches and called out. The captain knew of the situation, thanks to the scroll that Heracles had had delivered to the archon. He asked if they knew where the cult members might be, for their only known meeting place—the house of the widow Itys—had been vacated by its occupants with suspicious speed. Heracles did not squander words, for at that moment, with exhaustion hanging from his body like a hoplite's armor, they seemed like gold. He requested that some of the soldiers escort Diagoras back to the city, where he could be seen by a doctor, and offered to lead the captain and the rest of his men to the cave. Confused and exhausted, Diagoras protested weakly, but then he agreed. In the torchlight, the Decipherer soon found the path back to the cave.

Near the cave, which was in a forest near Lycabettus, one of the soldiers discovered a group of horses tethered to trees and a large cart full of cloaks and provisions. The cult members could not be far away, so the captain ordered his men to unsheathe their swords and approach the cave entrance with caution. Heracles had explained what had happened and told them what to expect, so it came as no surprise when they found Crantor's body, lying mute and motionless in a pool of blood, just as the Decipherer had described. Cerberus was a shriveled creature, whimpering quietly by his master's feet.

Heracles didn't wish to know whether Crantor was still alive, so he stayed back while the others approached the body. The dog growled at them menacingly. The soldiers burst out laughing, relieved at the unexpected greeting, for the combination of rumors about the sect and their own imaginings had terrified them. The ridiculous presence of the deformed little animal eased the tension. They taunted the dog for a while, feigning to strike it, until the captain dryly ordered them to stop. So they slit its throat without more ado, just as they had done to Crantor. Crantor's death had given rise to an amusing anecdote, which was to be repeated often among the regiment: While his companions were busy with the dog, one of the soldiers went to Crantor and held a sword to his thick neck. Another soldier asked, "Is he alive?"

And, as he slit Crantor's throat, the first soldier replied, "No."

The others followed the captain into the depths of the cave. Heracles went with them. The corridor opened out into a large chamber. The Decipherer had to admit that, with its narrow entrance, it was an ideal place for forbidden worship. And it had obviously been used recently: Clay masks and black cloaks were strewn about, together with weapons and a large supply of torches. Strangely, there were no statues of gods, no mounds of stones, no religious symbols of any kind. This didn't attract his attention at the time, for something else drew all gazes. It was found by a soldier in the vanguard, who alerted the captain with a shout. The patrol came to a halt.

They looked like lumps of meat hanging in the Agora, intended for the banquet of an insatiable Croesus. In the torchlight, they appeared bathed in gold. There were at least a dozen—naked men and women hanging by their ankles on hooks in the rock walls. Their bellies were slit open and their entrails hung out like mocking tongues or tangles of dead snakes. Beneath each body, there was a lumpy heap of clothing, and blood, and a short sword.[8]

"They've had their entrails torn out!" a young soldier exclaimed, and the echo repeated his words with increasing horror.

"They did it to themselves," somebody behind him said in measured tones. "The wounds run from side to side, not top to bottom, which would indicate that they cut open their bellies while hanging upside down."

Wondering who had spoken, the soldier turned and saw in the wa-

8. The macabre sight of the cult members' bodies mirrors, eidetically, the tree of the apples of the Hesperides, hanging "bathed in gold," as a final image.—TRANS.

vering torchlight the fat, weary figure of the man who had led them there. Who was he exactly? A philosopher perhaps? As if attaching little importance to his own reasoning, the man now walked over to the mutilated bodies.

"How could they?" murmured another soldier.

"A bunch of madmen," said the captain, settling the matter.

The fat man—a philosopher?—spoke again. Though he whispered, they all heard him clearly.

"Why?"

He stood beside one of the corpses—a woman of mature years, but still handsome, her intestines spilling over her chest like the folds of a peplos. The man, whose head was level with hers (he could have kissed her on the lips, had such an aberrant thought crossed his mind), appeared deeply distressed, so nobody wished to disturb him. While they began the unpleasant task of taking down the bodies, several of the soldiers heard him muttering in increasing desperation, still beside the corpse: "Why? Why? Why?"

Then, the Translator said,[9]

9. "The text is incomplete!"

"Why do you think that?" asks Montalo.

"Because it ends with the sentence 'Then, the Translator said.' "

"No," says Montalo. He looks at me strangely. "The text is complete."

"Do you mean there are pages hidden somewhere?"

"Yes."

"Where?"

"Here," he answers, shrugging.

My bewilderment seems to amuse him. He asks abruptly, "Have you found the key?"

I think a moment and stammer, "Is it the poem?"

"And what does the poem mean?"

After a pause, I reply, "That the truth can't be rationalized. . . . Or that the truth is hard to find."

Montalo looks disappointed.

"We already know it's difficult to find the truth," he says. "That conclusion *can't* be the truth . . . because, in that case, the truth would be *nothing*. And there has to be *something,* doesn't there? Tell me, what's the final idea, the key to the text?"

"I don't know!" I shout.

He smiles bitterly.

"Could your own anger be the key?" he asks. "Maybe the rage that you feel at me, or the pleasure you experienced as you imagined yourself lying with the hetaera, or the hunger you endured when I was late with your food, or the sluggishness of your bowels. Maybe they were the only keys. Why look for them in the text? They're in our own bodies!"

"Stop playing with me!" I shout back. "I want to know what the link is between this novel and my father's poem!"

Montalo's face becomes serious and he says wearily, as if reading from a text, "As I told you, the poem is by Philotextus of Chersonnese, a Thracian writer who lived in Athens in his later years and who visited Plato's Academy. Using his own poem as a basis, Philotextus created the eidetic images of *The Athenian Murders.* Both works were inspired by real events that took place in Athens at that time—in particular, the collective suicide of the members of a cult very similar to the one described here. It had a profound effect on him. He considered such things proof that Plato was wrong—we don't choose the bad out of ignorance, but on impulse, because of something unknown that lies within all of us and which cannot be reasoned away or explained in words."

"But history has proved Plato right!" I cry. "Men in our time are idealists, devoting themselves to thinking and reading and deciphering texts. Many of us are philosophers or translators. We firmly believe in the existence of ideas that we can't perceive with our senses. The best of us govern cities. Men and women are equals. The world is at peace. Violence has been completely eradicated and—"

The look on Montalo's face is making me nervous. I interrupt my emotional speech and ask, "What's the matter?"

Sighing deeply, with moist, reddened eyes, he replies, "That's one of the things Philotextus set out to prove with his novel: The world you describe—the world in which we live, our world—*doesn't exist.* And will probably never exist." And he adds gloomily, "The only world that exists is the world of the novel you've translated: Athens after the war, a city full of madness, ecstasy, and irrational monsters. That is the *real* world, not ours. That's why I said *The Athenian Murders* influenced the existence of the universe."

I stare at him. He seems to mean it, though he's smiling.

"Now I really do think you're completely insane!" I say.

"No, son. Try to remember."

And he smiles kindly now, as if we share the same misfortune. He says, "Do you remember, in chapter seven, the bet between Philotextus and Plato?"

"Yes. Plato claims that a book containing the five elements of knowledge can never be written. But Philotextus isn't so sure."

"That's right. Well, *The Athenian Murders* is the result of the bet. Philotextus thought the task a difficult one—how to create a work that included the five Platonic elements of knowledge. The first two would be easy: The 'name' is simply the name of things, and the 'definition' the sentences relating to those things. Any normal text contains both these elements. But the third, the 'image,' was more of a problem—how to create 'images' that would be more than mere 'definitions,' forms of beings and things beyond written words. So Philotextus invented 'eidesis.' "

"What do you mean, 'invented'?" I ask incredulously.

Montalo nods gravely.

"Philotextus invented 'eidesis.' It was a way of making his images fluent, independent—not linked to the text, but to the reader's imagination. One chapter, for instance, might contain the figure of a lion, or a girl with a lily!"

This is all so preposterous that I have to smile.

"You know as well as I do," I say, "that eidesis is a literary device used by a number of Greek writers."

"No!" interjects Montalo impatiently. "It's an invention and it appears nowhere but in this novel! Let me go on, and you'll understand. The third element, then, was dealt with. But the trickiest ones remained: how to achieve the fourth, 'intelligence or knowledge of the thing.' Obviously, a voice *outside* the text was needed, a voice that would 'discuss' the text as it progressed, a character watching the plot develop from a distance. But this character couldn't be alone, since a 'dialogue' was required. So it was essential to have at least two characters *outside* the work. But who could they be, and how could they be introduced to the reader?"

Montalo pauses and raises his eyebrows, amused. He continues: "Philotextus found the solution in his own poem, in the stanza about the translator 'locked up by a madman.' Adding several fictitious translators was the best way of providing that

---

fourth element. One of them would 'translate' the novel, commenting on it in footnotes, and the others would have some sort of relationship with him. This trick enabled our writer to introduce the fourth element. But there remained the fifth and most difficult: the 'idea itself'!"

Montalo pauses briefly and gives a little laugh. He goes on: "The 'idea itself' is the key we've been looking for from the start. Philotextus *doesn't believe* it exists, so that's why we haven't found it. It is there, though, in our search, our desire to find it." His smile widens and he concludes: "So Philotextus has won the bet."

When Montalo finishes, I mutter in disbelief, "You're quite insane."

Montalo's inexpressive face is turning increasingly pale.

"I am indeed," he agrees. "But I now know why I played with you and then kidnapped you and locked you up in here. In fact, I realized it when you told me the poem the novel is based on was by your father. Because I'm sure too that *my father wrote it*. He was a writer, like yours."

I don't know what to say. Montalo goes on, increasingly anxious: "We're part of the images of the novel, don't you see? I'm the *madman* who's locked you up, as it says in the poem, and you're the *translator.* And our father, the man who engendered both you and me, and all the characters in *The Athenian Murders,* is called Philotextus of Chersonnese."

A shiver runs down my spine. I look around at the dark cell, the table covered in scrolls, the lamp, and Montalo's pale face. I murmur, "It's a lie. I . . . I have a life of *my own*. I have friends! I know a woman called Helena. I'm not a character in a novel. I'm alive!"

Suddenly his face becomes distorted by rage.

"Fool! You still don't understand, do you? Helena, Elio, you, me—we all make up the *fourth element*!"

Stunned, furious, I pounce on Montalo. I try to strike him and escape, but all I manage to do is tear off his face. His face is another mask. But behind it, there's nothing, darkness. His clothes fall, limp, to the floor. The table at which I've been working disappears. So do the bed and the chair. The walls of the cell vanish. I'm plunged in darkness.

"Why? Why? Why?" I ask.

The space allocated to my words shrinks. I become as marginal as my footnotes.

The author decides to end me here.

TREMBLING, I raise my quill from the papyrus, having written the final words of my novel. I can't imagine what Plato—waiting for me to finish as eagerly as I—will think. As he reads, perhaps his radiant countenance will relax at times into a fine smile. At others, I am certain, he will frown. He might say (and I can hear his measured voice): "A strange work, Philotextus, particularly the dual theme—on the one hand, Heracles and Diagoras's investigation; on the other, this odd character, the Translator, whom you never name, who lives in an imaginary future, recording his thoughts in footnotes, conversing with other characters, and who is, at the end, kidnapped by the madman Montalo. His is a sad fate, for he is unaware that he himself is as much of a fiction as the work he is translating!"

"But you have put many words in the mouth of your teacher Socrates," I will say, adding, "Who has a worse destiny? My Translator, who exists only in the book, or your Socrates, who, though he might really have lived, has become as fictional a creature as my character? I think it preferable to condemn an imaginary being to reality than a real one to fiction."

Knowing him as I do, I suspect there will be more frowns than smiles.

But I fear not for him; he is not a man to be disconcerted. Enraptured, he looks out at the intangible world of beauty and tranquillity, harmony and the written word, that is the land of ideas, and offers it to his disciples. At the Academy, they no longer live in the real world, but in Plato's head. Teachers and students alike are 'translators' locked in their respective 'caves,' devoting themselves to the quest for the 'idea itself.' I simply wished to tease them a little (forgive me, for my intentions were good), to move them, but also to raise my voice (as a poet, not a philosopher) and cry, "Stop looking for hidden ideas, final keys, and ultimate meanings! Stop reading and *live*! Come out of the text! What do you see? Nothing but darkness? Stop searching!" I don't believe they will listen. They'll continue scurrying about, as tiny as letters of the alphabet, obsessed with finding the truth through words and dialogue. Zeus knows how many texts, how many theories written with quill and ink, will rule the lives of men in the future and foolishly change the course of events! But I'll abide by Xenophon's final words in his recent history: "As for me, my work ends here. Let another deal with what comes next."

The end of *The Athenian Murders,*
written by Philotextus of Chersonnese
in the year that Arginides was archon,
Demetriate was sybil, and Argelaus was ephor.

MYSTERY SO56A
Somoza, Jos*e Carlos, 1959-

The Athenian murders /
5/03

ALBANY COUNTY
PUBLIC LIBRARY
LARAMIE, WYOMING

DEMCO

HB